THE HAPPY LIFE OF Isadora Bentley

ALSO BY COURTNEY WALSH

ROAD TRIP ROMANCES
A Cross-Country Christmas
A Cross-Country Wedding

NANTUCKET LOVE STORIES
If for Any Reason
Is It Any Wonder
A Match Made at Christmas
What Matters Most

HARBOR POINTE NOVELS
Just Look Up
Just Let Go
Just One Kiss
Just Like Home

PAPER HEARTS NOVELS
Paper Hearts
Change of Heart

SWEETHAVEN CIRCLE NOVELS
A Sweethaven Summer
A Sweethaven Homecoming
A Sweethaven Christmas
A Sweethaven Romance (a novella)

STAND-ALONE NOVELS
Things Left Unsaid
Hometown Girl
Merry Ex-Mas

THE HAPPY LIFE OF Isadora Bentley

A NOVEL

COURTNEY WALSH

The Happy Life of Isadora Bentley

Published in Nashville, Tennessee, by Thomas Nelson. Thomas Nelson is a registered trademark of HarperCollins Christian Publishing, Inc.

Thomas Nelson titles may be purchased in bulk for educational, business, fundraising, or sales promotional use. For information, please email SpecialMarkets@ThomasNelson.com.

Library of Congress Cataloging-in-Publication Data

Names: Walsh, Courtney, 1975- author.
Title: The happy life of Isadora Bentley : a novel / Courtney Walsh.
Description: Nashville, Tennessee : Thomas Nelson, [2023] |
Summary: "What happens when a desperately lonely woman stumbles upon a magazine article outlining the '31 Ways to Be Happy' and decides to use it as a last-ditch attempt to turn her life around?"-- Provided by publisher.
Identifiers: LCCN 2023001361 (print) | LCCN 2023001362 (ebook) | ISBN 9780840712806 (paperback) | ISBN 9780840712882 (epub) | ISBN 9780840712912
Subjects: LCSH: Self-actualization (Psychology) in women--Fiction. | LCGFT: Christian fiction. | Novels.
Classification: LCC PS3623.A4455 H36 2023 (print) | LCC PS3623.A4455(ebook) | DDC 813/.6--dc23/eng/20230123
LC record available at https://lccn.loc.gov/2023001361
LC ebook record available at https://lccn.loc.gov/2023001362

Printed in the United States of America

HB 07.16.2024

For anyone searching for happiness. I hope it finds you.

The best portion of your life will be the small, nameless moments you spend smiling with someone who matters to you.

—Ritu Ghatourey

Chapter 1

Isadora Bentley is shopping for her final meal.

If I were a character in a novel, this is what the author would write.

Because it's true. I am. Not a character in a novel, of course, but a soon-to-be stiff. A dead ringer for a dead ringer.

Plus, if I were a character in a novel, my name would be Estella. Or Hazel. And I'd be thinner.

Okay, I'm being dramatic. Turning thirty isn't *The End.* At least not of my actual life. Just of my hopes and dreams. I'm pretty sure I saw them swirling down the drain last week along with my dignity.

I'm three decades old. I've spent 10,950 days on this planet, and I really thought my life would look a lot different by now.

When I graduated college, I was bound and determined to live a big life. To make a big splash with my significant contribution to the world of academia. I had a whole list of ways I was going to make a difference, a dent in the universe, *something*, and yet here I am, hours from the cliff of thirty with nothing to show for it but a job that's going nowhere and a life that's doing the same.

Actually, I stand corrected. My life *has* gotten somewhere. It's gotten to the parking lot of the Stop 'n Shop.

And now I'm staring at a neon-outlined sign on a brown brick building, knowing there's nothing terrifying about a grocery store.

I can practically hear the Funeral March as I blow out the thirty-candle inferno raging atop a store-bought cake.

Maybe to most people, turning thirty isn't that big of a deal. It's just another trip around the sun. Easy. All I have to do is stand here.

But it feels like I'm standing with my toes peeking out over a precipice. An Enter at Your Own Risk sign. A line in the sand. Life before and life after. A moment and a checkpoint. So I, of course, did what I always do. Last night, I carefully and objectively calculated my options.

Clinical. Scientific. Detached.

Isadora's work as an academic researcher gives her the tools to make decisions without emotion, fully based on facts and figures. And as she inputs the data into the chart, she sees the writing on the wall. Something in her life needs to change. There's just one problem—she has no idea what. And worse, no idea how to make that happen.

Man, my inner monologue sounds like Sir David Attenborough. It speaks with an elegant, calming, steady British accent. If I'm not careful, my inner monologue will lull me to sleep.

If only I were as well-versed in plotting a course of action or taking big leaps into the unknown as I am in studying other people's actions and leaps.

If you're around me for five minutes, you'll know I'm a rule follower. It's who I am. Envelopes stay un-pushed. Lines remain toed. I collect data, calculate outcomes, and act accordingly. The line from *A* to *B* is literally stick straight. Which is why I would never walk directly to Aisle 8 at the Stop 'n Shop.

Aisle 8 is, of course, where the candy is.

I love candy. But I don't eat candy. I know what's in it, and half of the things you can't pronounce on the label I can find in the lab. It's bad, and I won't allow it.

Correction, I *wouldn't* allow it.

Surely the narrator in my head would agree to skirt the Skittles rule just this once.

Today is a day like no other. Furtive, sugar-laden delicacies dot the landscape, and it is here we find Isadora Bentley foraging for the most delectable sweet treats. Today, Isadora would gather candy and chips and ice cream because turning thirty warrants an all-out junk food binge.

Skittles, Doritos, and Cherry Garcia. Not the fanciest birthday meal, but then, I'm not a fancy person. I don't want filet mignon or duck and mushroom foie gras. I don't even want vegetables. Let's be honest—*no one* wants vegetables. However, if we're talking about what to indulge in to make this birthday borderline healthy, ripe pineapple would certainly make the list.

It wouldn't be as high up as chocolate, or a whole box of Mike and Ike's, and it only makes it into my cart if it's fresh and already cut. I'm not wasting my time chopping up a pineapple, for Pete's sake. I've got life to avoid.

A man walks by me, and I realize I'm still in the parking lot. Good lord, how long have I been standing here? I see the look on his face. *Yeah, buddy, I know this looks weird, but listen, you've got no idea the confectionary decisions I've got weighing on me.*

Glass doors slide open. One foot in front of the other. Aisle 8. Candy.

Nope. First, pineapple.

If I were a different kind of person, I'd take my savings and go on a trip to celebrate my big day.

But then, a different kind of person would have an active social life. Or meaningful connections. Data to offset the negative side of the equation.

As it is, that's not my data. No matter how much I want it to be. And unlike people, data never lies.

What's worse is that I don't see a way off this path. I don't have what it takes to do anything about it. I keep waiting for something to change—or more accurately, someone else to just come and tell me what I need to change—but I'm stuck.

And look. All of the precut pineapple is gone. The empty spot on the shelf where the clear plastic cups stuffed with bright yellow chunks should be stares back at me, and I wonder if it's a metaphor.

Should Isadora wait for a better weekend, a weekend with pineapple, to note this landmark passage of time?

I sigh. No can do, Attenborough. Watermelon it is.

To the chip aisle next. And there I stand, repeating my parking lot posturing, surrounded by crinkly bags of goodness. I'm pretty sure that's the same guy who just walked past me again.

Like a drunken sailor looking for a good time, these chips make promises I know they will not keep.

In the end, I choose the Doritos, a bag of salt and vinegar kettle chips, and a canister of original Pringles to keep it classic.

And then it's like the Red Sea parts. I think I hear angels singing. *Aisle 8.*

Putting it like that suggests I've happened there by chance, which I can assure you I absolutely have not. I've been flirting with Aisle 8 for years. It's why I capitalize it in my head. Aisle 8. And now here I am, about to make out with it. A one-night stand with Reese's.

I hope he'll call.

I know I look like I'm prepping for the birthday party of a ten-year-old boy and fifteen of his closest friends.

But I'm elated. Who knew breaking my own rules could feel so decadent?

As I maneuver my cart into the checkout line behind an old woman who's searching her bag for what I can only assume is her alphabetized coupon file, I notice the cashier eyeballing my Cherry Garcia.

Today, I'm a rule breaker, Janice. Feast your eyes.

As a defense mechanism, Isadora Bentley often held full-on conversations with people in her unique and spectacular head. It made up for all the conversations she didn't have in real life. Let's zoom in and observe.

"Yep. Cherry Garcia. I've simply stopped caring, Janice. I've lost the will to follow any rules."

Janice's eyes will widen. *"Oh my word! Are you sick?"*

"Nope. In fact, I'm in perfect health. I'm just doing what I can to not have a horrible birthday."

Janice will pause. *"Well, only you control your destiny,"* she'll say, or some other simplified cliché that sounds like something on a poster under a picture of a dolphin or a light bulb or a herd of wild horses running on the beach.

Something like *"You are in charge of you,"* or *"You're just one decision away from changing your life."*

She'll pause again, likely for dramatic effect, and I'll do my best not to roll my eyes at this. As a rule, "dramatic effect" irritates me. As does office gossip and anything having to do with falling in love with vampires.

This is when the conversation will get awkward. I know this because nearly every one of my conversations turns awkward at some point. I'll do my best to explain my system to Janice—the variables I used, the data I analyzed, the conclusion I've reached. I'll point out that dolphin clichés help no one and "changing your life" isn't as easy as everyone makes it sound.

As if it's even up to me. I can't help the hand I've been dealt.

But, like most of the people I talk to, her eyes will glaze over, she'll start nervously laughing at the wrong times, and she'll get that pained smile people get when they're trying to escape a Chinese finger trap. I know this because most of what I do or say doesn't make sense to other people.

It's been hard to make friends.

"I have a coupon for that," snaps me back to reality. The old lady, as predicted, hands a paper-clipped stack to Janice. This could be a while.

For what it's worth, it's not for lack of trying. The friend thing. It's just that when it comes to me and other people—it's like I'm speaking a different language.

This could be because the things I love—science fiction and math and *Doctor Who*—aren't as popular as more socially acceptable interests like rock concerts or cute boys.

"You need to try harder to be friendly, Isadora," my mother would say. *"The other girls think you don't like them."*

Oh, Mom. If only you knew that I really *was* trying.

Connections at work are no different. The only one who congratulated me when I was promoted last year was a succulent I inherited when Frieda forgot to clear him off her desk when she retired. I named him Gary after my boss.

Being alone isn't a bad thing when it's your choice. But a lonely life, chosen or not, really isn't living. And frankly, I'm tired of my own company.

That doesn't mean I'm ready to "take the bull by the horns!" or listen to the frog halfway down the snake's mouth croaking, "Never give up!" Turning thirty has amplified my feelings on the subject—and now that I'm painfully aware of them, I don't know how to make them go away.

The Coupon Queen is through, and of course she's *writing a check*. I begin to pile my junk food onto the conveyor when a colorful magazine that looks more like a newspaper in the rack next to the checkout line catches my eye.

I'm slightly put off by the bikini-clad woman on the cover and the gaudy headlines sprayed haphazardly across the front. Bright pink letters shout: "Five Things Your Lover Won't Tell You—But Wants To."

I set a bag of candy down onto the conveyor belt, followed by a box of Twinkies.

The woman on the cover is smiling. If I looked like her, I'd smile too. Perfect white teeth. Tan, toned body. A full-time Photoshop editor on retainer. A playful, girl-next-door vibe men supposedly liked, though how would I really know? I could count on one hand the number of conversations I've had with a man this year about anything other than research.

And I wouldn't even need all my fingers.

Two pints of ice cream, onto the belt.

I wasn't exactly killing it in the dating department.

The woman's hand is pointing to a smaller, blockier headline: "31 Ways to Be Happy (Today!)."

I scoff a little louder than I intend to, and the cashier, whose name I now see is Linda, not Janice, tosses me a look.

I glance back at the magazine and softly snort again. Does this magazine actually think it knows something I don't? And then it hits me.

Are there really thirty-one ways to be happy?

Ridiculous. It's the same magazine that is telling me that eating chocolate in the morning will fix my metabolism. Which, incidentally, I'd totally be willing to try.

But . . . are there really thirty-one ways to be happy? I start plotting a graph in my mind as Linda slides my junk food over her scanner.

"Your son having a party?" she asks.

Oh no. Small talk.

I resist the urge to tell her the truth for all the reasons I've already been over with myself. Instead, I say, "Oh no, it's for me . . . and . . . um . . . a small gathering."

Linda stares.

"Of people. A small gathering of people."

I smile as if a small person inside my empty head controlling all of my autonomic functions ran the program for smile.exe.

Yep. Small. Just me and Gary, who I'm going to bring home from work for the weekend. My loyal cactus companion.

"This is a lot of junk food," Linda says with a laugh.

Doritos, slide, beep. *Oreos, slide,* beep.

I'm suddenly self-conscious of my purchases as I search for an answer that's not one word.

"Yeah. It *is.*"

Fail.

"Is that everything?" she asks, then adds, "Or did you want to wash this down with a Diet Coke?" She chuckles at her little joke.

My eyes are planted firmly on that headline. Attenborough? Any help?

"31 Ways to Be Happy." A simple yet profound conundrum. Like the birds of paradise finding their perfect mate in the jungles of New Guinea . . . Isadora Bentley, this was created just for you.

Linda pops her gum. "You okay?"

I turn and stare at her, and then, before I can give it another thought, I pick up the magazine and toss it on the belt.

Linda shrugs her eyebrows, rings it up, then hands it to me. I shove it into my purse and pay. And not with a check.

I push my cart through the glass doors leading to the parking lot and stand in the same spot where I stood before I came in. Only this time I'm not staring at the Stop 'n Shop.

"31 Ways to Be Happy (Today!)"

Maybe there's something I didn't consider in my research. Maybe there's one more variable to ponder.

And maybe, just maybe, I'll survive another year.

Chapter 2

The following morning, I find Gary—the person, not the plant—standing outside my office talking to a student researcher named . . . nope. Don't remember his name.

Ted? Fred? I think he has a superhero name. Clark? Bruce? Thor?

This is certainly something I need to work on. I've taken on a leadership role in the Behavioral & Social Sciences Research Lab here at Chicago University, and it's done wonders for highlighting my shortcomings, but forgetting names is perhaps my most serious offense. After all, nothing says "I don't really care about you" like not being able to remember a person's name.

These are students, and part of my job is to help train them. So far, most of my attempts at training them have ended with questions and me retreating to my office. I need to do better.

"Morning, Miss Bentley." Gary looks expectantly at me.

"Morning, Gary."

He's trying to grow a mustache again. Last year at this time, he ended up with something less Tom Selleck and more Steve Buscemi. Unfortunately, this in-between stage makes my wispy boss look like the kind of man who would drill a hole in the wall of a woman's bathroom.

I force a smile. *Focus on his eyes, Isadora. Do not look down.*

"Logan was just telling me about the sleep study he conducted this week," Gary says.

Logan. Wolverine. Very different from Clark.

"Yes. Logan. The sleep study." Not looking at Gary's peach fuzz is stealing all my focus.

The student researcher raises his hand in a half hello.

I open my office door. Even after all these years, the former janitor's closet still has a lingering lemony disinfectant scent.

Logan starts talking—I'm pretty sure it's something about studying the effects of sleep on the brain. Another one of my shortcomings as a leader—I'm not a good listener. Too many overlapping internal monologues to make space for other people.

Maybe I should work on that too.

Students need encouragement, Gary has told me, and I'm not great at giving it. Hasn't exactly been modeled for me.

Mine were parents who didn't subscribe to the idea of praising children.

And then, like the rain in Orlando, Logan abruptly stops. He stares, head cocked a little to the side, waiting for . . . what exactly? I feel like I've just been caught stealing.

Oh no. Did he ask me a question?

"I think that's . . . a great direction . . . Logan. Do that." *Smile. Nod. Encouraging, right?* I pat his arm for good measure.

Logan glances at Gary, then at me, then slumps his shoulders and walks off, leaving me standing there like an idiot. And because I'm not sure what else to do, I squeeze behind the too-big-for-this-space desk and pray Gary will walk away. He doesn't.

"You think it's a 'great direction' for him to shelve the last six months of research and start over?"

I look up, mostly to see if his nose breaths are ruffling the hairy bits above his lip.

"We've talked about this, Isadora." He keeps his voice low. "If we . . . if *you* . . . want to create the next generation of researchers, you have to build them up. Show interest. Train them. Actually care. For crying out loud, fake it if you have to. One of them could discover the cure for cancer, you know? Think of what that would do for the program."

To say nothing of all the people who would be cured of cancer.

"I know, Gary. I'm trying," I say. And I was—at least in my own mind. If I'm honest, there's a chance I've talked myself out of trying more times than not.

He sits on the edge of my desk. His butt cheek covers my expense report. "They look up to you so much, Isadora," he says. "Everyone knows how good you are at analyzing data, at digging up facts other people miss."

I blush a little under the compliment.

"They're all trying to win you over." His smile wants to be encouraging, but my mind trips over his words.

"Oh, are they?" I want to say. Is that why they go out every night after work without me? The thought is ludicrous. It's not like I *want* to go get pizza with Logan and the rest of them.

An unexpected wave of sadness washes over me.

It's been hard to make friends.

Despite that, this little office and the lab across the hall are the places I feel most like myself. Things make sense here. Problems have solutions.

I have this whole conversation in my head while Gary sits and waits for a response, and by this point, I've forgotten what he said.

"Anyway." Gary turns awkward, like he's not sure what to do with my silence. "Please consider what I've said, Isadora." He stands. "You have a good day."

After he's gone, I check the wall behind my desk for small,

camera-sized holes, then quietly chastise myself for thinking ugly thoughts about my boss. Mustache or no, Gary is a nice man.

Maybe he could date Roberta from the cafeteria. She has a mustache too.

I lay my bag flat on the floor next to my chair, and the magazine from the grocery store slides out. I kick it under my desk. It would destroy my professional credibility if anyone saw me with that thing.

Thirty minutes pass. Then an hour. I can't focus.

Now in her natural habitat, we find Isadora Bentley at her most serene, but also at her most vulnerable. Like the wildebeest tenderly reaching down for a drink, unaware of what toothy reptile may be lurking just beneath the surface, Isadora Bentley's mind is not focused on what it should be.

31 Ways! 31 Ways! It's thrumming in my brain like the telltale heart beneath the floorboards.

Giving credence to a tabloid fundamentally goes against who I am as a person. I'm surprised when I retrieve the magazine from under the desk and flip it open.

I scan the table of contents and find "31 Ways to Be Happy (Today!)" listed on page 43. I casually thumb past "Dating Dos and Eating Don'ts" and countless ads for miracle weight loss until I find it.

Written by Dr. Grace Monroe. Is this a real person with a real degree? And if yes, are we talking an associate's in communication or an actual PhD in behavioral psychology?

The article is a numbered list, the way most are these days, meant to be easily digestible for people who are too busy to read. The last time I took advice from a magazine was in the ninth grade when my mother left a copy of *Seventeen* on my bed with an arrow drawn on a sticky note stuck next to the headline "Make Yourself More Dateable."

Given how well that worked out for me, I have very low expectations for Dr. Grace.

Okay, Monroe. Let's see what you've got.

I push my glasses up and skim the list:

1. Smile more. *Really? Not a great start.*
2. Get enough sleep. *That I could get behind. I have a chart ranking thirteen different kinds of naps.*
3. Exercise regularly. *Well, that doesn't sound fun at all.*

I skim the rest of the list and grow irritated. This isn't rooted in data. Dr. Grace was paid money to write an article that's basically common sense? Anyone with half a brain would've already tried these things. I'm certain I've done at least half of them.

Okay, maybe a quarter of the things.

I read the list again.

Okay, a solid three of them. Maybe.

I've at least got step two down to a science. I am an excellent sleeper.

A laugh pulls me from the article, and through my open office door, I see Logan and one of the other students—a short, dark-headed girl named Shellie. I can't believe I remember her name.

All at once I'm fourteen again, sitting in the chemistry lab during my lunch hour because I don't have anyone to eat with.

Shellie smiles at Logan, and Logan smiles back at Shellie.

And that's when I get an idea. It's the kind of idea that comes seemingly from somewhere else, making you question whether you're the one who actually thought of it.

The idea is simple.

What if I disprove Dr. Grace Monroe and this entire ridiculous article?

Using a single test subject (me), I could put the steps into practice, calculating the effects of each step. I would keep detailed notes and, ultimately, prove that this article is, at best, an oversimplification. At worst, a beacon of false hope.

I'll treat it like I would any other research project. I'll observe, ask, hypothesize, predict, test, and iterate my way to happiness. Or not. That is where the mystery lies.

This experiment will determine whether or not Dr. Grace Monroe has any idea what she's talking about. And if she doesn't, I'll promptly send her my findings with a note to practice responsible journalism in the future.

I tear the article from the magazine and tuck it inside my calendar.

It seems Isadora Bentley, contrarily, and for the first time in a long time . . . has a plan for the weekend.

Oh, stuff it, Attenborough. I had a plan already. And I'm not wasting the junk food.

ꟹ

That night, surrounded by wrappers and Whoppers, I create a checklist. A procedure. A system.

Each of the 31 Ways has been broken down into solid, succinct bullet points. Over the course of the next however-long-it-takes, I'll try a new point. Monday, the experiment will begin with the very first item on Dr. Monroe's list.

Step one: "Smile more."

No problem. I have a lovely smile. I catch a glimpse of myself in the glass of my fireplace and try it out.

Hmm.

I try again with teeth.

Yikes.

But I can do this. Of course I can.

How hard can it be to smile?

Chapter 3

Turns out, smiling is hard.

I have a new appreciation for models. I'd always assumed it was easy to stand there and let someone take photos of you.

I now understand it is not easy.

My smile lands somewhere between "feeding hyena" and "painful constipation." So if I encounter anyone on the dusty African plain, I'll win the bigger zebra leg.

The next day, I arrive to work late. I don't want to stumble into this experiment haphazardly, and the two-liter of Coke I drank at 12:30 a.m. made it impossible to fall asleep.

Especially after consuming nearly three-quarters of an entire store-bought birthday cake. By myself. I'm actually pretty proud. I won't get into all the details of my pathetic birthday party, but it's worth noting that my advice to humans everywhere is to keep a random stash of birthday candles in a junk drawer in the kitchen. You'll forget all about them until you realize "candles" wasn't on your mental grocery list and you have to set a Clean Linen jar candle on top of your cake. The worst part is, the cake wasn't strong enough to support the jar candle, so I ended up with a giant crater in the middle.

And I discovered that I'm not above licking frosting off a jar.

I also chose the perfect blank notebook from my vast and varied collection for compiling data, and paper-clipped the article to the inside cover. On the top of the first day, I wrote:

STEP ONE: SMILE MORE.

Staring at it now, the directive feels so simple—but somehow . . . terrifyingly impossible.

I'm transported back to my first day of kindergarten. While many memories through the years have faded, this core memory has not. I'm back there again, six-year-old me, in pigtails and a red-and-white polka-dotted skirt that my mother insisted on buying.

She'd picked it up off the sale rack, claiming it was "darling."

I scrunched my nose. "I don't like red" was my way of saying, "Can I please wear something less bright?" How did a person hide while wearing red polka dots? It was as if even then I knew better than to draw attention to myself.

Mom wouldn't hear of it, of course. I was her baby doll, always a reflection on her, and she was going to dress me however she wanted.

We walked to school, and when we reached the edge of the playground, I pulled her to a stop, squeezing her hand. She looked down at me, and while I'd expected kindness, I was met with frustration.

"Isadora, what are you doing? You're going to be late."

Words were hard for me. Words *are* hard for me. I didn't know—and still don't know—how to put my fears into sentences. I stared at the kids laughing and playing and running around the grass and a tightness took hold in my chest.

They made it look so *simple*.

Every ounce of excitement I might've had about going to school and making real-life friends slowly fizzled away as fear took hold.

"Isadora. Come *on.*" My mother tugged at my hand, but I didn't move. My feet were cement blocks. She got down on my level. "What is the matter with you? *You're embarrassing me.*" She gestured with her hand. "All you have to do is go in there and smile! What are you so afraid of?"

As if it were easy. But it wasn't easy. A smile—that simple point of connection—wasn't easy. Smiles led to greetings and greetings to conversations.

Which, of course, led to some pretty epic awkwardness.

I snap back out of my mind's eye because I feel the trickles of sweat winding a path down my sides under my armpits. I'm flushed. The kindergarten tightness in my chest returns. I rush down the hall to the ladies' restroom and splash cold water on my face. That always helps people in the movies.

All it does for me is smudge my mascara.

Great. I've successfully combined the feeding hyena with a raccoon.

I groan, yank a paper towel from the dispenser, and do my best to clean my face, while my brain randomly tries to combine the words *hyena* and *raccoon. Racena? Hycoon? Hycoon is better.*

"Get it together, Isadora," I say out loud. A cursory glance around the restroom tells me I'm alone. Thank God.

I straighten my shoulders and stare. Time in front of a mirror is rare for me, and the last time I stared too long at my reflection, I noticed my bangs needed to be cut. Which I did myself. Badly.

They've mostly grown out, so now they're at a longer awkward diagonal.

I gaze, really looking. My eyes are big—blue. I like blue eyes. I'm glad I have them. But my hair is that weird color between blonde and brown, like none of my genes were strong enough to make a decision.

I blow out a sigh and the bangs scatter off my forehead, then land in their soft slant. I push my glasses up and force myself to smile. I hold it for a moment, then watch as it fades. Is there a way to force a smile without it looking forced?

I try again. Too gummy.

Again. Too toothy.

I channel my inner Tyra Banks—but my attempt at "coy" looks more "homicidal housewife." I adjust my lips and open my eyes a little wider. Still murder. I try again. And again. I try close-lipped, full-toothed, crooked, and everything in between. Just as I'm about to give up, I turn to find Miranda Barnett, professor of psychology who could moonlight as a Rockette, standing with her annoyingly perfect posture in the doorway.

The look on her face says she's been there for a while.

She would probably write "possible psychopath" on her yellow legal pad during our session, then scribble out the "possible."

Humiliated, I cower out of the bathroom and back to the quiet of my office. I open my notebook and scrawl the words: *Smiling is overrated.*

A few minutes later, Logan and Shellie show up in the lab. She's laughing at something he said on the way in.

This is it. Time to smile.

They'll walk by my office, and when they stop to say hello, I'll be ready. I'll ask them how their projects are going and see whether they need any help. I'll make myself *approachable.* But when they walk by my office, they don't stop to say hello. They don't even glance in my direction.

It dawns on me that sitting in the safe confines of my little closet is not the way to conduct this experiment. After all, there are no people in here. No offense, Gary. (The cactus, not the boss.)

Okay. Here goes nothing. Or everything.

I rummage around in my bag and pull out my wallet, forcing myself to do the only thing I can think to do. I go to the cafeteria.

This is a place I tend to avoid. When I was in college, I walked by a dumpster as a cafeteria worker was breaking down cardboard boxes with the words *Grade D but Edible* stamped on the side.

I haven't trusted cafeteria food since.

And then, of course, there are the stereotypical social ramifications of a cafeteria, especially if you have no one to sit with.

I'm standing in the line when a group of college boys walks in.

Here's your chance, Isadora. It's just data. A simple smile and you can rush back to your office and document how it makes you feel. The boys are all wearing Chicago University baseball spirit wear. They laugh and talk so loudly you'd think they were at a rock concert, desperately trying to be heard over the noise. Only there's considerably less noise in the cafeteria. It's not quiet, but it doesn't warrant this level of shouting.

My pulse quickens, and I swear I can hear my own heart thumping like a bass drum in my rib cage.

Smile, Isadora.

A simple greeting. Friendly. Polite. Nothing more, nothing less.

Just smile, you idiot!

Thump. Thump. Thump.

But all the willing in the world can't force my eyes to meet any of theirs. Men are terrifying, but college boys are a whole other level of scary.

Head down, through the line, nod at the cashier, then escape into the courtyard.

Outside, I finally breathe, aware that my behavior is utterly ridiculous. *I am a grown-up.*

I sit down on the first empty bench I see and practice yoga-style deep breathing.

Inhale, two-three-four. Exhale, two-three-four . . .

Once I've got my bearings, I look around. Chicago University sits at the center of Hyde Park, southwest of the main part of downtown

Chicago. Thankfully, the architect must've known humans would need nature among the towering steel and concrete, so he designed the school's quad. It's beautiful, covered with grass and trees and gardens of flowers that spring to life when the sunshine finally chases winter away. Red and yellow tulips outline a wide walkway and flowering bushes line the perimeter of the garden.

It's hard to believe I'm in the city at all.

A group of kids burst from the building, spilling out into the courtyard. One of the guys takes off and another throws a football in his direction. Two of the girls do that flirty laugh that seems to come naturally to every woman except me, and instead of burying my head in a book or my lunch or anything other than the scene playing out in front of me, I watch.

I never really look at people outside of work. Screens and spreadsheets, documents and data, but never people.

Mainly because people look back.

Even when I'm working, I tend to be a quiet observer, interacting with subjects as seldom as possible. My favorite project so far was a study on the effects of sleep as it relates to a person's charitable giving and empathy. It was far easier to spend time with people when they were sleeping.

My gaze falls from the far-off distance as the footballers escape into Old Main, the prettiest—and oldest—building on campus, and lands on an elderly man sitting on the bench on the other side of the wide walkway.

He looks up.

I want to look away, but something stops me. He's not intimidating the same way the college boys are, so I hold his gaze.

Smile, Isadora!

He watches me for a moment, and then . . . I do it.

I smile.

I don't know which of the smiles (the Smirking Psychopath? the

Upturned Talk Show Host?) is actually on my face at the moment. To my utter shock, the old man doesn't look away. Instead, he smiles back. A full-on toothy grin.

The heavens don't open and the angels don't sing, but it unexpectedly stirs something inside me.

I giggle.

I reach for my notebook and immediately start scribbling notes about this unexpected response.

While I'm not saying Dr. Monroe is correct (about anything), I can't deny that when my eyes met the old man's and he smiled back, an odd feeling came over me. I wouldn't call it "happiness" but it did make me feel something, which is saying a lot because what I typically feel could be summed up with a single word—"Meh." Still, the simple act of smiling—

"You're not making me a character in a book, are you?"

The old man has abandoned his bench and is now standing directly in front of me, holding a crumpled brown paper bag.

He waggles a finger at my notebook. "If you are, could you make me taller?"

What happens next shocks me. I laugh. A genuine laugh, because I thought what he said was funny. I cover my mouth with my hand, as if to stifle it.

He smiles. "Mind if I sit?"

I scoot my things out of the way and he sits down beside me. I can smell the faint hint of peppermint, and I'm thrilled to discover he doesn't have ear hair. A lot of old men do.

He sets his bag on his lap and looks over at me. "I'm Marty."

"Marty," I say, not as a greeting, just a little trick I'm hoping will help me remember his name on the off chance I bump into him again.

He sticks his hand out and I shake it. "I'm Isadora."

"Isadora," he says. "Pretty name."

"You think so?" I pull the tuna sandwich from my bag and set it on my lap. "I never liked it."

"Nah. It's pretty. It suits you," he says.

I notice that the lull in conversation that follows isn't awkward. He's eating. I'm eating. I suppose we're having lunch together. Marty is wearing a lightweight navy blue jacket, a flat cap—the kind a golfer would wear—and a pair of khaki pants.

"What are you doing here?" I blurt the question with zero tact. Marty laughs.

"You mean what's an old guy like me doing on a college campus?"

Yes. That's exactly what I mean. I watch a lot of crime documentaries.

I fumble. "Are you . . . a professor?"

"I'm not that smart," Marty says with a quiet laugh. "Or that patient." He sets down his half-eaten—I look over at the sandwich in his lap—bologna and cheese. He sighs. "I suppose I'm . . . reminiscing."

His gaze falls to the ground, but it's not sad. "I met my wife here on this very spot fifty-seven years ago." He's wistful, happy, settled in his thoughts, like a hammock. "I come every day to have lunch, right here where we met." There are tears in his eyes now, and I pay very close attention, pencil in hand.

I choose silence over questions. What do I say? Marty is a stranger—does he really want to answer questions from a woman he doesn't know?

"Would you like to hear about her?"

I look at him, and he smiles again. Involuntarily, I smile back.

What is even happening right now?

His is a nice smile.

"Yeah, I would."

Marty's face brightens, and something inside me does too.

I sit back on the bench and listen, and I realize fifteen minutes later that I set my notebook and pencil down without even noticing. As I'm finishing my bag of chips, I find I'm thinking less about data and more about a woman named Shirley who had "*legs that wouldn't quit*" and "*a smile that could light up the sky in a thunderstorm.*"

And there's a flutter in my chest, a flush on my cheeks. Both unfamiliar.

Happiness? Is—is that you?

HAPPINESS EXPERIMENT PERFORMED BY ISADORA BENTLEY

OBSERVATION:
People who live on this planet are existing in varying degrees of comfortability, contentedness, and happiness.

QUESTION:
What makes someone happy? Can happiness be derivatively reduced to a list of "things" to do, actions or mindsets, that will result in a deeper or higher state of happiness?

HYPOTHESIS:
People who follow a list of "Ways to Be Happy" will not be happier than those who do not follow a list.

PREDICTION:
Performing an in-depth look at happiness as described in the article "31 Ways to Be Happy" by Dr. Grace Monroe, I predict that accomplishing the tasks laid out in Dr. Monroe's article will not bring happiness but will prove that this article is comprised of false information that will mislead its readers into believing such an ingrained, complex emotion is easily attained.

Background information: Subject is a single woman in her early thirties with a stable yet unfulfilling job. She is in good physical health but reports a general malaise and feelings of discontent. No family history of mental illness that subject is aware of. Subject lives alone and has a limited social circle. Subject is introverted, thriving in comfortable, solitary spaces.

Presenting problem: Subject is determined to test the steps of an article written by Dr. Grace Monroe in an effort to determine its validity.

Will implement a series of suggested "ways to be happy" in order to prove that happiness is not a malady that can be treated. Will record subject's physical, emotional, and sensory responses to each of the thirty-plus suggested treatments to determine validity of article written by Dr. Grace Monroe. Subject is convinced some people simply do not have a happy disposition.

Subject believes herself to be one of these people.

Goals: To prove Dr. Grace Monroe is incorrect in her assessments. To find the root cause of happiness, if such a thing exists. Why are some people happy when others are not? Is happiness something to strive for or something your personality simply allows you to feel (or not)?

IS HAPPINESS ONLY AVAILABLE TO A SELECT FEW?

Chapter 4

I return to my office after lunch and find Logan and Shellie huddled over a table in the lab conducting an experiment. Or maybe she dropped a contact lens. Either way, they don't look up.

As I'm silently marveling at how I've perfected the fine art of being invisible, I round the corner and run straight into a chest.

If you want to get technical, a strong, nice-smelling man's chest.

I've knocked into him hard. Stumbling backward, I flap my arms as if I've suddenly gained the power of flight—and he reaches out to steady me.

Hand . . . on my shoulder. A thumb, grazing my cheek. Something inside me twists.

A tall man wearing a crisp button-down and tie underneath a tweed blazer stares down at me, holding me at a forty-five-degree angle, like the *Top Hat* poster with Astaire and Rogers. He has dark hair and a neatly trimmed beard, and I resist the urge to reach up and touch his chin.

What would that beard feel like underneath my fingers?

"Are you okay?"

Often, when confronted with the male of her species, Isadora Bentley's main defense mechanism kicks in. Muscles tighten, breathing slows to almost nothing, and brain activity completely shuts down. It's in this moment that Isadora Bentley is at her most vulnerable and most catatonic.

"Whurrr . . ." I slur some kind of sound out of my mouth, but it's more Klingon than English.

"Miss Bentley?"

His voice again. I mentally kick the side of my brain to jump-start the neurons.

"Yes. Ha. Sorry. About . . . that." I correct my posture to an upright ninety degrees and gingerly reach out and pat his chest, as if he were a good dog. "Hmm. There you go." I then barrel around him, head down, racing down the hall and into my office, holding my breath until I close the door behind me.

I look down at my arms. Goose bumps. *That man gave me actual goose bumps.* I struggle to ignore my brain, misfiring like Nicolas Cage's acting, which is to say, all over the place. I sit behind my desk, thankful there are no windows in my tiny room. My heart is racing. *Racing.* A little too quickly for a simple run-in.

I struggle to shut down this attraction—*the upending of my calm*—and my thoughts turn to Alex McEnroe, the man who solidified my belief that, where romance is concerned, I am certainly better off alone. There is no wistfulness clothing the memories of Alex. Only humiliation.

It's an emotion that's curled itself up beside me and decided to be my best friend.

But wait. Not all *men.*

Marty. The old man on the bench. Before he left, he asked if we could share the bench again tomorrow, and I found myself so charmed by him that I said yes.

I felt a kinship with Marty, almost instantly, as if the two of us shared something many people wouldn't understand. Loneliness, perhaps?

I don't like to think of myself as *lonely*. Ugh. Old women who smell like floral perfume and baby powder—the ones with orthopedic shoes and too many cats—are *lonely*. I mean, there's nothing wrong with flowers and baby powder. Or orthopedic shoes. Or cats, for that matter. But a combination of those four things? I might as well start writing checks at the Stop 'n Shop.

I'm not an old woman. I don't want anyone thinking I'm lonely. This is the life I've designed. It was my *choice*. Granted, I thought I'd be a little further along by now—published, revered, in charge of this entire department, global domination. But while those things still haven't come to pass, I can't deny that I like books and work and research and digging in on subjects of interest.

I do not, however, understand people. No matter how much I study their behavior.

People are complicated.

People are messy.

Not physically messy, like leaving half-eaten pizza crusts in boxes on the counter, though I suppose some of them are messy that way too. But *that* kind of messy doesn't hurt. The same can't be said about emotions.

Relationships are, by nature, not meant to last. They're fraught with conflict and dishonesty and, truly, I don't have any desire to clip my return address tag onto someone else's baggage.

One of the many reasons I prefer to be alone. The other reasons are best tucked away. No sense dredging up messy memories.

Just when my heart rate has almost returned to normal, a knock on my door spikes it again. Nobody ever knocks on my door. Nobody ever needs me. My coworkers have resigned themselves to avoiding me, which I'm thankful for. I honestly get so much more done.

I open my laptop and pretend to be busy before calling out, "Come in!"

My door opens. It's Gary, but he doesn't come in. Instead, he stands just outside, in the hallway, as if there is an invisible force field keeping him out. It's likely that invisible force field is emanating from me.

I barely look up.

"Excuse me . . . Isadora?"

I stop fake typing to give him a split second of my attention, and that's when I realize Gary is not alone.

I saw that chest up close about five minutes ago.

Gary is standing with the guy from the hallway. Gary and his lip foliage seem to know this man and his broad shoulders. I'm quite certain I'm staring. I do a quick mouth check and find my jaw slightly ajar. I snap it shut and clear my throat.

"Isadora, I'm sure you know Dr. Cal Baxter," Gary says.

Dr. Cal Baxter. Dr. Cal Baxter. Dr. Cal Baxter.

I repeat this in my mind three times. It's a trick to remember a name, but in my head, it sounds like a mooning teenager with a crush on Zac Efron chanting it into a mirror, hoping he'll materialize in my bedroom.

On the third chant, my brain snags on a memory.

The professor who was hired after Alex left.

Dr. Cal Baxter is Replacement Alex.

I push myself to my feet and proceed to knock over my pencil holder, and all of my No. 2 Ticonderogas clatter to the floor. I swear I see Gary roll his eyes as Dr. Baxter drops to his knees to collect them. I should be helping him, but instead I'm staring again, mouth agape, thinking Big Bad Wolf thoughts like, *My, what nice broad shoulders you have*, and *other* thoughts like, *I want to run my hand through that hair.*

Gary shoots me a look, and I bumble back to life. "Oh, just leave them. I'm so clumsy, I'm all arms and legs, you should see me ride a bike." *Shut up, shut up, shut up.* I word vomit a number of other sentences that would show up as "indistinct dialogue" or "guttural jabber" if my life were subtitled.

Then Replacement Alex stands, rendering me completely mute.

He's tall and broad, unlike many of the professors. Standing next to him, Gary looks like a child.

With a mustache.

He holds the pencils out like a bouquet of flowers, and I stare at them. He smiles. "It's so refreshing to see someone else who prefers real pencils. I can't stand those mechanical ones."

"Me *neither*!" I practically shout this because—*oh my goodness*—we have something in common. Then I way too excitedly go to grab the pencils and proceed to knock them out of his hand, spilling them across my desk and back onto the floor.

This event hangs for a moment.

Shockingly, he laughs. "They're the worst, right?" He bends down to pick them up a second time.

"They're the worst," I offer, hoping my assault hasn't derailed this conversation. "They shouldn't even be classified as pencils. Passable as a writing utensil, but not a *real* pencil. A real pencil needs to be sharpened."

He stands, offering the pencils again. I reach out, and he pulls them back, half smiling, with a look that says he's not sure he can trust me to take them.

His smile holds, and my Wolf brain growls, *What lovely teeth he has!* while my normal brain simultaneously wonders whether he had braces as a kid. I didn't, which is why I'm stuck with two crooked eyeteeth that often keep me from fully smiling.

Who am I kidding? As my "practice" indicated, there are numerous reasons I seldom smile. My teeth hardly top the list.

Gary clears his throat, and I gingerly take the pencils from Dr. Cal Baxter. Our hands touch briefly and the familiar goose bumps fleck my arms. I don't meet his eyes for fear of an impending full-body outbreak.

As a rule, I try not to notice members of the opposite sex. Gary doesn't count because (a) I *have* to talk to him, and (b) I don't really see him as a man but as more of a creature.

But even before the Alex calamity, other men around the university had become part of the background. I avoid eye contact. I fasten on my invisibility cloak to move about the campus, and up until this exact moment, it has always worked. At this exact moment, however, a pair of blue eyes is laser-focused on me.

Step one: "Smile more."

Yes! The experiment! And even though I've technically already collected data with Marty, part of the scientific method is iteration—repeating your experiments to produce similar, if not identical, results.

I give "demure" my best shot.

Judging by the horrified expression slowly contorting Gary's face, I've failed. I glance at Dr. Cal Baxter and his expression is like that of one who can't decide whether he actually saw Bigfoot or not.

Ah, Humiliation, there you are, old friend. You've been away a solid ninety seconds. I did not miss you.

"Dr. Baxter is a professor in the psychology department upstairs," Gary says through a confused frown. "He was hired after Alex—"

My eyes and my response both snap at Gary. "I remember." And that brief mention is enough to remind me that Dr. Baxter is cut from the same cloth as ex-Alex.

Al-*ex*?

"Have you brought him in here to do an evaluation of me?" I can hear the defensiveness in my own voice.

The professor half laughs.

"No," Gary says, "though I do wish I'd thought of that."

My frown deepens.

"I didn't bring him here at all—he's sought us out." Gary looks pleased with himself, like he's fallen in with one of the popular, cool kids in class. "And I'm assigning him to you."

If I'd been eating or drinking anything at that moment, I would've choked and died. "To me?"

I don't want to work with Replacement Alex.

I can't have a repeat of that experience. I can't.

It's been two years. I've barely recovered.

Not to mention *the goose bumps.*

"Yes, Isadora," Gary says with the patience of a big-box store manager dealing with a woman trying to return a tube top without a receipt. "Dr. Baxter is researching a book, and he's asked for our help."

I scoff. "I bet he did."

Dr. Baxter holds up his hands in surrender. "I have no problem admitting I could use your input."

But would he have a problem giving me any of the credit?

With all of the real-pencil-common-ground now sharpened to a nub, I say, "Sorry, Dr. Baxter. I work alone." I'm certain I don't have the right to say this. After all, Gary is my boss, and whether I like it or not, he can assign me to whoever he wants. But I say it anyway because the point must be made. *I don't want to do this!*

"Yes!" Gary says as if I've just gotten the correct answer on *Wheel of Fortune.*

I'm perplexed. My eyes dart over to Dr. Baxter, who I realize now is still smiling. "Gary says you're the best." On him, the smile is perfectly natural. I bet he doesn't even have to practice in the mirror.

"She is that," Gary says, and then to me, "But you're . . . particular, Isadora, and as you know, we'd love to get you to be more of a team player."

And once again, I'm confronted with my own dismal

existence. The truth is, I *should* be doing more with the people in our department. I *should* be taking student researchers under my wing. I *should* be doing something other than what I'm doing—alienating myself from everyone who might not understand me.

That doesn't change the fact that I don't want to do *this*.

"I *like* working alone, Gary," I sputter. "I'm better that way." I look at Dr. Baxter. "No offense."

He holds up a reassuring hand, shaking his head slightly as if to say, "*None taken*."

"The asthma sleep study is all wrapped up, and you've got some time. Now that you've sent Logan back to square one, and to his therapist probably, you're freed up to help the esteemed Dr. Baxter prove that technology is our enemy." Gary smacks Dr. Baxter on the back.

"Uh, that's not exactly . . . ," Cal says, but Gary isn't listening. He's issued his decree and now he's off.

"I'll check in with you periodically throughout the next few weeks, but for now, I'll leave you both to get acquainted and work out the details."

No! Don't leave! My insides are screaming out in panic, but on the outside I am calm. That's a lie. On the outside, I'm certain, I'm also panicked. Beads of sweat gather above my upper lip. Great. Now I'll have a sweat mustache and people will mistake me for Gary's twin.

The hum of the fluorescent light overhead seems loud all of a sudden, and I swallow to try to restore moisture to my mouth. It doesn't work. I might as well be chomping on cotton balls.

I drop into the chair behind my desk and motion for Dr. Baxter to sit in the chair on the opposite side. It's piled high with file folders and case studies and works in progress because my office is a literal closet, and there isn't enough room for everything. He picks up the stack and sets it on the floor. And then he sits.

I stare.

There's a very handsome, very nice-smelling man in my office. I tell myself to get it together—he's just a man—and despite my epiphany with Marty on the bench, I do not attempt another smile.

I rearrange the items on my desk. My water bottle. The jar of pencils. Straighten my laptop. A notepad. Clear my throat. Back to the water bottle.

"I don't think I'm going to be much help," I say. "I'm consumed with a few of my own projects right now."

"I understand," he says. "But I really could use the help."

I shift in my seat.

"Do you want me to tell you about the project?" he asks.

I look up and find his eyes fully on me. I hold that gaze for a three-count and then stand. "Can you excuse me for just one minute?"

His eyebrows pop up and his mouth opens to form a response, but before he utters a word I slip out from behind my desk, move quickly through the open door, and tromp down the hall to Gary's office.

It has a window.

He looks up from his computer. "Isadora?"

"Why did you assign me to this project?" I shout through the window before even reaching his door.

"Because you're an excellent researcher," Gary says loudly. "Because Dr. Baxter asked for a favor. And because you need a little help with your interpersonal skills."

"No. I don't." I come around to the doorway.

Gary nods toward the lab. "Need I remind you the only reason you haven't been required to teach is because you're supposed to be training them—"

I don't have to look to know that he's referring to the research assistants, interns, and students busying themselves with lord knows what.

"You know I work better by myself."

"And you know that's not the goal of this department. We work together to make each other better. No one can make you better if you're always by yourself. And you can't help teach them if you never speak to them. Besides, it's not healthy. People need people, Isadora."

I bristle. I'm sure team research is fine—*for other people.* But for me? People always get in the way. They always let you down. This job is the adult version of a group project in college where one person does all the work while the other participants sneak alcohol into the library. I decided a long time ago I don't have time for any of that nonsense, and that hasn't changed.

I'm better off alone.

I recall that one of Dr. Grace Monroe's 31 Ways is "Spend time with friends." At some point, I will have to confront this issue in the name of research, but only after having plenty of time to work myself up to it.

To quote Aragorn, "It is not this day." Today I am not properly prepped. I'm not storming the Black Gate of relationships without the entire Elvish army behind me.

Gary folds his hands on his desk and looks up at me with the same kind of quiet disappointment as my mother, who never did get over the fact that her daughter wasn't one of the popular girls. I'm sure there is much to unpack there, but as with many things, I've chosen not to.

"Did you even give him a chance to tell you about his book?" he asks.

"No."

Oh, quit tilting your head at me, Gary. If Dr. Cal Baxter is the author, he should do the research himself.

I decide to say that out loud.

"If he's the author, he should do the research himself. What is it with all these lazy professors coming to us to figure out the data they need to get published and then taking all the credit for themselves? It's maddening. Maddening! Doesn't it *madden* you?"

"He has done his own research, Isadora. The work is done. However, he's got a full course load this semester and a deadline. He's asking for our help organizing it, and we're in a position to give it. That's our job."

"Well, I didn't know that!"

"You didn't ask. And I'm guessing you didn't give him time to explain."

"If you really believe I'm an excellent researcher, then why are you wasting my time on some fluffy psychology book?"

His expression grows stern as he folds his hands on his desk. "This is your priority, Isadora."

I stand there for a few seconds, poised to respond, but it's clear Gary is finished with our conversation. He's dismissed me with his eyes.

Sometimes Gary could be a boss. Had to respect him for that, even though I really, really didn't like it.

Then I hear movement behind me, and my heart drops again.

Dr. Cal Baxter, standing in the hallway, has heard every word I've said.

Chapter 5

I should get a cat.

According to Dr. Monroe's sixth step, interacting with animals is a surefire way to be happy.

Cats are *technically* more work than dogs because, let's face it, a cat does whatever a cat wants. When you call a dog, that dog will happily come to you as if you've been gone for a year.

When you call a cat, it will give you the brush-off, walk the other way, and knock a planter off a shelf.

I wouldn't have time to try to train an animal, so by that logic, I should get a cat, which is going to do whatever it wants anyway. Also, because I think dogs might be too playful and energetic for someone of my disposition.

You won't see me talking baby talk to an animal.

Still, according to Dr. Monroe, playing with pets is statistically proven to increase the body's production of serotonin and oxytocin, two hormones associated with happiness. I make a note to research the validity of this statistic.

Sounds like something a dog person would say.

If I had a cat, I'd have something to look forward to when I got home from work, other than the sound of my noisy across-the-hall neighbors. I could sit with Cat and pour out all my embarrassing confessions, maybe even unload my frustrations, and he would respond by avoiding eye contact and going to lie on my keyboard.

I'm actually starting to think that *I* might be a cat.

Tonight's Cat Confessional would be long and angry and all about Gary and his *team mentality*. I'd share in great detail how much I'm dreading going to work tomorrow, and how I spent the rest of the afternoon completely worthless because I couldn't stop thinking about Dr. Cal Baxter and his stupid blue eyes.

Blue eyes and dark hair. Was that dominant or recessive? I make another mental note to research that, too, because it certainly feels like an otherworldly combination.

Not that it matters. I fully expect Dr. Baxter to request a new research assistant after my outburst. Typically, people don't love working with people who really, *really* don't want to work with them.

And judging by the look on Cal's face when I found him standing behind me in Gary's office, he was feeling slightly left of horrified. Or maybe he was amused?

As previously stated, I have a hard time reading people.

I open the door to my apartment as a text comes in.

Isadora, this is Cal. Hope you don't mind Gary gave me your number. Would love to meet tomorrow and discuss the project. Sorry we got cut short today. Coffee in the quad? I'm buying.

I stare at the block of letters forming what I'm sure are words, but something isn't computing. I want to type back: *"Thought for sure I ran you off. Don't like to be around people. Best get another assistant.*

Your eyes haunt my soul." But instead, I click the phone off and set it on the table next to my door.

As if that is enough to stop the nagging feeling that Dr. Cal Baxter isn't going to go away.

While my knowledge of Dr. Baxter is little, the similarities of my humiliation with *Alex* are enough to keep me from warming to the idea of working with him on anything.

I've never been one for wanting credit.

Okay, that's not *entirely* true, but I'm not one to go out of my way to make sure my name is on something—not really. But I'm absolutely convinced if Alex had kept his word, my professional life would look a lot different than it currently does.

To say nothing of my personal life. That'll teach me to pin my hopes and dreams on a man. Lesson learned.

After popping Hot Pockets in the microwave and cracking open a Coke, I open up my research binder.

In the front, I've rewritten the 31 Ways to Be Happy. I've given myself permission not to complete these tasks in order. After all, "Exercise regularly" is third on the list, and I'm in no hurry to implement *that* one.

Besides, I think it's smart to work my way up to the more uncomfortable tasks on the list. Baby steps. Small victories first. This is how I decide that my step two will be "Compliment someone" (even though it's step twenty-six on Dr. Monroe's list).

My mind, traitor that it is, seems intent on conjuring all kinds of lovely compliments I could pay Dr. Cal Baxter.

Your hair is so thick and wavy, I just want to run my fingers through it.

No. That would creep him out. That creeps *me* out.

Do you play the piano? I only ask because you have lovely, long fingers perfect for piano playing.

Equally as creepy.

There is no way to compliment this man without coming

across as a fawning dolt, which, let's be honest, is what I am. One simple brush up against his hand gave me *goose bumps*.

This is ridiculous of me! Good grief, Isadora, pull yourself together!

This man is most likely self-important, arrogant, and narcissistic. *Replacement Alex is just like Alex Prime.* Never mind the way he looks. Never mind the way he smells. Surely there's someone else I can compliment. Logan or Shellie or even Gary.

I applaud your effort at growing a mustache, Gary. Will you also be wearing seventies-style bell-bottoms with a turtleneck?

Funny how my compliments sound a lot like insults. I really should work on that.

I should tell Gary I respect him as a leader—after all, he put me right in my place today. Oddly, I don't feel like celebrating that fact.

I take out my journal and prepare for this next, important step in my research when my phone dings again.

On any given night I'm likely to only receive text messages reminding me to pay a bill or, occasionally, one from my mother with the link to an article about the latest fashion trend or celebrity gossip.

All these years and she still doesn't understand those things never have been, nor ever will be, of interest to me. I suppose it's to her credit that she hasn't completely given up on me yet, despite the fact that she has never, *ever* understood me.

I think Shawna Bentley expected that her life would turn out to be very different than it did. She must ask God daily what she did to deserve such a disappointing daughter, but I try not to think too much about it. I push those thoughts of her straight into a closet in the back of my mind, slam the door shut, and mentally lock it up tight.

I pick up my phone and see that it's not a reminder of a dental appointment at all. It's the professor. Again.

Me again, Isadora. If you don't like coffee, I'm happy to buy tea instead.

What kind of heathen do you take me for, Dr. Cal Baxter!?

Ah, I see I have your attention now . . .

As if that were ever a question.

I'm not flirtatious. However, I am considerably better at writing to people than talking to people. When texting gained in popularity, I thought the heavens had opened and smiled down on me—maybe for the first time ever. Finally, a method of communication that didn't make me look at someone. Or respond immediately.

Texting also doesn't make my palms sweat, my heart race, and my stomach vault.

I apologize for not responding sooner. I planned to text back after I ate dinner.

Oh, am I interrupting?

I snap a photo of my half-eaten Hot Pockets and send it to him.

Yes! My gourmet meal is officially ruined.

Ooh, is it pepperoni?

All at once, this familiar tone throws me. We aren't friends. Best if Dr. Cal Baxter doesn't think otherwise.

I'm happy to . . .

I erase that.

I will meet and discuss your project. Coffee is not necessary. Let's stick to my office. 10:00 a.m.?

I stare at the three dots as they appear, then disappear.

What? What did I do? I answered his question, right? Kept it profess—

The phone buzzes in my hand.

Before looking, I take a breath. Despite Dr. Cal Baxter's charm and good looks, he is a colleague. Nothing more. To him, I am simply a researcher. An anonymous assistant who has been given the task of helping him get published.

A twist in my belly betrays my true feelings. I *do* want him to like me.

I groan. I'm no good at this. I told Gary I wasn't! Why didn't he listen?

I look down at my phone.

10:00 a.m. sounds perfect.

I stare at these words, and a goofy grin spreads across my face. I'm thinking about ol' blue eyes and his perfectly groomed facial hair when the phone buzzes in my hand again.

But the coffee is nonnegotiable. Tell me your drink of choice or be subjected to whatever I choose.

My smile collapses as I remind myself not to read into this and I type:

Peppermint mocha please. I'll Venmo you for it.

He responds with a screenshot of his previous text with the words "I'm buying" circled in red. Then a wink face.

I realize it's silly to argue over this.

Thanks. I'll see you tomorrow.

Then, as if possessed, I type one more thing and hit Send before I even think about it.

What the heck is wrong with me?

Chapter 6

At exactly 9:57 a.m. the following day, I consider locking my office door and pretending I'm not in. Then I remember Gary has a key, and having him open the door to find me hiding inside would be so much more humiliating than simply having a conversation like an adult in the first place.

And for some reason, ever since I woke up, I've been thinking about the last real, meaningful relationship I've had that wasn't with a plant or an imaginary cat.

What the heck is that *about, brain?*

I don't like thinking about Alex. It's one of those topics I actively avoid. So why now?

Maybe it's my subconsciousness warning me off. If Alex taught me anything, it's that in this world, it's every man for himself.

I don't want to feel any of that again. Not the elation of thinking there might actually be another person in the world who understands me. Not the tingly hum or the excitement in wondering when I'd talk to him again. Not the foolish, idiotic idea that maybe I have something to offer after all.

You know—that I'm not broken.

I sit with this word—*broken*—for longer than I'd like, trying hard not to picture the fractured remnant that was left of me after I realized the truth about Alex. My face flushes and my chest tightens. I *should* let myself feel it—but I really, *really* don't want to. There's a knock on my door as the clock on my computer flips to 9:59 a.m. Dr. Baxter is punctual. Normally a quality I admire, but today, with the racing pulse, I curse it. I clear my throat and call out, "Come in!" noting the higher-than-usual pitch of my voice.

I'm unprepared for the reminder of his bookish good looks, and the second our eyes meet, I'm flustered all over again.

"Good morning, Isadora." He smiles.

Goose bumps. I try to rub them away. I fail.

He has a bag slung crossways over his chest and he's holding two cups of coffee. He cheers one into the air as he says, "Peppermint mocha."

"Ah, right." I clear away a spot on my desk, and he sets it down. "Thank you again for that. It wasn't necessary."

"It was, actually," he says. "I'm afraid I'm in a little over my head with this book."

I take a sip of the peppermint mocha and discover it's not a mocha at all. "Oh." I set it down on the desk. "I think this is yours."

He takes a drink from the cup in his hand. "Yep. This is definitely not mine." He switches the cups like it's no big deal, but all I can think is that our mouths will touch the same exact spot on these cups, which I learned in the third grade can get you pregnant.

I'm about to cup-kiss Dr. Cal Baxter.

"Make sure it's okay." He nods to the cup, and I do as I'm told and take a drink.

The warmth of the chocolaty, minty liquid makes its way down my throat and into my empty belly. "This is good."

He smiles his approval, and I feel it in my toes. I quickly look away. This man is turning me into a pile of goo, and let's be real, nobody's attracted to a pile of goo.

"Now, about the fluffy psychology experiment I'm too lazy to research myself . . ."

I half choke mid-drink. "I'm really sorry I said those things," I gargle. "I—"

He holds up a hand with a smile. "I'm teasing, Isadora."

When he says my name, I stop breathing for *one-two-three*. I want to ask him to say it again.

Remember Alex, you foolish girl! What are you thinking?

It should be noted that sometimes when I chastise myself, I speak to myself as if I'm an old woman.

I take myself more seriously this way. In my mind, the inflictor of these chastisements looks a lot like a schoolmarm, and I've named her Helga. She doesn't mess around.

"I understand that your department does a lot of the heavy lifting for professors on a variety of projects, and you're absolutely right to want credit for your work."

Oh, this old chestnut. I've heard this tune before.

The last time there was a "discussion" about me getting credit for my work, things didn't end well. I'm not even going to assume my name will appear anywhere in this book. That's not my role, not anymore. I am now nothing but a silent contributor. I make other people better.

The glory was never mine to crave.

Isn't that what Alex said?

It's better to go into this project with zero expectations. That way I'm far less likely to get hurt. This is a job, nothing more.

I shake my head. "No, I apologize for my outburst. I suppose I don't like change, and when Gary suggested we work together, well, frankly, I didn't like the idea. I was being juvenile."

Inwardly, I applaud the maturity of my answer. *Nicely done, Isadora.*

"Well, my hope is that we can work together to dig out some

really fascinating data." He opens his bag and pulls out a large stack of loose papers and plops it on my desk.

I frown. "What's this?"

"My research so far."

"How have you organized it?" I almost regret asking because I'm fairly certain I know the answer.

He grimaces. "By . . . um . . . how I stacked them when I brought them here?"

I raise my eyebrows.

"Yeah, this is where I need help." He pulls different papers and folders from the pile, seemingly at random. "I've conducted focus groups and surveys and studies. I've made copies of some applicable research that's already been done, but I'm sure there's more out there worth noting. The problem is, when I try to put it all together in a way that makes sense, I end up turning these pages into paper airplanes and seeing how far I can get one to go."

"Hmm. What's your record distance?"

"Haven't used a tape measure, but from my dining room table to the sink."

"For best results and maximum flight distance, you want to toss the airplane at an angle between forty-five and sixty degrees," I say. "Maybe your angles were slightly off?"

"Or maybe I shouldn't be making paper airplanes out of my research as a way to procrastinate."

I pause. "Or that, yes."

He smiles, and I involuntarily smile back.

I involuntarily smile back.

I take another drink and remember my own research project, which will never be published in any academic journal, but is as important to me as Dr. Baxter's is to him.

Step two: "Compliment someone." The thought vaults from the back to the front of my brain, bypassing the tact filter.

"Your teeth are amazingly straight."

I want to crawl in a hole and die.

He looks confused for a split second, recovers, then smiles and says, "That might be simultaneously the oddest and nicest thing anyone's ever said to me."

I haven't blinked yet.

"I had braces," he says.

I knew it.

"Though it has been decades since I got my braces off, and you're the first person to notice how straight my teeth are."

"Or maybe just the first person to comment on them." My laugh is laced with nerves. "So . . . tell me about your book." I desperately try to swim to the surface.

"Yes! I'd love to! I think it's a cool concept, and I haven't seen it before in a book." As he says this, his eyes brighten. I can see his excitement for his research from the moment he starts to speak.

"I don't want to demonize technology," he begins. "Gary got that part wrong."

"Gary gets a *lot* of things wrong." My tone isn't light, and I'm dead serious when I say this. I'd be a horrible poker player.

He laughs. "Let's hope he's right about you."

Yes, let's hope. While I'm confident in my skills as a researcher, I'm not confident in my ability to work on a team or my ability to stay focused when Dr. Cal Baxter is anywhere within ten feet of me.

The CDC has minimum safe-distance guidelines for everything else, why not for Dr. Cal Baxter?

I force myself to focus on what he's saying and not on the fact that he talks with his hands and smiles with his eyes.

"Okay. Big picture. This is a book about relationships. In it, I dive into the effects of technology on the human connection. I've been researching ways that technology has brought us closer together, and also the ways it's driven us back into ourselves. Pushed us farther apart. I think there's a direct link to—"

"Why?"

He frowns. "I . . . um . . . what do you mean, why?"

"Why are you writing about this? Why research it at all?" I straighten my shoulders. "I think it's important to understand the reasons behind a project like this one, don't you? If I know what kind of conclusion you're hoping to draw, I'll have a better idea how to focus the research."

"I hadn't really thought about it that way. I suppose . . ." He looks up, head tilted, thoughtful for a moment, then looks right at me. "I guess I want to prove that we need each other."

The air leaves my lungs.

He isn't talking about he and I needing each other. But for the briefest moment, his words hit me as if he is, and the backs of my knees tingle.

Tingling, in any form, is a warning sign. I quickly return to my coffee, a welcome, warm distraction for my useless hands.

He sits forward in his chair, and I can tell he's passionate about this.

"I believe connection, human connection, is directly related to finding a fulfilling life. Even animals live and operate in groups—herds, pods, flocks. On a basic biological level, humans are similarly designed to seek out other humans."

"And you think technology hinders that?" I ask. "One could argue that in many ways, it brings us closer."

"One could." He smiles. "And one would be right. I want to focus my attention on social media, how it challenges true, genuine connection. How it makes it easier to play a part, to pretend." He shuffles through some papers. "One study I found said that twenty percent of divorce cases due to infidelity name social media somewhere in the filing paperwork."

"I see."

"We're created to form connections. We're created to fit, to unite, to bond. But I believe it's important these are done in real life. The absence of human connection leads to loneliness, and loneliness can be toxic to the body."

"There's nothing wrong with being alone," I say. "Some people prefer it."

His brow quirks at this, and I'm certain he's recounting my words from yesterday: *"I work better alone."*

"Right. You work better alone. I remember," he says, confirming my thoughts. "Which honestly makes you even better suited to help me. You're choosing to being alone, but that isn't the same as loneliness. You wouldn't consider yourself to be lonely, right?"

Don't ask me that. Please don't make me admit it.

My palms are sweating, and I am mentally googling ideas on ways to remove myself from this project. It's hitting a little too close to home, and if I'm honest, I don't like it. I don't like that Dr. Cal Baxter is trying to prove the very thing I'm hoping to disprove.

Humans let you down. Repeatedly. Even the ones who are supposed to protect you—they still find ways to screw everything up.

As if reading my mind, Dr. Baxter holds up his hands and says, "I'm sorry, I shouldn't have asked that. And it's okay if you don't agree with this idea. In fact, it's better in a lot of ways. You can challenge this premise. You can keep me honest. It wouldn't be a very good book if we only found supporting data and left out the rest."

I put a hand on the stack of research he's set on my desk. "So this is a collection of your own research?"

"Mine along with other studies that have been conducted," he says. "We should probably perform a few more experiments and interviews, but it's a good start, I think. Maybe you could look it over and then we could meet back in a few days to discuss."

I frown. "You want me to read all these pages in a few days?"

He picks up the stack and pulls a page from the middle. On it is a single sentence: *"Do humans really need other humans to be happy?"*

"This giant stack is a bit misleading," he says. "Many, many pages look like this."

"Nearly blank?"

"Nearly blank," he echoes, slightly dejected. "I spend a lot of time talking to myself, and sometimes it's helpful to write every stray thought down."

I resist the urge to shout out, *"Me too!"* and commend myself for my restraint. *Excellent self-control, Isadora.*

Step two: "Compliment someone."

Oh no. Not again. The compliment that is forming in my brain has the inevitability of giving birth, and I have no idea what I'm going to push out. *Your forehead is pleasant? I want to poke your arm muscles?*

"I think—" I meet his eyes, and my brain—my very intelligent, highly developed brain—shuts off all inhibitions for a split second.

"I think this is really amazing and inspiring, and it's refreshing to see someone really passionate about their work."

Wait. What? That sounded like a real compliment. A good one too.

I remain silent, the absence of words taunting me. And then, finally, he smiles. And not in a mocking, you're-such-a-weirdo kind of way. There's kindness in his eyes.

"I can safely say that you're not like anyone I've ever met, Isadora Bentley," he says matter-of-factly.

And I can't be sure, but it seems like maybe—just maybe—he means to compliment me back.

I can't help it. I smile. Not a practiced-in-the-mirror smile either—a real one. And then I have to look away. Because the goose bumps are back, and all at once, ending the meeting is the last thing on my mind.

Chapter 7

A few days later, I'm sitting with Marty on our bench—he with his bologna sandwich and me with a turkey and cheddar from the cafeteria. We both have chips and I'm drinking a Coke.

We've met like this for days now, and I've mostly listened as Marty has talked, which is honestly just fine with me. The pressure to fill in gaps of silence has always hindered my conversations with other people, but Marty is perfectly happy to chatter on. Already, I can tell we're a good team.

Yesterday he told me a story about the day Shirley went into labor with their daughter, Miriam. According to Marty, Shirley was a little stubborn, and when she went into labor three weeks before her due date, she convinced herself it wasn't real, just a little discomfort she needed to work through. By the time she finally admitted her contractions were coming regularly, it was too late. Marty had to get a neighbor to help deliver the baby in their living room.

After hearing this, I thanked God I wasn't Marty's neighbor.

But today he must be all out of stories—that or he's decided I need to pull my conversational weight, because we've been eating only a few minutes before he starts asking questions.

"Tell me what you do here at the school," he says.

"I'm a researcher," I say.

"What do you research?"

"All kinds of things," I tell him in between bites. "Mostly I work in behavioral and social sciences."

"What's the most interesting thing you're working on at present?" He gives me a side-eye. I can see him working to engage me, and while I know I should make it easier on him, I can't help it. I've never seen the point in small talk.

Although, one could argue that's not what this is. Marty isn't asking me about the weather. He wants to make an actual connection with me. I'm aware of this, and yet I resist it. Like the Mandalorian, "This is the Way."

"Oh, a few different projects," I say.

"Anything that keeps you up at night?"

I turn to him, mouth twisted to one side.

"I'm really good at this," Marty says. "I've got all kinds of questions."

I think about the 31 Ways, and yes, they've kept me up at night. Mostly because there are steps I am literally dreading. Steps that have made me want to quit the whole thing. Steps that I'm not sure I want to do. Ones I don't think I can.

Step twenty-one: "Let go of grudges." Step nineteen: "Spend time with friends." And worst of all, step thirty-one: "Confront what is making you unhappy in the first place."

That last step has haunted me since the first time I read it. I almost tossed my research notebook then and there.

This experiment is about simultaneously proving once and for all that little steps like these don't result in happiness and disproving Dr. Monroe.

"I can practically see the wheels turning," Marty says. "Care to share?"

I look at Marty and narrow my eyes, like a cliff diver standing at the edge of Kahekili's Leap in Hawaii eyeing the water. As a rule, I don't share my feelings. Ever. Anytime I have, the results have been astronomically disastrous. But Marty isn't like other people. Something about him is safe.

You thought Alex was safe too.

I glance at Marty, who crunches a potato chip, then chews it quietly. Marty is *not* Alex.

"I'm . . . doing an experiment of my own," I tell him. "I'm testing the validity of an article I read called '31 Ways to Be Happy.'"

Marty's eyebrows pop up, and for the first time I realize they bear a striking resemblance to two fluffy caterpillars. But unlike ear hair, these eyebrows are endearing.

"I got the idea on my birthday," I tell him, "in the midst of a junk-food storm."

Marty chuckles, and I continue. I tell him everything. I explain about the clinical approach I'm taking, about how I'm the only test subject, and about Dr. Cal Baxter and his research. I tell him about how it's throwing me a little to be working on his project when it's slightly adjacent and counter to my own.

I realize I haven't stopped talking for a solid fifteen minutes.

I regroup. "I'm so sorry I unloaded all of this on you." I say this while simultaneously wondering why it was so easy to do so.

He's chewing slowly, and I wonder how straight *his* teeth are. *I am* so *weird*. I did leave out the part about the teeth compliment in my recap, but Marty is a perceptive guy, and I fear that maybe it's going to come up at some point.

Marty swallows. "I don't mind you unloading on me." He smiles. "I've been working on a little experiment of my own, if I'm honest. And I think it's good to get our feelings out there. Sounds like you've got quite a few feelings."

"No," I say. "I mean, yes, I've got feelings, I'm a human—" I pause. "But I don't like to be led by my feelings."

"Afraid where they might lead? I understand."

I'm convinced he doesn't really.

Feelings truly have no place in research. If a stray feeling does beg for my attention, I usually ignore it. Not unlike men with turn signals, I am an excellent ignorer. And I don't intend for that to change. Today's lunch hour was simply a momentary blip.

I bite into my sandwich, and the turkey and mayo squish out onto my cheek. This happens to be the precise moment when Dr. Cal Baxter is walking toward me.

Of course it is.

Cal lifts a hand in a wave and smiles while I scramble for a napkin and quickly wipe the mess off my cheek. I drop the sandwich back onto its wrapper in my lap and do a terrible job of composing myself.

Marty peers over at me. "You okay?"

I sputter around a mouthful of sandwich and mutter, "I'm fine," which comes out like "Ahmf fahn," and look up at Cal, who is standing on the sidewalk a few feet from our bench. I wonder if he would mind if I called him Cal, and I also wonder if he shops at J.Crew.

"We meet again, Isadora," he says, and it dawns on me that I've never, not once, seen him in the courtyard.

Or maybe I simply wasn't paying attention. Maybe he's been here all along.

"We do," I say.

He glances at Marty, a question on his face. "Is this your—?"

"This is Marty," I say. "He's my friend."

"Well, thank you for that compliment, Isadora." Marty beams.

Another compliment? I didn't even mean that one. I must be getting good!

I continue, confident. "Yes. My friend. He met his wife in this very spot. She's gone now, but Marty returns here to have lunch with her memory every day. We met a few days ago when I smiled at him." All at once the words stop, and the conversation sputters and splats to the ground like an ice cream cone dropped by a five-year-old.

I look away.

Marty clears his throat. "You must be Dr. Baxter."

"You can call me Cal," Cal says. "You know, I'd love to interview you sometime."

"What? No!" I scramble for a legitimate reason why this is a bad idea and come up empty.

"Why not?" Cal asks, and for a moment he looks at me funny. "It would be perfect to speak with someone who grew up without all the technological distractions. I bet you'd have great insight into the human connection."

Marty seems delighted by this, and for about five minutes, he and Cal enter into a conversation I am not a part of. Not because they've excluded me, but because I haven't reconciled the idea that Marty, my new friend and the only person in the world bored enough to listen to me pontificate, has now just entered Dr. Cal Baxter's orbit.

Oh bother.

When Cal finally excuses himself, he looks at me funny again and waves a goodbye. I'm left there with Marty and a barely eaten sandwich. I glance over at him and his smile shifts to a frown.

I should be the one frowning. "What?"

"You have mayonnaise on your cheek."

Of course I do.

I pull out my napkin and dab at my face, then look back at Marty, but he shakes his head, pointing to a glob of mayo so far away from my mouth you would think I'd been trying to eat my sandwich through my ear. I wipe it away finally and sigh.

"I take it you have a little crush on the good doctor?" Marty takes another bite.

"I do not!" I say it so loud that a flock of birds near us takes flight.

I hear the protest in my own shrieky voice, but I know it's pointless to lie, especially to Marty, who is apparently a wizard.

"Fine, I . . . might . . . have some . . . thoughts . . . about him."

"I can see why. He's a good-looking fellow. Smart too." He points at me with the last bit of his sandwich. "And he likes you."

"No, he doesn't!" I say. "And he *shouldn't*. He doesn't even know me. He doesn't know that I'm weird and awkward, and I hit him, literally, twice—once where pencils were involved—*and* I complimented his straight teeth."

Marty faces me. "Isadora. You're bright and intelligent and funny. Not to mention, you're a knockout."

I laugh heartily at this, and then I realize he's not kidding. He hasn't said these words to mock me. He means it. "Marty. I am very self-aware. Look at me. I'm gawky and strange."

"Isadora. You're not self-aware; you're just seeing yourself through a very specific lens."

This strikes me as incredibly profound.

"I don't know how to carry on a proper conversation."

"What do you call this?"

I pause at that. "This doesn't count."

"Why not? I'm practically a stranger to you, but you've been carrying this conversation since you sat down."

"Talking too much isn't the same thing," I say. "I do that when I'm nervous."

"But you're not nervous," he says matter-of-factly.

I check myself for the signs. My heart rate is unnoticeable. My palms aren't sweaty. I'm not jittery or tingly, and my stomach is perfectly free of knots. He's right. I'm not nervous.

"You should be kinder to yourself, you know?"

"I'm plenty kind to myself," I say, half believing it.

"Are you?"

I think on this. I know he's right. Arguing is futile, but I still try desperately to come up with some small, significant way in which I've been kind to myself.

I fail.

"You said the step you're on is 'Compliment someone,' right?" he asks.

I nod.

"I've got a great idea!" He looks almost gleeful as he says this. "Today, pay the compliment to yourself."

I frown. "I don't think that's what Dr. Monroe meant. I mean, I think the point is to reach out to someone else and see how the compliment makes you feel." A pause. "Or something."

"Forget Dr. Monroe. You know she's probably not a real doctor anyway."

"You just might be my favorite human for saying that. I thought the exact same thing."

Marty laughs. "This is *your* experiment. You can conduct it however you want. If you really want results, then I say this is an excellent way to start." He pauses. "So?"

I stutter a response, trying to get out of this, but Marty's expectant expression tells me he won't have it. And for some inexplicable reason, I don't want to let him down.

"Okay. A compliment."

"About yourself."

"About myself. Right."

So I think. I'm sure I can find one single thing to compliment.

"I'm a good researcher," I say with a nod, as if I've just handed in my paper and we can get on with our day, *thankyouverymuch.*

But the wrinkles in Marty's forehead deepen in disapproval. "You are not your job, Isadora."

"I sort of am, Marty."

"I beg to differ."

"If I were to lose this job, what would I do? What would I be? There would be nothing left."

He balls up his sandwich wrapper and stuffs it in his brown paper bag. "And you wonder why you're unhappy."

"Who said I was unhappy?" I ask.

"Why else would you do this experiment?"

"To prove it wrong," I say. "I like my work. I really do. I find it fulfilling most days and fascinating other days."

"Yes, but work doesn't make a person. You aren't what you do. There's so much more to this life than your job. There's so much more to *you* than your job."

I ponder this. It feels like a math formula that doesn't apply to my story problem. I finish my sandwich and take the final swig of my Coke. "Well, I think that's all I can come up with," I say.

"Then I'll wait here until that changes."

I stand. "I have to get back to work."

"That's fine." He pops another potato chip in his mouth and settles in. "I brought a book."

Chapter 8

The window in the research lab looks out over the courtyard, and throughout the afternoon, I peek in on Marty.

He sits, reading his book, unhurried.

All at once, it dawns on me how very much I like this old man. I like that he's wearing a hat and trench coat like a character out of a 1920s gangster movie, and yet he still manages to make it look grandfatherly. I like that his smile reaches his eyes, crinkling them at the corners, deepening well-earned wrinkles, reminders of the belly laughs of years gone by. And I especially like that against all logic, he seems to see something good in me—something I am still unable to grasp.

My view of him has gone foggy and I realize these thoughts have made my vision cloudy.

I walk out to the courtyard toward the old man, who is still reading, looking up occasionally to smile a hello at someone passing by. I reach the bench and sit.

He doesn't move.

"You said you're working on an experiment," I say.

His brow quirks. "Yes. I suppose I wouldn't have called it that, but I'm trying to speak your language."

I smile. "What is it?"

He hesitates, and I wonder if I've overstepped. "I'm working on visiting Shirley."

"Oh," I say. "I've never visited a dead person. How do you do that? A séance?"

He laughs softly. "You go to the cemetery," he says.

"You haven't been to the cemetery?"

He shakes his head. "Not since her funeral."

We sit in silence for a long moment, and I'm unsure how to respond. I'm not good with my own feelings, but I'm especially bad with other people's.

"I start every morning with a walk in the direction of the cemetery, but I never get any closer. I always expect to, but it never takes."

I ponder this and finally say, "Maybe tomorrow, work on going the length of one house closer, then the next day, maybe you get another house closer, and so on. That's how people begin to run—they just build up their distance a little each day."

"You think that will work?"

I shrug. "It's worth a shot, right?"

He nods. "I suppose it is."

There's another lull in our conversation, but my awkwardness calms, and then I remember why I came out here in the first place. "I don't have a compliment for me yet," I say. "But I was thinking inside about how much I like you."

He closes his book and turns toward me. His eyebrows lift. "Is that right?"

I look at him. I wait to feel awkward or out of place. I expect it, but it doesn't come, so I continue. "I don't have many friends, and I don't really enjoy other people's company. But you—I really like."

Marty beams. "That's so kind of you, I'll ignore the fact that you failed the assignment."

I smile. "I didn't fail it. I simply rewrote it."

He crosses one long leg over the other and sets the book on his lap. "Did you ever think maybe you don't enjoy other people's company because you've been trying to spend time with the wrong people?"

I consider this. Truth be told, I haven't been trying to spend time with *any* people. But in the past, before the world sullied me on the very idea of friends—was it possible? "I'm not sure. It seems like it's been pretty all-encompassing. People don't seem to understand my particular brand of existing."

"I think the right people are out there, Isadora. We just have to find them."

He says "we" like we're in it together, like we're a team. I've never been part of a team before outside the lab. I probably don't have to note that I was never athletic, but even teams that might've accepted me—chess club, mathletes, quiz bowl—were always just out of my reach, so his willingness to lump us together the way he has warms me from the inside.

"You'll have to keep me posted on your experiment," he says. "Maybe I could help you sort through your findings?"

"Really?"

"Why not?" He grins. "I'm just sitting around waiting to die anyway."

This gives me pause. "You're not really, though, are you? I mean, you have things to do and people you love?"

"Oh, of course I do," he says. "I have Miriam, my daughter." He harrumphs. "She's a pill."

I laugh.

"Miriam has David and they have three kids. So I mostly spend my time watching soccer games and being carted along to band concerts. I hate soccer, and my grandson James is better suited to playing the tuba than kicking a ball. Fact is, they're growing up now, and nobody needs an old man hanging around."

There's a wistful sadness in the way he says this that catches me off guard. Marty has awakened something inside me that I wasn't sure even existed—empathy. All these years of studying human behavior, I've always kept myself detached. It's the best way to conduct research. But this? It's something else entirely.

"Well," I say, "I'd be happy to discuss my findings with you. It's not a real research project, but it could be fun."

"It's a deal then," he says. "We'll be research partners in the quest for happiness. So what are we doing tomorrow?"

Chapter 9

A loud crash in the hallway outside my apartment shocks me from sleep the following morning. It's Saturday. This is an unwelcome start to my weekend.

The sound of a child screaming quickens my pace to the door, and when I open it, I see a toddler wearing nothing but a diaper, standing on the landing, pointing to the stairs and whimpering. This is the spawn of my across-the-hall neighbor, whose name I don't know. She's a short, pretty woman with dark hair and so many kids I've lost count.

At the moment, she's doing a very bad job of keeping track of this one.

The little boy looks at me, his big brown eyes brimming with tears. He points again and chokes out a sound only his parents would be able to decipher, but to me it sounds comically close to the mother of all curse words.

Hearing that word come out of a toddler's mouth once is jarring—but he is now saying it over and over again, jabbing a wet finger at the stairs.

I glance at the open door to my neighbor's apartment, certain that at any moment, the woman or her husband will notice their

R-rated toddler has gone missing. But there's no movement coming from inside.

The real concern here is that I have a yoga class at a studio down the block. I've moved on to "Exercise regularly," and despite the protest of every hidden muscle happily resting under a layer of fluff, I signed up. The class is this morning, and I have to get ready. Not only do I have to get ready, I have to mentally work myself up to attend this class. Me, in an exercise class? In public? With people?

This has all the hallmarks of another epic disaster.

But I can't just leave this toddler in the hallway.

I take a step toward him and he snuffles a few more times, then calms. Pointing toward the stairs and saying the swear word over and over again. I peer in the direction of his point and see an upturned toy dump truck on the landing. That must've been the crash that woke me.

"Oh," I say as I realize his meaning. "You want your *truck*."

He says it one more time.

The little boy sucks in his lower lip, and now that I've spoken to him, he must think we're friends because he's waddled toward me and latched onto my pajama pants with one of his snot-stained hands.

I stare at him as he lifts the other hand toward me.

Oh no, does he want me to pick him up*?*

The thought horrifies me. I can't pick up a stranger's child. Or any child. On holidays with my extended family, they have a running joke: "Nobody can make the children cry like Isadora."

"Swear at me all you want," I say. "I'm not picking you up."

This child, however, doesn't seem to care. He gives my pants a tug and they drop completely down to reveal my plain white, high-waisted panties.

I shriek and lunge to grab them just as my neighbor rushes out the door.

"Diego, no! Naughty!" She laughs at the horror on my face as I scramble to pull my pants back up. "Oh my goodness, I'm so sorry. They have no concept of personal space at this age."

My cheeks are hotly embarrassed. I don't tell her it's okay that her son has just pantsed me, but at least she's appropriately apologetic.

"Do you mind grabbing that truck for me?" She scoops up the boy and nods toward the toy. "Some kids have teddy bears. Mine has a big metal dump truck. Sleeps with it in his bed every night."

"Uh, sure." I plod down the stairs, giving a side-eye glare at the little goblin she's holding, still clutching the waistband of my pants. I retrieve the toy and hand it to Diego, who rewards me with the biggest toothless grin I've ever seen.

I notice the tiniest prick of emotion inside me and return the smile, temporarily forgetting that this little gangster drew me out here in the first place.

"You really should keep your door locked," I say. "And a better eye on your children."

The woman bristles. "You try keeping four kids inside an apartment all day."

"No, I don't think I will," I say. "I don't actually like children."

The woman's face goes blank. I assume she's taken offense, but when she throws her head back in a laugh, I'm caught off guard. "That was funny. You're funny. Why don't I know you? We're neighbors."

I shrug, though I know exactly why she doesn't know me.

I avoid her.

"I'm Darby," she says. "And this is Diego."

I scrunch my face in disapproval. "Are you one of those people who names all your kids with the same letter?" It isn't until that exact moment I realize I even have an opinion on the naming habits of mothers of multiple children.

I can see by her grimace that she *is* one of those mothers.

"Guilty," she says, giving Diego a squeeze. "There are three more—Delilah, she's a little mother hen, more old woman than child, then there's Danny and Dora, my twins. And then this guy."

"Dora?" I say absently. "I always wanted people to call me Dora."

"Just because you wanted to explore with a talking map, or . . . ?"

I meet Darby's eyes. "Oh, no, my name is Isadora. I always thought people who had nicknames were lucky."

It meant they also had friends.

She shrugs. "I never had a nickname either. It's kind of hard to shorten Darby."

There's a short lull, and I try not to freak out. Lulls are the gaps that my awkwardness sloshes in to fill.

I resist the urge to blurt out that she is the only adult to see me in my underwear in . . . well, ever.

"Well . . ." I release my death grip on the waistband of my pants and look at her.

"It's nice to finally meet you," Darby says. "I've seen you around in the building—at the mailboxes, in the elevator, in the courtyard. You never look up." She pauses for a moment, as if considering this. As if considering *me*.

"I should've introduced myself. We'd love to have you over for dinner one night. My husband, Dante, is studying to become a chef. Maybe you've smelled his cooking in the hallway?"

"He's heavy-handed with the garlic," I blurt.

"I tell him that all the time!" She laughs.

I don't say so, but I've also stood in the hallway outside our two apartments more than once, listening in on conversations seeping through the walls of the old building. While I have never envied Dante and Darby's life with their trail of troll children, I have envied the idea of an apartment full of people, of dinners that sound like celebrations despite being part of an ordinary day.

"So you like Italian food then?" Darby fills in the space I've left blank, highlighting the fundamental difference between the two of us.

I nod. "I do, actually."

"It's settled! You'll come eat with us next week. Sunday dinner is such a production, and the kids will love meeting you. Do you know they've made up stories about you? The mysterious woman in 318." She said that last part like a voice-over for an art house horror film.

"Mysterious? Me?"

Darby shrugs. "Anyone who doesn't talk incessantly is a mystery to them." She smiles.

"Well, I should go." I turn toward my door. "I have a yoga class in an hour, and I have to get ready."

"No way! Yoga?" Darby's eyes widen. "At Flow?"

I feel myself nod, and have a premonition. I don't like where this is heading.

"Do you go there often? I'm a regular! I have a punch card."

I should be a psychic.

"It will be my first time." Discomfort squeezes at my insides. The thought of exercising at all has me in knots, but my one saving grace was that nobody in the class would know me.

Darby squeals. "Oh, you're going to just love it! I'll come with you! Is it the nine thirty class? I'll come get you in a half hour! Just let me change and tell Dante he's on kid duty!"

"Oh, you don't have to—"

But it's no use. Darby has rushed toward her door, saying something about finding her favorite leggings, leaving me standing alone.

I feel more naked right now than I did when my pants were around my knees.

Chapter 10

True to her word, Darby knocks at my door a half hour later.

For the second time this week, I note that being punctual is a fantastic trait, except with people you're trying to avoid.

Despite the fact that she's birthed four children, she looks like a fitness model in her matching patterned leggings, a pink tank, and black zip-up workout jacket. Her dark hair is pulled back into a sleek ponytail, a black headband holding her hair in place. By contrast, I am wearing a pair of old gray sweatpants and my red Chicago University T-shirt, and my not-quite-blonde, not-quite-brown hair is pulled up into a messy bun—and not the cute kind. While Darby wears black-and-pink Nikes that match her outfit, I am wearing an old pair of Keds that are number eleven on the top ten list of shoes that cause plantar fasciitis.

Darby gives me a once-over, with an unspoken "*Is that what you're wearing?*" Or maybe I imagined that because she smiles brightly and says, "This is going to be so fun!" She peeks around my shoulder to get a look into my apartment, something that might be considered rude but somehow isn't, and I find myself moving aside so she can get a better look.

Is it possible I *want* her to know me?

Um, no, of course I don't.

Not only for obvious reasons, but mainly because I read her book cover and assumed everything about her story. Which is something I do on the regular.

I concluded that Darby and I have nothing in common.

Why, then, am I stepping aside as she inches her way across the threshold of my apartment?

"It's like a mirror image of ours. How many bedrooms do you have?"

"Just the one," I say.

"We have three. I wonder if my side of the building has larger apartments."

"Yes, this used to be an old hotel. When it was renovated, they wanted to offer larger spaces for wealthy people. And I suppose people with a million kids."

Darby laughs. "Well, I'm not rich. But some days it sure feels like I've got a million kids."

She stops in the middle of my tidy living room and draws in a deep breath.

"Wow. It's *so* quiet in here," she says. "I bet it's easy to think without a barrage of racket. Our apartment sometimes feels like—I don't know—trying to take a test inside a bag full of monkeys. Nonstop noise. Constant chatter."

"You probably have to dodge poop slung at you too."

Darby laughs again, full this time. I'm shocked. "You're hilarious! And sadly, not wrong." She looks around. "You probably have such an easy time reading a whole book in here."

She hasn't asked me a question, so I don't answer her. Instead, I take a step toward the door and say, "Should we get going? I don't want to be late my first day of class."

Darby waves me off and turns a circle in my home. "You don't have any photos on the walls."

I give a soft shrug as she walks over to my tall windows, looking out over our side of the city. In the distance, Lake Michigan stretches out, tiny white waves cresting, dotted with solitary boats.

"Wow," she sighs. "Look at that."

I stand beside her, and for a moment we're connected by mutual appreciation for the scene in front of us.

"I always feel so small when I think about how big and wonderful the world is," Darby says wistfully. "We're so lucky to be alive, don't you think?"

I'd never thought of it that way.

I glance at her and see she's completely caught up in the moment, the water, the sky—life. And I feel . . . comforted, maybe, but not overwhelmed with the awe of my place in the universe.

I look back out the window, hoping to be transfixed, transported, transcended, but instead, I only become more aware of the time.

Darby must feel my mental itching. She glances at her pink Apple Watch. "All right, time to go, but thanks for letting me see your apartment. Let me know if you ever want help bringing it to life."

I frown at this. Is an apartment something that needs a life? I'm having enough trouble getting one of those for myself.

"I'm not offering because I'm one of those annoying know-it-all people on the internet who thinks I'm a designer just because I painted a wall a bold color. I'm actually an interior designer. Or I was before I had all the kids. I have a pretty good handle on this space since I did my own and it's nearly identical. What would you say your style is?"

We're standing in the hallway now, and I'm locking the door, racking my brain for an answer to her question.

"I guess . . . minimalist?"

Darby laughs as if I've just told a hilarious joke.

"I have a quiz you can take," she says. "It'll be so much fun."

Clearly, Darby and I have different ideas of fun.

We walk in tandem down the stairs and out the door, and I turn toward Flow and notice Darby has stopped. She's standing still, eyes closed, arms loose at her sides, drawing in a deep breath.

"What are you doing?" It's not that I don't know what she's doing—she's obviously breathing—but I suppose what I'm really wondering is why? Is this preparation for the class, and if so, what have I gotten myself into?

"Taking it all in. Slowing down. Being present. Savoring this exact moment for exactly what it is."

"But we're going to be late," I tell her. "And we'll have to savor that awesome moment when everyone stares at us as we walk in."

Darby smiles and starts off in the direction of the yoga studio. "That's okay. I think it's better to be present than it is to be on time."

I couldn't disagree more. "I don't. I think it's better to be on time."

"I gave up hurrying a while ago," Darby says. "I want to feel myself in my body."

"Feel" yourself in your body? How in the world do you . . .

And then for the first time ever, I think of my own body and the way I feel in it.

I think about how my feet feel in my shoes. How my bag feels on my shoulder, and how brisk the air feels going in through my nose, down into my lungs.

If I had to describe my body, I'd probably use words like *fluffy* and *squishy*. Certainly not *toned* or *taut*, two things I don't care to be.

I bet it's easier to enjoy the way your body feels when you live inside toned skin. But at the same time, in this moment, I feel . . . *good*.

We arrive at Flow just as two women round the corner from the opposite direction. One of them spots Darby and waves excitedly.

"Darby! I thought you gave up Saturday morning classes!"

Darby waves back, and I brace myself to be left behind.

I had planned on coming to this class by myself. I don't need a yoga buddy. Step three: "Exercise regularly" isn't about friendship—it's about yoga.

Watching the two women smile and laugh and talk, I'm instantly transported back to the first day of middle school. I'm standing in the cafeteria, holding a tray of food I don't want to eat, wearing an outfit I didn't pick out, searching for an empty chair by my friend, Mia.

Mia was my only friend throughout elementary school—mainly because our mothers were friends. We were, I suppose, forced together.

Friends by proximity. But still, friends. Mia was my security blanket.

Our moms would get together and we'd play with Barbie dolls or watch the Disney Channel, and there were times I thought I was the luckiest girl in the world to have a friend. It really was all I'd ever wanted.

For her birthday, I bought her one of those necklaces with a charm split in half and the words *Best Friends* engraved across two pieces. I gave her one half and kept the other for myself.

I reach up and touch the charm as the cafeteria worker swipes my card. Turning with my tray of food, I search the tables. I spot her across the room, sitting at a big round table with three other girls, and let out a breath when I see there's still an empty seat next to her.

I walk toward her, anxious to thank her for saving my spot, when Ashley Hull slips into the empty seat just as I reach the table. They all—Mia included—stop what they're doing and look at me.

"Can we *help* you?" Ashley asks, eyes wide under raised brows.

"Uh . . . I was . . . um . . ." But I don't have words.

"You . . . uh-uh-uh . . . what?" She laughs as if she's just made a hilarious joke.

I look over, but Mia isn't looking at me. And she isn't wearing the necklace.

"I think there's room over there," Emilia Roberts says with a smirk. "At the loser table."

They all laugh. Heat rushes up my cheeks, and I wait for Mia to come to my defense, all eyes except hers fixed on me.

"Mia . . . ?"

"Get a clue, weirdo," Ashley says. "She doesn't want to be friends with you anymore."

Finally, Mia meets my eyes. But instead of kindness, they flare with disgust. "She's right, *weirdo.* I was only your friend because my mom made me hang out with you. The loser table has your name written all over it."

I feel my shoulders slump, and my eyes burn hot with humiliation. My tray clatters to the ground, and I run through the doors into the hallway, the sound of their laughter at my back. I slam open the bathroom door and close myself in a stall, where I stay, crying, knees to my chest, for the rest of the lunch hour.

After the bell rings, I reach up and hold my half of the charm necklace, dangling from the chain around my neck. I rip it off and drop the necklace in the toilet. It *clinks* on the bottom of the porcelain.

I flush the necklace along with all the feelings I don't want to feel.

After school, my mother can tell something is wrong. I explain what happened at lunch, and her response—*why did I think it would be anything else?*—was simple: "Well, honey, you can't blame Mia for wanting to be popular. I told you to try harder to fit in."

And now I'm standing on the street outside of a yoga studio, hearing the *clink* again.

Darby knows people here. She's popular and friendly. She's got a seat at the table.

One look at what I'm wearing will tell these other women that I do not.

I turn toward the door, but before I can open it, Darby grabs me by the elbow and tugs me toward her. "Meg, Stacy, this is Isadora. She's my neighbor. She's *hilarious*."

My heart races. These women are clearly also regulars at the yoga studio. My face flushes with heat, and I brace myself for another humiliating exchange.

The one on the left, Meg, smiles at me. She has a blonde bob, skin so pale it's almost translucent, and is as skinny as a stick figure. The one on the right, Stacy, is curvier, with dark skin and a nearly shaved head.

"Your first class?" Stacy asks.

I nod.

Meg chimes in, "Are you ready?"

I pause and say matter-of-factly, "I would rather be in bed."

I'm shocked again when they all burst out laughing.

"I like you already, Izzy!" Stacy says. "Are you in for a *treat*!"

Izzy? Did I just get nicknamed?

Darby pulls open the studio door, where a rush of cold air and the smell of lavender incense welcome us inside.

Isadora, normally a solitary creature often left to her own devices, has found herself welcomed, with open arms, into the flock. Despite her prickly exterior and her inability to emote, the other animals have accepted Isadora as one of their own, and they set out on a journey of exploration, discovery . . . and adventure!

Yeah, I noticed that too, David. Nice observation there.

I appear to now be a part of this little group. Nobody dismissed me. Nobody made me feel like I didn't belong.

They moved over so I could sit at their table, and that has

never happened before. Not in middle school with Mia. Not in high school. And not even in college when I made one last paltry attempt at finding a friend.

"You think it's going to be easy because you're just stretching, but wait until Samira gets finished with you." Stacy nods toward a woman at the front of the room.

Samira is small, dark-haired, buxom, and toned. Those are four words that have never appeared in a sentence with my name.

All at once, I think this might've been the worst idea I've ever had. My muscles tense like a gazelle that sees the tall grass move. I could've gone for a walk. A walk, Isadora! A nice, long, brisk walk. That could've easily been classified as regular exercise, right? Especially given the fact that I'm not classifying Dr. Grace Monroe as a real doctor. There is obviously a sliding scale of legitimacy here.

There are suddenly two hands on my shoulders, put there from behind. "Don't even think about bolting, Isadora," Darby says with a laugh. She leans in close to my ear. "You're stuck with us."

Do . . . do I have friends now?

As the class begins and we all take our spots on the floor, those words linger through every single painful pose Samira forces my body into.

Stuck. Adhered. Glued.

Joined.

Being stuck with Darby and Stacy and Meg sounds, surprisingly, really, really nice.

And then Samira introduces me to lowered planks and I hate them all.

Chapter 11

"I never knew my muscles could hurt so much just from trying not to fall over," I say as Samira ends the class.

The other women laugh. I have no idea why.

"But how do you feel now?" Darby stands and starts rolling up her yoga mat.

I take stock of how I feel—for Darby (and my research). I know I'm supposed to say that I feel enlightened, or energized, but I don't.

"I feel tired," I say. "Yoga is exhausting. And way harder than it looks."

"Told ya." Stacy laughs.

Samira enters the conversation in a sneak attack, and when she stands next to me, I feel like the Amazons who trained Diana in *Wonder Woman*, but with less than half the strength. I slouch a little to make myself smaller.

"Yoga isn't for everyone," Samira says, making me feel like I've just been caught passing a note in class. "Find something you like, something you'll stick with."

"Like kickboxing," Stacy says, holding up a fist, flexing a bicep. "Makes me feel *strong*."

Samira smiles. "Yes, like that." She then puts her hand on my shoulder. "Don't be afraid to occupy your space. You have as much of a right to exist in this world as everyone else."

I instantly stand to my full height at this, the words in a holding pattern in my mind, looking for a place to land. When they do, they land hard, and an unexpected emotion pushes forward.

It feels strangely like confidence.

Tears prick the edges of my eyes and I look away to avoid being noticed.

Samira leaves, like a sweet, quiet monk who has doled out her wisdom and now must go pray for six hours.

"That was *deep*," Stacy says.

"She's so wonderful," Meg adds, then says brightly, "Well, I have to run! Mike is taking me out for our anniversary."

Darby and Stacy coo over this, but I can't bring myself to do the same. This kind of gooey girl talk has always deepened the divide between me and other women. Not that I'm *not* happy for Meg and Mike and their impending celebration—I'm sure they're wonderful people with wonderful anniversary plans and future babies whose names all start with the letter *M*—but my response is a simple nod and a smile. I see no reason to gush.

Meg and Stacy leave, and Darby tucks her rolled-up mat under her arm. "Let's stop by Mal's on the way home."

"Mal's?"

"Coffee?"

I know Mal's. Who doesn't know the little neighborhood coffee shop named after my favorite character in the short-lived, gone-too-soon TV show *Firefly*? I've just never gone there with another person before. "Um, yeah. Sure."

We start the block-and-a-half walk to Mal's, and Darby talks to me in a familiar way, as if we are longtime friends and not two people who just met this morning.

"Listen, I have to take advantage when Dante has the kids. I'm sure they've torn up the apartment and created a big pillow fort by now. God knows where I'll find the Nerf darts this time." She laughs, you know, as friends do. "I doubt he's even fed them. The man's a chef, but the number of times he forgets to feed his own children is borderline criminal."

I offer an observation. "Kids eat way more than their own body weight would suggest they need."

Darby turns, practically hitting me. "Right?! Like, I just fed you at noon, you're hungry again at four? What the heck is that about?"

We arrive at Mal's, people bustling in the caffeinated atmosphere. There is an autographed photo of Nathan Fillion dressed in his *Firefly* costume hanging near the cash register. I make eye contact with Mal and swoon a little, as if the renegade space captain can see into my soul.

I like the coffee—and the celebration of science fiction—at Mal's and often swing through on my way to work.

I never sit and stay, though.

For the first time, the purple velvet sectional tucked in the back corner looks more cozy than intimidating. Maybe because I'm not here by myself.

We order our drinks and move to the end of the counter.

"What about you, Isadora?" Darby turns to me.

"What about me?"

She laughs. "What do you do? My kids have speculated that you're either a secret agent or you're building a bomb in your bathroom."

I'm not sure how to take that, but Darby's tone is kind, so I choose not to be offended.

"I'm an academic researcher," I say. She's staring at me, expectant. "I . . . research things."

"That's cool! What kinds of things?"

I fish for a vague answer, mostly because I don't want to get too heady with what I do. I'm self-aware enough to know that when I talk about my job, people's eyes glaze over.

I'm also wishing I was the kind of person who could wear colorful yoga leggings and a tank top into a coffee shop and not feel like I'm on display in the circular glass pastry case.

"All kinds of things, really. Questions about the human condition, behavior, responses. Right now I'm working on a few different projects about relationships, happiness, human connection."

"I never would've guessed!" She picks up her drink from the barista. "Do you enjoy it?"

Now there's *a question.*

"I think so," I say honestly, which surprises me. "I . . ." I briefly pause, and in that pause decide to trust Darby. "I . . . actually decided to conduct my own experiment. Not for work, just for me."

"Like, for fun?" Darby asks.

"I guess so," I say, though I've never looked at it that way. "Fun" for me consists of books, obscure science fiction movies, and the occasional junk food binge. Is it strange that my work excites me more than anything else?

We sit on the purple velvet sectional, and Darby's eyes are wide and hopeful. "Is it a *secret* experiment?"

I smile. "I'm not building a bomb."

She breaks a piece off her scone and pops it in her mouth. "My kids will be so disappointed. That was the top guess." She smiles. "Well? Tell me."

And that's how I end up spilling the whole idea of the 31 Ways to my neighbor—practically a stranger—over a peppermint mocha in our neighborhood coffee shop.

I didn't plan to tell her about the experiment. Or about Dr. Grace Monroe. Or Marty and our bench, but maybe years of *not* talking has finally caught up with me. Before I know what I'm saying, it's all out there.

And Darby isn't running away. In fact, she actually seems interested.

"So every day is like a new adventure," Darby says.

I sip my drink. "I don't know—do you call smiling at someone an adventure?"

Just then, a group of men enter Mal's, and we both look. Darby leans in close and practically whispers, "Depends on how cute he is."

A memory skitters through my mind. *Cal. He's holding out the pencils. Our fingers touch.* I can feel my face flush as I swat the thought away.

"Ooh. That hit a nerve," she says. "Because whoever you're thinking about just turned your face the color of a summer-ripe tomato."

Caught, I widen my eyes and shake my head. "Oh, I do that. My face . . . it's hot in here . . . and my coffee . . ." I splutter. "It's nothing."

She squints as she looks me over. "Well, it's clear you're not an actress. Or a poker player." Darby holds up a hand. "I'll let it slide. I get it, I'm new, and I can tell sharing about yourself isn't your favorite."

I'm stunned. She's caught on to this—to me—in one morning. I'm even more stunned it doesn't seem to bother her. It's as if she's got a handle on who I am and she's fine with it.

Maybe Darby is the kind of person who simply allows people to be who they are. I might as well be having coffee with a unicorn.

I haven't met someone like her in, well, maybe ever. People at work, Ashley and Mia from grade school, Alex, even my mother; they, on varying levels, were all trying to change me from who I was to who they wanted me to be.

My mother tried to turn me into Mia and Ashley. Mia and Ashley tried to turn me into a loser. Alex tried to turn me into a doormat.

Marty was right. Maybe I didn't enjoy spending time with

people because I hadn't found the right people to spend time with.

But as soon as the thought enters my mind, I remember the pain of losing a best friend, a boyfriend, my parents' approval.

And I've accepted that I'll never, ever be enough. Not even for someone as seemingly accepting as Darby. Nothing against her—that's just how these things always end. Still, knowing it doesn't keep me from wanting to try.

"It's all so fascinating," Darby says, pulling me from my thoughts.

"What is?"

"You. Your job. The fact that I've lived next to you for years and never knew you. I'll be honest, the most interesting thing I've discussed with anyone lately was the conversation I had with Delilah about which nineties boy band really *was* the best. She came up with a scoring system and everything." She gives me a look. "She's really into nineties music for some reason. I blame her father."

"Her father likes boy bands?"

Darby barks a laugh so loud that people at nearby tables look over. I'm beginning to learn that Darby is a loud laugher. "No. He introduced her to Nirvana, which led her to discover nineties grunge, which led her to New Kids on the Block, and the rest is history. Delilah was very likely born to the wrong generation."

"I always say the same thing about myself," I tell her.

"What generation do you see yourself in?"

"The late 1800s," I say without hesitation. "I would be a 'New Woman,' someone who pursued a self-sufficient life and who was not dependent on a husband."

Darby stares, her mouth curved up in a disbelieving smile.

"I'd also take on various low-impact sporting activities, like bicycling. Though I don't think I would like having to wear a corset, so maybe I need to rethink my answer." I take a sip of my coffee, then set it down. "Can you imagine life before yoga pants?" I shudder at the thought.

Darby is still staring. "Isadora. You are, by a mile, one of the most fascinating people I've ever met."

I have no idea what she's talking about.

Darby grins. "I want to do these adventures with you. The experiment. The 31 Ways. What's next?"

"I'm not sure," I say, not really wanting a partner in all this. I've already agreed to keep Marty in the loop—adding Darby to the mix would be tricky. The irony of this predicament doesn't escape me. Who would've thought I'd have two too many research partners? "I haven't picked yet."

"You'll have to text me tonight and let me know. It sounds fun!" She grabs my phone, takes a selfie, and clicks around, presumably to add her contact information. A few seconds later, her phone dings. She holds it up and I'm too late to realize she's taking a photo of me. "There. Now we have each other's numbers. Just text me when you run out of toilet paper or you see my naked child falling down the stairs." She takes a long sip of her iced coffee. "I'm willing the caffeine into my bones. I hardly slept last night. Even in the middle of the night, someone shorter than me always seems to need me."

I turn my cup around in my hand. "You're lucky that way."

She stills. "Huh. You think so?"

I hadn't before, but I do now. When Darby goes home, she'll be met by five other people who need her. They'll have noticed her absence and be thankful she's returned. When I go home, the only thing waiting for me is silence.

And bare walls, which I can now never unsee. Thanks, Darby.

I nod my reply and draw in a breath. "Anyway, that's why I went to yoga today," I say. "Step three: 'Exercise regularly.'"

"And?"

"And what?"

"And what did you think?"

I think on this for a long moment before finally saying, "It didn't make me happy at all."

Chapter 12

For the next week, in between catching up on Cal's research and avoiding seeing him in person, I make a point to exercise every single day, for research—and research only.

I go to three more yoga classes with Darby, and my hamstrings are unionizing to plan to stage a coup. I take long, if somewhat slow, walks at lunchtime with Marty.

One of the days, I strolled into the university's gym with the intention of trying out one of the exercise machines for a little variety, and after three seconds I walked back out.

I'm totally counting that as a full-on workout, though, because the calories I burned worrying about it warrant it.

Sunday, after completing step four: "Declutter your space" (which *did* give me a sense of satisfaction that, I think, could be described as happiness), and in order to keep my mind off of the impending Sunday dinner with Darby and her family, I dove headfirst into the stack of papers Cal left on my desk over a week ago.

I spend most of the afternoon culling through this research and organizing his thoughts in a way that makes sense.

Spending that many hours with his pages—sticky notes on

nearly every sheet with hand-written notes to himself—makes Dr. Cal Baxter, professor of psychology, more than just a pretty face.

He'd left himself a trail of thoughts that seemed almost personal. For instance, one page—interviews with couples who claimed social media had ruined their relationships—had a yellow note stuck to it with the word "Sasha" written in black marker.

These sorts of crumbs had me wondering if this book was simply his stab at publication or if there was a deeper reason for it. Why would a person conduct experiments on the human connection?

Isadora, dear, isn't that kind of what you're doing?

Why was it important for him to prove that technology, arguably the greatest tool for bringing people together, was also responsible for driving us apart? And didn't it bother him that he'd practically given me a ticket to the inner workings of his mind?

I have to admit, Dr. Cal Baxter has become as intriguing as the research itself. A puzzle I want to solve.

Around five o'clock, the smell of garlic wafting over from next door stirs me from my thoughts, and when I remember that I get to sample one of Dante's best dishes for dinner—gnocchi with pomodoro sauce—I'm far more excited than a person should be because of food. This excitement nearly eliminates my nerves at the thought of sharing a meal with people who are mostly strangers.

I find the chaos of my neighbors' apartment slightly overwhelming, and the pointed glare of her oldest daughter, Delilah, slightly unnerving. Darby reprimands Delilah twice but eventually gives up, telling me, "Ignore her, Isadora. She's still trying to decide if she believes you're not a secret agent."

I give Delilah my best mysterious smirk and do as Darby has told me to. The little girl seems unfazed by my disinterest, and twice I catch her scribbling what I assume are thoughts about me in a little notebook.

I am curious about what she's writing but pretend not to be. I survive the whole ordeal and leave an hour and a half later with a tinfoil-topped container of very tasty leftovers.

As I try to fall asleep that night, I realize I haven't had dinner with anyone but my television since Alex left, and for the first time, I wonder if he made me even more reclusive than I already was. In retrospect, of course, I realize he wasn't good for me.

Compromise is easier when the pain is familiar.

I wish Hallmark would reach out—I've got hundreds of these zingers for their Cards for All Occasions line.

And why in the world am I still letting him affect me two years later? Am I so incapable of moving on?

The following Monday morning, when Logan and Shellie walk in, I purposely look up, and when they pass by the door to my office on the way into the lab, Logan stops.

"Did you have a good weekend, Miss Bentley?" he asks.

"I did yoga," I say dryly.

"Oh, I love yoga!" Shellie gushes. "I always feel so energized when I'm done. Did you love it?"

"No," I say. "I don't know why I keep going." This isn't entirely true. I'm going because there, with Darby and Meg and Stacy, I feel like I'm a part of something. Also, I really want a punch card. Even if my head starts spinning every time I try downward dog.

Shellie's face falls, and I try to read the emotion that's landed on her as a result of my reply.

"But I'm glad I went," I add. "It was my fourth time going,

and I think my muscles just happen to hate the instructor. I keep thinking I'll get better."

She smiles then, as if the sting of a barb I didn't know I'd inflicted has been soothed. "You will. That's why they call it a practice."

I smile back—I'm getting better at that, by the way—and I wonder if this is what *human connection* looks like.

This idea has me thinking about Cal's research again. Or maybe Cal's research has me wondering about this little interaction. Or maybe I'm just thinking about Cal.

The exchange with Shellie normally would have gone unnoticed, but I'm hyperaware now. Maybe there's a part of me that knows I've stood in my own way when it comes to human connection. Or maybe I'm still that middle schooler, desperately looking for someone to wear the other half of my Best Friends necklace.

As Logan and Shellie head off to the lab, I pick up Cal's stack of research, much of which I still haven't touched. So far, I've concluded that while he's thorough and has a good foundation for his project, his thoughts are like a chimp found a dictionary and a shredder.

At least he was honest about his lack of organizational skills.

The morning drags on, and I find myself peeking at the courtyard through the windows in the lab to see if Marty has arrived. I'm so thankful I have someone to eat lunch with again.

At noon, I head through the cafeteria line for a turkey and cheese sandwich, and when I exit the building into the courtyard, the sun hits my face. The warmth of it stops me in my tracks. I inhale a deep breath and exhale slowly, closing my eyes as I let it warm me from the outside in.

Step five: "Breathe deeply." And I do.

I breathed plenty deep in yoga, but it doesn't count if one is gasping for air.

I stay still for a few minutes, inhaling on a three-count and exhaling just as slowly. Long, deep breaths just the way Darby did that first day when we stepped outside on the way to yoga—something she does regularly, I've learned.

I wonder how some people inherently know to do this while others, like me, walk through life head down, not paying attention to any of it.

I also wonder if this paying attention thing is going to make me any happier. Let's be honest—with my life, it could go either way. I have reasons why I've never bothered to engage.

After another moment, I look up to find Marty sitting on our bench, brown paper sack on his lap. As I approach, he grins at me. "Isadora, you look radiant this afternoon."

I do a little curtsy with an invisible dress and return his smile. "Why, thank you. You're looking quite dapper yourself."

"Miriam made us cookies." He holds up the bag, giving it a little shake.

"I love cookies." I sit next to him and set my food on my lap. "Wait, does that mean you told her about our lunches?"

"She thinks it's fabulous I have a friend." He pauses thoughtfully. "Really, I think she's happy that she's not the only one responsible for entertaining me anymore."

"What makes you say that?"

He pulls out a plastic bag of cookies and sets them on the bench between us. "Because these are guilt cookies." Another smile accompanies his sideways glance. "So . . . I haven't seen you in two days. Tell me where we are in the happiness experiment."

"I met another friend last week." I pull half of my sandwich from my wrapper. "Darby. She's my neighbor. She has a little naked demon child who woke me up on a Saturday morning and pulled my pants down in front of her, but then she went to yoga with me."

He pauses. "There's a lot to unpack in that sentence."

"I'm an enigma, Marty."

He laughs. "Yoga, huh?" Marty sounds impressed. "How was that?"

"On a scale of one to ten, it comes in at a solid two." I take a bite of my sandwich, careful not to reenact the mayonnaise fiasco.

"That's okay," he says. "Not everything you try is an instant way to happiness."

"If I'm honest, it wasn't all bad," I say. "Darby and I went for coffee after at this little shop in our neighborhood called Mal's. We sat on the purple velvet couch, and I blabbed about my experiment to her too."

"And here I thought you didn't like talking to people." Marty grins. I can smell that his sandwich today is salami and cheddar.

"I think I prefer our walks to yoga," I say. "But being with Darby is as nice as being with you." I smile at him and add, "Almost."

He rewards me with a grin.

"Well, lunches and walks with an old guy north of seventy," Marty says. "Not hard to rate higher than that."

"True," I say. "But you don't come to lunch with eighteen kids all under the age of four. That's a win."

He chuckles to himself and takes another bite of his sandwich.

"I also decluttered my apartment," I blather on, noting that I like telling Marty about my life. I like having someone to share these things with. Someone who seems eager to listen. I imagine most people would see us as a mismatch, but I think something divine brought us together.

I wonder if Marty needs me as much as I'm starting to realize I need him.

What an arrogant thought. I can't think of a single time someone has needed me for something other than work.

I'm still talking—telling him that decluttering was good for my soul, though, in truth, there wasn't much to get rid of—when someone catches my eye across the courtyard.

"Oh my gosh. That's Darby."

Marty follows my gaze to where tiny Darby is pushing a giant stroller and towing another child alongside her. Delilah, carrying a book, trails behind.

"Neighbor Darby?" Marty chuckles at the sight of Darby and her brood and eats half of an oatmeal raisin cookie in one bite. "You weren't kidding—she certainly has got her hands full."

Darby spots me and waves. "Isadora!" She's still a good distance away from me, so she's shouted this, drawing the attention of several people in the quad. My shoulders slump, and the desire to hide overwhelms me.

Why? Why do I do that?

I remember what Samira told me on my first day of class. *"Occupy your space."*

I stand and wave back at Darby but make no move to help her haul her tiny humans into my lunch bubble. Two worlds are colliding, like inviting band kids and football players to the same party—and I'm not sure how to feel about it.

Chapter 13

When Darby reaches us, she's out of breath, but not surprisingly, she's grinning.

"Had to get out and enjoy the day. Whew! It's a teacher institute day, so everyone's home, and these rug rats need their vitamin D. I was halfway here when I remembered you said you eat in the courtyard at the university," she says through huffs of breath. "It's okay that we're crashing your lunch, right? Thought I'd show the kids you're not a bomb maker."

I shift at this and notice Delilah, Darby's oldest, is eyeing me again, as if still trying to uncover my secret life. Without thinking, I narrow my eyes at her and rub my hands together, villain-style. "Or am I?" I say flatly.

I believe what I just did was make a joke. On purpose.

"Isadora, you're a nutcase," Darby says, not unkindly. "Is this Marty?"

"I am," Marty says. "I'm flattered Isadora mentioned me! Come sit, come sit. The more the merrier." Darby spreads a large, multicolored blanket on the grass next to the bench.

"So you're the one who saw Isadora in her skivvies." Marty says this as I am mid-drink, and I proceed to choke and spit a mouthful onto my lap.

Darby laughs and pulls juice boxes from a bottomless bag, handing one to each of her kids. "And you're the one who met his wife in this courtyard."

"Correct," Marty says.

Darby smiles at him and I breathe a silent sigh of relief that my two worlds are going to get along just fine. It's odd, though. I'm not a connector of people. But listening to a friend I made on a bench share his story about the first time he saw his wife with my neighbor I met in a hallway because her son swore at me and pulled down my pants—well, it's kind of wonderful. These two never would've met if it hadn't been for me.

After Marty finishes his story, Darby clutches her hands to her chest like a woman in a soap opera and wipes an actual tear from her eye. "That is the sweetest story I've ever heard."

Marty tosses her a slight shrug, hands up, as if to say, *"What can I say? I'm a romantic."*

Danny, now securely fastened by child-leash to the stroller, is shouting and trying to walk toward some kids in the quad playing disc golf, pulling the stroller sideways almost to the point of tipping over. Darby stops the tip with one foot while simultaneously quieting Diego with goldfish crackers. Impressive, actually. She then turns her attention to me as if it's perfectly natural for her to have performed this little move.

"Okay, so what are we doing today?" she asks.

"Well, I'm working," I say, motioning to the buildings all around us.

"I mean for our experiment," she says, clapping her hands together. "What step are we on?" She turns to Marty. "I thought yesterday would be something fun I could jump in on, but when I went to her apartment to tell her dinner was ready, I found her cleaning. I have to do enough of that in my own apartment, so I left."

"Are you a scientist, Miss Bentley?" Delilah asks between

bites of her peanut butter and jelly. I notice that she is now single-handedly keeping her middle brother, Danny, from running off, while Dora and Diego are still strapped into the stroller.

"I'm a researcher here at the university," I tell her.

"Isadora is researching how to be happy," Darby explains.

"How do you research that?" Delilah asks.

I swallow my potato chip. "Mostly by conducting experiments."

"She throws herself into new things every few days," Darby says. "That's why she started going to yoga with Mommy."

"And that works?" Delilah has abandoned her sandwich now and seems genuinely interested.

"I guess we'll see," I tell her. "I'm on step five of thirty-one."

"Wow." Delilah considers this for a moment, then says, "When you find out, can you let me know? I would like to test it out for myself."

I stare at the girl in silence and admiration as Darby shakes her head. "I swear, she's a seventy-year-old woman in a ten-year-old body."

"I'm afraid you'll be bored by my step today," I say. "Step five: 'Breathe deeply.'"

Darby frowns. "That *is* boring. Aren't there any 'go skydiving' type steps? Something to get you out of the house? Heck, even Bingo is more interesting than cleaning and breathing."

"I'm sure there are more exciting steps, but I'm working my way up to those."

By now, Dora has crawled halfway out of her stroller and onto Marty's lap. He seems perfectly unbothered by this, which fascinates me. If a child tried to latch onto my lap, I'd probably call for security to have it removed.

Our group of two has multiplied exponentially, and my quiet lunch hour has turned into an event. I munch on my carrot sticks while Darby peppers Marty with questions and her children clamor for her attention. Except Delilah. She's pulled out her book and seems perfectly content not to be a part of any of it.

I love her.

I watch as she thoughtfully turns a page. In the out-of-focus distance of my gaze I notice Cal is striding toward us.

It takes a second for this to register in my brain.

Cal. Is walking. Up.

My pulse races. *Breathe deeply. Breathe deeply. Breathe deeply.*

Note to self: repetitive deep breathing will result in lightheadedness and hyperventilation if done in rapid succession.

I'm thinking about his scattered research and the way it led me from one subject to the next, and all those questions that had popped up about Cal are back. Who is Sasha? Why *this* research subject? What does he have against social media? Does he have a girlfriend?

"Hey, Isadora, it's our friend!" Marty says as Dora swipes half of a cookie from his hand and shoves it in her mouth.

"Whoa, hot professor alert," Darby says through a closed mouth when she sees him.

"Darby!" I hiss at her.

"Do you have a crush on this guy?" Darby asks, low and quiet.

I momentarily pull my attention away from Cal to drill a shut-up stare into Darby's forehead. I've gotten a good enough look at him to know he's wearing jeans and a simple blue button-down, sleeves rolled to the elbows. He's got his glasses on, which makes him look smart *and* attractive at the same time.

I do a quick mayo check on my cheeks and ears, resisting the urge to take a napkin to everything above my neck.

"Dr. Baxter is Isadora's coworker." Marty is trying to rescue me, though he already knows the answer to Darby's question.

Cal stops in front of our group, surveying the assortment of people gathered around this perfectly ordinary bench. "Wow, quite the group! How is everyone?"

"We're good—we're more than we were an hour ago," Marty says, laughing heartily.

"Hey, Marty, good to see you."

I don't look up, but I can feel Cal's eyes on me.

"Isadora."

When he says my name, I snap to attention like something is physically wrong with me. I catch Darby's expression, which seems to be saying, *"Hold it together!"*

"Hi, Dr. Baxter," I say. At least I think I said it out loud.

"It's Cal," he says. "Even my students call me Cal."

"Well, that's disrespectful," I blurt. "Hard work deserves respect, and it's hard work to get your doctorate. These kids don't know that."

He smiles. It's a kind smile, not a patronizing one. "I appreciate the sentiment, Isadora. We should probably connect today or tomorrow about that research," he says. "Did you have a chance to look it over?"

"Yes. It's a mess."

He chuckles. "I warned you."

"I color-coded it for you," I say. "And began organizing it into categories. I noticed you have a chapter outline, but I think it needs tweaking, and some of the chapters simply don't have enough material yet."

"Ah," he says. "I was afraid of that." Cal looks at Darby, her kids, then at me. Then at Darby, then at me again.

He's trying to tell me something, I know it.

Darby jumps in. "I'm Darby, Isadora's neighbor." She's standing now, Diego on her hip, stars in her eyes. "So"—she flicks her hand between Cal and me—"you guys work together?"

I shoot her a look, but she ignores it. She's completely smitten with Cal. Or maybe—and I'm just guessing here—she's smitten with the idea of me having a crush on Cal. Because there is something in her stance that makes me think she's going to try to play matchmaker.

My fight-or-flight reflexes are on high alert at this realization, and I reenter the conversation like a stagehand accidentally falling onto a stage through a piece of scenery.

"My boss assigned me to him. To it. To the project." *Idiot.* "I'm . . . helping organize his research."

"And what's it about?" Darby asks.

"It's about the human connection," Marty says with a snicker.

"That's right," I say, aware of the irony of *me*, Isadora Bentley, researching anything having to do with that particular topic. "Nothing you'd be interested in, I don't think. Cal"—good grief, his name feels weird in my mouth—"I think I'm free tomorrow."

And every day for the rest of my life, if you want.

"So, wait, is that what your '31 Ways to Be Happy' project is for?"

I widen my eyes at Cal and slow turn to Darby. *Shut. Up.*

Darby continues, either oblivious or on purpose. "I mean, I can kind of see the connection. It all relates to happiness and relationships and, you know, interpersonal connections, that sort of—"

Cal interrupts. "What's this now?"

I want to dive under the bench and hide.

I've already told two perfect strangers about my experiment—and neither Marty nor Darby have the kind of effect on me that Cal does. Frankly, I don't care if they think I'm a weirdo.

But I care what Cal thinks.

"You didn't tell him?" Darby shoots me a look. "You should totally tell him. It would be perfect research for this social experimentation, or whatever you call it."

Inwardly, I groan. Outwardly, I take a breath and hold it.

"Did I say something wrong?" Now Darby looks worried. "Was it a secret? Oh no, I'm so sorry. I just assumed, since you told me the same day we met, that it wasn't a big deal."

Forcing a smile to my face is like trying to extract a woodland creature from a bear trap. "It's not a big deal, it's just—"

"Just what?" Cal's eyes are trained on me, waiting for an answer and truly the same color as a summer sky.

"Nothing," I say. "Just, nothing. I've . . ." I sigh. I'm not getting out of this. "I've been doing a little experiment of my own. That's all."

At that, Cal moves over to the picnic blanket and sits down next to Delilah, who barely notices him.

My life would be so much easier right now if I were ten. And had a book.

"I can't wait to hear about it," Cal says.

Darby grins open-mouthed at me like this is the best thing that's ever happened.

Marty holds up his bag. "You look like you need a cookie."

Chapter 14

It turns out that Dr. Cal Baxter finds my experiment fascinating.

Of course he does.

I've given him a very brief overview of my experiment, and now he's asking questions. Lots of questions. I suppose this is to his credit, given his line of work, but I don't like being the center of anyone's attention—especially his.

"How far into the experiment are you?" he asks.

"I wouldn't call it an experiment," I hedge. "It's more of a project. Just for me. Really. I got the idea because I am determined to prove the author of an article I read wrong."

"How many steps have you done?"

"Just four," I say. "Today is my fifth. So far I've smiled at someone, complimented someone, started exercising, and decluttered my apartment. And your research. I decluttered that too."

"And I'm eternally grateful." When he smiles, the heavens open and a stream of sunlight falls on his shoulders.

I might've dreamt that last bit.

"And step five is . . . ?"

"'Breathe deeply,'" I say.

"Let's do it now," Darby says, and they all close their eyes, inhaling and exhaling as if Samira had just instructed them to do so.

After a few seconds, Cal opens his eyes and looks at me. I feel caught.

I feel seen.

He grins at me and mouths, *"Close your eyes!"*

I do as he tells me, trying not to laugh, aware that this almost feels like we have just shared a moment. An inside joke. I can't keep from smiling at the thought. I've always been on the outside of inside jokes.

I stay like that, eyes scrunched shut, listening for cues that I could be done deep-breathing, before I finally dare to peek again. When I do, I think maybe Marty has fallen asleep, but Darby and Cal are both watching me.

"That's a good one, Isadora," Darby says. "You should do that often. Anytime you feel overwhelmed or, you know, anxious."

Ah, Overwhelmed and Anxious, those old friends. I wonder how she's seen them hanging around me, but I don't ask. I don't want her to tell me any truths that might humiliate me in front of Cal.

I don't need any help in that department.

Danny and Dora are now taking turns spinning and wrapping themselves up yo-yo style in the tether. "Yeah, I should go." Darby stands. "It's about one, and one is when I duct-tape these kids to the wall." The kids protest loudly, and Darby hugs them close. Delilah stands but doesn't put her book down.

I love her.

In the midst of gathering and packing and separating kids referee-style, Darby says, "Thanks for letting us come eat with you!"

"Oh, we weren't . . ." I stop myself before finishing with *"given that much of a choice."* I scramble for words and end with, "bothered at all that you came." C- on the recovery.

I simultaneously realize I like that she joined us. It felt nice to be sought out. Darby came here because she knew Marty and I would be here. Maybe she and I really could be friends.

I bet she *would've worn the Best Friends necklace.*

She looks up at me, and I realize I've been staring at her.

"You okay, Isadora?"

I smile involuntarily and look away, but unfortunately for me, I turn in Cal's direction. There are a million things out here he could be looking at—the robin in the tree beside us, the group of students playing disc golf (terribly), a maintenance worker driving a golf cart at what has to be its max speed—but Cal isn't looking at any of those things.

Cal is looking at me.

When our eyes meet, my breathing stops and I wonder how long I can hold this breath before I need mouth-to-mouth.

I look down. Down is always safe.

"Isadora?" Darby has packed up all her little people in record time and is now also fully focused on me.

I see Delilah's eyes dart to mine. The corner of her mouth lifts in a slight smile. Somehow it comforts me, and I lift my chin to look at her mother. "I'm good." I glance at Delilah, lean in, and say to her, "Just having conversations with myself in my head."

Delilah leans in to me and quips dryly, "My mom knows a good psychiatrist for that."

Against my will, a laugh escapes. I really do love this little girl.

"Oh, D, I swear." Darby shakes her head, amused. "Marty, it was so nice to meet you, and Dr. Baxter . . . *Cal*." She looks up all gooey and holds out a hand, which he takes and shakes.

"Darby, you're married," I practically shout.

Darby, without missing a beat, retorts, "But *you* aren't, Isadora." If emojis were able to be vocalized, she would've put that obnoxious winky smiling face followed by three or four heart-eyed faces.

She waves a hand at me. "Oh, stop it, I'm just teasing. You know I like you so much! We'll see you all later, I hope!"

And with that she's off, her exit leaving me embarrassed but cozy, like a warm blanket left out in the sunshine. Darby likes me *so much.*

"I should go too. Soccer game this afternoon." Marty grunts as he stands. "But you should have these." He hands me the bag of cookies. I start to protest, but he hands them closer. "Miriam made another batch, so I have plenty more."

I take his offering with a quiet "Thank you" and watch as Marty goes.

"Same time tomorrow?" he calls over his shoulder.

"I'll be here!" Only then do I realize that they've all gone, and I've been left alone with Cal.

"And then there were two . . ." Cal stuffs his hands in his pockets, which somehow transforms him to adorable.

I start off toward the building, and he falls into step next to me.

"So . . . what do you think about sharing your research with me?" he asks.

"At this point, you really need to worry about organizing the massive number of interviews and surveys you already have into some sort of cohesive, digestible, readable format—not add more to the mess."

"Okay, harsh," he says with a laugh. "True, but harsh. You really don't beat around the bush, do you?"

I stop moving and look at him. "No, I . . . don't. I know, I'm sorry. My mother says I need a filter, and that if I had one, ninety-nine percent of what I say would go unsaid."

He gives me a quizzical look. "I'm sorry she says that."

His apology is so sincere it knocks the wind out of me. "She's probably right," I say when I finally find my voice again. "I never learned how to censor myself, I guess."

He pulls open the door and holds it until I walk through. "It's refreshing. Most people never say what they really think, but you speak your mind."

"To a fault."

"Nah. You should own it. It's a pro, not a con. Like, if you hated my beard, you'd probably say so. Out loud. Without a second thought."

I stop again. "I don't hate your beard."

My fingers are twitching again, and I force myself not to reach up and touch his face. I've never touched a beard. My father has never had one, and I can't imagine ever being close enough to touch him anyway. He isn't a touchable kind of dad.

I really need to say something. Thank goodness Cal steps in to save me.

He chuckles. "It's okay, you don't have to say that. I was speaking hypothetically."

"Oh." I start back down the hall toward the elevator. "Right."

The elevator dings and the doors open, and when Cal follows me in, my mind flashes to the many, many episodes of *Grey's Anatomy* I've watched and the pivotal role the elevator always seems to play. Of course, those doctors don't need an elevator to hook up (they don't seem picky about location), but for whatever reason, it's practically impossible for two attractive medical professionals to take a simple elevator ride that doesn't end in a make-out session.

My heart rate quickens at the thought of being locked in a three-foot by four-foot box with Cal, and seconds before the doors close, I jump out into the hallway. I successfully dodge the retractable sensors that would make the elevator think it was crushing someone in its doors, and rush away. I hear Cal call out, "Isadora?" but I'm down the hall, away from him, and dart straight into the bathroom. This is all getting to be too much. Somehow, my feelings, which are normally so controlled and obedient, are starting to spiral out of my control.

I blame Dr. Grace Monroe for this. That dumb article has dredged up feelings I didn't even know I had.

I realize as I walk into the bathroom that I am breathing deeply again, this time without even trying.

I walk over to the mirror and look at myself.

Isadorkus.

The taunt assaults my memory without my permission. It's what they chanted at me in the hallways throughout high school. I look closely at my reflection. Has anything really changed since then?

I was supposed to prove to them all how wrong they were. I was supposed to return triumphantly, all Julia Ormond in *Sabrina* or Drew Barrymore in *Never Been Kissed.* But when I look at my reflection, I see that same girl. Different glasses, maybe. Longer hair, for sure. No poorly cut bangs—thankfully—but at the heart of me, she's still there.

"Stop it, Isadora," I say out loud. "You are not that girl anymore."

There's a knock on the door.

Threatened with the possibility of discovery, Isadora Bentley regresses to her basest of instincts—standing . . . absolutely . . . still. She might believe that her enemy's vision depends on movement, like the T. rex, so muscles tightened, breath barely audible, Isadora hopes to elude capture by simply becoming . . . part of the furniture.

Another knock. Who knocks on the door of a public restroom?

When Cal calls out, "Isadora? Are you in there?" I have my answer.

A panicked Isadora looks back at me from the mirror.

"Are you okay?" he calls through what I think is now a crack in the door.

My reflection looks as clueless as I feel. "You're no help," I hiss at it.

Breathe deeply. Good grief, this step is getting a workout.

I breathe in and blow out a breath and then cross the bathroom to the door. When I pull it open, I find him standing there, and I immediately and involuntarily slam it shut. I scold myself silently, take another breath, and then open the door again.

The genuine concern on his face surprises me. It stirs something deep—an emotion I don't immediately recognize. It feels dangerous, like I shouldn't be feeling it, so I force it to go away.

I run my hands over my dress pants and bring my gaze to his. I clear my throat, and as if everything is A-OK, I say, "Sorry."

"No, it's okay, it's just . . . you ran off so fast, I was afraid you were going to throw up." He's waiting for me to say something next because that's how conversations usually go. But for the life of me, I can't think of anything to say. My mind has gone as blank as a school whiteboard in the summer.

"Isadora?"

"Hmm?"

"Are you okay?"

"Mm-hmm." I eke past him into the hallway, and finally I can breathe again. After a moment, he starts after me.

"I'm good," I call over my shoulder. I pull open the door to the stairwell and head up the two flights, the promise of solitude spurring me on. "Not sick!"

"So . . . ?" He's caught up to me now, and we've reached the third floor. We're standing there, in the stairwell, the only two humans in sight, and I realize this is every bit as intimate as the elevator. "Are you claustrophobic?" he asks. "I once got trapped in an elevator, so I understand if you have a phobia or—"

"You make me nervous."

Blurt: transitive verb. *To utter abruptly or impulsively.*

I am an expert blurter.

He takes a step back. "Oh. I'm sorry."

I smile awkwardly and fold my arms over my chest defensively.

"Can I ask why?"

I feel my shoulders drop. "No." *No, you cannot ask me why.* The myriad reasons run through my mind. *Because you have the hands of a piano player. Because I want to touch your face. Because when you look at me, I feel like you really see me.*

"No?"

"I like my comfort zone, and the last couple of weeks, I've been pushed outside of it too many times to count."

"Because of your experiment?"

"Yes. I don't exercise. I don't normally smile that much. Decluttering was fine, but I like things how they are. I've settled into a nice routine that doesn't involve . . ." I trail off, waving my hand as if I'm going to grab the right word to put at the end of the sentence.

Cal says the silent thing out loud.

"People?"

He has an uncanny ability to read my mind.

"I mean . . . no. But . . . kind of. And when Gary assigned me to you . . ." I flounder. "I'm just used to working alone."

"Ah, so maybe it's not *me* that makes you nervous but people in general?"

No, it's you. I respond with a shrug.

He pauses, then says, "Isadora, what made you decide to do this experiment in the first place? Is it because you're unhappy and you want to know why?"

Warning bells go off at the back of my mind. Suspecting he actually sees *me* is very different from giving him a front-row seat to my particular brand of crazy. That's not what I do. It will be far easier to avoid any messy feelings if I don't share them.

"I just think maybe if it is, and you *are* unhappy, then getting outside your comfort zone could be a good thing." His slight shrug punctuates the sentence, and I can tell he's used great caution in addressing this issue with me. He seems to have a rare sixth sense that, against all odds, understands what it is I'm not saying.

What it is that maybe I don't want to admit. That proving Dr. Grace Monroe wrong is only part of my reason. But what if there's more to it than that?

"Maybe," I say.

"Just do what you do best. Look at the facts. Empirical data. Categorize. Color-code, if you must."

A smile pushes through—I know he's referring to his bird's nest approach to note-taking. "It's bad," I say.

He smiles. "Yeah. It's bad. I know. I am *very* aware that organization isn't my strongest suit."

He leans back against the wall. I notice he's no longer wearing his glasses. And as much as I like his glasses, I also like this unobstructed view of his blue eyes.

"Look, Isadora, if we're going to work together, I want us to be friends."

"Friends," I repeat.

"Yes. Friends." He smiles. "I don't want you to be nervous around me, and if I made you uncomfortable, I—"

"No, you didn't," I interrupt.

And there's a moment—a brief flicker of a moment—when our eyes meet, and my breath catches in my throat and my heart does the two-step.

"It wasn't you." I look away. "Sorry, it's me. I'm not great with people."

"Well, if your lunchtime crew is any indication, your days of being alone are over, Isadora Bentley." His smile widens.

He's right. I've gone and gotten myself a "lunchtime crew."

Marty and Darby and Delilah and the twins and the baby who talks like a sailor.

Chapter 15

"I saw your chapter breakdown, which isn't actually half bad," I tell Cal.

"That sounds like a compliment, but I'm actually not sure," he says back.

"And I've begun to arrange your research into those categories. I've made notes here—" I hold out the pages, pointing to the pink sticky note stuck to the side. "Just some ideas for additional research that could be done or, in some cases, taking out surveys I don't feel you need."

"Wow." Cal is leaning forward in his chair on the opposite side of the desk. "This is awesome, Isadora."

I feel my cheeks flush at the words. "It is?"

"Yeah," he says. "My mind doesn't work like this. I love the research and the data and the information, but when it comes to categorizing it, I get . . ."

"Lost in the weeds?"

He laughs. "Very. I love the details but hate the distribution. It's uncharacteristic for someone who loves the finer points to be so cluttered."

"Well, that's okay, because now you've got me." As soon as the words are out of my mouth, I want to reel them back in. "You know, to help. With the . . . organizing and stuff. I'm fresh off a stint of decluttering and . . ."

If my mouth were sitting next to me, I would've kicked its shin under the table.

When he smiles at me and says, "Thank goodness," I relax a little.

I realize in that moment I'm walking a familiar tightrope here. This situation is not unprecedented. *Alex welcomed my help too.*

"You know," he continues, "about your research—one could argue that you'd benefit from an unbiased assessment of your findings."

I consider this. And darn it, it's a fair point. My judgment could cloud the results. Am I too biased? Am I too close to the work to expect accuracy? Am I fooling myself in thinking I have a singular reason for starting the project in the first place?

"Ah, you agree," he says when I don't argue.

"I don't . . . disagree," I say.

"Isn't that the same thing?"

"Yes. And no."

Cal stares as if I'm an AP Calc test and I've barely finished Algebra I.

"It isn't that formal of a project. I'm really only doing this for myself."

"I know," he says. "But it's hard to evaluate yourself when you're the only test subject."

"True."

"And you're helping me with my book, so I could repay the favor."

"No."

He smiles. I can actually see the wheels turning in his head, and I don't like it.

"Isadora . . ." He says it like I have a cookie that I'm not supposed to, and I have to put it back.

I shift in my seat. "It's not a favor. It's my job."

"Still," he presses. "I'd like to help if I could."

I stare. He stares back. I furrow my brow, and he lifts his. We sit like that for a few seconds, and before I even know what I'm saying, my mouth says, "If I do decide to give you access to my research, there will be stipulations."

He leans back in his chair. "Name them."

I clear my throat. "I'm not going to show you everything."

"Understood," he says, hands up in surrender. "Only what you're comfortable sharing."

"I'm not comfortable sharing *any* of it," I say. Yet despite all that, something has made me want to invite him in to this experiment I'm conducting.

As if I instinctively knew he might be able to help me decipher my findings, the same way I might be able to help organize his.

"Like I said, I don't want you to be uncomfortable with this. A good working relationship is important to me, and we won't have that if you feel pressured to share more than you're willing to share."

I fold my hands on the desk and look at him. "No. I'm fine with it. I think you've made a good point. Having a psychologist help could make my study more accurate. And accuracy is important to me."

He nods once firmly, as if we've struck a deal. And just like that, I feel a little less alone. I have a sort of makeshift partner in this happiness project, and I don't hate that it's Cal. Marty and Darby hardly count—they're only in it for entertainment purposes. But Cal may actually have expertise to contribute. Never mind that he makes me feel gushy on the inside.

"I have to go teach a class," he says, standing. "But stay in touch. I can't wait to hear what your next step is." He smiles at me, and I look away.

"Goodbye," I say.

But he doesn't leave.

I look up, and he catches—then holds—my gaze. "Have a nice afternoon, Isadora."

Then he turns and walks away, leaving only the hum of electricity behind.

That night, I'm standing in my kitchen, heating up a Lean Cuisine meal in the microwave. It's nothing but high class with me—usually I go for the tried-and-true Vermont White Cheddar, but tonight it's Savory Sesame Chicken & Vegetables.

I'm about to peel back the steamy plastic sheet on my pasty green beans when I hear a knock on the door. I open it, expecting Darby.

Instead I find Delilah. She's carrying a lunchbox and a notebook.

"Hi, Delilah," I say, puzzled. "What can I do for you?"

"You're not building a bomb."

My insides smile, but I hold a straight face. "Not today."

She continues stoically. "I wondered if I could spend the evening here, where it's quiet." She looks back at the door to her apartment. "It's so hard to think in there with all those *children*."

I love her.

"Does your mom know you're over here?"

She shrugs. "She won't even notice I'm gone."

She doesn't say this sadly or like she's looking for attention. Simply stating a fact. *Nobody will notice if I'm not there.*

I understand.

"Sure, come on in." I text Darby and let her know her oldest child has invaded my space, and turn to find Delilah seated at my kitchen table, opening the lunchbox.

"I hope you're not planning on eating that tray of microwaved chemicals," she says.

I glance over at the Lean Cuisine meal, still steaming through the holes I poked. I've read the research on processed foods. I know Delilah has a point. "I was planning on it, actually."

"Miss Bentley, that is *not* real food." I remember that her father is a chef as she tosses me a side-eye that reminds me of her mother. She's a feisty one, this Delilah.

My phone buzzes with a text reply from Darby:

Oh, Isadora, send her back! I'm so sorry she's bothering you!

I glance over at Delilah, who has arranged her dinner on the table in front of her so perfectly it's as if her place has been set by a professional restaurateur. I text her mom back:

No, it's no trouble. We're going to eat together, and then I'll send her home.

I pick up the cardboard tray, peel the plastic back, and flip the whole thing over onto a plate, as if that will transform it into "real food." I sit down across from Delilah. She looks at me.

"I packed enough for two people," she says. "My mother says single people never properly take care of themselves."

"Your mother is shockingly accurate."

"Plus," she says without an ounce of tact or hesitation, "I'd feel better if you'd eat real food."

"I see." I have to admit, the spaghetti and meatballs she's dished up for herself look and smell much, much more appealing than the defrosted trash sitting in front of me.

"My dad made the pasta himself, and the meatballs are a family recipe," she says. "I can't tell you how many times he's told me about his great-great-grandmother who perfected the meatball a million years ago back in the 'old country.' She passed it down to his grandma, who passed it down to his mom, and his mom passed it down to my dad." She looks up. "I mean, you get the point."

I smile.

"You'll need to get a plate," she says. "I doubt you want to eat this out of a plastic container."

"I don't mind," I say.

But when she looks at me again, I can see that she wasn't making a suggestion. I stand, retrieve two plates from the cupboard, and hand them to her.

"I think it's a great idea for your dad to share your family history with you," I say.

"Really? Why?" She loads up my plate and pushes it toward me.

I shrug. "Well, I research all kinds of things for my job. If people didn't pass things down, like a meatball recipe, I wouldn't have anything to research."

I'm having an actual conversation with a ten-year-old.

"It's good to know where you came from."

"Do you know where *you* came from?" She takes two napkins from her lunchbox and hands me one. Next, she affixes hers onto her lap so properly I'm certain she's been to finishing school.

I refrain from telling her I came from a narcissistic mother and a father who never really wanted children in the first place and say instead, "Some." I pick up my fork. "My parents aren't big on sharing stories."

As I lift my fork to cut into a meatball, Delilah makes a sound that stops me cold. "We have to say grace."

"Oh, right." It's been forever since I've done *that*. In my defense, I've never had any reason to believe anyone *up there* was listening. My parents were submarine Christians—they only came up for air twice a year, on Easter and Christmas. That bit has been left up to me for so long, I'm not sure how I ever would've come to any other conclusion.

But as the little girl sitting across from me touches her bowed forehead to folded hands, eyes squeezed shut, I wonder if this is simply something else I've missed out on.

Delilah prays in a hushed tone. She thanks God for the food and "for my new friend, Isadora," and when she says "Amen," she opens her eyes and looks at me.

"You didn't close your eyes," she says.

"I never understood that part," I say. "I mean, it would be weird if I closed my eyes right now, talking to you."

"Well, I'm not Jesus."

"Jesus requires closed eyes?"

Delilah shrugs. "I'm only ten. That's what everyone else does."

After a few silent bites (I really am following Delilah's lead here—she clearly has better manners than I do), I say, "You really believe in all that stuff?"

She frowns. "All what stuff?"

"That someone is listening to you when you pray?"

Delilah chews thoughtfully for a few seconds, then nods. "Sure. I mean, I prayed for a friend who would understand me, and then we met you."

She's so certain of it, as if she's just solved for *x* with only one outcome, or even more scarily accurate, as certain as I am in my work. Measuring data makes sense—it's easy to quantify. But this? God? Faith? There's no certainty in faith.

It's easier not to hope. Easier to assume I'm on my own.

And yet this ten-year-old is saying that *I* am an answer to her prayers. And that's something I've never been before.

"Aren't you going to eat?" She looks up at me, her eyes wide. "It's going to get cold."

I take a bite. "It's really good."

"I know," she says. "Better than that garbage you were going to eat."

I laugh a real laugh and pull apart a piece of garlic bread. "Let me get this straight . . . you prayed for a friend who would understand you—and you think that's me?"

She shrugs. "Yep."

"How do you know?"

Another shrug. "I just do."

"So the kids at school . . . ?"

She shakes her head and cuts me off. "It's not any of them."

"They don't understand you," I say. A statement, not a question.

She looks down, and I see a familiar loneliness in that posture. I want to take it away. I want to tell her that in ten years, none of those people will matter—they'll be working trivial jobs while Delilah is off making a real difference in the world, but I'm not sure that's true. After all, it's been more than ten years for me, and the words of my peers still play out in my mind far more than they should. And if I'm honest, I'm not sure anything I'm doing will ever make a difference in the world.

What I am sure of, however, is what I say next.

"You know, Delilah, just because you're different, or you like getting lost in a book, or you aren't into the things the other kids in your grade are into . . . that doesn't mean something is wrong with you."

Her eyes dart to mine. I've hit on something.

"I know, because I was exactly the same way. And I thought something was wrong with me. In fact, the other kids let me know all the time. It was—"

"Delilah Pigsty-la."

I stop. "What?"

"That's what the kids call me. Delilah Pigsty-la. It's so stupid. It doesn't even rhyme."

I smile and point to myself. "Isadorkus. Sometimes, if they were feeling extra, it would be Isadorkus Maximus."

Delilah sits with that for a moment.

"That's actually kind of smart."

I nod ruefully. "I know. Which made it somehow worse."

We look at each other, and it's an actual moment. A connection. It's like I've time-traveled to talk to my younger self. Delilah's face turns a combination of pained and hopeful. "When will it get better?"

I don't have the answer, but I offer, "I don't know, but I know it will. I can tell you with absolute certainty, there is nothing wrong with you. I turned out okay, right? And now I read books for a living, and thankfully the amount of name-calling has died down to almost zero."

Her shoulders drop, only slightly, as if she's just allowed herself to let go of something that's been weighing on her. She cuts another piece of meatball and pops it into her mouth. "I'm glad I prayed for a friend."

I spin my pasta in a circle on my fork, trying not to cry.

A scene flashes in my mind, a forgotten memory, of me in the back seat of my parents' car on the way to school. I'm ten, and I'm praying to meet a friend who understands me.

And here she sits. Just a few years late.

Chapter 16

It's Sunday afternoon, and I'm sitting at my kitchen table with Cal's research spread out in front of me. It's still a lot to sift through, but I respect how thorough he's been. Or maybe I'm just looking for reasons to admire him.

I make notes:

Think about focusing these three points into one—they're pretty similar. Dig deeper on the effects of social media on people's sleep cycles—it's good. Go deeper on the points about how social media has given us confidence to say things we would never say in real life—both the pros and cons of this.

I leave questions on sticky notes for him to find. Through his writings, his scribbles, his sketches—he apparently likes to draw this one particular face but with eyes up, eyes down, or eyes crossed—I try to form my own hypotheses about Dr. Cal Baxter.

It mostly just involves hypothesizing about how he smells.

I wonder if he's also spending his weekend working.

I'm doing what I do best and hoping that he appreciates his full access to my big brain.

There's a knock at my door. When I pull it open, Delilah walks right in and past me without saying a word. It's like I just held the door open for her to enter.

She's holding a notebook and wearing oversized glasses, bib overalls, a pair of high-top tennis shoes, and a bright pink backpack.

She enters the conversation just like she entered my apartment. "I thought we could go exploring."

"Well, hi, Delilah."

"Hi." She raises her eyebrows. "Exploring? Get out into nature? Isn't that one of our steps? I heard you and my mom talking."

"Yes, that's one of the—wait, *our* steps?"

"I think I can help with your experiment," she says. "Plus, Diego won't sleep and Mom is ready to lose it, so I think it's best if I disappear for a few hours." She stands behind me in the living room. "You won't need a jacket. The weather today is sunny and clear. A balmy sixty-two degrees. Uncharacteristically warm for April." She faces me. "I heard a weather guy say that on the TV."

"Indeed."

"So . . . ?"

"Right," I say. I consider telling her I'm right in the middle of something, but for some reason I can't explain, I say, "Let me grab my bag and text your mom, and we'll go."

"You can text her, but I already told her," she says. "She's fine with it."

I text her anyway.

Are you okay if I take Delilah for a walk?

YES! It would be a huge help. She's a pill when she's bored.

Okay, I'll keep my phone on me if you need us.

Don't let her con you into spending money on her. She's really, really good at that.

I have no idea where Delilah wants me to take her, but I do get the impression it will be an adventure.

I realize, though, that I'm not going to be able to "get into nature" without getting out of the city.

Unabashed, Delilah leads as we trudge down the stairs and outside. I notice she doesn't stop to inhale the fresh air or feel the sun on her face.

I have to jog every few steps to keep up with her, which serves as a sad reminder of just how out of shape I am.

"Why are we in such a hurry?"

"This is just how I walk." She tosses a look over her shoulder, then stops abruptly. I nearly trip trying to sidestep her. "Do you need me to slow down? Are you okay?"

I frown. "I'm new to exercise."

"I'll walk at your pace," she says matter-of-factly. "It'll take twice as long to get there, but if that's the way you want to do it."

If someone else had said this to me, I might have been offended. But since it's a ten-year-old with dark hair and sad eyes, I find it interesting. She doesn't see the world the way other people see the world.

Then again, neither do I.

We walk several blocks, and when we reach a neighborhood with a row of tidy shops, Delilah begins to slow her pace. I do my best to cover up the fact that I'm using this as a chance to catch my breath.

I spot a toy store and assume this is where we're going, but, as I should've known, Delilah is anything but predictable. We stop in front of a comic book shop.

"Do you know anything about comic books?" she asks.

I shake my head. I know very little about them, though in that moment, I wish I knew more. Somehow, it seems important to Delilah. "But I bet the guy behind the counter does."

"Yeah, but he's a stranger," she says. "I . . . don't really like talking to people I don't know."

She sees the world like I do.

"But I was a stranger once," I say. "Not that long ago, in fact."

She looks troubled. "Maybe let's come back later."

I frown. "Okay."

She starts off down the block.

"Let's get a doughnut," I say. "That always helps me sort through things."

She spins around. "I'm not sorting through anything." Then, after a pause, "But I do like doughnuts."

We go into a bakery and make our selections, taking our treats outside to one of the small café tables. "Your mom isn't going to be mad I bought you sugar, is she?"

Delilah takes a giant bite of her chocolate-filled Long John, and whipped cream squishes out over her mouth. "We don't have to tell her," she says with a whipped cream–covered smile.

We sit for a few minutes in silence, and I take in my surroundings. I like living in the city, but I realize I don't get out and enjoy it enough. This is a cool place to live—why haven't I been paying attention?

"Isn't that Dr. Baxter?" Delilah points—her voice interrupts like a record scratch on my meditative-mood playlist.

I follow her finger across the street and spot where Cal is walking. At his side is a tall blonde woman wearing a sundress and a jean jacket with a wide hat and earrings that dangle enough that I can see them from where I sit. I could never pull off that look, I'm convinced, but it works for her. She looks perfectly put together.

And beautiful. She's beautiful.

I feel myself shrink in my own frumpy Sunday clothes. I look away. I look back. I can't stop looking.

"Are you upset?" Delilah asks.

"Me? No. What? Why? Why would I be?" I fumble with my

doughnut, which—and this is the real travesty here—has suddenly become unappetizing.

Not unappetizing, that's incorrect. *Prohibited*. It's as though it's suddenly become not okay to eat it because it won't make me look like her.

"Because you like him, and he's over there with that other lady." Another bite.

"Of course not." But I can't stop staring. They're perusing racks of clothing set out in front of one of the shops. The woman picks up a pair of sunglasses and puts them on, then turns to Cal, who nods his approval. She makes a face, then puts them back on the rack.

"You're staring," Delilah says, finishing her last bite of doughnut.

"I'm not." I force myself to look away, but when Cal and the woman walk on, it's as if a magnetic force pulls me out of my chair. "Let's go," I say, pulling on Delilah's arm.

"You didn't finish your doughnut," Delilah grabs at the plate.

But I'm already at the crosswalk, eyes fixed on the beautiful professor and this woman. Is this his girlfriend? His cousin? A woman he met on the train that morning?

I'm obsessed with finding out.

Chapter 17

It is not often we find Isadora Bentley on the hunt, but today she is out in force. A male has piqued her interest, and he's out for a stroll with what appears to be . . . a mate. Isadora—not the best at adapting to new stimuli or fitting in with her surrounding environment—follows gamely behind her prey, blending in exactly like a wildebeest doesn't.

I pull Delilah across the street as Cal stops in front of an indoor market and pulls open the door. The woman walks in, and he follows.

"Oh, perfect. Weren't we going to get a late lunch?" I ask.

"We just ate doughnuts," Delilah says. "I'm not hungry."

Next time I do this, I really need an older partner. She's not understanding me at all.

I walk over to the windows of the market and see them standing in line for ice cream. "Maybe he's taking his cousin for ice cream?"

I don't realize I've said this out loud until Delilah says, "There's no way that's his cousin."

I look at her. "It could be."

"Look again."

I look back and see them chatting as they wait in line. The woman puts a hand on Cal's chest, then throws her head back in a laugh. Okay, so "cousins" is a long shot.

The market is filled with displays and merchandise scattered in a maze throughout the open space. If we go in, there will be plenty of ways to hide.

"Come on," I say.

"I'm ten, but even I know this is a terrible idea," Delilah says. She follows me anyway.

"We'll just, you know, look around," I tell her. "If we bump into him, great. We can ask him how he's *doing*, what he's *up to*, how his cousin is liking her time in the *city* . . ."

"I think something is wrong with you," the little girl says dryly. "You're acting like the character in my book before his alternate personality kicks in."

Point taken. I need to act less like a maniac. We stroll through the doors as Cal and The Blonde get their ice cream. They head over to a table as Delilah and I skulk behind one of the pasta displays. Well, I'm skulking—Delilah is actually looking at something other than Cal. I suddenly wish I was short enough to go unnoticed.

I watch as Cal engages in what appears to be lively conversation with this woman, who is as pretty as I thought she was.

She's taken off her hat, and I see she's wearing cute wedge sandals. I'm wearing jeans and a baggy sweatshirt from college.

She's a damsel. I'm a troll demanding an answer to my riddle so she and her party can cross my bridge.

Definitely best to stay here in the shadows, hidden behind bags of homemade fettuccini.

I wonder what they're saying. I marvel at how easily she seems to handle her part of the conversation. They look perfectly engrossed in each other. I inch my way closer and settle in next to a display of fruit. I'm straining desperately to try to hear what they're saying, but it's no use.

"You could go say hi," Delilah says.

I glance at her and find her wide, innocent eyes trained on me.

If only it were that easy. "No," I say. "We should go." Before I make a fool of myself.

"Okay." She gives my arm a tug—I think she means to help me up from my crouched position—but when she does, somehow I lose my balance and knock into the fruit display I've been hiding behind.

The world turns to slow motion as the apples, oranges, and pears begin to avalanche off the stand and onto the floor. I'm helpless to stop it. It's like Carmen Miranda tripped and it's all headed toward Cal and The Blonde.

I'm horrified as one of the workers shouts out, then runs toward the display, shooting daggers at me with his eyes. It stands to reason he will be responsible for cleaning this up.

The fruit finally stops toppling onto the floor, and one lone apple rolls clear across the room and gently bumps the foot of an old woman. I look at her apologetically. But my concern is short-lived when I see Cal staring at me.

"Isadora?"

I've heard people speak of having waking nightmares, but I didn't think they were real.

Until now.

Cal walks over to the fruit carnage as the worker in the black apron crouches to pick up the fruit, but he happens to crouch at the same time I crouch, and we end up knocking into one another. He looks at me as if I'm doing this on purpose.

"I'm really sorry." In an effort to help, I set an apple back on the stand—and deftly knock three oranges back onto the floor.

"Just"—he holds up a hand—"leave it."

I leave it.

"What are you doing here?" Cal asks.

"Oh, hey, Cal. Hey, hi." I feel like my fakeness is coming off less as nonchalance and more "awkward middle school girl with a crush."

"Yeah, just, you know," I sputter, "Delilah and I are exploring." My sweat mustache is back. I can feel the beads gathering above my top lip. I dab at it with the back of my hand and force myself to stand.

"Delilah's with you?" Cal asks.

"Yeah, she's . . ." I turn a circle and see that she's not standing beside me anymore. "Delilah?" I look around in the immediate vicinity.

She's nowhere in sight.

"Delilah?"

Nothing. Now I'm panicked. This girl is incredibly self-sufficient, but she's still a child.

I scan the indoor market, calling out her name, moving through the displays, hoping she's just too short for me to see. I rush around the entire space when I realize Cal is doing the same thing on the other side of the market.

We meet back near the downed fruit, and he says, "Don't worry, we'll find her."

My skin splotches, red and hot. But what if we don't? What if I've lost Darby's daughter?

I glance over and see The Blonde is now standing, holding her ice cream and wearing a blank expression.

"No, I"—I toss a glance at the woman—"I'll find her." I start toward the door, hoping she hasn't gotten far, when I feel Cal's hand on my arm.

"I'm helping you find her." He turns to The Blonde. "Brooke, do you mind if I help my friend?"

"Of course not." She sounds like a cartoon character, her voice high-pitched and squeaky, but I manage to keep that to myself.

"I'll be back," Cal tells her.

We push through the doors and onto the street.

"Is there anywhere you can think of that she would've gone?"

The comic book store catches my eye. "Maybe there?" I point to it.

"She likes comics?"

"No, but she wanted to go in there before we saw you—" I realize what I've said *as* the words are coming out of my mouth. "I mean, before we ran into you. Before we went into the market."

Cal either doesn't catch on (*wishful thinking*) or chooses not to embarrass me. "Let's go look."

I'm usually a person who waits for a green light and a crosswalk to cross the street, but when Cal heads out into the road, I follow, feeling slightly rebellious and a little terrified. Chicago drivers are crazy! He holds up his arm to block me as a taxi zooms by, honking at us as it passes.

We reach the other side of the street and walk toward the comic book shop. When Cal pulls open the door, I rush in, and instantly I see her, standing at the back of the store, her pink backpack facing us.

"Delilah!"

She doesn't turn around. I hurry toward her and find her deep in thought. She glances over at me—unfazed—and says, "Do you think this comic book would make a good conversation starter?"

She holds up a copy of something called *Flashpoint* and waits for me to reply. Then she notices Cal is beside me. "Dr. Baxter. Where's your cousin?"

He frowns.

"Delilah. You scared me to death," I say. "You can't just go running all over the city by yourself."

"It's not all over the city," she says. "I figured you'd have to stay and clean up your mess, and I wanted to get over here before we had to go back home." She shakes the comic book at me. "Now, what do you think about this?"

I only stare. I have no words. This is why I don't take care of children. This is why I don't like children.

Only, that isn't exactly true, is it? Because I *do* like Delilah. And I like her very much. I wasn't only worried that I'd be responsible for losing her.

I was worried that I might lose *her.*

This is an emotion I've experienced before and one I thought I'd safeguarded against. I don't want to need anyone. People can't be trusted.

And yet, just looking at this small person with the soul of a seventy-year-old woman challenges that thought. More to the point—Delilah trusts *me.* That, I can't ignore.

"Uh, I think that's an excellent choice," Cal says in my silence.

"You do?" She turns to him. "And you're a man, so maybe you could tell me—if you saw a woman reading this, would it make you want to talk to her?"

Oh no. Delilah has a crush. And elementary school crushes can be brutal. I silently pray he isn't one of the kids calling her Delilah Pigsty-la.

Cal clears his throat. "I do, think that, yes. But are *you* interested in this comic book?"

She shrugs. "I'm not *not* interested in it. I mean, I don't know anything about it. Maybe I'll read it and find it's just the thing I've been missing in my collection of books."

"Okay." He nods. "But if you don't like it, don't pretend to like it because of a boy."

Her face reddens. "Who said I like a boy?"

"I'm just speculating," he says, smiling at me as if we're sharing an unspoken secret.

She doesn't flinch at his use of this word. In fact, she seems to be pondering it. "Well, you're right. There is a boy I like. His name is Leo. He's really into comic books."

Cal nods. "That's great, Delilah, and I think it's awesome you're taking an interest in the things he's interested in. But I don't think you should change yourself just to make some boy notice you."

The words capture me more than they do Delilah, and as with all things having anything to do with relationships, my thoughts turn to Alex. I wish it wasn't such a knee-jerk reaction—it's like all those memories and emotions are just there, under a thin layer of sand, revealed by the slightest breeze of an offhanded comment.

Is that what I did with Alex? Did I change myself to make him like me? Did I make myself small so he would feel larger than life?

Did I put myself aside to make room for him?

"I think I'll get it," she says. "But I'm taking your advice into consideration." Then she holds up her open palm in my direction. "Can you spot me thirteen bucks?"

"Don't let her con you into spending money on her. She's really, really good at that."

I muse for a moment and then fish a twenty out of my bag and hand it to her—mostly because I'm certain if I don't, I'll get into some sort of logical debate about why I should invest in her future.

She walks over to the counter and sets the comic book down.

"*Flashpoint*! Barry Allen, time travel, excellent choice," the clerk says.

"If you saw a girl reading this, would you want to talk to her?" Delilah asks.

I tune the rest out, mostly because I'm standing next to Cal, who has swooped in and saved the day, but also because I can't bear to hear this hygienically impaired sales clerk give Delilah romantic advice. "Thank you."

"You're welcome," he says.

"Not just for helping me find her but for what you said. I'm worried she's going to get her heart broken."

He looks curious. "Why would you automatically think her heart is going to get broken?"

"It's inevitable."

"Inevitable?"

"Yes. It's bound to happen." I'm on a train here, and I can't jump off. "You give your heart to someone in the form of a comic book and they will undoubtedly, at some point, leave that comic book on a shelf and never pick it up again."

I'm praying he doesn't catch on.

"That's an unfortunate outlook." He looks right in my eyes. "I wonder who hurt you." He says this as if he's simply musing over it out loud, not asking me a question.

In my silence, thankfully he moves on. "The good thing is that's part of life, right? Unfortunately, hearts break. Fortunately, they mend."

A bell signals the door has been opened. We both turn and see The Blonde standing there, an expectant look on her face.

"Oh. Brooke," I say. "You should go."

"Right." He squeezes my arm. "Have a great rest of your weekend."

He leaves with the cousin I am certain is *not* his cousin, and all at once I realize this man is a whole lot more than a handsome face with a book idea.

Chapter 18

For the next several mornings, I wake up earlier than usual. Darby has insisted on early morning yoga, claiming it's the best way to start the day. The truth is, Dante is working nights, so if we don't get up at the crack of dawn and haul our butts to Flow, we won't get to go together.

I guess Darby wants to go to these classes with me as much as I want to go with her. If it weren't for her, I would've quit a long time ago.

It's almost seven o'clock on a Thursday morning and we're walking to Samira's class. "I think this is starting to become a habit, Isadora," Darby says.

"It's not a habit I intend to keep," I say. "It's not like I exactly fit in with the yoga crowd. It's like going to watch a marathon. There are the spectators and there are the athletes—and the differentiation is clear."

Darby frowns over at me. "Are you kidding? You totally fit in. Look at you."

I give myself a quick once-over. My outfits have improved immensely since that first class. I traded in the '90s-style sweatpants (which are apparently back in style?) for black leggings. I've paired these with an oversized Jonas Brothers T-shirt, but my look is saved by a sleek new pair of black Nikes.

Still, I'm unconvinced. And I insist repeatedly that yoga is maybe not my thing.

Darby won't hear of it. "Yoga is everyone's thing."

"We've been doing this for almost two weeks now, Darby. If it were going to stick, I think it would've by now."

"Hmm. Yet here you are, back again." Darby smiles at me as she pulls open the studio door. Meg and Stacy wave at us from their mats, and we quickly join them. After an update on Meg's love life and Stacy's story of her promotion at work, I'm set to feel my muscles quiver at me.

This social part of exercise I find I truly enjoy. Shocking that I like the part where I don't exercise.

I'm pleased to report I don't die.

I hesitate to report that I continue to find no happiness in the actual practice of yoga.

After the class, Darby and I swing through Mal's for coffee, then walk back to our apartment building.

An hour later, I arrive at my office, showered and ready for a new day.

I exit the elevator and find Cal standing in the hallway near my door. We've communicated about his book over email the past few days, and I've dropped my notes by his office when I knew he'd be in class. I haven't been able to bear the thought of facing him after crashing his date with Brooke. I imagine at some point he'll tease me over what a fool I made of myself. Sometimes, at night, I replay the moment all the fruit toppled and I get sweaty with embarrassment all over again.

I force myself to look him in the eye, and when I do, he smiles. Has anyone ever smiled at the sight of me?

Maybe the guy taking my school photo, trying to get me to smile.

My stomach flip-flops. I swore to myself I'd never act the fool over a guy again, but he's making it very difficult to keep that promise.

I've spent many moments replaying his words to Delilah. *"I don't think you should change yourself just to make some boy notice you,"* he said. The words were gold waiting to be mined. And still, no matter how many times I turn them around in my head, I can't bring myself to believe anyone could actually accept me just as I am.

"Good morning," he says brightly, reminding me a little of a golden retriever puppy—the kind of person who wakes up happy no matter what's going on in the world.

"Oh no. You're a morning person, aren't you?" This is more of a statement than a question.

He winces through the smile. "Yeah, I am. And you're . . . ?"

"Not."

"Ah." His gaze latches onto mine. "Mornings are the best time of day, Isadora. A clean slate. A chance to do better than you did yesterday."

"I think I did just fine yesterday."

He chuckles quietly. "I was speaking hypothetically."

"Oh."

"So let's try this again." He turns around, his back to me. He then turns slowly, acts surprised to see me, and says, "Good morning, Isadora!"

"Hello," I say, frowning.

He points at me. "Okay, so we'll work on that."

He turns and swings his arm widely, as if to usher me onto a red carpet. I roll my eyes and start toward my door. "I worked through some of your notes on the book last night," he continues, "and I have to say, your insight was pretty inspired. I finished the first chapter." He pulls a small stack of paper-clipped pages from his bag and hands them to me.

"Great." I open the door to my office, walk around my desk, and set my bag down. I then look up to find that he hasn't left—but is now standing in my office. I still haven't gotten over the fruit debacle, and I find his nonchalance toward me odd.

"Is there . . . more?"

"I have a light day today, so I thought maybe I could jump in on whatever step you're doing today. Might be good for me to watch and assess."

"Watch what?"

"You." He sits in the chair on the other side of my desk, like it's the most natural thing in the world for him to be here.

Nothing about this feels natural to me. I'm beginning to feel like all my spaces are being invaded by other people, and I'm not sure where the escape hatch is.

He must sense my apprehension because he is immediately apologetic. "Wait, I'm sorry. Will that make you uncomfortable?"

"You? Watching me?" I blow out a long breath, hands on hips, then arms down, then hands on hips, then one hand on one hip and the other one appearing to hail a cab. "Nah."

I'm a terrible liar.

I try to fill the awkward moment. "Anyway, you're supposed to be just an 'assessor of findings,'" I say. "You're not involved in my experiment at all. But by just observing, you are altering the outcome."

He sits forward in his chair, piqued now. "You're talking about Heisenberg's Uncertainty Principle. Okay, I hear you. You want me to be less observer and more active participant?"

"What? No!"

"It's totally fine, and a great idea! Plus, I need a diversion," he says. "Writer's block."

"Writer's block is just a myth," I say. "The great television writer Shonda Rhimes doesn't believe in it. She says, 'Writer's block just means you're not writing. So get off your butt and start writing.'"

He doesn't respond.

"Do you know who Shonda Rhimes is?"

"Yes, Isadora, I've seen *How to Get Away with Murder.*"

"Have you also seen *Scandal*? *Grey's Anatomy*? *Bridgerton*? She's really one of the most prolific creators of our generation, so it would be wise to take her advice to heart."

The look on Cal's face seems to be one of amusement. "Well, I maintain that I'd be a positive addition to your research today." He sits back in his chair. "I know a lot about being happy."

This I don't doubt. I seem to repel happiness. If happiness were a person, I'd be the lady in the mall with a clipboard that happiness takes the stairs to avoid. Cal, however, seems to embody it.

Two days ago, during my lunch break on the bench with Marty, I saw him walking through the courtyard. A few of the regular disc golfers were out playing.

Don't get me started on disc golf. How is this a sport? How does a person perfect their disc throwing to ever make progress in this sport? Why is it so popular on college campuses, and why is it that when I walk through the quad, I always, always feel like I'm going to get cracked in the face with a disc?

Cal must not share my sentiments because when he spotted the kids, he threw his bag down and asked for a turn. He spent the next several minutes trying to hit the disc in the goal, and every time he missed it, he laughed. The boys laughed. They made fun of him and bartered for better grades in his class. Cal wasn't embarrassed by any of this—he simply tried again.

I admired that about him then, and I admire it now. How can I get that sort of happiness to stick to me the way it does to him?

I remind myself that to properly conduct this experiment, I can't wish for certain outcomes. I can't wish for it to work or not work. It simply has to be what it is, positive or negative.

Still, I can't deny that I have been learning. I began my experiment wanting desperately to prove Dr. Monroe was wrong—that her advice was faulty. That was the hypothesis, that someone could do every single thing on her list and *still* emerge unhappy.

But then I smiled at Marty on that bench in the courtyard, and ever since, even I can admit, a small part of me has been wishing for a different outcome to my experiment.

But so far, nothing has worked—not *really*. There've been emotions that seem adjacent to happiness. For instance, last night after dinner, Delilah and I spent a solid hour debating which *Doctor Who* was the best (David Tennant, and it's not even close), and through it all, excitement bubbled inside me as we recounted our favorite moments.

But was that happiness?

If so, why didn't it hang around after Delilah left?

If happiness is a state of being, how does a person continue to exist in that state? How do I hold on to it when it seems so fleeting?

I shelve the thoughts and focus on Cal. "So you're procrastinating."

"Absolutely."

I laugh at his resolve and pull my notebook from my bag.

He sits forward, like he's ten and I have just pulled out a cake. "Is that . . . ?"

I pull it slightly back. "You don't get to read my thoughts, but I will show you the article." I take the pages torn from the magazine and hand them over to Cal. He skims them thoughtfully, then sets them down.

"Interesting. You know, you never told me why you decided to conduct this experiment in the first place." He props an ankle on his opposite knee and leans back in the chair.

"Yes, I did," I say. "I want to prove Dr. Grace Monroe doesn't know what she's talking about."

"Nothing more?"

The fact that he is an expert in psychology unnerves me. There's a very good chance he's reading my mind in the lulls of this conversation. Is it possible he can hear what it is I'm *not* saying? I don't even know what it is I'm not saying.

"Could I . . . ?" His eyes narrow. "Could I pick the next step? I mean, unless you're going in order."

"I'm not, actually. But I was thinking I'd do the chocolate one next," I say. "I need an easy one, and what's easier than eating a ton of chocolate?"

He glances down at the article. "It says 'Eat chocolate (in moderation).'"

"I've been avoiding Aisle 8 for years. Now that I have a scientific reason for eating candy, I'm not going to waste it."

He laughs, a real one. I have no idea why—I was being totally serious.

A lull settles in, the kind that makes me say stupid things.

"I'm sorry I crashed your date," I say, staring at my folded hands. "And the fruit, and the whole thing . . . not my finest hour."

I glance up and find him smirking. "You mean my afternoon with my 'cousin'?"

"Was she actually your cousin?" I try to temper the hopefulness in my voice but fail.

"No," he says. "She wasn't my cousin."

I feel my cheeks flush. "Brooke was a good sport about you helping me. Tell her thank you," I say.

"I'm not sure that'll be possible," he says.

"Why not?"

"I don't think I'm going to see her again."

"Ever?"

"It was just a first date." He shrugs.

"And you don't want a second?"

He shakes his head.

"Why not?"

"We don't have anything in common," he says. "Plus—" He stops. "I don't know, there was just something . . . you know . . . off."

I don't know. I never know.

I pause. "I thought maybe it was because she sounded like a cartoon character."

He laughs out loud.

"I don't mean that as an insult," I say genuinely. "Just something I noticed."

"No, I'm sure she'd be thrilled to hear it." He grins.

This troubles me. I honestly didn't mean it as an insult, just a statement of fact. Her voice was made for a small animated animal like a chipmunk or a meerkat. Is that an insult? Who wouldn't want to be a meerkat?

Now I fear I've gone and made myself sound like the exact kind of person I don't like.

"Where did you meet her?"

"She's a coworker of one of my buddies," he says. "I guess it was kind of a blind date."

I pull a face. "I can't think of many things worse than a blind date. Except maybe a dating app. Why would I give people the opportunity to reject me?" I look at him. "Plus, I don't really believe in love."

His eyebrows shoot up. "Like, as a principle?"

"Like, as a truth," I say.

"Uh, I'm pretty sure it exists," he says.

"As a concept, sure. As a tangible thing? Not really. It's like faith, or hope—those concepts simply can't be scientifically proven." Even as I say the words, contradictions fire off in my own mind. What about Marty and Shirley? What about Darby and Dante?

Love does exist—it just hasn't found me yet.

"You said the other day," I continue, "that hearts break but they mend."

He nods. "I did say that."

"So I assume you've had your heart broken."

Another nod.

I study him. He's engaged me with his eyes, as if he's enjoying our conversation, even though it's taken a slightly personal turn. "Aren't you afraid that will happen again?"

He leans forward as he quietly ponders this. "Sure. Having your heart broken is one of the worst things that can happen to a person. But it's not enough to make me want to be alone for the rest of my life."

You've never met Alex, buddy.

"Haven't you ever heard 'no risk, no reward'?" he asks.

"Yes, but that usually refers to financial investments, not life partners," I say.

"Isadora, the principle works for both. Love is a risk. Every time. But to have something like"—he thinks for a moment—"like Marty and Shirley, for example. You have to be willing to put yourself out there in order to have something real like that. Think how his life would've turned out if he'd never said hello to her."

"Actually, I think she was the one who approached him," I say. "Brave woman, that Shirley."

After a moment of silence, Cal brightens. "I have an idea," he says.

I'm immediately apprehensive, and I don't know why.

"I mean if you're okay with me picking your next happiness step . . . ?"

"Uh, sure," I mumble.

"Great. I'll meet you at lunch."

And without telling me his idea, he's gone.

Cal Baxter, everyone. Simultaneously the best and the worst.

Chapter 19

The rest of the morning is wasted. I can't stop thinking about Cal's idea—whatever it is. I pore over the list, trying to guess what he's going to pick and, moreover, what he's going to do.

Maybe he's going to help me with step twenty-two: "Plan your week." That's not terrible. Or step seventeen: "Create a self-care ritual." Good grief, is he going to take me to get a massage?

Wait. Is he going to massage *me*?

Wait! Am I going to massage him? Stop it, Isadora!

Lunchtime. Finally. I've been so restless, I've straightened the same six things on my desk fourteen times.

My lap drawer is actually pretty organized now.

I hurry through the line in the cafeteria and walk straight to our bench, where Marty is already sitting.

I plop down beside him. "Hey, Marty."

I notice he's not moving.

He clutches a brown paper bag in his lap with both hands, his face shaded underneath the brim of his hat. He stares out across the courtyard, and I get the sense he sees nothing at all.

"Marty?" I say his name more quietly this time, but he barely stirs.

I reach over and put a hand on his shoulder, and I feel the tug of concern. It's been a long time since I've been so aware of another person's feelings. I'm ashamed to admit that, but it's true. Feelings are messy, and I've always believed it's best not to get involved.

But sitting here on this bench with this old man, who in only a matter of weeks has become a friend, I can't help it. It's not like I don't have feelings—it's just that I tend to keep them in a nice box, under a few more boxes, tucked in the corner behind another very big box.

There's a knot in my stomach. I need to make sure Marty is okay.

He crinkles the bag in his hands. "It's our anniversary." His voice breaks ever so slightly.

My heart sinks. I realize the depth of his pain, and once again I'm reminded why *my* approach to people is the best approach. If you don't get close, you can't get hurt.

That is selfish and you know it.

If Marty and Shirley had never met that day in the courtyard, he wouldn't be feeling this pain now.

Isadora, what is wrong with you?

"I keep thinking about all the little ways she made my life better," he says. "She would enlist my coworkers to hide cards in weird places at my work. These handwritten love notes would drop out on my desk from the middle of a report folder. I'd spend the rest of the day side-eyeing people to try to figure out who was her accomplice."

"That's really sweet," I say.

"Shirley was a terrible cook." He sighs a laugh through his tears. "Used to burn everything." He looks at me then. "Do you know how many blackened pot roasts I ate over the years?"

I smile.

"She couldn't make anything without setting off the smoke

alarm," he says. "It scared the heck out of the dog so many times, anytime Shirley would turn on a burner, poor old boy would run upstairs and hide in the closet."

He looks away, and I wonder if he's imagining Shirley walking toward him, the way she did the day they met. The mind is a powerful thing, and our memories can easily play out like movies on a screen.

Marty speaks forcefully now, holding back what I'm sure is a tidal wave of emotions. "We didn't have enough years together. We didn't have enough time. It could've been a hundred, and it still wouldn't have been enough."

He looks up at me, right in the eyes. "I miss her so much, Isadora."

I try to comfort him with a weak smile, but I don't know how to help.

After a moment, I shift in my spot. "Do you regret it?" I pause. "I mean, knowing how it would end . . . ?" My voice trails off when I realize I'm not sure how to finish my insensitive question.

He sniffs. "Do you mean, do I wish we'd never met because of the pain I'm feeling now?" he asks.

I nod quietly. "Yes, that."

He draws in a breath and lets it out slowly, and then the expression on his face changes, as if he's just remembered something amusing.

"She used to light candles to hide her burnt meals," he says with a laugh. "I knew if I walked in the door from work and smelled vanilla bean or pine trees that she'd been cooking. Another trick she'd try is turning out the lights, like trying to make it romantic. She thought I wouldn't notice it if we ate it in the dark."

I smile at that, because that's actually clever and incredibly sweet.

"She never let me off the hook, you know?" he says. "Never let me get away with phoning in a birthday or an anniversary. If she thought I was going to forget, she'd find not-so-subtle ways to remind me." He stills. "She didn't do that for her own benefit, though. She did it so I wouldn't feel bad when I realized I'd forgotten."

"She sounds so wonderful," I say.

"She was." He pauses. "And my life was better because I knew her."

Marty gazes out into the middle of the courtyard. I look too, and we sit. As friends. Sharing an emotional moment.

After several minutes in silence, he turns to me. "So to answer your question—no. Even if I'd known the end at the beginning, I wouldn't have traded a minute of it for anything."

My parents don't love each other like this. I have never loved anyone like this. Until this very moment, I haven't believed this sort of love exists.

Maybe Cal was right.

"Isadora," he says now. "I know you said you didn't start this experiment because you were trying to find happiness."

I don't respond. I myself have been questioning why exactly I started my experiment.

"Happiness isn't that hard to find, you know. It's everywhere. It's all around us. But it's not something that happens *to* us. It's something we seek. It's something we pursue. And you'll never find it if you never let anyone in."

The words hang there between us, and I'm still unsure what to say. I could get angry that Marty has made such a broad assumption about me, but I don't.

Because his assumption is correct.

I open my mouth to start saying something, then stop.

I never let anyone in. I *can't.* I just can't. When I do, bad things happen.

And just because Marty is right about certain things, that

doesn't mean his approach to finding happiness is also correct, right? Surely there is more than one way to be happy. For Marty, his life with Shirley brought him happiness, but this emotion I'm witnessing right now is anything but.

For someone like me, maybe a life without complication—a life without the flip side of the coin—would bring happiness. Solitary people are happy, right? Wasn't there a whole movement about women not needing men?

And yet, if that were true, wouldn't I have already found it?

I choose not to argue. We sit again in silence, and Marty doesn't appear to have an ounce of fight in him at the moment. I can see a sad wistfulness on his face that's done nothing but tighten the knot in my belly.

"Marty," I start. "Maybe when I get off work today, we could take some flowers over to her grave," I suggest. "I'd be happy to go with you."

"No," he says. "I don't want to be reminded of the day we put her in the ground."

"I understand," I say.

While I haven't buried someone that close to me, I mentally buried Alex. I understand not wanting to go to the place where the bad memories are. It took me over a year to step foot in our lab without replaying the time I spent there with him, usually at night, because Alex never did make our relationship public. Major red flag there, but I always explained it away.

Oh, we work together, so we have to keep it hush-hush.

Hindsight is always 20/20, they say.

"I wish I could go—I do. I feel like I'm letting her down," Marty says quietly. "She would've been at my graveside every day if the roles were reversed."

"But you come here," I say, trying to line it in silver, "where the good memories are."

He nods slowly. "But it's not the same. I should be strong enough to visit her final resting place."

I look down at my lunch, not the least bit hungry, and I wonder if Marty would rather be alone with his memories.

Just as I'm about to ask Marty that very question, I see a man walking toward us, wearing the same clothes Cal had on that morning. I squint to get a better look, certain there is no way it's Cal.

Because why on earth would he be walking eight dogs?

Chapter 20

Correction, the eight dogs are walking Cal.

It appears the puppies, of varying sizes, breeds, and colors, are dragging him toward us in a tangled pile.

Marty spots Cal and his furry-footed frenzy a few seconds after I do, and it's as if a light has moved from his mouth to his eyes underneath his skin, like a flashlight under the covers in a dark room.

As he approaches, Cal calls out, "Step six! 'Spend time with animals'!"

What. The. Heck.

One of the dogs—a smaller, golden-colored one—jumps up onto my lap and drags its cold, wet nose across my mouth. When I pull my face away, it licks my cheek and neck, and before I can react, I burst out laughing.

"Oh my goodness, aren't you just the best boy!" Marty chuckles next to me, then sets his lunch aside so he can pick up one of the smaller black dogs.

"That's Olive," Cal says.

Marty looks up at Cal. "Best *girl*—sorry, Olive." He scratches under Olive's chin with both hands.

"And who's this?" I squeeze the ears of the dog currently burrowing into my armpit.

"That's Honey," he says. "She's a sweetie. I had a feeling she'd like you." Then he winks at me and says, "I guess it's true opposites attract."

I let out a fake gasp.

Dr. Cal Baxter is teasing me. And I don't hate it.

I can't linger long with that realization because Honey's head is fully under my armpit and digging around my back. I'm shocked to discover I don't mind. I actually kind of love her. The others are clambering up on the bench, or chewing the grass, or winding around Cal's ankles. "Where did you get them?"

"I help out at the animal shelter on weekends," Cal says.

Of course he does.

Really, Cal? On your off days, do you give blood to orphans, lend your carpentry skills to construct housing for the homeless, then jet off to the African savanna to distribute your new, inexpensive invention that distills clean drinking water from muddy rivers?

"They let me take them out for their afternoon walk." Cal nods at Honey. "Looks like a match made in heaven."

Honey has lost interest in my armpits, thank goodness, and is now full-on French-kissing my face. I can't keep from giggling. Beside me, Olive has nestled into Marty's lap as if she's just found her place in the world. Marty looks down at the dog, stroking her head and back as her tail wags in approval.

While I'm sure the twinge of sadness still hovers over him, there's a contentment there too, as if the two emotions have decided to coexist. I make a mental note to write this idea in my notebook—*Can happiness exist in the midst of profound sadness? Can two emotions share the same space?*

"Dr. Monroe may've been right about this," Cal says as he sits down on the ground and a giant, fluffy, gray-and-white dog lumbers over and plops down in his lap. "Studies do suggest that animal therapy can reduce stress hormones while also increasing—"

"—oxytocin, dopamine, and endorphins," I cut in. "I read that study too."

He smiles at me. *Connection.*

"I thought maybe I should get a cat, but now—" I lean over to pet a tiny, rat-looking dog. The small animal flinches. "It's okay, Rattie," I say in a calming voice.

"Her name is Bertha," Cal says.

I burst a single laugh. "This dog could not look less like a Bertha."

"And you definitely don't want a cat," he says. "You need an animal that will be excited to see you every time you come home, not one that will judge you while it knocks a full mug of coffee on your floor."

Cal catches my eye and nods over at Marty, who is completely smitten with Olive. Honey nips at my hands, desperate for attention, and while I'm certain I could never keep up with an animal this energetic, I can't deny that she's had an instant effect on me.

"Dogs accept us for who we are," Cal says, holding the fluffy gray dog's face close to his. "Don't you, buddy?"

He gives the dog some quality skritches, and the animal turns full over in Cal's lap to let him rub his belly. "There's nothing like the unconditional love of a dog."

The dog lets out a snorted sigh, and Cal pats his belly. "You okay there, Hank?"

Some of the college kids in the quad stop by to pet or play with this pack of dogs, and for today anyway, our lunch spot has become Happiness Central.

For a moment, I wish Delilah were here. I think she would love this.

I marvel at the way these animals, simply by existing, bring joy to the faces of stressed-out college kids and overworked professors. I think back to what Marty said about happiness being a choice, and I decide to stop overthinking any of it, and let myself feel whatever I feel.

You know, just for today.

Mostly, I'm in awe of the way Marty's mood has changed, like someone switched his light on. I wonder if Olive might be exactly what the old man needs.

When it comes time for Cal to take the dogs back to the animal shelter, both Marty and I decide to join him. We each take a couple of leashes and start off down the sidewalk toward the direction of the street.

Cal dips his head toward mine and whispers, "If I didn't know better, I'd say maybe Honey won you over."

Honey tugs on her leash, then veers off the path, and I give a little yank to get her back on track. "What makes you so sure?"

Cal turns his attention back to the sidewalk in front of us. "I just haven't seen you laugh like that before."

I'm suddenly embarrassed he witnessed this little outburst of emotion.

He bumps into my shoulder with his. "You should do that more often."

"What? Laugh?"

He nods. "It looks good on you."

"I agree," Marty says from the other side of me. "You're far too beautiful not to smile."

I feel my cheeks flush at this. As if Marty calling me beautiful will call attention to the fact that I absolutely am not.

"He's right," Cal says.

I glance over and find him looking at me.

"Far too beautiful not to smile."

When I don't look away, something passes between us, and

I wonder if this is what Marty felt when he met Shirley all those years ago.

"It's a zinger," he told me that first day we met. *"It comes out of nowhere and hits you like lightning. And when it does, you're never, ever the same."*

Is that what this is? A zinger?

I tell both Cal and Marty they've got it wrong. "I'm not beautiful."

I got the message loud and clear, ages ago.

By my junior year of high school, I'd mastered the fine art of blending in. I thought I was safe—long forgotten by Mia and the other girls who'd made my middle school life a living hell.

But someone found out about my crush on Noah Johnson.

We're sitting in homeroom, and a series of video announcements is droning on from the television set mounted on the wall in the corner of the room. I'm half listening when the shot cuts away and Katy Perry's "Teenage Dream" starts to play.

As with the other kids in the class, this gets my attention. After all, there is rarely any music on the video announcements, just perky Tiffany and her cohost, Caleb, telling us all the "super-fun things happening this week."

The kids in the class start moving along to the beat of the music when suddenly there is a video of a girl in the hallway. I'm horrified when I realize the girl is me.

My cheeks flush instantly, and I know I've turned beet red. Because I don't remember anyone filming me.

The camera pans haphazardly to the middle of the hallway where Noah and his friends are walking toward the frame. They're laughing about who knows what, and he looks so cute with his backward baseball cap on.

Then I'm back on the screen, and it's as if I'm hypnotized by the sight of him. I stop pulling books from my locker and watch him pass by, slowly and with a look on my face that tells the entire classroom—the entire school—exactly how I feel about this boy.

There are more moving images like this, and I realize someone has been filming me watching Noah—in class, on the track during PE, in the cafeteria—for days, maybe even weeks. And they've put it all together in a video that ends with text in a thought bubble over my head that reads:

Make my teenage dream come true, Noah.
Go to prom with me?

Hot tears burn my eyes, and I can feel everyone in my homeroom looking at me, including Miss Anderson—the line of worry across her forehead is unmistakable.

The worst part is that Noah is sitting diagonally from me, and his friends have erupted in laughter.

By the look on his face, it's clear this video has embarrassed him too. He shifts in his seat, then leans over toward me and says one word: "Woof."

I want to explain that I didn't do this, but before I can say anything, tears sting my eyes, and I can't keep them from falling. As I run out of the room, I hear the snickers and giggles in my wake.

I don't remember most of the rest of the day. I spent the morning locked in the bathroom stall, and the afternoon back in Miss Anderson's class. She said she'd report whoever did this, but I told her the truth—I didn't know. Not for a fact. Besides, I didn't want any more attention. I just wanted it all to go away.

Maybe it was that day that I realized it was useless to even think about things like beauty. Miss Anderson said I had something much better—I had brains. And if I channeled my intelligence, I could be something really great. I could make a difference in this world.

So I made up my mind to do just that. Brains over beauty. I *was* an intelligent, competent student, and if I focused on that, I could do something really amazing one day.

And maybe once I did, it would be enough. Maybe *I* would be enough.

But I'm thirty now, and I'm still waiting to do something great. Still waiting to prove myself.

So these two very kind men have got it all wrong. Isadora Bentley is not beautiful. Not when she smiles or any other time.

I know what I am—and what I'm not. And nobody is going to convince me otherwise.

Although, isn't that exactly what's happening? A piece of me wants to believe it—and then I'm reminded of my own words to Delilah.

"Just because you're different . . . doesn't mean something is wrong with you."

Now if I could just get me to listen to me, I'd be fine.

Chapter 21

I never expected when I started this project that I'd accomplish any of these steps with anyone but myself. But it's been three weeks since the day of the dogs, and the next two steps I checked off in that time were with other people.

Step seven: "Daydream."

First, Delilah and I spent an afternoon daydreaming together. Initially, it was hard for me to let my mind wander—I like to keep my brain occupied, after all. And doing nothing doesn't come easily.

The other difficulty was that after about ten minutes, I noticed Delilah was staring at me. When I met her eyes, she smiled at me and said, "Bet I know what you're daydreaming about."

"Oh, really?" I asked, certain she'd guess something like Little Debbie snack cakes, which, let's be real, were exactly what I was thinking about.

"Dr. Cal *Bax*ter," she singsonged at me, completely out of character. When she waggled her eyebrows, she looked like her mom.

"I was not!"

Not exactly a lie, but not exactly true either. I *was* daydreaming about Little Debbie snack cakes—but Cal was there.

I got to that point by thinking about the way he'd walked all those dogs back to the shelter; and then I thought about how he convinced Marty to adopt Olive; and then I thought about how he set him up with everything he'd need to take care of the little dog—food, a leash, a collar. He'd taken such care with both Olive and Marty, and then I just jumped right to him also taking care of me, which in that moment meant addressing my growling stomach.

And what better way to solve that problem than with Little Debbie snack cakes?

Apparently, the junk food bender on my thirtieth birthday has unleashed a sugar monster inside me.

With Marty and Olive and everything really, I sit on the sidelines watching, wishing I were a different kind of person.

If I weren't so *me*, Cal might see someone other than just a colleague.

He'd shown up to eat lunch with us almost every day since, checking in on Olive. Chatting about his research. Asking Marty questions about life without technology, a world that seemed foreign to us, having basically grown up with it.

I didn't tell Cal I found another one of his notes to himself in his research the night before—this one said: *"Statistics make me wonder is infidelity to be expected with the accessibility to old flames on social media?"*

I had to hold myself back from repeating his words from that day in the comic book shop: *"I wonder who hurt you."*

When Cal speaks, I home in on every word. I notice his mannerisms. I secretly hope his smile finds its way to me simply because he likes that I exist.

I know it's dangerous to daydream about any of this. I know because I used to do the same thing with Alex. Listening to him talk about his work used to thrill me. I'd never met anyone more passionate, more ambitious.

But that ambition played out in ways I'd rather forget.

Maybe Cal is the same. Maybe he's all about building a name for himself, about professional success.

But no, his passion is different, and even I haven't been able to convince myself otherwise. Over and over, it seems that what Cal is most passionate about is people.

And that was never Alex. We had that in common, he and I. Alex and I were both driven and loved the research. Cal and I have other things in common—he's also an avid *Doctor Who* fan, for instance, and sometimes to unwind, he plays video games, which is a little guilty pleasure of my own.

Not that I should compare. Not that it matters. Cal and I are colleagues. Nothing more. I need to stop imagining otherwise.

Of course, I didn't tell Delilah any of this. That girl is too smart for her own good. I wasn't about to let her know it.

"If you must know"—I offered my best serious face—"I was dreaming of being published one day. Of making a big discovery that would change millions of lives."

She stared, clearly not buying it. "You had that dopey look on your face."

"What dopey look?"

"The one you get when Dr. Cal comes around."

I made a mental note to take stock of my expressions when Cal was around, just in case Delilah was right.

Step eight: "Participate in activities that will put a smile on your face."

The following week, I went to a soccer game with Marty. Historically, I've never seen sporting events as a place that could usher in any feelings other than anxiety or claustrophobia. Maybe because of all the years I was forced to play dodgeball in gym class—that's legit trauma, you know.

This was different, though. Good different.

Namely because I wasn't in any danger of being blindsided in the face with a rubber ball. I swear, how does that not qualify as organized bullying?

We sat in the bleachers—Marty's daughter, Miriam, and I on either side of Marty, who was surprisingly rambunctious with every pass, kick, and goal. Before long, I was cheering for the Yellow Jackets too, and specifically for Miriam's son, James, who as it turns out *is* better suited for playing the tuba than playing soccer. But when the kid kicked the game-winning goal, the crowd went wild. Marty went wild. *I* went wild. It was pure elation unlike anything I've ever experienced.

I've never even met James, but this was infectious joy, and when I went home that night, I wrote it all down in the notebook.

Chapter 22

A week later on Thursday, after yoga (still no joy), I'm on my way to work when I get a text from Cal.

I've got your next step handled.

I smile down at my phone. He was thinking of me. Not only to send this text but to handle the next step.

Last time you picked a step, I went to second base with a golden retriever.

😂 Lady killer, that one.

For sure!

So you're good with me stepping in?

Yes, today was going to be "Let go of grudges" and I didn't really want to do that anyway.

No, you don't. Our grudges keep us warm at night.;)

😂

I'll meet you in your office after lunch.

I can't deny that my heart flip-flops at this. Unfortunately, my most basic emotions are tied to some bad core memories.

The familiarity is sounding an alarm: *Remember Alex. Remember Alex.*

So I do. I remember Alex.

Like Cal, Alex was also a professor. He wasn't conventionally good-looking, which I think is why I let my guard down in the first place. His intelligence was what drew me to him.

And like Cal, Alex sought me out to consult on an academic paper he was writing for publication. I was floored and I was flattered.

No, it was more than flattered. No one had ever sought me out before.

He said he'd asked around, and I had a reputation of being brilliant (*brilliant! me?*) and he could really use my help. In return, I'd be credited for my research. We'd be partners, equal billing and accreditation, along with two other professors.

This was it. My chance to be published. It's not unknown in my line of work that everyone wants to contribute something great to the larger academic sphere. And here, walking right in my door, was my chance. My chance to put Isadorkus Maximus in the rear-view mirror for good.

We were tireless in our research, and Alex was tireless in his pursuit of me. He complimented me every step of the way—not just my work but me. He told me he'd never met anyone like me. He praised my research. He tucked my hair behind my ear one night when we were working late in his office and kissed me after walking me home.

Alex had fallen . . . for me.

And I was just as upside-down in love with him.

Never in my life had I expected this. I'd given up hoping, really, that another person would ever see me like that. Want me like that.

I gushed about him to my mother, who was far happier about

the fact that I had a boyfriend than she was about the fact that I was going to be published, and who insisted on meeting him.

"Soon," I'd told her. "Let us get through this research, and then we can think about next steps." I won't lie. Sharing Alex with her almost—*almost*—felt normal. The way I imagined other girls were with their moms, trading secrets and having girl talk. So what if it had taken over twenty years for that to happen? We had finally arrived.

Weeks and months flew by in a whirlwind. Third, fourth, and final drafts were printed, edited, and scoured. Alex and I grew inseparable, spending days at the office working and nights at each other's apartments *not* working.

And then, finally, the paper was published.

And my name was nowhere to be found.

Not in the foreword, not in the reference notes at the beginning, not even in the acknowledgments at the end.

Nothing. Nowhere.

At the publication party, Alex had the nerve to stand in front of the entire department, claiming all my work—*my work*—my hours and hours of research, conclusions, and intelligence. For himself.

And nobody questioned it. Didn't any of them realize what had just happened?

Or was it so easy to believe that I was nothing more than Alex's little assistant, contributing so little after all this time?

He stepped off the stage into a throng of curious academics, and when he made eye contact with me, he actually smiled.

He made his way through the crowd to where I stood against the back wall. "We did it, Isadora!"

I think he was high on the adrenaline of everything going right in his world. I was dumbfounded at the realization that everything was going wrong in mine.

"Bob, I'll be right there!" He waved at someone over my shoulder, distracted. "We'll chat later," he said. "Dinner tonight?"

I nodded numbly.

He grinned. "I have something important to talk to you about."

At that, my insides shifted. My anger about the paper began to dissipate, replaced by a certainty that this was it—the moment I'd been silently waiting for.

"You . . . you do?"

"Yes, super important, can't wait to talk to you—" His attention darted to the side. "Hi, Dr. Weir! I know, I know, so glad you could make it!" And he was off.

Hindsight being what it is, I couldn't see this for what it was. From those nine words, *"I have something important to talk to you about,"* I firmly believed that he was going to take our relationship to the next level.

I was certain Alex was going to propose.

And while I was disturbed by him taking all the credit for my work, that could be dealt with later—I was happy to support him in his dreams. We could be an academic power couple—I could jump onto his star and ride all the way to the top with him.

That night, before I clocked out for the evening, he showed up in my office. One look at him, and I convinced myself to forget about the lack of credit he gave me on the paper. It didn't matter that much anyway—it *was* his project.

And relationships were about building each other up, right? Sacrificing and compromising and all that? If I could help do that for Alex, why shouldn't I? His dreams were a lot bigger than mine, after all.

"Hey," I said. "Big day."

He smiled. Remembering back on this now, I would say that his smile was forced. I didn't notice it then.

"Yeah." He shoved one hand in his pocket, and I held my breath. "I've got things to say, Isadora."

I braced myself for this. I wanted to remember every moment of it. I wanted to be wide-awake as I lived out the moments of a story I would tell for the rest of my life. I sat on the stool in the lab and drew in a deep breath. "Okay, go ahead."

His smile shifted. "I've been thinking about us, Isadora. A lot. You've been amazing . . ."

"You too, Alex." I wanted to hit the fast-forward button to the good part.

He paused. "And, well, I think . . ."

"Yes?"

"I think maybe it would be better if we go back to being colleagues."

There are moments in everyone's lives where, when you recount them to others, you include the line, "I can't believe what just happened." Those moments might include a police chase that ends in a wreck on your front lawn, a lightning strike that topples a tree onto your neighbor's house, a whale that swallows your guide's kayak on your Alaska trip . . .

. . . and what Alex had just said to me.

I breathed. At least I think I did.

"What?" I whispered.

He kept talking, I think to repeat what he just said, and I whispered again.

"What?"

Colleagues? He was supposed to meet my parents next week. We were supposed to go on vacation together over summer break. He was supposed to be proposing to me right now.

He was supposed to put my name on that paper.

I looked at him as if he was speaking some form of ancient Greek. "I think I need someone a little more fun," he continued. "And come on, Isadora. We both know that's not you."

I didn't hear his criticism mostly because I was already sorting out in my head how to get my favorite cardigan and slippers from his apartment.

"I thought we were a team," I said in a fog.

He covered my hand with his. *No goose bumps.* "We were. A good one too. But maybe not a great one. At least not personally. Professionally, we were perfect."

"Professionally?" I repeated.

"Yeah, I mean, the paper is getting a lot of attention."

I could've said something then. Something about his lack of integrity or the fact that he practically stole my work, but I didn't. I didn't say a word. I just sat, and watched, and listened, and breathed.

And then I guess he was done saying what he needed to say, because he walked out the door, leaving me sitting there alone.

It wasn't until later that I realized I was sad he was leaving me. And even later that I realized his professional betrayal had just as many implications as this personal one.

Alex was revered. That paper catapulted him into a whole new world. He was offered a job in Boston, traveling, teaching, lecturing. He turned his findings into a book. He was living the high life.

Meanwhile, I was still in the same closet office researching other people's projects.

So, no, Cal Baxter. Hearts flip-flopping and goose bumps and sweaty palms are nothing but warning signs. He might as well be wrapped in caution tape.

Chapter 23

That afternoon, I'm leafing through Cal's second chapter, marveling at how focused it is—and feeling pleased every time I see my fingerprints on his work—when a knock on my open door pulls my attention.

I keep my door open now, and I've been practicing smiling this whole time. I'm trying to move away from *recluse* and more toward *approachable*. A key indicator that things are progressing in the right direction is that nobody's been grimacing at the sight of my teeth lately. Not Logan, not Shellie, not even Gary, who checks in with me every few days to make sure I'm properly connecting with my coworkers.

And that I'm not messing things up with Cal's book.

I'm doing well on both fronts, by the way. Two days ago, Shellie and Logan even joined Marty and Cal and me for lunch on the bench. We talked about their projects, and I think I even gave them good advice.

I glance up to see Cal filling the doorframe, holding a thin white box, and unlike when I first met him, something inside me relaxes at the sight of him. As if a part of me has been waiting all day to see him, and now, here he is.

I remember my pledge to remain distant, but I also feel the

effects of the way he looks at me, with such earnest eyes, and I wonder if I'm already too far gone.

"Am I interrupting?" he asks.

Never.

"Obviously," I say. "I'm hard at work on your book."

His eyes widen. "Oh?"

I nod to the box in his hand. "What's that?"

He gives it a shake. "I promised you I'd handle the next step."

"Are my grudges in that box?"

He laughs at that and takes a seat—his seat, I realize it's become—then sets the box on my desk.

"When I read the list, I knew there were a few steps I'd be especially good at helping with." He lifts the lid from the box to reveal a dozen pieces of gourmet chocolate.

And now Isadora is on the alert. When presented with the finest delicacies, Isadora Bentley's defenses wane, her jaw goes slack, and she is reduced to her most primal urges. To eat as if this is the only meal she will have for the entire year. There are few things in this world that can stop her in her tracks; and one of them is chocolate.

"You're already salivating, aren't you?" He lifts a brow to punctuate the sentence.

I absolutely am.

I reach. "Which ones are caramel?"

He shrugs and pulls the box back slightly. "Half of the fun of this is not knowing."

"I disagree." I frown. "I don't like surprises."

"Even when they taste like chocolate?" He affixes the lid underneath, keeping the box open, and catches my gaze. "Don't try to solve a puzzle that doesn't exist. Overthinking is not required. This isn't a big deal. Just chocolate."

"I know that," I say with a twinge of defensiveness in my voice. "But I know what I like."

"Maybe you'll find something new to like? Like marshmallow or hazelnut or praline."

It was a silly thing to wish this candy came with a ridged cardboard pictorial to tell me what each piece was, but I can't help it if I prefer my life to be a little predictable.

I do better when I know what's coming.

He slides the box toward me. "You pick first."

I survey the candy, inspecting each small square and circle and rectangle as if they will tell me where to begin. Finally, I choose a simple brown round one.

Cal picks up a white chocolate and then mocks apprehension. "I wonder what's inside," he says, bringing it up really close to one eye.

It occurs to me that this entire scene highlights the difference between his personality and mine. Cal seems excited just to be living. Most days, I'm just getting through it.

Not lately, though, I realize.

"Ready?" He grins.

I reluctantly go along, mostly because I don't want him to think I'm a killjoy, even though I know I am. We each take a bite of our chocolates, and I'm thrilled to learn the gooiest, most wonderful caramel is inside of mine.

Cal's is some sort of nougat and almonds and he practically moans as he closes his eyes to taste every single flavor.

I watch him enjoy his chocolate for a solid ten seconds until he finally opens his eyes and looks at me. "Mine's better."

"Not a chance," I say.

"I'll tell Sarah."

My heart sputters. *Who is Sarah?* I cough to clear my throat. "Sarah?"

"My sister. She has a little coffee and chocolate shop, but most of her business is shipping out boxes like this. She put together her favorites for us."

For us.

For some reason that changes the way I look at the box of chocolate—and the way I'm eating them.

He nods toward the box. "How about this time I pick one for you and you pick one for me?"

Go with it, Isadora. "Deal," I say. "Just make sure you pick one with caramel."

He chooses a green rectangular piece for me, and I pull out a pink circle for him.

We lift both pieces in a mock toast, nod, and bite. We chew in silence, and once again, Cal treats the whole experience like he was born for this exact moment.

"Oh my giddy aunt, I love chocolate."

I laugh because I have never heard that expression before.

Is it the chocolate that's spiking my endorphins or the company? Unclear.

He goes in for another piece, then pushes the box toward me.

"Fine. One more." I choose one and he smiles, like I've just made his day by going along with this.

He chews and swallows another white chocolate–covered candy. "That one was cookies and cream. I should've split it with you because everyone needs to taste that."

I bet I could taste it if I kissed him.

Cal is handsome. Handsomer than a professor should be allowed to be, really. But also, he's kind. Genuinely kind. He didn't need to do this.

In a fleeting thought, it occurs to me that Alex never would've done this. And the very next fleeting thought somehow flies right out of my mouth.

"Do the girls in your classes have trouble focusing?" *So that's out there now.*

"Pardon me?"

"Because you look like—" I wave a hand in his general direction as if to explain.

"I look like . . . ?"

"You look like you. Like you're selling Rolex watches on a magazine cover."

He laughs. "I don't think I've ever been given that exact compliment. It . . . it *is* a compliment, right?"

I wish I would stop verbally painting myself into these conversational corners. "Yeah, no. Yeah . . . it is a compliment." Was it possible to get drunk on chocolate? Because I feel like I'm drunk on chocolate. "Is it hard on them? The girls? In your classes?"

"I couldn't honestly say," he ponders, amused. "Is it hard on you?"

"Of course not," I lie. "But I'm an adult. I'm past the point of raging hormones."

He narrows his perfectly blue eyes, a little grayer today than when he's outdoors. "Is that right?"

See, this is the problem with having a big imagination. It's easy for me to read into this—to hear a challenge in his innocent question. It's easy for me to imagine that all the way out to the point where we're walking down the aisle, raising babies, and growing old together in a little house in the suburbs with a porch swing and a white picket fence.

That's not where this story is headed. I don't even want those things.

When I simply nod in response, he says, "I'll keep that in mind." He picks up another chocolate and pops the whole thing in his mouth. It's obvious he isn't giving a single thought to his waistline. I'm a bit jealous of that.

"I just finished your second chapter," I say, mostly to fill the silence.

"And?"

"I'm impressed. Very focused." I smile. "But I noticed . . ."

"What?"

"I'm not sure I should say," I tell him. "After all, you're the author. I'm not. It's not my voice."

"No, Isadora, please." He sits up straighter. "We're partners in this. I value your opinion."

Partners?

When he says this, fireworks explode in my mind and I actually let myself imagine what it would be like to kiss him.

The connectors in my brain are misfiring. His valuing my opinion should in no way make me think of kissing.

"Are you okay?"

The memory of Delilah's accusation—*dopey look*—rushes through my mind and I straighten my expression to what I hope is blank.

"What you've got"—I'm verbally flailing for a fingerhold on this conversation—"is really well organized, really focused . . ." I pause.

"But?"

"But I think you should put more of *you* into this," I say. "It reads a little . . ." I search for the right word. "Clinical, I guess? And you . . . aren't. Clinical."

"Huh." He seems to be pondering this.

"Like, why did you decide to investigate this topic of social media and how it relates to human connection in the first place? You're writing a book about relationships, about personal connection, but you aren't including anything about your own."

He looks away. Did I hit a nerve?

I wonder who hurt you.

"That's a good question," he says. "Just not one with an answer I'm sure I want in the book."

I nod and say, "I understand." But I don't understand. I'm more curious than ever what it was that made Cal want to write this book on this subject in the first place. Maybe we're both conducting experiments because we have something to prove.

"It's a strong start, though. I got really caught up in it last night."

"You did?"

I nod. "Yeah. I like reading your notes in the margins. Helps me see your train of thought."

"I'm surprised you can follow it."

"Well, I'm good at puzzles."

He inches the box of chocolates toward me. "Got one more in you?"

I shake my head but slowly reach for a rectangular piece with a chocolate drizzle on top.

Cal grins.

I nod toward the box, and he takes another piece.

"Wanna split this one?" he asks.

If my inner thoughts came with sound effects, this exact moment would have an audible *gulp*. If cup-kissing got my pulse racing, I don't stand a chance with chocolate-sharing.

Still, I manage a "Sure."

We each bite our pieces in half. Mine is marshmallow with a graham cracker crust. His is white with a pink center. When we switch pieces, my fingers brush against his, and I swear he lingers for at least five beats of my wildly racing heart.

My eyes dart to his, and he lifts a brow. "I don't know if you're ready for white-chocolate raspberry." He says this like a challenge, and now that I've locked onto his gaze, I can't look away.

But he doesn't look away either.

We both slowly eat our chocolates, chewing, savoring, smiling. And I'm proud of myself for not running from the room, even though I felt that look all the way to my toes. *Zinger.*

"So how do you feel?" he asks.

Like I need a cold shower. "How do I . . . ?"

"Did the chocolate make you happy?"

Oh, right. The *experiment.* "Sure. Yeah."

"I don't believe you," he says.

I draw in a deep breath. "I don't know. I like chocolate. I like chocolate a *lot.* I like the way it tastes, and I even liked trying the new flavors."

He looks expectant. "But . . . ?"

I shrug. "Part of me wonders if I'm predisposed not to feel happiness the way other people feel it."

His forehead crinkles as he considers this. "When was the last time you were truly happy?"

Now *there's* a question.

He leans back in his chair, and my resolve begins to crumble. He's looking at me like he's genuinely interested, and I could be way off base, but it doesn't seem like that interest is purely professional.

Maybe it's because he's a psychologist who understands human behavior, but his eyes are intent on mine, waiting for an answer, waiting to hear about the last time I was truly happy.

But my mind is blank. I can't remember a single thing. I have no silly anecdote, nothing to share. "Can I get back to you on that?"

"Come on," he says. "There must be something."

My gaze falls to my desk as the pressure inside me mounts. Yes. There must be. Why can't I think of anything?

"You know what I think, Isadora?"

I'm scared to hear this.

"I don't think you want to prove Dr. Grace Monroe wrong at all."

"Oh yes, I do," I say. "She's spreading false hope to the masses."

"Well, first of all, I don't think *masses* of people are reading that magazine, but second, why do you think it's false? Is it possible that maybe—just maybe—you started this experiment because you want her to be right?"

"Of course not," I say matter-of-factly, but I slightly don't believe it. Marty didn't believe it. Darby didn't believe it. Even I've had my doubts, so why am I holding on to this false narrative so tightly?

"You want to figure out why *you're* unhappy." He sounds convinced. As if he's made up his mind about me. "You're hoping that if you do these thirty-one things, you'll figure it out."

"That's not true," I say. "I don't like fake science."

"I looked up Dr. Monroe. She's legitimate."

"She's a psychologist," I say.

He stops. "Which is a legit science." There's an air of defensiveness in his voice.

"A soft science," I mutter. "There's a lot of room for human error. Your interpretation of your findings is subjective."

"Isadora, that's not true. Not exactly."

"It's not like there is ever definitive proof of anything. Not like solving a math problem anyway."

"There are still ways to examine data and reach a conclusion," he says. "Previous diagnoses and behaviors can help inform and predict future ones. Human personalities and emotions are complex, I get that, but there are definite guidelines to helping someone navigate self-discovery. And I know you know this. You're one of the best researchers I've ever met."

He has a point, and I know it. "You're right. I didn't mean to offend you. I'm sorry."

"You didn't. A lot of people look at my profession like I just doodle on a yellow pad while some poor guy pays me to tell me about his mother."

A pause. And then I say, "I'm not hoping she's right. I'm going to disprove her ideas. These steps can't make a person happy."

"Independently, maybe not. And maybe every step isn't going to have the same effect on every person. But would you really say that you're no happier now than when you started the project?"

I think back on the past several weeks. Darby. Delilah. Marty. The eight slobbery dogs. Yoga. Mal's. The purple velvet sofa. Spaghetti and meatballs. A bag full of cookies. Cheering at soccer games. Daydreaming again.

I meet his eyes and steel my resolve. "It's too early for me to make that deduction. Just like it's too soon for you to make up your mind about me."

He watches me too intently. "Oh, I made up my mind about you the day we met." He smiles then, and it unnerves me.

"What's that supposed to mean?"

"Do you have plans Saturday?"

"What?" Why is he suddenly acting like we're friends? Or maybe . . . is he acting like we're *more* than friends?

"I have an idea."

I frown. "What kind of idea?"

"For another one of the steps. Dress casually and come hungry." He stands. "Text me your address, and I'll pick you up a little before lunchtime." He fixes his messenger bag crossways over his chest and nods. "Sound good?"

"Uh, no."

"Great." He turns to go.

"I just said no!"

He smiles. "Okay, is it a real no or a talk-me-into-it no?"

I'm exasperated now, but I feel the smile crawl across my face.

He rewards me with one of his own. "Keep the chocolate. And learn to enjoy eating it, would ya?" His smile holds for a count of three, and then he's off.

I don't like this one bit.

I don't like him making assumptions about me. And I especially don't like that I fear maybe, just maybe, he's right about all of it.

Chapter 24

Saturday morning, I'm standing in my bedroom, surrounded by a mountain of clothes that simply won't do for a day with Cal. I'm beginning to realize that my wardrobe is slightly outdated and—I hate to say it—frumpy.

He said to dress casually. That isn't a problem given the fact that I don't own anything dressy except work clothes. But I'm certain the tapered '90s sweatpants should not make an appearance.

I'm lamenting this when there's a familiar, frantic knock on my door—one I've grown accustomed to over the past several weeks. I don't have to open it to know Darby is on the other side.

I could pretend to be annoyed that she and her children never seem to leave me alone, but the truth is, I like it. I like that they include me. I almost feel like part of the family.

On the nights Darby doesn't come over, I can almost certainly count on Delilah showing up—and while she's only ten, I consider her a friend too.

Is that weird? A grown woman being friends with a ten-year-old?

I already know. It *is* weird, but I don't really care. I'm starting to feel like my apartment is a safe space for Delilah. What I wouldn't have given to have had that when I was her age.

Another knock.

It really does me no good to romanticize my new friendships. My nature is to keep everyone at arm's length, but it is nice to have someone to talk to other than Cactus Gary.

"Isadora? Dante made cannoli!"

Well, who the heck am I to turn down cannoli?

I yank the door open. Darby is looking down and rummaging through her bag when she starts talking. "I told him to make extra because I figured you— *Oh my gosh*!" She takes one look at me and frowns. "What is happening here?" She waves a hand from my ankles to my shoulders, then makes a circle in the air around my head.

I maintain eye contact, slowly reach out and gingerly take the cannoli, open the container, and shove a whole one in my mouth.

"Whoa," Darby says. "It must be serious."

I stare and chew.

"I get it. Intervention." Darby takes me by the shoulders and moves me back into my apartment and over to the kitchen table, pushing me to a seated position. "You don't eat cannoli like that. They're meant to be savored."

"I'm too stressed to savor," I tell her with my mouth full.

"Okay, Isadora. Spill it."

I grimace. This is the kind of girl talk I don't enjoy. I don't want her to squeal or fan her hands in front of her like butterfly wings the way celebrities do when they're fake crying. "It's nothing, really. I'm just . . . getting ready to go out."

"You're going out? Like *out*?" Darby takes a step back. I shrink under the weight of her gaze. "Is this why you couldn't go to yoga?"

"I'm too stressed for yoga." I reach for another cannoli and Darby smacks my hand like I'm one of her kids.

Her eyebrows pop up just as Delilah appears in the doorway. "Are you going out with Dr. Cal?" the little girl says.

Traitor.

Darby gasps. "Are you?"

"She is," Delilah says, making herself at home on my couch. She props a picture frame on my coffee table, right next to the lamp, but I have no idea what's in the frame because it's facing the opposite direction. "She's making the face again."

I reset my face to factory settings and sigh. "It's not like that. He's going to help me with one of the steps. He's assessing my findings." I point at Darby. "This is your fault, you know."

"Yeah, yeah. You can thank me later." She stands. "You can't wear"—another dismissive wave in my general direction—"whatever this is." I give myself a once-over, and I know she's right. The jeans are out of date, and the short-sleeved floral button-down is the color of vomit. There's nothing appealing about this outfit.

Darby walks into my bedroom, takes one look at the mess, and turns right around and closes the door.

"I'll be right back."

I look at Delilah, who shrugs innocently. "She's going to fix you."

"I don't need to be fixed. It's not like this is a date."

"Yes, it is."

"No, it's not."

"Yes, it is."

I'm losing an argument to a ten-year-old.

I walk over to the armchair facing the couch, where Delilah is sitting with an open book she's not reading. The new picture frame catches my eye. It has a photo of the lunch crew—me and Marty on the bench, Darby and the kids off to one side, and Cal sitting on the ground next to me.

"Where'd that come from?" I nod toward it.

"I took it on my phone," she says.

"You're too young to have a phone," I say.

"I'm practically an adult." Delilah looks at the photo. "Plus, if I didn't have a phone, you wouldn't have this photo and your apartment would continue to be devoid of life."

I stare at her. I assume this is something else she's overheard her mother say.

"It's true," she says. "Mom is always talking about bringing more life to this space. I thought the best way was with a photo."

I glance over at the framed image and suddenly, like the Grinch, my heart grows three sizes. I'm used to keeping my distance from everyone, but I'm overcome with gratitude for these people in my life.

Was it really only a few short months ago that I had no one?

Now I can hardly imagine eating lunch at my desk, or dinner without my nosy neighbors.

"I can take it back," Delilah says with a nod toward the framed photo in my hand, a line of worry etched into her forehead.

"No," I say. "I love it. Thank you."

She smiles then, and I wonder how anybody in the world could ever make this girl—so smart and kind—feel like anything other than what she is. I'm angry on her behalf, I realize. And on my own.

Once upon a time, I *was* Delilah.

Darby strolls back in carrying a laundry basket of clothes. "Let's get you ready for your date."

"Not a date," I say.

"It's a date." Delilah doesn't look at me when she says this.

"If it's not a date," Darby asks, "then why did he ask you to go somewhere with him on a Saturday?"

"For research." I haven't moved from my spot in the armchair, and all at once I think maybe this would be a better place to spend the day.

"Uh-huh." Darby sets the basket down and starts pulling out loud, busy-patterned, bright clothing.

"I cannot wear any of those," I say.

She frowns. "Why not?"

"I don't wear magenta, Darby."

She narrows her eyes, amused and skeptical. "Well, maybe you should."

I'm certain magenta is not my color, because magenta isn't actually a real color—fun fact. It's a color your brain fills in when confronted with a gap between red and purple. "He said to dress casual. He's just going to help me with the next step. That's all. This is not a date. We're colleagues."

"Are you finished trying to convince yourself?" Darby plants her hands on her hips and stares me down. "You can call it what you want, but either way, you can't wear that."

I take off the floral button-down and toss it aside, feeling slightly self-conscious in my white cami.

"Delilah, grab that and put it in a giveaway pile," Darby says. "Quick!"

Delilah does as she's told, dropping my shirt in a pile by the door.

"Stand here," Darby says, pointing.

I do as I'm told but suddenly feel more naked than the day we met in the hallway. Delilah comes to her side, and now they're both staring at me.

"Are you kidding me, Isadora?" Darby is looking at me the way I've seen her look at Danny, usually when he's done using the potted plants as a toilet.

"What?"

"You've been hiding *that* figure under these giant clothes this whole time?" Darby groans.

"I don't like to draw attention to my body," I say. "I'm not a fan. Of my body. I'd rather show off my brains, in case you haven't realized by now."

"There's no reason the two can't coexist," Darby says.

Delilah plops back down on the couch.

"I want to be taken seriously as a professional," I say. "I don't think there's anything wrong with a little modesty."

"Okay, there's 'modest' and then there's 'Puritan.' Isadora, you don't have to be professional all the time. You can be a woman too." She stuffs an outfit into my arms and shoos me off. I walk into my bedroom, closing the door behind me. Seconds later, Darby flings the door open.

"Tell me what he said," she says. "When he asked if you could go out today."

I'm standing in the middle of the room and instinctively cross my arms over my chest.

"Please. I have four kids."

"Do your kids have boobs?" We aren't close enough for her to watch me change my clothes.

She shakes her head. "Who knew those were hiding underneath your oversized shirts. Where do you shop anyway, the thrift store?"

I frown and try to tug the shirt over my head. "There is nothing wrong with thrift stores, Darby. I don't like waste."

"Then you shouldn't waste your figure hiding under those tents you call shirts." She tosses me a pair of jeans I'm certain won't go over my hips.

"Darby, we are not the same size."

"They have stretch," she says. "Just try them. Also, you have a warped perception of your own body."

Hiding it is simply part of making myself invisible. I don't want to be looked at—ever. I push her out of the room, worried about trying on too-tight jeans in front of another person (even if she is a mom), and close the door.

I turn away from the mirror and pull on the pants. They go

right up over my hips and button easily. Darby's right—they stretch. Denim has come a long way.

"They fit, don't they?" she calls from the other side of the door.

I pull it open and she looks at me. "Look at you, Isadora. You actually have curves."

"Must be all that yoga," I say sarcastically.

She laughs, then pulls a black jacket from her fashion basket. "Here, try this."

I layer it over the loose gray T-shirt.

Darby turns me toward her—forcefully, I might add—and tucks the very front of the gray shirt into the jeans. I feel slightly violated as she fusses with it, then finally stops. "Perfect," she says as she spins me around to face the mirror and smiles at my reflection.

"Look at you, Isadora," she says. "Your date's not going to know what hit him."

"Not a date," I say. I shake my head. "I don't know if I can do this."

All this "date" talk has me fidgety. I didn't agree to a date. I am permanently, as in always and forever, *not* dating. Thank Alex for that. Never mind what Marty said. And never mind how drawn to Cal I am. The inevitable heartbreak is so much worse than any momentary joy.

I look back into the mirror and see that my face has fallen.

"He's just a guy," Darby says. "And he likes you. *And* you have a lot in common, right? You both love research and that crazy *Doctor Who* show."

"And chocolate."

She smiles. "Just go and have fun! Say yes to new adventures! Calculate how happy it makes you later, if you want, and then when you get home, tell me all about it."

"And me," Delilah calls from the couch.

I draw in a breath.

"Isadora, what is it?" Darby looks genuinely concerned for me. I'm unsure how to process this. Do I tell her about Alex? About all the ways he chipped away at my self-esteem? The ways he made me feel like I was lucky to be dating him? That he was somehow taking pity on me to be with me in the first place? How foolish I felt that I didn't see through him sooner?

"Nothing," I say. "I think I'm just nervous."

Delilah has appeared in the doorway like a tricky little ghost, and she clucks her tongue at us to get our attention. "You're going to do her makeup, right?"

Darby's eyes snap to my face. Her eyes narrow.

"I don't wear much makeup," I say.

"I *know*," Delilah says pointedly. "But we can fix that."

Darby scrunches her nose and smiles at me, and we share a brief moment of amusement over the ten-year-old.

"Makeup is just a way to adhere to society's superficial standards of beauty," I say. "I'm fine with ChapStick."

"It's okay to like girly things, Isadora," Darby says. "It's fun to dress up and put on makeup. It doesn't take away from your ridiculously high IQ."

"How do you know about my high IQ?" I ask seriously.

Darby silently walks over to my nightstand and thrusts both hands at the small stack of books piled there. *A Short History of Nearly Everything* by Bill Bryson, *Teaching and Learning Discrete Mathematics Worldwide* by Eric W. Hart and James Sandefur, and *The Worth Expert Guide to Scientific Literacy* by Kenneth D. Keith and Bernard Beins.

"Call it a hunch."

Darby stares at me for a moment. "This isn't the kind of makeover where we change your whole appearance and—boom!—now you're a whole different person. All I'm going to do is bring out what you've already got going on. Because there are so many good things about you, Isadora. Inside *and* out."

As she walks back over to me, I think about my mother. She was always trying to push her "superficial beauty standards" on me. All the times she tried to "fix me up," the only message I got was, "You're not good enough as you are."

But that's not the message I'm getting from Darby. To her, this is just fun. Just two girlfriends playing dress-up.

"If you hate it, just wipe it all off and go back to your ChapStick," she says. "You're beautiful either way."

"Fine," I say. "But don't make me look like a showgirl."

Darby's face brightens. She pulls a small makeup bag from her basket, then walks me into the bathroom. I feel like her pet project, and for whatever reason, I don't hate it. The outfit *is* significantly better than anything I could've put together. I'm wearing jeans I didn't think I could fit into, which is, shockingly, an instant mood boost.

"Someone hurt you, right? Who was it, some guy?" Darby isn't looking into my eyes when she says this. She's focused on getting my eye shadow *just right.* Maybe that's why I'm able to respond honestly. I find it easier to confess when I'm not looking directly at someone. Or maybe I simply want her to know.

"His name was Alex," I say. "He wasn't the first person to hurt me, but . . ."

"That's the one you're still not over?"

I blink. "Oh. I'm over him." Am I, though? "But he made me much more cautious."

Darby stands back and surveys my left eye. She must be pleased with it because she gives a nod and turns her attention to the other one. "I get that. Before I met Dante, I dated a guy named Chaz." She laughs. "Chaz. Ugh, just by his name I should've known he'd turn out to be a tool."

"He hurt you?" I ask.

"Broke my heart," she says.

"But then you met Dante?"

"No, then I met Ricky."

"Ricky? Darby, these are terrible names for boyfriends," I say. "I'm beginning to question your judgment."

"Hey, you don't have to tell me," she said. "When I met Dante, I was *not* interested. I didn't want anything to do with anyone after what I'd been through." She takes a step back, this time not to look at my makeup but to look at me. "But I don't know, there was something different about him. He was sweet. He wasn't driven by the same things other guys were driven by. His family was important to him. *Is* important to him. He was kind. You can tell a lot about a guy by the way he treats his mother."

She shrugs, then pulls a small compact from her bag. "Just because one guy didn't handle your heart with the care it deserves doesn't mean every other guy will do the same thing."

"I hear what you're saying, and logically, it makes sense. One person doesn't represent the whole group," I say. "But in my experience, nobody handles my heart with care."

"That's just about the most honest thing I've ever heard you say, Isadora." She swipes blush over my cheeks with a large brush. "I promise you, I will. I'll put a Fragile sticker on it myself." She smiles.

"Darby, why are you friends with me?" I ask. "Is it just because you feel sorry for me?"

She frowns and puts away the blush. "What? Are you kidding? You're thirty, single, and get to go to work at the university every day. I'm thirty-two, raising a bunch of kids, and if I'm not careful, can waste weeks at a time staring at the same four walls every day."

"But you love your life."

She smiles. "You're right. I do. But it's nice to see how other people who've made other choices live. Besides, I like you."

Before I can ask her why, she goes on.

"You're funny and smart and kind. Honestly, you remind me of my daughter. And you wear granny panties, which basically makes us kindred spirits. I'll never understand people who wear uncomfortable underwear." She laughs. "The real question is . . . why are you friends with me?"

I don't have to think very hard to come up with a list of reasons—Darby is like sunshine. Every time I'm with her, I feel like I have a place where I belong. And I never, ever feel like I have to be anyone other than me.

But saying that out loud feels risky, so instead, I pause for a moment, then say, "Cannoli."

Our laughter fills my small bathroom, and after a moment she nods toward the mirror. "Okay, you can look now."

I'm doing far too much looking into the mirror for my liking, but I do need to make sure she hasn't made me look like a cast member in *The Rocky Horror Picture Show.*

When I finally meet my own gaze, I'm stunned.

The makeup is subtle. Somehow she's managed to bring out the blue in my eyes. My skin is smooth, and I look more awake than I ever have.

"Is it okay?" Darby asks.

I know I'm thirty years old. I know playing dress-up and giving each other makeovers isn't something women my age typically do. But I can't help but think that this is one of those rites of passage I never got to participate in.

I never had a girlfriend do my makeup or help me pick out clothes. And it wasn't about the actual clothing or makeup—nothing as superficial as that. It's not like I'm wishing I'd spent my adolescence with *Seventeen* instead of my chemistry textbook—I'm not.

But Darby and I spent the morning doing the kinds of things

girls do together, the kind of things friends do together. I have a friend. And she's liked me from the very start.

"It's perfect," I say.

"So you're not so nervous now, right?"

I think about this for a moment. "No," I say. "Now I'm even more terrified."

Chapter 25

Just before noon, my heart rate skyrockets.

I'm pacing across my living room floor, noting where it creaks under the weight of me.

"You're stressing me out," Delilah says. She stands. "I need to go meditate."

I look at Darby, who has pulled a tablecloth from her fashion basket and is creating some sort of Instagram-worthy display in my kitchen. She's unfazed by her daughter's need to access a higher plane. I imagine she's used to it.

Delilah pulls open the door and Cal is standing on the other side, just about to knock.

She grins and looks at me, then back at Cal. "Good afternoon, Professor. I'm glad to see you're on time."

He smiles down at her. "Hello, Delilah. Thank you, and yes, I believe punctuality is important." I love that he doesn't treat her like she's ten. He treats her like she's a highly intelligent girl because that's exactly what she is.

Delilah crosses her arms over her chest. "And what are your intentions toward Isadora? Do I need to set your boundaries?"

"Delilah!" Darby rushes over to the door and shoos her daughter into the hallway. "So sorry about her. You two kids have fun!" She exits my apartment but catches my eye from behind Cal. She gives me two thumbs up with an open mouth before disappearing into her apartment.

I smile cautiously at Cal.

"Wow." He smiles at me. "You look really nice."

I try to occupy my space, but I feel myself wanting to shrink. It's hard to make myself believe I belong anywhere but behind my desk at work. My brain is on break, per usual, when Cal is around, so I fumble and say, "You're welcome."

I mentally smack myself on the forehead and recover with, "I mean, thank you. Thanks. And you look . . . really nice too." But then, doesn't he always?

Today he looks more relaxed than he does at work. He wears gray pants and a blue Henley that brings out the color of his eyes. He looks ready to go hiking or build a campfire.

"We're not hiking or building a campfire, are we?" I ask. "The great outdoors and I aren't exactly friends."

"No, you're safe there. No outdoors. Wait, why do you think we're hiking?" he asks.

"Oh, because you look like you just stepped out of an Eddie Bauer catalog."

He laughs. "Thanks?"

I look directly at him, not understanding what's funny. "You're welcome. It's a compliment."

He smiles again, then takes a few steps into my apartment. Sirens go off in my mind—the European kind you'd hear when the *Polizei* are chasing an amnesiac spy through the streets of Berlin. *Cal is in my apartment.*

He looks around.

I look around.

I try to see my place through his eyes, but mostly I just see all the little touches Darby has added that I resisted at first but have now gotten used to. There's the patchwork picnic blanket she draped over my gray sofa the day after she joined us for lunch in the courtyard and the two turquoise throw pillows she piled into the corner of the couch. There's a big plant near the window that she thankfully waters every day. And a basket of decorative nonsensical turquoise burlap balls on my coffee table.

But Cal doesn't seem to notice any of these things. Instead, he walks over to my bookshelf and peruses my collection, which, I realize, is the most *me* thing about my apartment.

"Quite the eclectic reader," he says.

I stuff my hands in the pockets of Darby's jacket and try to relax.

"I like books," I say.

He turns to me. "Me too." Then back to the shelves. He pulls one out. "*The Hitchhiker's Guide to the Galaxy*?" He looks at me again. "You're full of surprises."

"I don't know what you mean," I tell him.

"I didn't realize you were a science fiction lover," he says.

"Are you also a science fiction lover?" I ask.

His mouth turns up at the corner. "'What's the answer to life, the universe, and everything?'"

I smile and then, as if it's the most obvious thing in the world, reply, "Forty-two." After a moment, I add, "'But you really won't get the answer if' . . ."

". . . 'if you don't know the question,'" he finishes the quote with me.

It's a real nerd moment. *West Side Story* dance in the gym meets Comic-Con.

He shelves *Hitchhiker's Guide*, and I feel myself relax. Maybe Darby was right. Maybe we do have a lot in common.

"You ready to go?" he asks.

"Sure," I say. "But first, tell me where we're going."

"It's a surprise," he says.

"We've been over this, Dr. Baxter." I follow him out of my apartment and into the hallway.

"I know," he says. "But I'm testing a theory that a surprise is a great endorphin rush. And endorphins . . ."

"Contribute to happiness," I say. "I know. But I disagree. Some people"—I indicate myself—"are predisposed to loathe surprises."

"Just go with it this once?" he asks. "Trust me, it'll be fun."

Trust me. The words hang there at the back of my mind. I look at him and realize I do.

From behind, I hear Darby's doorknob *click*. I glance over and see the door is barely cracked. My gaze drops to meet Delilah's one watchful eye.

"Goodbye, Delilah," I say loudly.

She shuts it, and I have to laugh.

"Seems like a great kid," Cal says.

"She is," I agree, looking back at her door. "A really great kid."

We walk downstairs and into the sunshine of the warm spring day. Cal inhales a deep breath. "We couldn't have asked for a more perfect day."

"But the springtime weather in Chicago is unpredictable. We should hurry and do whatever you have planned so we don't get rained on."

His forehead scrunches in confusion. "Rained . . . ? I have no intention of hurrying. It's Saturday."

"What difference does that make?"

"Saturday is a day off," he says. "What do you usually do on Saturday?"

I don't want to say. Before I met Darby, I didn't even leave my apartment unless I needed to restock the potato chips. I shrug a reply.

"Saturdays are for refilling your tank. Getting out into the world. Enjoying your life. We work hard, Isadora. We deserve to play hard."

"I don't believe in play," I say.

"As a practice or as a concept?" he quips.

I roll my eyes. "Funny guy," I say. "I've just never . . . been really good at it."

He looks contentedly resigned. "Well! That's something we'll have to remedy. We're going to have fun today, whether you want to or not."

He walks over to a convertible parked on the street and opens the passenger-side door.

I stare at him for a moment as if I'm trying to decipher a Picasso painting. "That's a nineteen-sixty-five Ford Mustang."

He raises his eyebrows in surprise. "Impressive. A Douglas Adams fan *and* a vintage car enthusiast?"

"Not an enthusiast," I say. "I was involved in a research project about the safety of convertibles."

"And? What did you conclude?"

"Convertibles are no more dangerous than any other car," I say. "The death rate for drivers was eleven percent lower in a convertible, but the rate of driver ejection was higher. Twenty-one percent compared to seventeen percent in a regular car."

"It's a good thing for you that I'm driving, then, right?"

"Is this your car?"

He shakes his head. "Borrowed it from a friend."

"Out of curiosity, which step is this we're doing today?" I ask.

"There are two," he says.

"But that's cheating."

He laughs. "Are you coming with me or not?"

I hesitate but eventually get in the car. He closes the door and walks around to the other side. I glance up and see Darby and

Delilah watching from their window. They both wave and smile, and then Darby mouths, *"Relax!"*

Cal gets in the car beside me, and I try to follow her advice.

"Step ten," he says. "'Get out in the sun.'"

He pulls away from the curb and before long, the city is an image in the rearview mirror. I struggle as the wind whips through my hair, and Cal reaches into the space behind my seat. He pulls out a navy blue baseball cap.

"It'll keep your hair off your face," he says.

"You came prepared."

I don't bother telling him my mother made it clear I don't have a face for hats. My hair is getting stuck in the lip gloss Darby applied, so action must be taken.

I put on the cap and glance at myself in the passenger-side mirror. I'm still recognizable, and yet somehow different. I don't feel like I've been erased. It's almost as if Darby saw something inside me that needed a little coaxing to come out.

Maybe I could get used to being a little brighter on the outside.

Maybe I could find a way to feel a little brighter on the inside.

I glance over at Cal, who is wearing sunglasses and no baseball cap. The wind tousles his wavy hair, and there's a look of pure contentment on his face.

I try to set my expression to match. I want to embrace these little adventures the way he does.

"What a perfect day," he says, almost to himself.

Beyond that, Cal isn't talking much, and that's okay because I'm getting the impression the goal here is to simply enjoy the ride. So I settle in and try to do just that. I take note of my surroundings.

We're on a highway—not an interstate—surrounded by freshly planted fields. The smell of dirt is surprisingly comforting, and the sky is the bluest it's been in a long time. Somehow the sunshine keeps the air from being too cold.

I take note of the way all this makes me feel.

Alive.

Cal turns on his Spotify playlist, and I laugh when "Manic Monday" by The Bangles comes on.

He gives me a side-eye. "No laughing. This is a classic."

When he pulls into the parking lot of a small-town park, I realize I've lost all track of time, and I have no idea where we are. There are no people around, and frankly, this would be a great place to commit a murder.

As a lover of true crime documentaries, I survey Cal and wonder if I need to plan for my escape. "What is this place?"

He nods toward the playground and says, "It's a park. Don't tell me you've never been to a park."

"Of course I've been to a park, but why are we here?"

His grin is boyish as his eyes widen. "You'll see."

Right. Surprise. Endorphins. Although, I can't deny, the first surprise was a pretty good one.

"Is this still 'Get out in the sun'?" I ask.

"You just have to know everything, don't you?" He exits the car, and I follow.

"I do like to be kept in the loop," I say as if this is new information.

"Well, you're gonna have to go with it today." He grins. He's at the back of the car, about to open the trunk.

"You're not going to pull out an axe and murder me, are you?"

Cal laughs and points at me. "I knew you were a true crime fan."

"You didn't answer my question."

But he's ignoring me. He pops open the trunk and digs around for a few seconds, emerging with . . .

"Are those kites?"

He closes the trunk and walks over to me, holding two plastic kites with long tails.

"It's a great day to fly a kite, don't you think?"

"I don't know," I say. "The physics of kite flying is actually quite complex. Just to get the kite up in the air, the force of lift has to overcome the force of gravity. But then to *keep* it in the air, the force of thrust has to be equal to the force of drag."

Cal stands, shaking his head slightly.

"Or so I've heard."

"Yeah, we're just going to let the wind take control." Cal hands me a kite. He starts off toward a large open field, and I stand dumbly, staring at the kite. I just know I'm going to be terrible at this. Kite flying involves running.

I begin to calculate all the ways I could make a fool of myself while trying—and failing—to fly a kite. I could trip and fall. I could drag the kite on the ground because I can't run fast enough to get it up in the air. I could snap the string in half or get it caught in a tree.

"Isadora?" Cal calls out, and I follow him. "You look panicked."

"I'm pretty sure I'm going to embarrass myself," I say. "That's kind of how these things go for me."

"When was the last time you flew a kite?"

I stare at him. "I've never flown a kite."

"Never?"

I shake my head and wonder if this gives him a clear picture of my childhood.

"Well then, you *are* in for a treat." He grabs my hand and pulls me out to the middle of the field. I try not to freak out over the fact that he's holding my hand, and try equally as hard not to look disappointed when he lets go.

He sets his kite on the ground, then takes mine from me.

"Okay, you're going to hold the string," he says. "And I'm going to take the kite and try to get it in the air."

"Okay, but the force of lift—"

He holds up a hand as if to silence me. "We're just going to let the wind take control."

It's a strange sensation, not trying to figure out the reasons for things that are happening. I've been doing that for as long as I can remember. But maybe knowing how the sausage is made, so to speak, ruins the chances for enjoyment.

So I make up my mind to try.

My first attempt is fruitless, but before I have a chance to get frustrated, Cal runs over, picks up the kite, and lays it on the ground.

"Maybe I can help." He takes the string from my hands, then moves into the space behind me, positioning my body next to his like this is where it was born to be. His arms are around me, and he leans in so his face is next to mine. I can feel the stubble of his cheek against my own, and I inadvertently hold my breath.

"All right, you take the string," he says, his breath warm against my skin.

I do as I'm told, and his hands wrap loosely around mine.

"Okay, hold the kite up and let the wind catch it," he says.

After a moment, the wind gets underneath my kite, and it climbs.

"Now let out a little of the string," he says, stepping away. I feel the absence of his body against mine immediately.

I try not to panic as I follow his instructions, giving the kite a little more freedom to fly. It occurs to me in that moment that maybe in doing so, I've also given myself a little more freedom to fly, but I don't say so because the string goes from taut to loose in a matter of seconds, then the kite tips nose-down and crashes straight to the ground.

"Let's go again." Cal runs over to pick it up.

So we do. And it's oddly exhilarating, getting my kite into the air, figuring out how to keep it there, seeing how high we can go.

Over the next hour, Cal and I fly kites. I don't think about lift or thrust or directionality. I simply follow his lead and let the wind take control.

It's strange how fully I feel this metaphor of flying a kite. The wind takes control of the kite without the kite doing anything except existing—and I want so badly for that to be true for me too. I can feel myself fighting against it. I can feel all the ways I still want to hold the reins. I don't want to be *too* happy because it will make any impending sadness feel that much worse. I don't want to like Cal *too* much because I don't want to be disappointed if he decides he doesn't like me at all. I don't want to settle into the idea that my life has people in it now who really matter, people who may actually care about me, because people always, always let you down.

I watch my kite soar; I see Cal smile; I feel the sun.

And, for a moment, it's enough.

Chapter 26

"Well, that was pretty successful," Cal says after we've packed our kites into the trunk and gotten back in the car.

"It was fun," I say, meaning it.

He widens his eyes and gasps. "Wait. Isadora Bentley had fun?"

I look at him steadily for a long moment. "You're teasing me."

He grins. "Yeah, a little. Should I stop?"

As a rule, I don't like to be teased, and yet, since I know his intention isn't malicious, I think I'm okay with it. "No," I say. "It's okay." I look straight ahead as he pulls out of the parking lot. "Thanks for making me get outside my comfort zone."

"Anytime," he says. "Are you ready for step eleven?"

I'm still processing through the feelings of step ten. If left to my own devices, "Get out in the sun" likely would've meant sitting on the small fire-escape balcony outside my bedroom window and eating a bowl of Lucky Charms. Instead, I experienced two things I've never done—riding in a convertible and flying a kite.

My shoes are a little muddier, but my heart is a little happier.

Not because of a step. But because of the company. The kite flying. The other side of my comfort zone.

"Isadora?"

"Yes, I'm ready," I say.

"You might not like it at first," he says.

"I'll be okay." And I mean it. I will be.

We drive down the highway, and I close my eyes, letting the warm wind wash over me. Cal cranks the music—"You Oughta Know" by Alanis Morissette—and I want to sing at the top of my lungs, but I resist because I'm really not a very good singer. I am moderately comfortable with Cal—I'm not *that* comfortable.

It's important to protect my dignity.

But then, as Alanis hits the chorus, Cal busts out in unison with her, so loud it startles me. I glance over at him and he's full-on singing, as if he were on a stage in front of thousands of people, holding an air microphone and everything.

He looks over at me, grinning. "Come on, Isadora. You know the words, right?"

I do. I know every single word. Delilah isn't the only one with an affinity for '90s music.

Alanis goes into the next verse, and Cal lowers his voice as he continues to sing along. He has a nice voice, actually, and Alanis's range seems to be in line with his own.

"Okay, here comes the chorus," he says. "It's your turn." He passes me the invisible microphone, and at my hesitation, he urges me on.

I hold a fist in front of my mouth, thumb up, and start to sing. I'm quiet at first, but Cal joins in, and before I know it, we're both belting the song at the top of our lungs.

We're still singing when Cal turns down a gravel road and drives us straight toward the horizon—a wide, open road with nothing but the blue sky and perfect, puffy clouds in front of us. He slows the car and turns again, this time down a long driveway that leads to a big white farmhouse in the middle of nowhere. Not a run-down one but a beautifully restored, perhaps newly built farmhouse, complete with large trees out front and a wraparound porch.

I stop singing as the song ends, and Cal turns down the volume.

"Where are we?" I ask.

Two dogs rush out toward us, barking and jumping, and Cal brings the car to a stop. "We're at my parents' house."

I frown. "Wait. What?" This was not supposed to be a date, but he brings me to his parents' house? I'm meeting Cal's parents?

"Is that okay? Step eleven is 'Spend time with quality people.' I thought of the most quality people I know. My family. I wanted you to meet them. It's my sister Sarah's birthday."

A birthday party? I'm attending a *birthday party*?

I'm meeting his parents and going to a birthday party. Without a gift. I feel like I'm going to hyperventilate.

"Uh-oh," he says. "I can see this is freaking you out. I knew it was a risk, but maybe I miscalculated." He looks away as a woman rushes through the front door and onto the porch. She waves in our direction, and Cal waves back. "That's my mom."

Unlike my mother, Cal's mom doesn't appear to be hiding the fact that she is, in fact, a mother. She's wearing jeans with a lightweight, long-sleeved floral button-down over a white tank top. I'm instantly thankful I didn't wear *my* floral button-down, but also a little nauseous over this whole situation.

"Maybe this is too far out of your comfort zone." Cal turns toward me, a distraught expression on his face. "I promise they are really great people."

"You actually want to spend time with them," I say mindlessly.

"'Course I do, they're my family," he says. "But I realize it was presumptuous to think you might be okay with this. I'm so sorry." I can see that he's trying to save the situation. I hate that my reaction is making him feel that way. "I get the impression you don't love being around people you don't know."

"What gave me away?"

"Well, the panicked look on your face for starters," he says. "But I promise we'll leave the second you give me the sign that you're not okay."

"What's the sign?"

He glances back at his mom, who is petting one of the big black dogs. He meets her eyes and holds up one finger, letting her know we'll be there in a minute.

"How about this?" He clears his throat, then in a super-loud voice shouts, "Hey, Cal, I'm not okay!" Then says in a completely serious tone, "Would that work for you?"

In a flash, all of my worry vanishes, and I can't help it—I laugh.

"Too much?" he asks, face blank, voice deadpanned.

"Just don't leave me alone," I say. "Unless I have to use the bathroom."

"Right, because that would be weird."

I can do this, right? I've gotten much better at being around people. My new friends have helped me realize that there really are good people out there. Maybe they were there all along, but I wasn't looking.

Some days, when I'm lying in bed after a day with my lunch crew or an evening in Darby's apartment, I close my eyes to try to sleep but end up replaying moments from the day. Moments when I didn't feel awkward or out of place. There have been many of those moments.

He tilts his head down at me. "You ready?" he asks.

I breathe and nod and we exit the car. I try to mentally prepare myself to spend an afternoon with the people who probably know Cal best of all. I wonder what he's told them about me—if anything. I wonder if I can be friendly the way Darby is friendly. I also wonder if, when I leave, his parents will ask him why on earth he's wasting time with someone like me.

I have a tendency to overthink things.

I realize my self-esteem is in the toilet here, and I would say I'm working on it, but the truth is, I've sort of resigned myself to it. I know what I'm good at—interpreting data, facts, figures; organizing charts and graphs; thinking through problems in ways that other people don't; and I'm also very tidy.

On the flip side, I also know what I'm not good at—meeting new people being at the top of that list. And yet, what if that isn't true anymore? What if it's an old belief I've held on to but one that isn't supported by evidence? The old Isadora might've struggled to meet and connect with people.

But maybe that isn't who I am anymore. Is that too much to hope for?

"Isadora," he says as he meets me at the front of the car. "Just breathe. It'll be fun."

By now, Cal's dad is also on the porch, and when the dogs notice we're no longer in the car, they rush back out to meet us.

"That's Rizzo," Cal says, pointing to one of them. "And that's Bryant. You can probably guess I come from a long line of Cubs fans."

One of the dogs hits my hand with its nose. "I don't understand."

"The Cubs?" he says. "The year they won the World Series? Anthony Rizzo? Kris Bryant? Javy . . . ?"

"I know there's a team called the Cubs, but I don't watch sports," I say.

"This is a tragedy," he says. "I mean, at least you're not a Sox fan . . . right?"

Before I can respond, Cal's mom rushes over to us. She pulls Cal into a tight hug. "Hey there, stranger," she says, squeezing. I notice Cal doesn't shrink away; he hugs her back.

"Hey, Mom."

When she pulls away, he motions toward me.

"You must be Isadora," the woman says before Cal can introduce me.

"That's right," I say.

"Cal's told us how invaluable your help has been on his book," she says.

Right. The book. This was all starting to feel a little too much like a date, so I appreciate her reminder that Cal and I are colleagues. Nothing more.

"Oh, I haven't done much," I say. "Just organized a few things."

"That's not what my son says." She smiles at me. "Sounds like you were an answer to prayer."

That's the second time I've been called that, and I'm unsure how to feel about it.

"I'm Brenda, by the way." She motions toward Cal's dad. "And this is Craig."

I reach out to shake her hand, but she waves me off. "We're huggers in this family." She pulls me in tight—so tight I almost melt.

When was the last time I was hugged with such intention?

"All right, Mom, don't make it weird," Cal says.

When I pull back, Brenda looks me in the eyes. "We're so happy you're here."

This stirs up my insides like a pot of soup, and I have to blink back tears. "Thanks for having me," I say.

Craig shakes my hand. "Good to meet you, Isadora."

I nod in reply, and Craig looks at Cal. "You've been away too long. Your sister was convinced you wouldn't make it. She said something about some new research project?"

I feel my cheeks flush. Am *I* the research project?

"The book's been keeping me busy," Cal says. "But now that I'm working with Isadora, it's going a lot more smoothly."

My insides do a somersault at this, and I don't even bother to tell myself to calm down.

Brenda smiles over at me, then puts a hand on my shoulder, patting it. "Let's go in. I'll get you something cold to drink."

Inside the house, I'm struck by the smell of . . . cinnamon? It smells like a home should smell, and I inhale it deeply to mark it in my mind. My parents' house always had the smell of sterility—clean, yes, but clinically so.

A petite brunette woman is bustling around the kitchen, and at the sound of the door, she looks up and smiles. She shares Cal's bright blue eyes. A tall man with sandy-colored hair is on the other side of the kitchen.

They all start talking at the same time. In the mix of conversations, Cal ushers me toward the woman and introduces her as his sister, Sarah.

"You're the chocolatier," I say.

Sarah laughs, and only then do I notice she is mixing something in a bowl that smells amazing. "Yep, that's me. Did you like your assortment?"

"They were so good," I say. "I really liked the one that sort of reminded me of a Twix bar."

"That's one of our most popular," she says. "This is my boyfriend, Tim."

The conversation volleys across the room from one person to another, and, as promised, Cal doesn't leave my side. We jump in to help prepare what they tell me is Sarah's favorite meal—burgers on the grill, a giant taco salad (seriously, the bowl is bigger than anything I've ever seen), and hand-cut French-fried potatoes with rosemary and garlic.

"It's not the most cohesive meal," Brenda says. "But whatever the birthday girl wants."

I absently think about my last birthday, and I'm overcome with jealousy. The scene unfolding in front of me is so foreign. Growing up, my birthdays were always low-key affairs. My mom tried having a party for me when I was in the second grade. She invited the children of all her friends, and I got so overwhelmed I spent the entire afternoon in the closet.

The worst thing? My mom didn't even notice I was missing. After everyone left, she said, "Wasn't that the best birthday party ever?"

After that, I asked her not to throw me parties anymore. I told her I wanted to spend the evening eating Chinese takeout with her and my father. I didn't want a big, beautiful bakery cake—just a small, handmade one.

She told me if I was going to be that ungrateful, we'd just ignore my birthday altogether.

I know that sounds harsh. And I suppose it was, but truthfully, I was okay with it. I started my junk food birthdays a few years later, and I've been doing them ever since.

Just me and a pile of candy.

My eyes drift over to a lopsided pink birthday cake in the corner of the kitchen, and my heart aches. It's all I can do to swallow my emotions.

A small family gathering. A handmade cake. If Chinese takeout were on the menu, this would be the birthday celebration of my dreams.

"You okay?" Cal whispers this in my ear, his breath tickling my neck.

I nod and whisper back, "I hope you know how lucky you are."

His gaze locks onto mine. "I do."

I'm not sure we're talking about the same thing, and the uncertainty sends a shiver up my spine. I'm beginning to like being locked up in his gaze. Cal's attention still unnerves me, but in a different way than when we first met.

"Isadora, would you like some lemonade?" Brenda is pouring me a glass I don't dare refuse, and just like that, I'm pulled into the mix.

As she puts the finishing touches on the meal, Brenda tells me story after story about Cal jumping off the back deck as a child. "He thought if he tied a towel around his shoulders, he'd be able to fly like Superman."

"Oh no," I say.

Cal looks away sheepishly. "Broke my arm."

Sarah laughs. "And he still tried it again two weeks after he got his cast off!"

The laughter is natural—unforced. I'm engrossed in the storytelling, the banter, the kindness. Sarah gives them all an update on her little shop, and I put together that her parents are the investors who helped her get it off the ground.

My father would say they did her a disservice not letting her raise the capital herself.

They've invested in her. Last year her business doubled, and she expects the same this year. They believed in her and gave her an opportunity she wouldn't have had otherwise.

It wasn't shortsighted—it was kind.

Tim beams as his girlfriend shares her latest ideas for growth and expansion, obvious pride on his face.

I realize somewhere along the way that if Cal had left me alone with these strangers, I would've been okay.

Cal jumps in to help his mom, and everyone—even Tim—razzes her about her lopsided cake.

Sarah catches my eye and winks, then says lowly, "That's why I always make another dessert."

"I heard that," Brenda says.

Craig announces that the burgers are ready, and we all make our way to the back deck and sit around a large table. The view, though not the ocean or mountains, is Midwest breathtaking. Fields and trees and green and blue. Instantly, I feel at peace.

"Your house is beautiful," I say.

"Thank you, Isadora," Craig says. "Do you enjoy living in the city? We keep trying to convince Cal to come back here, but he won't hear of it."

"I do like the city," I say. "More now than I used to."

"Oh?" Brenda piles some potatoes on her plate and passes the dish to me. "How come?"

"Because now she knows me," Cal says with fake bravado.

The others give him a little grief over his comment, but I'm not sure he's wrong. Not just Cal, but also Marty and Darby and her entire family.

I feel like there's a point there I should try to sort out, a hitch in my thinking I need to unhitch. But I can't quite make sense of it.

"Tell us about your little experiment, Isadora," Brenda says with a smile.

"You can't say that, Mom," Cal says.

"What? What did I say?"

"You called it a 'little' experiment." Cal puts a hand on my knee, and I almost jump out of my skin. "To a researcher—or a psychologist—that's kind of condescending."

"Oh," Brenda said. "I'm sorry." She looks me square in the eyes. "I didn't mean for it to be."

I can't find words to respond. I'm in kindergarten again in the red-and-white polka-dotted skirt, and my mother tells me, "*Just smile.*" I'm in middle school, crying in the car, and my mother says, "*You can't blame Mia for wanting to be popular.*" I'm upset at every age with no one to defend me, my feelings constantly belittled and pushed aside.

But here, now, in the simplest, smallest way—Cal has done the exact opposite.

"It's okay," I say quietly. And I mean it.

"Well, I've gone and put my foot in it, haven't I?" Brenda says. "I would never belittle your work."

"Don't even worry about it," I say. "I know you didn't mean anything by that."

The conversation picks back up, but at the back of my mind, I am thinking only one thing. Cal stuck up for me.

And nobody has ever done that before.

Chapter 27

Dinner carries on, despite the barrage of emotions racing through my mind.

I'm trying to understand why such a simple gesture has moved me so deeply, and I'm coming up empty. It doesn't make sense. I shouldn't be this affected.

The conversation winds back to Brenda's original question about my experiment, and while I still haven't sorted out my feelings, I am able to explain what I'm doing.

What I'm not able to explain is why. Like Cal and Marty, Craig has asked me what made me do this in the first place, and my stock answer doesn't ring true.

"It started out as a way to prove the author of the article wrong, but . . ."

"But?" Brenda smiles at me.

"But Cal thinks there are other reasons I'm doing it."

Sarah scoffs. "Well, he should know."

"What do you mean?"

"Nothing," Cal says.

"I mean because he's got ulterior motives for writing his book too," Sarah says as if I've already been let in on a secret I very much have not been let in on.

"Sarah—" Cal shoots her a look.

"What?" Sarah frowns. "Is it a secret?"

"Let's clear the table and get the cake," Brenda says.

My curiosity over Cal's reasons for writing his book was already piqued, but now? It just skyrocketed. Still, we clear plates, rinse them off, and make way for a pathetically lopsided yet perfectly wonderful strawberry cake. It's brought onto the table with much hilarity and fake fanfare, and I marvel at how easily this family gets along with one another. If this home had a soundtrack, it would be the sound of laughter. It permeates the air. It's as if the walls are holding secrets they can't wait to share because they know they'll make someone smile.

"Hey, are you okay?" Cal is standing in the doorway, a concerned expression on his face.

"I am," I say. "I'm just having some feelings." I prefer to keep them to myself, but as expected, Cal asks:

"Oh? What kind of feelings?"

"Ones that require sorting," I say. "I'm not used to this. I prefer rational thought."

He steps into the room and stops only a few feet away from me. "But those pesky feelings get in the way."

We stand like that for a long moment, and I realize my throat has gone dry. "Could I have a glass of water?"

"Of course." He leans toward me and opens the cupboard behind where I'm standing. He's so close to me for *one-two-three-four* that I can smell his body wash—it's *lovely.* He fills the glass with water from a pitcher on the counter and hands it to me.

His nearness makes me nervous, but despite that, I want him to move closer.

"You look . . . pensive." Cal crosses his arms over his chest and watches me. He's still standing so close, studying me so intently I have to look away.

In the beginning, he was handsome—but now he is so much more. This scares me a little, and I know I need to keep my heart guarded. How much do I want to tell him? "My family isn't like yours."

"We should probably unpack that," he says.

"Um, I'm fine with not." I smile and look away. "Thanks for sticking up for me. I mean, I wasn't offended by what your mom said, but nobody's ever done that for me before."

He waits until I meet his eyes again, then says, "Well, I'm sorry no one protected you, Isadora." His gaze is steady as he reaches over and tucks a strand of hair behind my ear. His thumb trails down the edge of my cheek, his hand resting at the nape of my neck. His eyes dip to my lips, and he makes the slightest move toward me, and I tuck my fear away and let myself feel what I'm feeling.

It's more than attraction, though I suppose that's there too; it's genuine affection.

I'm pretty sure I've stopped breathing, and my senses are back on high alert. I've all but forgotten what we were talking about.

I'm pretty sure I've also forgotten my name.

"Hey, it's cake time!" Sarah's voice draws our attention, and Cal snaps his hand back.

"Be right there," he says. He turns back to me. "I'm sorry, we should probably—"

"Were you going to kiss me just then?"

His face dips toward mine, and he laughs.

"Sorry, it's just—I don't want to misinterpret anything, and you had a look, and I think there was a moment, maybe? Or maybe not. Maybe I'm wrong."

"The thought did cross my mind," he says.

"So this *is* a date," I say—a statement, not a question, which I follow up with, "Is this a date?"

"I thought so," he says. "But is that okay? I mean, I know we work together."

"Right," I say. "That could be problematic. Maybe we should keep this professional."

He nods and takes a step toward me. "Absolutely. Is that what you want?"

In addition to forgetting my name, I've now also forgotten the date, my birthday, and what town I live in, but I do know the answer to his question.

No. It's not what I want. I don't want to remain professional with this man who gives me goose bumps. A man who listens to my opinion like it matters. A man who stuck up for me—even though really, I was never offended in the first place.

"Cal!" Sarah's impatient voice severs the connection between the two of us.

He takes a step back and says, "I guess your answer will be another surprise."

Chapter 28

It's late afternoon by the time we finish the cake and clean up, and I haven't been able to stop thinking about my conversation with Cal.

Darby was right. This is a date. A good date. My first "date" with Alex was spent in the lab where we talked about his research over a box of pizza from the cafeteria. Most of my "dates" with Alex were like that because we always had to be ready to pass it off as work.

"I don't think we should tell anyone about us," he'd said. *"Don't want our professionalism being scrutinized."*

I went along with it, but now it felt like a cop-out. He couldn't have planned a single nice dinner for us?

This was planned. Thought out. Intentional. Cal had put time into it. For me.

"Does anyone want to go into town?" Sarah asks. "There's a new jewelry store and you know I have to get some Mad Cow ice cream while we're here."

"We just ate birthday cake," Cal says.

"Calories don't count on your birthday," I say. I firmly believe this.

"Yes! I knew I liked you!" Sarah says. "Let's go."

My cheeks flush at the idea of Cal's sister liking me, and I have to conceal a smile.

We all pile into Tim's SUV, Cal and I in the back seat, and I try not to hyperventilate when he reaches over and takes my hand.

This is a date.

We drive into a town with a big sign that says Welcome to Woodstock, and I realize this is the first time all day I've had any idea where we are.

"Woodstock." I turn to Cal. "This is your hometown?"

"Yep," he says.

"He was the king of this place when we lived here." Sarah turns around, then rolls her eyes as she says, "One of those guys everyone loves."

"You were popular?" I ask.

Cal shrugs modestly. "I had a lot of friends."

I look down at our two hands, intertwined, and I note the way he rubs his thumb over mine. For a moment, I can think of nothing else.

"No, he was literally the king. Like, the prom king. The homecoming king. The King of Woodstock."

"Oh?"

"He was on a float in the Fourth of July parade every year he was in high school."

I look at Cal, and he looks embarrassed.

I raise a brow. "Oh really?"

"You know how many times that's come up in conversation since I graduated?" Cal asks. "Once. Right now." He squeezes my hand, and for a moment all my nerves migrate to that one spot. "I've never really been into stuff like that. I just like people."

"I think I'm going to need more stories like this about Cal. You know, for research purposes," I say.

"Please, no," Cal begs.

"Oh. We've got *loads*." Sarah beams.

I smile, but secretly I'm trying to balance the math of a guy who was popular enough to be voted prom king deciding to spend any amount of time with a girl who never even went to her prom.

I'm also trying not to move my hand for fear that he'll let go.

"Did you know Cal was an extra in the movie *Groundhog Day*? I mean, he was a baby, and my mom had him in a stroller, but he was there!" Sarah says. "They filmed the whole thing here in Woodstock."

"And *Planes, Trains and Automobiles*," Tim adds.

"And everyone's favorite, *The Bloody Rage of Bigfoot*," Cal says.

They launch into a memory about one of these movies while I watch the historic downtown come into view. There's an actual town square with a wide gazebo, surrounded by shops with tidy awnings. It looks like a painting. Idyllic small-town America.

Part of me wishes I grew up in a place like this. It's never even occurred to me to seek out a place like this. I bet there aren't many academic researchers living here, after all. When I graduated, I applied for a bunch of positions and took the first one that offered me a job. I've been at the university ever since.

Tim parks on the street, and we get out and spend the next hour walking around. Tim and Sarah. Me and Cal. To onlookers, we probably look like two couples on a double date.

I'm one half of a couple.

I'm not sure how I got here, because (1) I vowed not to date again, (2) my heart is neatly wrapped in Bubble Wrap, and (3) I should be conducting this happiness experiment dispassionately. Instead I'm sweating from a guy holding my hand in the back seat of a car.

I'm starting to think that Cal and Marty were right to question my motive. I didn't realize it fully until now, or maybe I was just denying it.

Maybe I don't want to disprove Dr. Grace Monroe. Maybe I want her to be right.

"I have to admit it," I say as Tim and Sarah disappear inside a little jewelry store. "Step eleven. These are quality people for sure."

"Can I plan or what?"

I wonder if his smile will always have this effect on me. He leads me over to a bench outside the store, and we sit.

Our knees are touching, and he stretches an arm around me, resting it on the back of the bench. I'm really unsure how to start talking, but I feel like if I don't, I'll explode.

"Cal."

"Yeah?"

I just open my mouth and words come out. "I . . . I don't know what I'm doing here. I don't know how to act, and I don't even know about this experiment anymore. I mean," I sputter, "I *thought* I knew why I was doing it. I was so sure."

He angles his body toward me. "But now you're not?"

"It's a lot," I say. "I don't like not being able to figure things out."

He sits, thoughtful for a moment, and I notice another difference between Cal and Alex. Alex was a fixer, so if I ever needed to vent, his response was always advice on how to proceed. Cal doesn't seem to want to fix anything for me. He only seems to want to understand me.

"Maybe," he starts, "it's okay not knowing. Maybe it's okay that you don't have all of the answers yet—and that you don't know the end from the beginning."

I smile weakly. "It's very unnerving. I like things how they are. I like data and spreadsheets and fixed points in space." I look up at him. "And now I . . ." I pause to try to explain it. "I'm untethered."

His brow crinkles, seemingly understanding but unable to help.

"I also think maybe you were right," I say.

"I usually am." He grins, and I feel the mood lift. "About what?"

"Why I'm doing this experiment," I say. "I thought it was because I wanted to prove Dr. Monroe wrong, but maybe I really wanted her steps to work. Maybe I really did want to be happy."

"You weren't before?"

I think. Was I?

"No. I really don't think I was." I shrug. "I mean, I didn't really think about it on an everyday level. How many people actually do that? Take stock of their happiness on a day-to-day basis? I just figured this is how it is. I like my work. I'm good at it. I stopped questioning if there was more, I suppose." I pause. "But shouldn't I be further along by now? I mean, I was going to do something amazing."

He draws in a thoughtful breath. "Maybe happiness isn't about what you do, Isadora. Maybe it's about who you do it with. Or simply about accepting who you are."

"That one is hard for me," I say.

He picks up my hand and turns it over so my palm is facing up. Then he traces the faint lines running from the side to the bottom with his finger so gently it's like a whisper across my skin. He meets my eyes. "I wish you could see yourself the way I see you. Then it would be easy."

My pulse quickens, and once again I find myself in uncharted waters. But before I can break it all down into digestible pieces, a woman on the sidewalk says Cal's name.

He turns and says "Sasha" so quietly under his breath that I'm sure the woman didn't hear him. But I did.

"Sasha?" I say.

Cal's expression changes, and he stands. "Hey."

She smiles wide at him, and I'm suddenly the goofy kid whose mom made her older brother take her to the party. Everything about this woman makes me feel inferior—flawless skin, trendy outfit, aviator sunglasses, giant purse, perfect hair.

Sasha. I half expect her to speak with an accent saved for Russian spies or clandestine, off-book government agencies.

She steps forward and pulls Cal into a hug. I notice he seizes up but endures it. Odd.

The hug is so awkward it could've been me giving it. He pats her three times gingerly on the shoulder, then takes a step back. "You're in town . . . ?"

Her eyes flash as she tosses long brown waves behind her shoulder. "I am. It's my parents' anniversary, so . . ."

"Right, right. Um, I guess say congrats from me?"

"I will." Then, for the first time, she notices there's another human being in the proximity. She looks at me and says, "Is this your . . . ?"

Her voice trails off, the question in it undone.

"Oh, yeah, sorry." Cal motions toward me, and I stand. "This is Isadora. We work together."

"We flew kites," I say idiotically.

Sasha laughs and looks at Cal as if to ask whether he's lost a bet having to spend time with me, but she says, "Aw, that's so cute."

"It's actually quite difficult getting a kite to stay up. It took us an hour. I ran in a field." It's like I just discovered the English language and decided to take it out for a spin.

Sasha stares as if I just asked to buy her necklace by offering a goat as collateral. "That's . . . amazing, I guess?"

It was the kind of awkward that makes other people's skin hurt by just watching. I have to escape, so I wrestle my brain to the ground and hog-tie it.

"Yes. Well. Hmm. I'm going to check out this jewelry store with Sarah," I say. "I'll be just . . ." I retreat across the sidewalk into the little shop, stopping just inside the door, wondering if that little scene actually happened. I turn and look through the glass in the door just in time to see Sasha roll her eyes and keep talking to Cal.

"Isadora?" Sarah is at my side like a protective hen. "What's wrong? You look pale." But when she looks past me onto the street, she has her answer. "Oh. Sasha." She says the other woman's name like a swear word.

"*The* Sasha?" Tim joins us near the window. Thankfully, we're still obstructed by a tall display of merchandise—I don't want Cal knowing this bothers me in the slightest. I'm not sure why, but I don't. And I also don't want a repeat of the runaway fruit incident, so I keep my distance from the display I'm hiding behind.

This shouldn't bother me, after all. It's not like he's my boyfriend. Up until an hour ago, I didn't even know this was a date.

"Who is she?" I ask, not sure I want the answer.

"His ex," Sarah says. "They were together all through high school and most of college."

"Whoa." That was a lot. My relationship with Alex was so short by comparison, and look how messed up I am from that.

"She broke his heart," Sarah says.

"She didn't just break his heart," Tim says. "She ran over it with her car, then put it in Reverse and backed over it again."

"How so?" We're all peeking out the window, where Cal and Sasha are engaged in what appears to be polite conversation, though his body language is completely different from hers.

"She left her Facebook page open on his computer once when she was visiting him at school," Sarah says. "There were a lot of messages back and forth with some guy in her music program. It was pretty obvious they were together."

"While she was with Cal?"

"Yep. It was brutal. She said some pretty terrible things about Cal too. I'm not sure what was worse, the heartbreak or the humiliation. Turns out, it wasn't the first time she'd done it."

I'm suddenly angry. I find myself rising and wanting to defend him, though I don't exactly know why. How could someone treat a relationship with Cal so callously? He's just so . . . good.

Sarah sighs. "But don't worry. He's so over her."

Watching Cal and Sasha, I think she's right. He looks like a cornered animal, ready to engage his fight-or-flight response.

But maybe that's just the way I'm seeing it. Maybe this chance encounter would remind him of what they had. Maybe it would make him want to rekindle whatever it was—back when it was good.

"I'm going out there," Sarah says, but Tim puts an arm out to stop her.

"No," he says. "He can handle it."

Sarah frowns. "This is Sasha we're talking about. He took her back once—what's to stop him from doing it again?"

Tim's eyes dart to me, then back to Sarah. "I think he's finally moved on."

The comment stirs something in me. Is Tim talking about *me*? Cal has moved on with *me*?

Sarah stills, but she's a little like a bull in a pen waiting for its chance to escape.

Across the street, Cal points to the shop, and I duck for cover. As I peek out from behind a display, I see Sasha move in for another hug, and Cal step back and wave, avoiding it.

At long last, Sasha walks away. Sarah is out the door, a woman on a mission, and Tim and I follow her.

"What the heck, Cal?" she says incredulously.

His eyes go wide. "What?"

"Why were you talking to the actual devil?"

He laughs. "A little louder, Sarah. I don't think the whole town heard you."

"I don't care!" Sarah says. She's livid. "I'll tell her straight to her face what I think of her."

I'm in awe of how emotionally worked up Sarah is over this. Her brother was wronged, and she's ready to fight on his behalf. Their family is good at sticking up for each other.

Step eleven: "Spend time with quality people."

"I'm sure you would. I'd kind of like to see that, actually." He turns to me. "Don't freak out," Cal says. "That was all small talk—nothing more. I'm sorry, Isadora. I'm sure that was awkward."

"Not really," I say. "I don't even know her. And you're not my boyfriend or anything."

"Right," he says, looking slightly dejected. "You're right. I'm not."

"Just promise me you didn't agree to meet up with her later or anything stupid like that," Sarah says.

"No, *Mom*, I didn't agree to meet up with her," Cal says. Then he gives me a pointed look. "I told her I couldn't because the girl I'm seeing needed to get back to the city."

If I'd been chewing gum, I would've swallowed it.

Chapter 29

"The girl I'm seeing."

He called me a girl. Not a woman, not a friend. And are we seeing each other? When did this happen?

You held hands, Isadora—you're practically engaged.

Surely him saying that was the verbal equivalent of gnawing off his own arm to escape the trap that was the conversation with Sasha.

That was it, right? What other explanation could there be?

I sit in the back seat of Tim's SUV stewing on this when it hits me.

"Oh my goodness. So *that's* why you believe technology is destroying relationships," I blurt.

He sighs. "Sarah told you."

Sarah whips her head around to look at her brother. "I'm not sorry. What she did was the crappiest thing ever. And the fact that you still gave her a second chance after she did it was the stupidest thing ever." She turns on the radio, and I'm thankful because it drowns out what I'm about to say.

"I wish you'd told me," I say quietly.

"I don't like to talk about it."

I understand this. I don't like to talk about Alex either. In fact, Darby is the first and only person I've told about him. Even my mother didn't get the full story. Only a simple "*It didn't work out.*" To which she responded, "*Sweetie, did you make him up? We never met him. We never even saw a photo of the two of you together.*"

Which was true, because Alex and I were a secret.

It's better to keep it all to myself. Locked up tight where it can't hurt me anymore.

"She's just a part of my past," he says. "Not part of my future."

"Yes, but if you're exploring this subject matter in a book, she's definitely part of your present." I say this straight, as a fact.

Sarah turns around, smiling. "Wow, Cal. She's got a point. Care to respond?"

Cal purses his lips, kind of like a toddler. "No. I wouldn't." His tone is quasi–mock hurt, so I can tell he's at least partly amused.

But I understand now. I understand his *why* when it comes to his book. It's personal—but he hasn't put anything personal in the pages.

I understand that too. It's not like I'm writing pages about what a colossal jerk Alex was, or using that as a reason why I'm not happy. Maybe neither one of us wants to give our past that much power over us.

Both Cal and I are processing through our research. Another thing we have in common. This makes my heart squeeze, like it's just been hugged.

Cal slowly reaches across the seat to hold my hand again, and I let him. My thoughts betray the moment and I wonder about what will happen when we say goodbye tonight. Will he try to kiss me? Would I be okay if he did? *Yes.* My heart starts pounding in my chest, and I draw in a deep, slow breath.

"You okay over there?" he asks.

My reply is unintelligible—a mix of something close to

"mm-hmm" and "yeah," and it comes out like "yeahmm," but not quite. I'm staring out the window, getting more nervous with every mile closer to goodbye.

We return to his parents' house, where we dole out hugs and thank-yous and hope-to-see-you-soons, and then it's Cal and I, alone in the Mustang, driving back to the city as the sun slowly makes way for the moon to take its place.

We sit in silence for a bit, occupied only by the sounds of the road.

Finally, Cal says, "It was a good day."

I smile over at him. "It was."

"What will you write about it in that notebook of yours?"

I know I should hold up my end of the conversation, but I'm back to imagining what will happen when we reach my front door, so I'm finding it very hard to concentrate. My skin is hot, and I resist the urge to jump out of the car. A desire that's wrestling with the exact opposite inclination—to stay right here, beside Cal, so close I can smell his aftershave—and look at that, now I'm covered with a fresh set of goose bumps.

There haven't been many of these moments in my life. Moments when I'm on the edge of my seat, expectant about what comes next. That mixed feeling of nausea and exhilaration, of wanting to heave but also wanting to be fully present, feeling every tingle, electrical charge, sensation.

I've shut those feelings off. I don't like them. They're supposed to make someone feel a certain positive way, but with all my experiences, they're anchored to the opposite. Feelings like this make me feel lost, adrift, or more to the point, like the control is in someone else's hands—and that's not something I ever want to feel again.

But even as I think this, I remember the kite. The soaring in the air—the freedom of dipping into the wind and out of it again.

Being lifted up and carried on the breeze. The way it felt to close my eyes and let the sun wash over me as we drove down a country road with the top down.

The wind is in control of the kite, but the kite doesn't mind. It's what actually makes a kite a kite.

I'm starting to think I need to let go to soar.

It's such an odd feeling for me. It's so different from what I'm used to. It's like I'm being magnetically pulled in a completely new direction.

And it's a nice change not to think about the eventual *snap* that happens when two opposite poles attract and click together. It's almost too much for me to process, and of course, my awkwardness fills the silent gap like molded Jell-O flopping into a dish.

The anticipation of our date's end has cast a spell on me—and not in a good way. My toes are tapping inside my shoes, completely on their own—nervous fidgeting over which I have no control. My palms are sweating. My nerves are too many to be contained.

Worse, I've made up my mind that I want Cal to kiss me. So now these nerves are also compounded by the worry that he might not.

Finally, without thinking, a single question bursts from my mouth. "What are your intentions for the end of this date?"

I snap my jaw shut, mortified and wishing there were a place to hide.

Good grief. It's surprising Cal hasn't started clawing at the door handle to escape.

Cal half laughs, then looks at me. "Uh . . . I haven't thought that far ahead yet."

"I know it's probably better not to discuss it, just to let it happen," I say. "But I . . ."

"Don't like surprises."

"Exactly."

"I'll keep that in mind." He squeezes my hand, and the Chicago skyline comes into view. All lit up, the buildings stand tall and proud, and from here, you'd never know there were thousands of people teeming among them, each with their own life, their own set of problems, their own moments that take their breath away.

It occurs to me that these moments are mine too.

This car. This man. The memories of this day. This is *my* life. And for the first time in a really long time, I am an active participant in it. I settle into my seat and take in the view, feeling grateful for all of it and mentally writing out my journal entry for the day.

When we reach my street, I straighten, my back pressed firmly against the seat of the car. Cal pulls into a spot in front of my building and turns off the engine. "I'll walk you in."

I nod, but my brain is working overtime, as if there's a hamster spinning a wheel in my head. I wish I were better at this. I've never been comfortable with romance. Does this part ever get easier?

I go through the motions of getting out of the car, but my knees go weak.

What am I, a twelve-year-old girl? Get ahold of yourself, Isadora. Look for signs. Read the body language. You should be able to figure this out—it's like any other equation. Find the variables and solve it.

He meets me on the sidewalk and takes my hand, leading me up to the front door. I reach for my keys, but my fingers stop working, of course, and I fumble them and drop them on the ground.

Then, as if scripted, Cal and I both bend down to pick them up simultaneously. I crunch my nose on his shoulder, and he's knocked sideways.

Yeah. This is pretty standard fare.

"I'm so sorry," I say as he utters his own apology. He's holding the keys and my hand is on his as our eyes meet and we stand.

"I don't think that's actually ever happened to me in real life," he marvels.

"It's a daily occurrence for me. I routinely walk into things. It's practically my superpower."

He smiles. I notice for the first time that his smile is asymmetrical. Endearing. Lovely.

"Thanks for going with me today," he says.

"Thanks for inviting me," I say.

A man walking a tiny dog strolls by on the sidewalk, and we both unplug from one another's gaze and pretend like it's completely normal—us standing outside my door. A streetlight flickers. A car horn honks a few blocks away. It's like my senses are heightened to the world around me, and even as this thought enters my mind, it all goes blurry because Cal is so focused on me, I can no longer hear or see or feel anything else.

Only him.

He reaches out and brushes his thumb across my cheek. "Isadora," he says.

"Yes?"

"I know you hate surprises, so I'll try something I've never done before." He gathers up what looks like confidence. "I'm going to kiss you now," he says as if he's a doctor preparing me for surgery. "I didn't want to make any sudden movements."

I bite back a smile. He's not making me feel silly or stupid or ashamed.

It feels safe. I feel safe.

"Is that okay . . . ?"

Without another thought, I summon a braver version of myself and interrupt him with a kiss. It's a quick one—a peck, really, on the side of his mouth, because I kind of miss. "Wait. Sorry." I talk with my hands. "I can do better."

I frown as I go in again, this time with a bit better aim. I hold it a little longer, and something starts to happen. I relax, and I can feel him starting to kiss me back.

I pull away. But I don't know why.

He looks puzzled. "What? What happened?"

"I . . . started to like it, I think." I start blathering. "It's just been so long since I've done this, I don't exactly know what I'm doing, and you seem like you've probably had a lot of practice, and I'm thinking now that I have to read a book or watch a video on how to make this happen because . . ."

"Isadora."

". . . I'm thinking about holding it longer, or maybe moving around a bit, like in the movies, or do I tilt? Should I tilt? People tilt, right?"

"Isa*dora*."

He stops me by taking my face in his hands and looking straight into my eyes. I can feel it all the way down to my toes. It's as if every nerve ending in my body is exposed, and I resist the urge to cover them up. For the first time in a long time, I let myself feel it all.

"*We* can do better. Let's try again."

He leans in and brushes his lips across mine.

For a brief moment, it's like I'm floating outside my body, watching the scene unfold as an onlooker instead of a willing and active participant.

I imagine the way we look, standing on the front steps bathed in the light of the lamp above the door as Cal kisses me.

He pulls away and looks at me. "Stop thinking so much, Isadora. If you overthink it, you'll miss it."

I don't want to miss a bit of it, so I do as he says. I let myself go. A kite carried on the wind.

Cal pulls me closer, and the exposed nerve endings fire. His kisses are deep and kind and attentive. Never once do I get the feeling he wants to be anywhere but right here. With me.

A thought hits me.

I pull back and look at him. "Why are you with me?"

He opens his eyes as if coming out of a stupor. "Wh . . . what? Why am I with you?"

I continue, because it makes perfect sense to me. "I mean, now that I've seen Sasha and Brooke, I have a pretty good idea of the kind of women you date. I'm not like them, so I guess I'm wondering . . . ?" There's a question in my voice, but I'm not sure how to finish my thought.

He leans toward me, to force eye contact. "No. You're not like them. That's part of why I like you." He shakes his head. "You do not make this easy, that's for sure. I thought you weren't going to think so much."

"I did pretty good for a few minutes there," I say. "You are an excellent distraction."

He smiles.

"But my question."

A laugh then, before his expression goes serious. "I don't want to be with Sasha or Brooke."

"But why?"

"You *really* always have to know how everything works, don't you?"

I shrug. "Yes," I say as if it's the only answer.

"This one I can't explain in a way you'll understand," he says. "But I'll try. I love the way you process things. I love the way you see the world. I love that you're highly intelligent and you don't pretend you aren't. I love seeing you with Marty and Delilah—people you feel protective over."

I realize I do feel protective over both Marty and Delilah as he says it. They've brought out something in me I didn't even know was there.

"It's a feeling. I'm drawn to you. I like you." He frowns. "I think quite a lot."

"You don't know how rare this is." I don't go into all the things that are wrong with me—things he will inevitably figure out. "I think just for tonight, though, I'm going to choose to take you at your word."

He chuckles and shakes his head again. "You are like no one I've ever known, Isadora."

I smile, and I try not to think about how all this will make me feel tomorrow.

"I should probably go get the car back," he says. "And you probably need to go capture your data from today."

I smile. "Right. Data. You've given me a lot of . . . data."

"Or maybe you'll just ask them for their input." He looks at me and points up. I follow his gaze to see Darby's and Delilah's faces in the fogged-up window.

"Told you it was a date!" Darby practically screams. What a lunatic.

I look at Cal, who laughs. "Good night, everyone," he says with a wave. And as I watch as he gets in the car and drives away, I think one last thought before I walk in.

I should've tilted. People tilt, right?

Chapter 30

It's Monday morning, and I fully expect to feel weird seeing Cal for the first time since our date, mostly because of the kissing.

Darby, face pressed up against the window like a dog trying to eat a treat through the bottom of a glass table, saw how my date ended. Even still, she made me recount the entirety of the day—the kites, the party, the running-into-his-ex, the moment he told me it was, in fact, a date, holding hands in the car . . . everything. Sharing it all in detail made me feel like a teenage girl with too much energy to fall asleep.

It was the first of many, many times I relived every single moment.

And now, sitting in my office, I'm practically perched on my chair for a better view of the hallway.

Just in case he decides to pay me a visit.

The negative side of my brain wonders if he's had a change of heart in the one day it's been since I last saw him. It also reminds me that I'm doing an experiment, and there's no step thirty-two: "Hook up with a hot professor from work." I don't even bother to tell myself to keep my feelings in check, because it's much too late for that.

I like him. I fear I like him a lot.

My feelings have a mind of their own.

I go into the lab to check in with Shellie and Logan, who both seem oddly happy to see me. Gary has told me before that the students respect me, but they're intimidated. I am hoping they see me as more approachable now. Logan shares the findings of his new sleep study, while Shellie shares about a new hot-yoga class she thinks I should try.

I smile and thank her for the suggestion, knowing full well I have no intention of ever checking it out. As if I don't sweat enough as it is. During our conversation, Gary walks by the lab, and when he sees me in there, he smiles and gives me a thumbs-up.

I must be doing something right.

About an hour and three cups of coffee after I've arrived, Cal appears in my doorway, shooing away all of my fears over seeing him again.

He looks handsome in a pair of navy blue pants and a pink and white button-down with the sleeves rolled to the elbows. I bet he's the type of person who could wear a bow tie and make it look sexy.

He smiles at me. "Good morning."

I smile back. I've perfected my smile, by the way. The trick, it turns out, is not to overthink it.

Apparently, that's the trick to a lot of things.

"I've got a few more chapters for you to read." He sets a stack of papers down on my desk. "But first, let's hear about what steps we're working on next."

"Oh, I think your book is a little more important," I say.

"You think so?"

"Of course it is! You have an actual publisher and an actual deadline and it's far more legit than what I'm doing. You're about to be an author—and I'm just a researcher."

"You're not *just* anything, Isadora," he says with such conviction I almost believe him.

I shrink ever so slightly, and he takes my hand from across the desk. "Don't belittle who you are or what you do. It's annoying."

I laugh out loud at the directness, and I wonder if he's trying to learn my language. In an effort to keep him from feeling like he's in therapy or something, I quickly change the subject.

"Since you asked, I do have an idea of what I'd like step twelve to be," I say as brightly as I can.

His eyebrows perk up. "I'm listening."

∽

At lunch, we meet Marty on the bench, and today is one of the days Darby brings her crew to join us. Delilah's at school, but the other kids are in tow, and once we've all assembled, I pitch my idea.

"So you wrote out a bunch of encouraging notes," Darby says. "And you want us to hide them around the campus?"

"That's the gist of it," I say. "Step twelve: 'Spread encouragement to those around you.' It's almost finals week, so I thought maybe a little extra positivity was in order."

"Look at you bringing the sunshine," Darby says, giving me a little push.

"Are you going to track what kind of effect they have on people?" Marty asks.

I shrug. "I thought about that, but I'm not sure that's the point. I think this is about planting, not harvesting. We give these out and we might never see how it affects someone. On the other hand, maybe we'll find them trampled on the sidewalk or thrown away in the trash."

"Or maybe the right note will fall into just the right hands at just the right time, and it'll make all the difference," Marty says. "I'm in." He holds his upturned hand out to me. "Give me some."

I've rubber-banded my sentiments in small stacks, handwritten on colored paper I stole from the copy room, and I hand one over to Marty.

He flips through the words, reading over the quotes—some from famous figures in history like Winston Churchill, and others from pop stars like Kesha. "This is a wonderful idea, Isadora," he says.

I beam at the compliment. I can't help it. It feels good to do something kind for no other reason than to be kind.

We all take a bundle, and after we've finished our lunches, we split up and distribute the notes. I head to the library where I hide mine in books, on shelves, in the bathroom. I'm on the way out when I spot a girl at a table where I've taped a note to the back of the chair. She peels it off, reads it, and looks around. She reads it again and looks up, thinking. She reads it a third time, sighs as if a weight has been lifted, and then tucks it inside her textbook.

I have no idea how this note actually made her feel (does she like to take advice from Justin Bieber?), but I have to hope it's done its job. I wouldn't have expected spreading joy to strangers to have any effect on me at all, but I'm oddly excited by it.

So much of the world is dark. People are cruel. And maybe Cal's right—maybe social media has made us bolder in our cruelty. After all, it's easier to snipe a comment from behind the allure of online anonymity. Maybe it's eroded our sense of decency.

But for all the darkness and cruelness and selfishness, that doesn't mean there isn't good in the world. That doesn't mean there isn't light to be found.

The crazy thought now that is starting to creep into my consciousness—what if *we* are supposed to be that light?

What if *I* am supposed to be that light?

That isn't something I've ever wanted—or needed—to be before.

It shames me now to think of how much time I've spent wallowing in my own mess. I've spent years hiding myself away so I wouldn't get hurt. But what if there really is something inside me—more than *just* a researcher—that I could share?

Maybe these simple, little, ordinary things *are* the big things I'm meant to accomplish with my life.

The lunch crew meets back at our bench after all our bundles have been distributed. Marty is the last to join us, and while I initially thought it was because he moved more slowly than the rest of us, the truth is, he spent the entire time we were gone chatting with a young history professor who apparently "looked like she needed the whole bundle of encouraging words."

"Did you just hand the whole stack to her?" Cal asks.

"No, I tucked one in her computer bag when she wasn't looking." He holds up the rest of his bundle. "I'll have to do these after you all go back to work."

I laugh and shake my head, thinking it's just like Marty to brighten the day of just one person. He did that with me, and look at me now.

I would never think his kindness was a small thing. By living his life and being himself, he opened up a whole world for me, reminded me that I'm alive.

"What's your secret, Marty?" I ask him after Darby and Cal have gone—Cal to teach, Darby to pick up Delilah from school.

"What do you mean?" he asks.

"How do you stay so positive all the time?" I know there is deep sadness inside of him, but he manages not to let it infect him. How does he keep it from stealing his joy?

Marty leans back against the bench and watches some birds fighting over a discarded potato chip. "Wine. Lots of wine." He pauses, then glances sideways at me and starts to laugh.

This makes me laugh, and I realize I laugh a lot when I'm around Marty.

After a moment, he offers, "I suppose I focus on the good things in my life."

"Good things like springtime in the city? Or Miriam's cookies?" I smile.

"Ooh, definitely the cookies." He sighs. "Good things like my daughter and her family." He looks at me. "And you."

"Me?"

"It's good to see you smiling so much these days." Marty holds the bundle of colored papers in his wrinkled hands. "It looks like you're starting to get it."

"What am I getting?"

"The secret to happiness," he says. "It's becoming clear for you."

I frown. "The secret?" I don't feel like I've landed on anything specific yet. It still feels more like an unfinished puzzle.

"I should go." He stands. "I have to share these brilliant words from someone called"—he squints at the paper—"Eminem."

I watch as he walks a ways away, then hands the Eminem quote to a college kid who reads it, immediately recognizes it, and laughs, closed fist to his mouth. They stand there, chatting like two old friends, and I marvel at this—a human connection—and the happiness it seems to bring.

And then I make a mental note to listen to more Eminem.

Chapter 31

A few days later, Marty and I are flying solo at lunch.

I love that we have a whole crew sometimes, but I also love spending time alone with the old man. There's a fatherly something about him that I never had growing up. My dad wasn't one for doling out advice, or even carrying on a conversation with me, for that matter.

I've made my peace with that.

Mostly.

"So your experiment has got me thinking," Marty says.

"About the music, the moment?"

He looks at me quizzically, not following my Eminem reference.

"Sorry," I say. "Go on."

"I know your experiment is supposed to be about happiness," he says. "But I've noticed an interesting byproduct of doing all these steps."

"You have?" I pull a giant chocolate chip cookie from my bag and break it in half, then offer both to Marty for him to choose.

"You see? You don't even realize what an effect this has had on you."

"What do you mean?"

He turns toward me. "Why did you offer me both halves of the cookie?"

I ponder this a moment. Normally I would've just handed him one piece without thinking about it. "I thought that since I broke it in half, you should get to choose. That way I'm not taking the biggest side for myself."

He points at me emphatically. "*Exactly.* Isadora, you *thought.* I can safely say that not a lot of people think before they act. It's affecting even the smallest of gestures."

Good grief, he's right.

He eyes the smaller half, takes it, and raises an eyebrow. "Next time let's see if we can split that more down the middle." He takes a bite, and I smile at him.

"You said there's a byproduct. Is that it? Thinking?"

"Well, I guess there're two," he says, laughing. "There are probably a hundred."

"What's the other one you were thinking of?"

"Bravery," he says.

"Bravery," I repeat.

"Bravery." He nods. "I don't think you had it the first day I met you, but now? Look at you doing all these things that take you right out of your comfort zone. Didn't I see you throw a frisbee to some boys last week?"

I smile. "Ugh, I was hoping no one saw. It was a terrible throw."

"It was indeed." He smiles. "But it was still brave."

I hadn't thought of it that way. I hadn't thought anything I was doing could be categorized as brave. But Marty had a point. Just a short time ago, I practically hid from college boys in the courtyard.

Marty chews and swallows a bite of his sandwich. He takes a moment and looks down to the ground between his knees. "I want to be brave too, Isadora."

I go still. It feels like a confession. "You are plenty brave, Marty."

He looks up at me, but only for a moment to say, "No. I'm not."

Instinctively and immediately, I know what it is he's been scared to do. The idea that anything I've done could inspire him to face that fear humbles me.

He is still looking down. I place a hand over his.

"Marty. I'll go with you."

He looks up, equal parts pain and relief on his face. Though his face is lined with years, he looks like a kid wanting his mom to hold his hand as they walk into a new school in a new town.

He nods just once, then I send a text to Gary to let him know I'll be back soon.

On the way, we don't say much. We honestly don't need to. I stop for Marty to pick out a fresh bouquet of red tulips. He spends careful moments inspecting each bulb before settling on the perfect arrangement.

He carries the cellophane-wrapped treasure like a nervous teenager about to pick up his crush for their first date.

As we walk toward the cemetery, he finally speaks. He begins by telling me a story about the time Shirley sprained her ankle falling out of bed. This leads to another story about the time she surprised him with a karaoke birthday party, where she dressed up like a hula dancer and sang his favorite Beach Boys song, "Surfer Girl."

"Who knew a grass skirt could be sexy?" he says, and I can see the push and pull between heartache and wistfulness on his face.

After several blocks and several more stories, Marty stops. When I look up, I see we are standing underneath a gate that says Briar Stone Cemetery. It's almost as if an invisible force has stopped him from moving any farther.

He's clutching the flowers to his chest.

I'm typically bad with this sort of thing, but somehow I know exactly what Marty needs in that moment.

He simply needs me to be there. So I am.

"A few weeks before she died"—his voice breaks as he stares off across a field of gravestones—"we were watching a Cubs game, and she looked over at me and said, 'You've given me such a good life, Martin.'" He peers over at me. "Sometimes she called me Martin. Mostly when I was in trouble."

I smile.

"She said, 'We may not have the biggest house, or the fanciest cars, but you still make me feel like the richest woman in the world.'" His lip trembles, and so does mine. He manages a smile as he says, "Well, after a compliment like that, and she was looking so pretty . . . let's just say that we never did see the end of that game."

"Marty!"

"I'm a sucker for a compliment, what can I say? Plus, it wasn't fair, her walking around being as pretty as she was. I could hardly stand it some days."

I look straight ahead, trying to imagine someone looking at me the same way.

Then I bump my shoulder into his. "I'm sure she thought the same about you."

"Oh, she did," he says without hesitation. "I was a catch."

I laugh, and Marty does too, and it feels good in the moment. It helps to mask the deep sorrow I fear is lingering just below the surface.

"I think I'm starting to understand," I say. "Happiness really has nothing to do with stuff. I mean, that's such a cliché, but it's true." I pause for a moment and then say, "Happiness is not finishing a Cubs game."

The sadness I'm sure Marty feels in Shirley's absence weighs on me, and I have a fleeting thought—now that I have someone in my life who matters to me, the thought of *not* having him stings. My heart aches even entertaining it.

I can't imagine that feeling multiplied by a lifetime of moments.

Marty takes a step . . . through the gate and into the cemetery . . . then stops. He looks at me, his eyes pleading. "I don't like it here."

I slip my hand in his and squeeze. "We've got this."

He doesn't look so sure. "We do?"

I nod. "Yes. We do. You can do this."

He looks straight ahead, and I see him steel his gaze and straighten his shoulders ever so slightly. He takes a deep breath and lets it out. "I owe this to her."

We walk down the road in silence, hand in hand, and I can feel him trembling as he fights back tears. It's almost too much for me to bear—but I do. Because I sense that he needs me, and because I want to be there for him.

When we reach a fork in the road, he turns right, into the grass. He stops a few feet away from a big gray headstone with his last name—*Miller*—etched in bold black letters. On the left side is Shirley's name and on the right side, a blank space where one day, Marty's will go.

Well, that is depressing.

No wonder he didn't want to come here. It's a morbid reminder of your own mortality, etched permanently in stone.

I stand quietly for a few seconds, then realize maybe it would be better if I gave him some privacy.

"I'll just be over by the road," I say.

"Please stay," he says. "Please."

I stay. Because he's my friend.

He takes a few steps toward the headstone, then places the tulips on the ground in front of her name. I see his tears have left small discolored splotches on the tissue paper inside the cellophane.

"Red tulips, just like the ones around the tree in the backyard."

He removes his hat, holding it in his hands for a few long, silent seconds. I look around the cemetery. It's quiet. Empty. We're the only ones here.

Marty glances at me. "I've been avoiding this for so long and thinking about what I would say when I finally got here. But now that I'm here . . . I'm not sure what to say."

"I'm not going to lie, Marty," I say. "I don't have a lot of experience with this. But I suppose you can just talk to her if you want to."

I bend down and clear some leaves from the headstone. "What would you say if she were here?"

I stand and he nods tentatively, as if gathering courage to start. I step back a bit, and he shares an update on Miriam and the kids. He tells her about Olive—and about our lunchtime crew. "You'd really like Isadora, Shirl," he says, turning slightly to look over his shoulder at me. "She's your kind of people."

I smile at that.

He takes a hitched breath. "I'm so sorry," he whispers. "So sorry, Shirl. I . . . just couldn't make it here without—" He puts his hands to his forehead, and I instinctively take a step forward and place a hand on his shoulder. He reaches across his chest and grasps it, like a man overboard desperately reaching for a lifeline. He takes another deep breath, gathering himself. "It's taken me so long to come see you," he says. "It's not because I didn't want to be here. I promise. I think it's just that"—he draws in a breath—"well, grief is a funny thing, isn't it? I'll be perfectly fine, going on about my day, and then I'll call for you in the other room."

Oh, Marty.

"When you don't answer, it's like I have to relive it all over again. I'm pretty sure I'll never get used to the fact that you're gone."

A lump forms in my throat. My heart is breaking.

He lets go of my hand and wipes his face. "Ah! Look at me, I'm a mess."

I feel the tears on my face, but I let them stay.

His tone changes, and it sounds like he's on the other side of the worst of it. "But I know you'd want me to stop being such a sad sap, right, Shirl?" He chuckles through his tears to himself. "What is it you always used to say? 'Life is beautiful and horrible and wonderful and awful all at the same time'?" He looks at me then. "And *that* is the adventure."

The words hang in the air for a moment.

Marty turns back to the headstone. "This is the horrible part, Shirley. But it doesn't erase the wonderful and the beautiful. Not by a long shot. In fact, I think this awful part makes those happy days even happier."

We stand in silence for several more minutes. I am sure he's replaying some of those happy memories, and I'm basking in what he's just said.

Is it possible that the happy days and the sad days, I don't know, *need* each other somehow? As if the two things have to coexist for either to matter at all?

I get an idea. I don't exactly know how Marty is going to take it . . . but he said I was brave. So here goes nothing.

I silently pull out my phone, open the Spotify app, and search. Then I take a few steps toward Marty as I hit Play.

The harmonies of the Beach Boys ring out from the small device as the opening notes of "Surfer Girl" begin to fill the air.

Marty's laugh is loud, like an explosion of a million different emotions, and then he begins to sing along. I don't know the song, but I sway to the music, and before long we're dancing around Shirley's grave, and I am certain she's up in heaven dancing right along with us.

Maybe even wearing a grass skirt.

Marty twirls me in a circle, and we laugh and he sings, and all at once I see it—sadness and "Surfer Girl," heartache and hope, melding together to create an entirely new, deep, indelible emotion.

And while it has no name, it is so much sweeter than either is on its own.

Chapter 32

If this were a movie, this would be the part with the montage to show all the fun, romantic things Cal and I did together after that first date. Normally every good romantic montage needs a jaunty underscore, or a Taylor Swift song, but mine has a narrator. Mr. Attenborough, if you please.

Now that Isadora has found a suitable mate, she endeavors to win his heart with numerous displays of interest. It is the simple pleasures in life that seem to entertain Miss Bentley the most. FaceTiming from nearby offices, laughing at the delay in their voices, hiding a sticky note or two in a manuscript, hoping the other will find it, and the latest excursion . . . a movie in a park.

Cal took me to see a movie in the park. We sat on an old quilt his mother made for him when he was a boy and ate from a picnic basket. When the film ended and almost everyone had gone, we stayed. We lay in the darkness, looking up at the stars.

"They're so much easier to see at my parents' house," he said. "Less noise from the lights. Next time we're there, I'll show you."

I count this as step thirteen, "Get out in nature," even though we were still in the city and this "nature" didn't even require insect repellent.

His kisses are growing familiar, but not common. I find myself missing him almost immediately once we are apart.

I'm gushing. I can't help it.

I've never had a relationship like this; I mean, I was pretty serious about Noah Calhoun from *The Notebook*, but he was a fictional character. Cal is real and in front of me. He's not just a boyfriend, he's my friend. He cares about me in a way that no one ever has.

I've paid close attention for any sign that Cal might secretly be Alex 2.0, and I've found none. He's genuine. And honest. And good. There isn't an ounce of selfish ambition in him. He's writing his book to understand something personal. Alex was writing his book for the sake of his name and his reputation.

It scares me, but I believe in me and Cal. I've doodled our names on various scratch pieces of paper (and one expense report I had to turn in to Gary).

And little by little, corner by corner, I'm giving him my heart.

Over the next few weeks, we spend countless hours together. He even comes to yoga with Darby and me, and it makes me feel better that he hates it.

There's no pain like shared pain.

We walk around campus holding hands, stealing kisses behind the big oak tree in the quad, in the stacks at the library, in my office with the door closed. We work on his book—his research spread all over the floor and table in my apartment—only to end up kissing on the couch way past my normal bedtime.

He tells me he sees my fingerprints all over his chapters, and I try not to think of the uncredited hours I put into Alex's work, only to be tossed aside at the very last minute. And it dawns on me that I still haven't told Cal about Alex.

In fairness, he wasn't the one to tell me about Sasha either, but that doesn't change the fact that I know. He knows nothing about my past relationships.

Maybe it doesn't matter. What matters is that Cal is different. And also that I'm wiser now. I have no delusions that my name will appear anywhere on his final product. I've set my expectations appropriately, as I determined to do forever and always, amen. Lesson learned.

Besides, I *like* working with him on this. Not just because it's with him, but it's actually interesting work. I enjoy digging, editing, critiquing, cross-referencing. He took my advice and included his personal story about Sasha—changing names to protect the not-so-innocent.

On the subject of my (our?) experiment, I prod him for more information, but he's locked up tight over the whole thing. He promises that one day he'll share his deductions about my project.

With Cal's help, I work my way through the happiness list. And he works his way through his chapters. And he also has worked his way into my every waking thought, it seems.

We eat dinner with Darby and her family, and Marty comes too. We laugh over conversations that crisscross the table, all of us interjecting like we're selling wheat on the stock exchange. It's familial and fun, and I'm settling into a life I never even realized I desperately wanted.

Cal takes me out on dates (outside the lab!) and walks me to the door after every single one. I'm getting the feeling he takes me out just to get to my stoop.

I don't hate it.

I discover he has a problem setting boundaries when I find his desk piled high with a colleague's work, but I choose not to say anything. He also gets distracted easily, takes frequent breaks, and sometimes hums while he eats. None of these are dealbreakers, of course, but it's nice to know the King of Woodstock has things to work on like the rest of us mere mortals.

When I look back to the beginning of my research notebook, I almost don't recognize the words I'm reading. It's like a completely different person wrote them. While it would be easier to criticize the person I was, the truth is, I simply want to give her a hug. She was doing her best.

I'm still not sure what the secret of happiness is, and I still don't put huge stock in every bullet point of the 31 Ways—but I can't deny that these steps have led me to Cal.

And to a shape of happiness that fits me.

Somehow, though I hesitate to admit it, I think my experiment has made me a better person.

I'm not even mad I may have to conclude that maybe—*maybe*—Dr. Grace Monroe had an inkling of what she was talking about when she wrote that article in the first place.

When I see Shellie has one of the notes we left around campus taped to the outside of her planner, I'm practically clamoring to find new ways to spread encouragement. I host an inter-office/lab celebration of Logan's acceptance into a prestigious grad school program that will surely kick his career up a notch or three—and I'm not even jealous. I find myself smiling and complimenting and congratulating without a shred of insincerity.

It's as if the quote I wrote on one of those cards—"Someone else's success is not your failure" (*thank you, Jim Parsons*)—has been embedded in my mind. Gary notices and compliments me.

"Isadora, I have to say that you have really, truly become a team player," he says.

And I beam at this because I am. I really, truly am.

Who knew it would have such an effect on me? Well, Gary knew, I guess.

Cal and I get all dressed up and take ourselves out (step fourteen) to a symphony, the one where they play the movie score to *Star Wars* as the audience watches the film on the big screen. I'm transfixed by the whole experience. It fills the hollowness in my bones.

I share a selfie of me and Cal in our formal attire with my mother, along with a text that says:

Heading out for a night on the town! This is Cal. He's

Her reply:

Don't mess this one up! 

I'm not even bothered. Mothers, with a single sentence, are adept at transporting their kids to the way they felt when they were ten—but I stay firmly in the moment and refuse to be moved. Normally I'm assaulted by those kinds of memories, having to physically shake them off—but not today.

Not today.

Chapter 33

We return from the symphony, and I take off the black and silver heels I borrowed from Darby (whose feet are about half a size smaller than mine, unfortunately). As I go to unlock the front door, Cal steps in front of me and stops.

He looks straight at me, and I feel his gaze zip a bolt of electricity straight down my spine. Will I ever tire of him studying me the same way he studies his research?

"You look beautiful tonight," he says. "I mean, you look beautiful all the time, but especially tonight."

I wrap my arms around his waist, my hands resting casually on his back. "It's Darby's dress. I think it's magic."

He gives his head a tiny shake. "No, it's not that."

"No?"

He leans in and kisses me. "No, it's you. No matter what you wear."

My inclination is to correct him, but I force myself not to. Instead, I smile up at him and whisper a quiet "Thanks."

He takes my face in his hands, and I let him look at me—I'm not even uncomfortable under the weight of his full attention. "I think I'm falling for you, Isadora."

I want to ask him why. Or say something like, "Are you sure?"

But again, I resist. I don't want what I believe about myself to spoil the moment.

His kiss, soft yet strong, makes me grateful I chose silence. As his lips move across mine, I feel it in my toes, and I think how lovely it would be if it never had to end.

But then he pulls back and grins. "*Doctor Who*?"

I respond with a grin of my own.

Cal takes my hand as we head up the stairs, but when we reach my door, we find Delilah sitting there, hugging her knees.

There's a stack of comic books on the floor beside her.

"Delilah?" I kneel down in front of her. "What's wrong?"

She looks up at me with big crocodile tears in her eyes. "Boys are stupid."

I look up at Cal, whose brow is knit in a tight line of concern.

"Let's go inside," I say. "Does your mom know you're out here?"

Delilah shakes her head, and Cal nods toward the door of my friend's apartment. "I'll let her know."

I usher the little girl into my apartment, and she plops down on the couch. I don't want to pry, but it feels like she's here because she needs to talk about whatever it is that's upset her.

"So . . . ?"

"No offense, Isadora, but I'd like to wait for Dr. Cal."

"You would?"

"Yes, he's a boy."

A man, actually.

"Maybe I can help," I offer.

"Can you help me understand why Dylan Moffat told me I was a try-hard and I needed to get a life?"

I sit beside her. "He said that?"

A flash of familiarity. Dylan Moffat for Delilah, Noah Johnson for me. Both boys have four-syllable names and apparently four brain cells between the two of them.

After the phony promposal, and probably to protect his reputation, Noah made sure everyone in school knew he thought I was "a dog." And he "woofed" at me more than once in the hallway. (What did I ever see in that kid?)

She sniffs. "In front of my whole class."

I hate this for her, and I feel anger rise. I want to help, and I want to protect her.

I know I can't keep other kids from being mean, can't keep Delilah from experiencing a series of humiliations like the ones that I was subjected to—but I know they shaped me into the person I've only just now begun to understand.

I've always wondered how differently things would've gone for me if someone—anyone—would have stuck up for me.

Having just one ally could've changed everything.

At the same time, though, now, with so many years between me and the Noah Johnson debacle, I can see this for what it is. An immature boy who could never appreciate the unique gift of a brilliant girl. I think back all those years and wonder why I ever let small-minded, bullying boys have any effect on me at all.

I couldn't see it for what it was then. Can any ten-year-old?

I know any moment, Darby will rush in. I want to warn her not to belittle Delilah's humiliation the way my mom did. To an adult, this whole scene may seem "amusing" or "adorable." Maybe Darby will try to brush it off like it's some rite of passage to have your heart trampled by a boy.

I know from experience that if she says anything that makes her daughter feel like this is her fault, it will scar Delilah. Maybe for life.

Okay, so I'm projecting. But I think I understand Delilah in a way that maybe other people don't. I know these feelings, intimately, and can pick that emotional scab open like a fresh wound.

I want to find a way to show her that anyone who doesn't see the magic inside her doesn't deserve her time or her tears.

My thoughts are interrupted when the door flings open and Darby and Cal rush in. Her face is aflame with anger, and I stand to intercept her.

But when Darby kneels in front of Delilah and takes her hands, I step back. A tear streams down the little girl's face.

"Oh, my sweet girl, what happened?" Darby wipes Delilah's tears away.

"He told me I was ugly, Mom," she says, sobbing a little.

Darby stands and pulls out her phone. "Give me this boy's name. I'm going to call his mother and tell her what a little monster her son is. Better yet, I'm going to go over to his house and demand he apologize for being such a cruel, hateful little troll."

My eyes widen at Darby's outburst. Delilah lets out a giggle. "A troll, Mom?"

"It's not funny!" Darby says. "This kid sounds like the human version of period cramps!"

I glance at Cal. He shrugs. She's on a roll.

She shakes the phone at Delilah. "Nobody talks to my girl like that and gets away with it!"

"Mom. Calm down."

"Calm down? *Calm down?!* And let this little . . ." She's searching, and I can't wait to hear what comes out of her mouth. ". . . tick-infested, sleepy-eyed butt monkey call my daughter *ugly*?"

Yeah. Darby doesn't disappoint. Delilah, Cal, and I burst out laughing.

"Oh my *gosh*, Mom!" Delilah's mood has completely changed. "You look like a cartoon character with smoke coming out of your ears," Delilah says.

"Well, I am." Darby sits on the couch and wraps an arm around her daughter. "Nobody gets to say those things to you, Delilah Rose."

Delilah frowns. She sits for a moment and blinks. "I did everything right. I bought these comic books and read them at recess right in front of him." She looks up at Cal, eyes pleading for some insight. "I even dropped one in the hallway when I was walking past him."

"And?" he asks.

"He didn't even stop to pick it up."

"Butt monkey," I say. I make a mental note to use that phrase more often, even though I have no idea what it means.

"He doesn't deserve your time," Darby says, stroking the girl's hair.

"I just don't understand why he doesn't like me," Delilah says. She looks at Cal. "Why isn't he nice to me like you are to Isadora?"

My ears perk up at this. Delilah has been paying attention. Although, that shouldn't surprise me. Nothing gets by her.

Cal sits on the coffee table opposite the little girl. "I'm going to tell you a secret, Delilah."

Her eyes are fixed on him. Heck, *my* eyes are fixed on him. I want to know the secret too.

"Sometimes boys are stupid," he says.

Delilah scrunches her face. "That's not a secret."

"No," he continues, "but some are also blind." He glances over at me. "Sometimes we just need our eyes opened to how amazing some girls are."

"But that's what I was trying to do! Open his eyes!"

He smiles. "Do you remember what I told you in the comic book store?" he asks.

She thinks for a moment, then her face shifts in realization. "You said not to change myself for a boy."

"Good advice, Dr. Baxter." Darby pats his arm approvingly.

"So did you like the comic?" he asks.

Delilah sits up a little. "Well . . . yeah. I did. The characters in

The Flashpoint Paradox one are really cool, and it shows the possibilities when messing with time travel."

"So you bought more of them."

She nods.

"Because you like this boy?"

"Because I like the story," she says.

"Hmm. How about that," Cal says. "Granted, you never would've found that story if you weren't looking to impress the—what did your mom call him—a butt monkey?"

Delilah snickers, and Darby shrugs as if to say, *I call it like I see it.*

Cal continues. "But the way I see it, you found a whole new genre to explore. Not a bad deal."

"That's true, I guess."

"Delilah, the thing you have to realize about boys is that we *never* stop being stupid. We do dumb things all the time, and we definitely don't mature as fast as you girls," Cal says. "So maybe one day he'll catch up to you, or maybe he never will. Either way, right now, he's just a kid who doesn't get to have an opinion about you at all."

"He doesn't?"

Cal shakes his head. "No. The only opinions that really matter"—he opens his arms wide to indicate all of us in the room—"are the ones of the people who love you."

"And we think you're pretty special," Darby says.

Delilah lifts her chin so slightly I almost miss it. She looks straight at Cal and says, "I am pretty special. And smart."

"And unique," Cal says.

"And beautiful," Darby adds.

They look at me, as if I'm supposed to add something here, but I can't.

I'm emotionally tongue-tied. I simply can't speak. And I know why.

This scenario played out far differently from what I experienced as a little girl. Somehow, Darby and Cal knew how to protect Delilah's heart. They knew, instinctively, what to say to keep her from believing—like I did—that something was wrong with her.

"Are you okay, Isadora?" Delilah asks.

I nod, but I still find myself unable to respond. Darby's kindness to her daughter, her fierce protectiveness, has stunned me to silence.

Everything Darby and Cal said to Delilah, I claim for myself. As if simply by doing so, I can heal old wounds—wounds I don't want to face.

Wounds that have been making me unhappy in the first place.

The last step on Dr. Monroe's list. It's step thirty-one: "Confront what is making you unhappy in the first place." I have been avoiding that like the plague. I don't want to drag all the packed-away emotions out into the open, let alone face anything. Who does? Pain is bad at any time, but at least if it's familiar pain, it's tolerable.

Or is it?

My hurt has been there for so long, I'm not sure how to let it go.

The little girl stands and walks over to me and then throws her arms around my waist and squeezes.

I hold back tears at the tender kindness, and I hug her back, thinking that yes, she is absolutely an answer to prayers I fell asleep praying all those years ago.

Please, God, just bring me one good friend.

Delilah pulls away and gives me a sad smile.

I kneel down in front of her, look her straight in the face, and say, "I really love you, Delilah."

I know to a ten-year-old, having the love of your weird neighbor does nothing to quell the pain of a boy's rejection, but it had to be said. I had to say it.

Darby steps forward and takes her hand. "What do you say we let these two get back to their date, huh, Li?" Darby leans toward me. "You look beautiful, by the way."

"Thanks, Darby," I say quietly.

She thanks Cal, and after they leave, a deafening silence fills the room.

He walks over to me and takes me in his arms, holding me for a long moment. He kisses the top of my head and then leans down and whispers, "Who hurt you, Isadora?"

And there it is.

Chapter 34

I'm not sure where to begin.

Alex? College? Third grade? My mom?

A lot of things have happened to me that, logically, would give me the justification for never loving, never revealing, never living. I have so many reasons not to try, or even care.

But there's one reason to let it all go—and he's currently holding my trembling body.

The wounds, even as old as many of them are, somehow still feel heavy. A mother who never protected me still has an effect on me years later. Alex's betrayal kept me locked within myself for over two years.

But I'm not sure I should say any of this out loud. At some point, Cal may realize it's too much. That *I'm* too much.

We stand like that for what feels like forever—my mind spinning, my tense body struggling to relax, and then he inches back and looks at me. "Whoever it was, I can call Darby. We can make it look like an accident, no questions asked."

I laugh.

I look into his eyes—the same ones that used to leave me unnerved now leave me undone. I realize I want him to know. I want him to know about my childhood and my parents and my unfulfilled dreams and even Alex. I want him to know *me.*

It's just so incredibly hard. Secret hurt has a way of making a person feel falsely protected—as if being the person holding the keys to the door ensures that no one can get in and nothing can get out.

The problem with holding in that hurt is that you're stuck at that door, hand on the doorknob, every day. You don't move forward because you're too busy holding things back.

I never want to admit those things that have kept me feeling small because I don't want to give any new person I meet any inkling that they should think them about me too. I don't want Cal—or anyone—to see me through the eyes of the people who only saw my flaws.

I mentally take my hand off the handle that's been keeping the hidden things at bay.

And the door cracks open.

"There was . . . someone," I say. Words are hard to find in this moment. "I thought maybe he was someone I could . . . that he was *the one*, you know, for me to . . ." I trail off and look down.

Cal doesn't move—he just breathes with me.

"But it turned out, he was just using me." I pull back slightly and look up. "He hurt me." I exhale as I say the words—words that have been bottled and hidden for years now.

I see Cal clench his jaw and his muscles tense.

"He made it hard for me to believe anyone could ever really see me, at least as anything other than a researcher."

He pulls back and looks me square in the eyes. "You're so much more than that."

"I'm not fishing for compliments," I say, pulling away. I sit on the couch and he sits down on the coffee table, our knees touching.

"I'm not in the business of just handing out compliments, Isadora." He smiles. "I just wish I could make you see you like *I* see you." He reaches up and pushes my hair back over my shoulder. "What will it take for that to happen?"

I shrug. "Therapy?"

He laughs. "That is one of the steps, right? 'Consider therapy.'"

"I considered it. Decided it wasn't for me. There, step fifteen done."

I can feel him watching me as I try to decide how much I want to tell him about Alex. How much detail do I want to share? How much detail does he want to know? He's told me very little about Sasha—mostly his sister has filled in the blanks—and yet it has only drawn me closer to him, knowing he's had his heart broken too.

"I was like Delilah when I was younger," I say. "A lot, actually. I understand her in a way that I don't think even Darby does. I was different. I was . . . weird."

"Unique," he says.

"Yeah. Maybe. But like you said, kids that age really can't appreciate people's *uniqueness.*" I sigh. "But the way Darby came in . . . and what you both said to her, I just . . ." I start to tremble, holding back tears. I really do not want to cry right now.

The door cracks open a bit wider.

"You both stuck up for her. That—I mean—that never happened for me. My mom wanted me to be popular more than anything in the world. The more I've researched, the more I've realized she is a narcissist, and someone like that maybe shouldn't have a child. She criticized my clothes, my face, my friends. The fact that I was smart didn't matter. That wasn't good enough." I take a deep breath. "She never stuck up for me. Ever. Kids would be mean to me and she would tell me it was my fault."

He takes my hands in his.

"I didn't have any friends. The one I did have dropped me the second the popular kids came calling, and"—I groan—"this is all stupid. It's so stupid. It was childhood. Everyone has horror stories from childhood. Shouldn't I be over this by now?"

Cal watches me. "I don't know—have you dealt with it? Have you told your mom how it made you feel?"

My laugh is humorless. "No way."

"Why not?"

"You haven't met her. If I tell her she did anything to hurt me, she would launch into, 'How could you do this to me, Isadora?' Or 'You know all I ever did was try to make you the best you could be!'" I shrug. "I don't want her to make my pain about her."

He seems to accept this answer, at least for now.

"And yes, I had my heart broken a couple of years ago," I say. "I was stupid and fell for an egomaniac who kept our relationship a secret, turned all our conversations back to his needs, and told me my feelings were ridiculous."

I pause. "Oh my gosh, I was dating my mother." I half laugh at this, then look at Cal seriously. "Is there something wrong with me?"

He tilts his head slightly. "Are you asking that as a serious question?"

I really want to know. "Yes. Is there something wrong with me?"

"No." No hesitation, no pause, all conviction, and I want so desperately to believe him.

"Here's what I know, Isadora. We all have our stuff. We all have holes, and we all have scars. And we all have things we'd rather keep hidden, because we think it's easier not to burden someone else with our baggage." He takes my hand. "None of that makes you 'weird' or 'wrong.' In fact, in clinical terms, it makes you pretty normal."

I shake my head.

"You know," he says, "your experiment is kind of incredible, really. I know you started it as a way to disprove the article, right?"

"Yes."

"What if you actually tried to do something with it?"

I'm confused. "Do something with it? Like what?"

"Publish."

Now the shock on my face is real. "Publish? Are you nuts?"

He smirks. "Why not? It wouldn't be the first time somebody has studied the subject."

I know this is true. When I started the project, I discovered there was a massive, long-standing study through Harvard University on happiness. It's been going on since the 1930s and is still being conducted today. If the folks at Harvard have the topic covered, they certainly don't need my voice in the mix.

And yet, what if I have something *unique* to offer to the conversation? I frown. "Publish?"

"Yes. Publish. Put your name on it and put it out there."

I didn't read the findings of the Harvard study because I didn't want them to influence my own experiment, but I can't imagine my steps will lead me to any new data.

"Think about it, Isadora," he says. "It has wide appeal. It has a personal viewpoint. It has real-world data and marked experiences. You could add multiple test subjects and track their results."

I'm still stuck on what he just proposed.

"But . . . publish?"

Cal laughs. He can obviously see that my train of thought is still boarding at the station. "If you'll let me help you put it together, I'm all yours."

That snaps me out of my mental loop. "Did you just say that you're all mine?"

He nods as he leans toward me. He takes my face in his hands and kisses me. He then leans close to my ear and talks so softly it's barely a whisper.

"All yours."

I smile, but only for a moment. I sit back and look at him.

"But . . . publish?"

Chapter 35

The next day, Darby comes to pick me up for morning yoga, and I'm a sloth. The previous evening was later than I'm used to, and these early sessions are kicking my butt.

As I rush around to fill my water bottle and find a clean outfit to wear, she stands in my living room, waiting.

"Cal is pretty great, Isadora," she says from the other room. "Do you think he's the one?"

I stop moving. "The one?" I call out.

"Oh, come on, don't act like you haven't thought about it. Heck, even I thought about it *for* you after seeing him with Delilah last night. Who wouldn't want to marry a man as sensitive and kind as that?"

"He's a psychologist," I say. "They're trained to be that way."

"Oh, is that right?" Darby asks. "Is that how you feel when you have conversations with him, like you're on his couch?" She pauses. "Maybe you'd *like* to be on his couch."

I can hear the smile in her voice and poke my head out of my bedroom. "Darby!"

"It's okay to be happy, Isadora," she says. "You should embrace this. This is the fun stuff—the falling-in-love stuff."

I step out into the living room, still trying to pull on my shoes while standing. "Who said anything about love?"

"Oh please, it's written all over your face," Darby says. "You don't hide your emotions very well."

"I always thought I was good at hiding my emotions," I say simply.

She gives me a look that seems to say "*Yeah, right.*"

"A curse, to be sure." I stand, arms out, looking for approval of my mismatched outfit.

"It'll do. Let's go." Darby opens the door.

We walk down the stairs and head outside. We both stop, inhale a deep breath, and let it out slowly. "It's a beautiful day," I say on an exhale.

We start off toward the yoga studio. "I have to thank you for being so sweet to Delilah. You didn't even seem to mind that she interrupted your date. And you looked smoking hot and everything."

I laugh. "I did not."

"You absolutely did."

My cheeks heat. "Thanks. And I didn't mind at all. She needed us."

Darby peers over at me. "You relate to her in a way that I can't."

I laugh. "That's because I *was* her when I was little." I glance over at my friend. "But I didn't have a mom to stick up for me like you do for her."

"Really?"

I shake my head.

"That's sad," Darby says.

"Yeah," I agree. "It is. I mean, it *was*." I feel embarrassed. "I kind of got the short end of the mom stick."

"Where are your parents now?"

"Phoenix," I say. "She said if I wasn't going to give her

grandkids anytime soon—or ever—there was no reason for her to stick around here."

"Ouch."

"Yeah, most of what she said to me over the years was a big 'ouch,'" I say. "She never once got fired up over someone being mean to me like you did for Delilah. Somehow those things were always my fault."

Talking about this is way easier with Darby than with Cal.

"I'm so sorry," Darby says.

"I don't think she means to be so harsh," I say. "I honestly think she has an inflated view of herself and no idea how she comes across."

"Don't do that, Isadora," Darby says. "Don't defend her if she hurt you."

I shrug. "She's my mom."

"Yeah, but you didn't pick her," Darby counters. "And you certainly don't have to let her keep making you feel like you're a failure."

I see her point, I hear her point, but I can't bring myself to even think about doing anything about it. "I guess I just don't want to let it make me bitter."

"You can be hurt and not be bitter."

I wasn't sure how. All these years, my hurt has kept me locked up, and it's like it has turned me into a shell of the person I was supposed to be.

"And maybe you should let her know how much her words have hurt you over the years."

That pesky last step on the list. Step thirty-one: "Confront what is making you unhappy in the first place."

I shake the thought away. "I can't do that," I say. "It's not worth the agony of hearing her turn it around and make it all about her."

Darby stops and turns toward me. She puts her hands on my

shoulders and spins me to face her. "I'm really sorry you didn't have anyone to stick up for you when you were younger. I can't think of anything more horrible than that. But you have friends now." She gives my shoulders a shake. "Friends. And we care about you."

I don't know how I got here. For the first time in my life, I have safe spaces. Plural.

And I'm discovering that safe spaces equal happiness.

In the middle of a sidewalk, on a balmy morning, standing in a yoga outfit that doesn't match, being shaken at the shoulders by a crazy lady with four children, I'm beginning to understand what happiness feels like.

Chapter 36

After yoga, I head into campus. I attempt step sixteen: "Take a new route to work." Normally, I take the straightest route to the university. I have it all mapped out, and I know the quickest way to get where I need to go.

In fact, I get slightly annoyed when people don't take the most direct route somewhere. It feels like wasting time.

But now, in the interest of research, I take the long way. The scenic route. It's late spring, and there's a special kind of smell in the air. It's that *outdoor* smell, a mix of grass and flowers and dirt all bathed in warm sunshine. If green had a smell, this would be it. The trees have filled out, and as I walk down the city streets, I take note of the big, puffy, white clouds set in a crisp blue sky overhead.

Some days, the city feels claustrophobic. It strangles with its busyness. Other days, like today, it feels like the top of the world, and I'm just floating along. I start to hum "Good Day Sunshine" as I turn down another street I've never been on. How could these adorable rows of houses be so close to the university and I've never seen them before?

I'm thinking about life and where I am in it as opposed to where I was—when I realize I've arrived at the west end of the university. I'm still humming as I start off in the direction of a shortcut through staff parking when something stops me.

A 1965 blue Mustang convertible pulling into the lot.

And behind the wheel—a very familiar silhouette.

Alex.

His sandy-colored hair is a little longer, but that's definitely him. As much as I've tried to forget him, I still recognize that profile.

I can't breathe for a second.

Panicked, I rush over to hide behind a parked car so Alex doesn't spot me. He pulls the Mustang into a Reserved parking space.

My head and my vision are literally spinning. *What is he doing here?*

After he published his paper, he took a job in Boston. The last I heard, he'd begun guest lecturing at colleges throughout the country. It was his dream to travel and speak and get up on the stage like an academic rock star, all of the pretty college students hanging on his every word.

Every circle has its celebrities, and it meant everything to him that he was one of them.

I guess his dream came true. And it was, in large part, thanks to me.

Wait. Cal picked me up in that car.

He said it belonged to a friend.

My stomach drops as I see Cal appear on the sidewalk, walking out to greet Alex.

Alex who kept me a secret.

Alex who stole my research.

Alex who broke my heart.

Cal extends a hand in greeting, and Alex shakes it, then pulls Cal in for one of those bro hugs, even though Alex is about as far away from a "bro" as a person can get.

I'm terrified of what this could mean.

Happy Isadora, breathing in the sunshine, taking the long way to work, laughing through tears, handing out inspirational cards—she's gone now.

She's replaced by cautious Isadora—the one behind the door.

They planned this. They must have. They're friends, right? Did Alex tell Cal that if he sweet-talked me, I'd do all that work on his book for no credit?

But Cal took me to meet his family. We flew kites together!

Then again, Alex was nothing like Alex—not until *after* I turned in the last of my research. Once he had what he needed, everything changed. That's when I saw him for who he really was.

And I still said nothing.

I hug my bag to my chest. Inside is the last of my work on Cal's book. Once I hand it over, that's it. He'll pull the same thing.

It's the same. It's all the same.

I think about what Darby said to me this morning. *"You can be hurt and not be bitter."*

And I realize that I'm not bitter. I'm angry.

"'Those who cannot remember the past are condemned to repeat it,'" I mutter under my breath. Santayana's words were never truer than in this moment for me, crouched behind a car, wondering how I missed all the signs.

I don't deserve this. I didn't deserve to be cast aside by Alex, and I sure don't deserve to be cast aside by Cal.

I push aside all of the feelings I have for Cal and look at the situation clinically. Logically.

Like I always do.

The facts are plain. Alex treated me a certain way to get what he wanted, then humiliated me in—what was for me—the worst way possible. Long nights and stolen kisses.

Cal has, so far, done the exact same thing, right down to the sticky notes in manuscripts.

Conclusion? The similarities are too great. At some point, somehow, Cal will do what Alex did. Maybe not in the same way—but I can't take that chance.

I storm inside and don't exhale until I reach the safety of my office. I pull Cal's pages from my bag. I'll drop them off with his assistant, and then, I suppose, he can be done with me.

Just like Alex.

Those three words reverberate in my mind, rhythmically pounding as if keeping time in a marching band.

I pull out my happiness notebook and struggle not to rip out the pages upon pages I've written about Cal. How he makes me feel, how he understands me like nobody else has. How I might even take him to meet my family because I'm pretty sure they won't run him off.

I could replace his name with Alex's name and change the dates and it would still all be true.

Just like Alex.

I let myself get caught up in a guy all over again. So much so that I've forgotten who I am.

I push the notebook aside and try to get my head around all of this. A part of me knows it's ludicrous for me to jump to conclusions about Cal simply because he's friends with Alex. For all I know, Alex kept me a secret from him, the same way he kept me a secret from everyone else. Cal has done nothing to make me think his intentions toward me are anything but genuine.

But the what-if floating around at the back of my mind isn't going away.

I can't concentrate. I'm angry. Frustrated. Full of questions.

Why didn't Cal tell me he was friends with Alex? Was any of it true? Would I ever recover if this ended in heartbreak?

Gary walks by my open door and peeks into my office. "Did you hear your old friend Dr. Alex McEnroe is guest lecturing today?"

"My old friend?" I practically spit the words.

Gary frowns.

"Gary, can I ask you something?" I push myself up out of my chair. I don't want to ask this question, and I don't want to know the answer.

Gary's frown deepens, and I see genuine concern on his face. "Okay . . . ?"

"Did you assign me to Cal or did he request me?"

I can see he's unsure whether or not he should answer because he looks like he's swallowed a pigeon.

"I'm just curious how it all came about," I say, trying to sound less psychotic.

"Well, as a matter of fact, yes, he requested you," he says. "I wasn't sure how he knew so much about you, your methods, or your passion for your work, but . . . yes. He asked for you by name."

I clench my jaw. The imagined conversations between Cal and Alex start to swirl.

He continues. "I went along with it for all the reasons I said. And it turns out, my gut was right. You've blossomed. You've changed, and we're seeing real potential in you—the kind we saw when you first came on board."

This stops me and my mental gymnastics. "What do you mean?"

"I mean you were on a very specific track when you arrived, Isadora. We had high hopes for you. I thought you'd be running this whole place by now, if I'm honest—you are the smartest one here."

I don't respond. Truthfully, I'd thought the same thing.

Gary continues. "Then, I don't know what happened—you shut yourself off, and—" He sighs. "Well, you—please forgive me for saying this—you became difficult to work with."

"I did?"

Gary nods. "There was no question your work was good. You're great at finding and analyzing data—but this job is about more than data. And your interpersonal skills left a lot to be desired."

I can feel my face change; it's like when you're reading an intense book and a half hour later you realize you've been holding your face in the same position—and then it relaxes.

Gary smiles. "Frankly, it's good to see you like this. More open. More interested in your coworkers. More connected."

I am assaulted by emotion. It takes a fair amount of strength—and chewing the inside of my cheek—to keep myself from crying.

I'm struggling. "Did Cal say why he wanted me on his team?"

Gary shrugs a little. "Said he'd heard you were the best." He chuckles lightly. "At first, I didn't agree. I told him you'd be great at the research but prickly to work with. He said he had friends who spoke highly of you and that he'd take his chances."

"Friends who spoke highly of me? Who . . . ?"

Gary says nonchalantly, "You apparently have a good reputation and have made some marked impressions. You've worked with several professors around here, Isadora. And professors talk."

"Right," I say. Professors talk. So by that logic, I should assume that Alex talked to Cal. Should I also assume that Alex convinced him to enlist my help? Gave him a play-by-play on how to get me to take on his research as my own?

"Why didn't you tell me that in the first place?" I ask.

"He asked me not to," Gary says. And then, at my reaction, he adds, "Miss Bentley, are you okay?"

I'm staring down at my desk, trying not to freak out, so I don't see Alex until he's standing right next to Gary, as if he's materialized out of thin air. Like a demon or a vampire or one of those Death Eaters in Harry Potter. He slaps two hands on Gary's shoulders from behind, squeezing them.

"Oh! Dr. McEnroe!" Gary is like a teenage girl at a Harry

Styles concert. They shake hands emphatically, Gary laughing and gushing in the presence of the university's superstar.

"You're drooling in your mustache," I mutter to myself, and then I pretend to be highly engrossed in something on the other side of my computer.

The two men make small talk for a few minutes, followed by the lull that comes in every bit of small talk where both trail off a laugh and say, "Anyway . . . ," and then Gary promises to give Alex whatever he needs while he's here, and leaves.

Alex, however, does not.

"Isadora," he says, emphasizing the third syllable in my name with a *"Well, well, well"* tone in his voice.

I don't look up.

"Still here in this same office, I see."

"Where else would I be, Alex?" I mutter.

"Yeah, yeah. Totally." His tone makes my teeth hurt. "I hear you and my old buddy Cal have been working together." Alex comes in and sits down in Cal's seat, as if he has every right to do so. My face heats under his watchful eye.

Finally, I look at him. I force a tight smile. "What do you want?"

He smiles back, and my skin crawls at the sight of it. "Wow, you look different."

"I am different," I say, even though I'm not sure that's true. A day ago, absolutely. I was a much more confident, happier Isadora Bentley. But seeing him here—with Cal—it's like all those things I've been learning about myself have disappeared.

He nods. "Cal says you've been a huge help with his book. I told him you were the ticket."

"The ticket?" I ask.

"The golden ticket." He grins. "Sounds like I was right."

And there's my answer. Cal and Alex discussed me, my work, how to get the best out of me.

But then, as if a light bulb literally blinks on over my head, I realize that this really isn't about Alex at all.

It's about me.

It's a revelation. Things click in my mind.

Isadora Bentley, through the struggle and strife of living through the vast landscapes of emotion, is now focusing her gaze on an old foe. Normally, Isadora would choose flight—hiding in the tall brush until the danger has passed. But now, girded with years of experience and emboldened by confidence, Isadora Bentley stands to fight.

That's right, Attenborough. I'm done hiding.

I made myself small so Alex could feel important. And he let me.

He practically required it.

I never said a word about his lack of integrity, never demanded my name be added to his paper because I was so afraid if I did, I'd lose him.

Which, as it turned out, is exactly what happened anyway.

I was more afraid of being alone than I was of losing who I was.

All the walls I so expertly constructed around my life—all of them—I am reducing to dust and rubble.

Only now do I realize that the true tragedy of Isadora and Alex wasn't the fact that he used or betrayed me. It was that *I* allowed him to. I convinced myself that I must've done something wrong. I was so ashamed that I'd believed Alex might actually have feelings for me that I excused his bad behavior on account of a foolish, romantic notion, and I convinced myself I'd gotten what I deserved.

And *that* was the truth I didn't want to confront.

Step thirty-one. It's time to kick down that door.

"The golden ticket," I repeat, slowly standing.

He holds his hands up in a shrug. "You have the magic touch—what can I say?"

"You know, Alex, I *feel* like you think you're complimenting me, but really"—I look right at him—"this is one of the biggest insults of my life."

"Whoa, Isadora," he says, hands in the air as if I've just declared this to be a stickup. "I'm not insulting you here. I'm saying you're good at what you do."

"As long as no one knows *I'm the one who did it*," I say a little louder.

I feel renewed. I think my eyesight is even better.

I can't remember when I've ever felt this enlivened. It's like backward, awkward, get-along-to-go-along Isadora just woke up. And she's sick of being everyone's stepladder to the top.

Alex didn't put me in the back seat—I did that all on my own. I'm stuck where I am because of me.

The horrible realization washes over me, and I feel a little sick over it. It does not, however, wipe away my resolve. It just makes me angry. I'm done underestimating myself.

I verbally launch at Alex like I'm shot out of a cannon.

"It was *my* research that tied your entire thesis together. Mine. *My* research that took all the pieces of your little *paper* and made them make sense." My voice grows, as if I'm discovering it for the first time. "When you brought it to me, it was a *disaster*. A mess. *I* fixed it. *Me*. Because of me, you have a vintage *mustang*!"

I hear silence outside my door, and that means that the others in the lab have stopped working and are listening.

Good. I've kept the secret for too long.

"Isadora, calm down—"

"Calm down?" I cut in.

"I didn't mean anything by it. I just—"

I cut him off again. "I know you think you can romance favors out of grad students and research assistants and lord knows who else, but guess what, Alex. Not anymore. That's not how this works. Your actions have consequences."

He tries to match my tone. "I didn't do anything wrong, Isadora," he says. "That was your job."

I don't back down. "The worst part is, I think you actually believe that." I take a step out from behind my desk. I'm done hiding. "If you think passing off someone else's work is perfectly ethical, great. But you're wrong. You told me it was a 'team effort.' You told me you 'couldn't have done it without me.' You told me this was 'our paper.' And the biggest irony is that I wouldn't have allowed it if you hadn't convinced me that you and I had a future!"

He scoffs. "Okay, say I couldn't have done it without you. That doesn't mean you deserve credit. You're just a researcher."

A gut punch. I narrow my eyes. "What did you just say to me?"

The look of shock on his face pleases me more than it should.

"Look, Isadora, I'm sorry—it was my project—my paper."

"Stop talking. It was *my* research," I say. "Almost *exclusively* mine. You had no idea how to interpret the results you found. You needed my brain to do that. And you've been riding my coattails as far as you possibly can."

He scoffs again. "That's not true!"

"Prove it!" I practically shout. The lab is undoubtedly all ears on doors right now. "Tell everyone where you found the contrasting studies on diametrically opposed characteristics. List out the news sources, the peer-reviewed journals, the primary source interviews. Explain how you made your findings accessible and comprehensible enough to put them in a book that a fifth grader could understand! Tell me that, Dr. McEnroe!"

I'm shaking with adrenaline. Alex looks shocked. Heck, I'm shocked. But I'm also proud of myself for finally—finally—confronting what has been making me unhappy in the first place.

I don't want to hear his excuses. I've said my piece. I'm done. Besides, it's almost lunchtime, and I have a standing date with a seventy-year-old man.

I pick up Cal's book and shove it toward Alex. "Here, give this to your old buddy Cal. Unless you want to slap your name on his work too."

I walk out of my office, leaving Alex standing there, jaw slack.

As I pass the lab, I glance inside and see Shellie standing there, smiling ear to ear and giving me two thumbs-up. "Good for you, Isadora. It's about time one of us stood up for herself."

Chapter 37

I need air.

Never in the two years I knew Alex, never in my life, did I ever speak to him—or anyone—like that. I never had much of a voice with him at all.

In the hallway, I nearly barrel into Gary, but as I do, I look up and find Cal standing there. Did he hear my outburst? Heat rushes to my cheeks as I try to decipher the expression on his face—is he upset? Caught? Surprised I finally stood up for myself? Is he . . . proud?

I need air.

Hot tears sting my eyes as I push open the door to the stairwell and disappear inside.

I lean against the wall for a few brief seconds and try to let myself process what just happened. I don't know if Cal set out to hurt me the way Alex did. I don't know if my standing up for myself will ruin everything with him.

But I *do* know that seeing Alex reminds me why I vowed to myself never to let this happen again.

Cal's intentions aren't the issue—my promise to myself is.

I lost sight of that, but now it's all I can think about. This is the exact pain I was trying to spare myself from.

I rush down the stairs and out into the courtyard. I need to talk to Marty. He'll dole out his wisdom in small, digestible pieces and set me back on the right path. Maybe he'll tell me I'm overreacting or that I'm jumping to conclusions. I hope there's a cookie involved somewhere.

I reach the bench, but Marty isn't there.

I pull out my phone and look at the time. He's late. Eight minutes late. Marty is never late.

My pulse quickens as I scan the courtyard, hoping that maybe he got into a conversation with another professor or is regaling a new group of students with tales of his time in school here.

But he's nowhere.

For the first time since the day I met him on this very bench, he's not here.

I pull out my phone and send him a text.

Hey, Marty! I could use your wisdom today, old man. Are you close?

I know he hates texting as much as I hate talking on the phone, so when my phone buzzes an incoming call, I'm not the least bit surprised. I'm relieved, in fact.

"Marty! You're late! You are not going to believe what is happening right now—are you almost here?"

"Isadora?" It's a woman's voice.

"Hello? Who's this?"

"It's Miriam," she says.

"Miriam, what's going on?"

"Isadora, it's my dad . . ." She pauses long enough to make me think we've been cut off.

"Miriam? Where's—"

"My dad had a heart attack."

No. Please. No.

Chapter 38

I race back to my apartment and close the door behind me. I don't understand what's happening. This small circle of people I've allowed past the gates is falling apart. It's all coming undone.

I'm a building in an earthquake.

Darby, who vowed to protect me. Delilah, who looked up to me. Marty, who always accepted me. And Cal—who stuck up for me. Who held me. Who *saw* me.

These are the people in my life now. Some barged in and stayed. Some broke through barriers I'd hidden behind for years.

And now I think these people need to go.

I can't keep going through this. This feeling of being lured in and romanced by the idea of acceptance, only to be left out in the cold. It's as heavy on my shoulders as piles of snow on a rickety roof.

I feel selfish thinking this way—looking at it only from the perspective of how it affects me—but I'm overcome with grief I wouldn't have to feel if only I'd kept everyone at arm's length, the way I'd successfully been doing for so many years.

I walk into my kitchen and stare at the refrigerator, where Delilah practically created a photographic shrine to me and my new friends. Smiling images, frozen in time. Snapshots to prove that I am here, I am alive, I have people I love.

I remove one of Marty and me sitting on our bench out from underneath the Tardis magnet and stare at the old man's smiling face.

"This wasn't part of the deal," I say to the image of him. Tears well and threaten to spill over, but I hold them back. I reject all of this.

I refuse to think that Cal could ever, ever turn out to be like Alex. I refuse to think something bad could happen to Marty. I refuse all of it while simultaneously building a safe house for myself in my mind. If I can put myself back behind the walls, maybe I can make it all go away. Pretend I was never a part of this circle at all.

I'll move. Get a new job in a new city. Start over fresh.

Get a dog.

Which reminds me of Olive. Which reminds me of Marty. Which reminds me of Cal.

Stop. It.

The thought of being separated from these people makes me ache.

A knock on the door. Instantly, I realize that on the other side is someone I do not want to see.

"Isadora?" Darby's voice calls from the hallway. "I know you're in there. Please let me in."

I don't want to open the door. I'm sure by now my mascara has trailed black lines down my face. More importantly, I know that Darby will be able to see through any guarded lie I try to tell. *I'm okay. It's no big deal. Everything is fine.*

Lies. Lies. Lies.

The knocking persists. I know she's not going away.

Finally, I move my feet, trudge over to the door and open it, but refuse to meet her eyes. I don't want to see the maternal look of concern. My mind is made up. I am bowing out of this new life.

Halfway through the happiness steps and the experiment got the best of me. I win, Dr. Monroe. I've proven you wrong.

"Isadora!" I walk away slowly as she steps into my apartment. "Cal texted me and said something about you losing it on a guy at work?"

"A guy?" I slump onto the couch. "Darby, it was *Alex*."

"Wait. Ex-Alex?"

I look up and raise my eyebrows as a reply.

"You saw him? What happened?"

I tilt my head and say matter-of-factly, "Apparently he's Cal's friend with the convertible."

Darby's eyebrows draw together, a look of confusion on her face. "Okay. So? Cal knows Alex. It makes sense if they both worked at the university. Is that a big deal?"

"Is that a . . ." I shake my head. She's not seeing the cataclysmic collision of two completely separate worlds that I see. "Alex recommended me to Cal." I emphasize every word. "He sent Cal to me." I bury my face in my hands. Darby sits on the coffee table and puts her hands on my shoulders.

"Did Cal know about you and Alex?" she asks.

I sniffle and wipe tears from my cheeks with my palms. "I sure didn't tell him. But it's not a leap to think that Alex did."

"Look. You know Cal and Alex aren't the same person, right? Not even the same type. Cal is kind. Alex is a tool."

I peer up at her. I can feel the slightest shred of dangerous hope. I've already decided these relationships have to go—all of them—and I don't want her to convince me otherwise.

"Cal would never do that," Darby says. "I've seen you two together. You're a real couple. This is a relationship. Cal would never hurt you the way Alex did."

"Are you sure?" I say through a soft sob. "I *think* I know that. Cal and Alex aren't alike. And I hope Cal would never intentionally hurt me. I'm guessing he had a reason for not mentioning Alex to me in the first place." I look at her then. "But, Darby, seeing Alex sitting in my office? In that chair? With his smugness and his obstinance and his stupid face? It felt the same as two years ago. The humiliation. The hurt. The pain. I'm sorry, but I can't go through that again."

"Who says you will?" She squeezes my hands.

"Statistics say I will," I say. "It's logical to assume that this relationship with Cal will end. Most do. When it does, I will be heartbroken. Again."

"Aren't you going to be heartbroken if it ends now?"

I open my mouth to say something, then close it.

My lower lip trembles. "Yes."

Darby presses, but softly. "Then why not just wait and see what happens instead of cutting things off too quickly?"

I would be broken if things ended now. I already am. But not nearly as much as if I let it continue. My feelings for Cal would grow exponentially with every single day, making the inevitable crash that much worse.

"I knew better than to get involved," I say. "With any of it."

She pulls back slightly. "What do you mean 'any of it'?"

I look up and sigh. I want to stop myself from pushing her away, from pushing any of them away—but I'm in self-preservation mode. "Before you met me—"

"You were alone," she interrupts. "All by yourself up here in this drab apartment, building bombs in your bathtub. No photos on the wall. Not even a colored drape." She pauses. "There was no laughter. No joy. No—anything. Can you honestly say you were happy?"

"That was my choice," I say. "That *is* my choice."

She frowns. "What are you saying, Isadora?"

"I'm saying I don't have what it takes to handle loving other people. I'm saying I don't want to get hurt again. I'm saying . . ." I pause and look at her. This isn't what I want at all. I know it. She knows it. Am I going to be stubborn and let myself go through with pushing everyone away when all I've ever wanted is to belong?

"Darby, Marty's in the hospital."

She gasps. "What? *What?!* You kind of buried the lead there. Why didn't you tell me that sooner?" She stands. "Get up. Let's go. Do you know which one?"

"I can't go," I say, and then I meet her eyes, staring at her through fresh tears. "I'm not strong enough to say goodbye."

~

That afternoon, there is another knock on my door. Different. Tentative.

This time, I don't answer. Because I know that as much as he wants to come in, Cal would never push past me the way Darby did. Cal will take the hint.

I lie in my bed, listening to the knocking. He calls out my name twice, presumably to let me know he's there. And then I hear voices in the hallway.

Darby starts pounding, pleading for me to open the door, but I physically can't move from the bed. I'm worried about Marty. I'm afraid to go see him. I'm afraid to lose him.

It's paralyzing.

I know being with Cal and Darby would probably ease that pain. I know they are probably exactly what I need. They'd build me up and hold my hand and give me faith that things could still turn out okay.

But fear right now is stronger than faith—and I can't come out from behind this wall.

~

Cal sends me a text message from the hallway:

Darby says you haven't left your apartment, so I know you're in there.

Can we talk?

I didn't know Alex was the guy who hurt you.

I would never, ever treat you the way he did.

After a few minutes, I hear him leave and my heart clenches.

I'm being stupid, and I know it. I'm overreacting, and I know it. If I could open the door and talk to him, all of this could go away.

But I'm playing the long game here.

And the long game means protecting my heart—today and down the road.

~

Later, I get another text message from Cal. He's probably back at his apartment.

When you're ready to talk, I'll be here.

Chapter 39

For the next three days, I call in sick to work.

It's not a lie. I've eaten so much junk food I've made myself sick. I ate frozen waffles at one in the morning and fell asleep with hands sticky from syrup.

The fork was optional.

I haven't showered.

I haven't gone to yoga.

I haven't gone outside.

I've quit living my life.

I've turned into an even more pathetic version of the person I was before I started the 31 Ways. I've lost all desire to finish my project—and I've never left anything half-finished in my life.

Worse, Cal hasn't stopped texting me.

> Smiled at the lunch lady today. Did you know she has a gold tooth?
>
> Made me think of you.
>
> The smiling, not the gold tooth.
>
> You okay?

And later:

I think I finally got the angle right on the paper airplanes.

It's all in the fold.

Thanks for the physics lesson.

Can we talk?

They're unbearable to read, and even more unbearable not to answer. He can see that I've read them. I tried just looking at them as notifications on my phone so they would stay unread, but sometimes they're too long and I have to open them. I want to answer. I want to give him a chance to explain everything, but I know better. This isn't about what Cal knew or didn't know. What he did or didn't do. None of that matters.

Just like Alex. The pounding is back.

This is about what I've always known to be true: if you let them, people will hurt you. I'm tired of being hurt.

I'm lying on the couch watching the same soap opera I used to watch in college, and I'm shocked to find that I can follow the current storylines as if I'd been watching all along. Some of the actors are still the same—one guy died in an avalanche, but here he is, toasting his sister's wedding in Barcelona.

The hair rises on the back of my neck when I hear what sounds like scratching at my door.

I stare at it, as if I might be able to see through it if I watch long enough, and the noise stops.

I breathe out my held breath.

Skritch, skritch, skritch. The noise returns. The handle jiggles back and forth.

Is someone trying to break into my apartment?

I grab the closest thing to me—an empty Pop-Tarts box—and toss it aside because it's not going to help me defend myself. I grab a small ceramic figurine of a toad, and in the back of my mind I think, *What in the world is this going to do?* but I creep toward the front door anyway.

Skritch, skritch, skritch.

I reach out, slowly, and in one motion unlock the door and yank it open while simultaneously raising the frog over my head.

"Hi, Isadora."

It's Delilah.

She's holding two bobby pins like a tiny robber.

Delilah, whom I haven't seen in days. Delilah, who has come to my door after school every day, then come back at dinnertime every night. Delilah, who has left me care packages to *"help you feel better"* on the floor outside my door.

Delilah, who calls me her friend.

Looking at her wide eyes now, I slowly lower the frog.

"Well, look who finally answered her door," Delilah says as if it were the most natural thing in the world to be confronted by a maniac with a knickknack for a weapon.

"Are you trying to pick my lock?"

She puts the bobby pins neatly away in a small plastic baggie. "I watched a YouTube video. I almost had it."

"That is equal parts terrifying and impressive."

"Thank you."

"Aren't you supposed to be in school?" I ask.

"It's summer." She plows straight through me and into my apartment, looking around with a judgmental, upturned nose. "It's disgusting in here."

"Thank you." I close the door and pull my long cardigan around my waist.

"Mom says you're hiding," she says.

"I am. You found me. You win." I move into the kitchen, vigilant of her every move, mostly because I feel like she's trapped me and I'm looking for a place to hide.

"She says you're making a big mistake."

I pull open the refrigerator and take out a Coke.

"It's ten in the morning," Delilah says.

"So?"

"We don't drink Coke at ten in the morning."

"Well, *I* do." I crack it open like a belligerent child and take a long drink while staring at her.

Delilah scrunches up her face. She's like a little grown-up, and reprimands me as such. "Isadora, I hate to tell you this, but you're acting like a baby."

I gently set down my can of soda and look at her. She looks back. It's like a standoff at the O.K. Corral. I don't argue. I know she's right. I know it's immature and childish for me to lock everyone out when they've done nothing wrong, to punish these beloved people for someone else's mistakes. But I also know that some people are better off alone. I am one of those people.

"We went and saw Marty," she says.

His name stings. I know my reaction should be different, but I can't help it. "You did?"

"He asked about you." She folds her arms over her chest like a tiny mother hen. "Probably wonders why in the world you haven't bothered to come see him."

My stomach is hollow at that. Does this mean he's going to be okay? "Is he okay?"

"You should go and ask him yourself," Delilah says. "That's what friends do, Isadora. And if you want to have good friends, you have to be a good friend."

The simple, powerful truth stuns me to silence.

"You're pushing everyone away," Delilah says. "Why do you do that?"

I don't know if she overheard Darby say this or if she's come up with it all on her own, but she's right. I know she's right. She's ten years old, and she's got a better handle on all this than I do.

What am I doing?

"And . . . I miss you."

I look at her then, and I see her eyes, fixed on me and filled with tears, and my heart twists in my chest. I've been such an idiot. Worse, I've been a lonely idiot.

We stand in silence for a few minutes. It's my turn to speak, but I have no words. I walk into the living room with my Coke, and Delilah digs her heels in, waiting for me to say something.

When I don't, she turns and starts toward the door.

"Delilah, wait."

She stops but doesn't face me.

"I'm . . . I'm sorry." It's all I can say. I've got nothing else.

She turns to me then. "I don't need you to be sorry. I need my friend back."

And with that, she's gone.

She closes the door behind her, and my heart grieves. My attempt to protect myself from getting hurt is hurting everyone else. I'm becoming exactly the person I'm trying to avoid.

What is wrong with me?

I sit with that question for half an hour, replaying Delilah's reprimand. I know my actions have been selfish. I know it isn't the proper way to deal with any of this. I know my ten-year-old friend is right.

It's time for me to grow up.

Chapter 40

Once again, I'm embarrassed.

But this time, I own it.

It's my own actions that have caused that embarrassment. It turns out, in this case, I didn't need anyone else to humiliate me. I took care of that all on my own. I'm moving up in the world.

I shower off three days of depressing, self-pitying sludge. I get myself dressed and even put on makeup. Shocking.

I walk outside.

Without even thinking about it, I stop on the sidewalk and draw in a deep breath. "It's a beautiful day," I say to myself, and all at once, it helps. I feel better. I'm emotional again, of course, because it dawns on me that Darby's fingerprints are all over my life.

I can't possibly believe giving her up is a good idea.

The hospital is only several blocks away, so I walk. I need the sunshine. I need to be outside. Within mere moments, both fill me up.

By the time I reach the entrance of the hospital, I am energized. Slightly winded, but better for it.

It's as if there's been a hazy film over my eyes for the past few days, and it's finally fallen away. I'm seeing everything more clearly somehow, and yet my brain is still shuffling pieces of this puzzle around, trying to solve it. There are lessons I'm supposed to learn here—certainly to *grow up*—but I know there's more.

I walk up to the counter and get Marty's room information. He's on the fifth floor. Room 529.

All at once, I'm worried to see him. Worried I've hurt him in my absence. Worried he won't want me to visit.

But I have to at least try. *"That's what friends do."*

I find the elevators and say a silent prayer that Marty won't kick me out for bad behavior, and when the door opens and I step onto the fifth floor, my heart starts to race again.

I don't like thinking of him here. More than that, I don't like thinking that I abandoned him while he was.

I walk around until I find room 529. I then proceed to stand in the hallway for three solid minutes, trying to think of something—anything—I might be able to say to explain my absence.

Normal people rush to hospitals when their friends and loved ones are admitted. They wait long hours, pacing the floors of waiting rooms for news on whether or not that person will be okay. They show up.

I hid.

The door to Marty's room swings open and Miriam walks out. She takes one look at me and I see her shoulders drop. I interpret that as disappointment and brace myself for a lecture on what a horrible person I am. Instead, she gives me a soft smile.

It wasn't disappointment. It was relief.

"He's going to be okay, Isadora," she says. "And he'll be so glad to see you."

The tension in my body begins to disappear. "I'm sorry I—"

Miriam holds up a hand. "Don't even give it a second thought. Your timing is perfect. I have to go pick up kids and get everyone fed and shuffled, but I'll be back in a little while. You can keep him company while I'm gone?"

I nod softly and watch her go. Then I stand in the hallway for several minutes, as if I've been frozen by Queen Elsa.

"Are you lost?" A nurse stops beside me.

"No," I say.

"Oh, are you here for Marty?" She smiles, and I can see Marty has worked his magic on her.

"Yes," I say.

She squints at me then. "Are you Isadora?"

"Yes. How did you know that?"

"He's been asking for you," the nurse says. "He'll be so glad you're here." She walks away. Her words give me the courage to push Marty's door open. There's light flooding in through the windows, and despite being a hospital room, it's cheerful.

Vases of flowers are positioned throughout the space, and handmade Get Well Soon cards pinned up on the walls. It looks like his grandkids and Darby's kids have drawn many pictures for the old man—one with a rainbow and the heartfelt sentiment *"I hope you don't die"* written in purple crayon.

Marty is lying in the bed, wearing a hospital gown. He's hooked up to machines, but mostly, he looks good. There's color in his cheeks, so that's a good sign, right?

When I clear my throat, his eyes flutter open. At the sight of me, he smiles.

I smile back. Oh, how I've missed him.

"Isadora," he says hoarsely. "You came."

"Sorry I'm so late," I say.

He gingerly raises a hand and waves me off. "I was worried you'd go to our bench and think I'd deserted you," he says.

"I did think that for a minute." I'm trying hard to forget that day. "But I knew better. You would—"

"I would never not show up for you," he says.

While he doesn't mean for his words to hit me sideways, they do. Because I didn't show up for him.

"Right," I say quietly.

He motions to the chair next to his bed. "Sit. Stay."

I hang my bag on a hook by the door and take a seat, looking over at him with the greatest regret. "I'm really sorry. For . . . you know, not being here for you."

His eyes smile. "You're here now." He's too kind to do anything but give me the grace I absolutely don't deserve.

"Cal was here," he says. "Twice so far. He came to visit me, but I think he might've been hoping to run into you."

"I doubt he ever wants to see me again," I muse. He'd finally stopped texting me, which is what I thought I wanted, but, funny thing, I want exactly the opposite.

"He looked lost," Marty says. "And sad. He misses you."

I fold my hands in my lap, unsure of what to say.

"You know, Isadora, I've watched you the last several months," Marty says, slowly and carefully. "We were strangers that day we met on the bench. But we're friends now, wouldn't you say?"

"Yes," I say with a smile. "I would say we're friends."

"I watched you take on those 31 Ways to Be Happy, and it seemed like every day, you became a little more . . . you. A little more Isadora. Like you were on this journey and it led you to the person you were always meant to be."

I nod softly but say nothing. I didn't originally consider that this experiment could have any impact on my identity, but I've noticed it myself. It's not surprising that Marty has noticed it too.

"So now . . . the question remains," he says. "Are you happier?"

I sit and think. For the first time through this whole experiment, I honestly attend to that question. That's the point, isn't it?

Is Isadora Bentley happy?

"I don't know," I finally say. "I thought I knew, but now I'm not so sure. I'm not happy at all at the moment." My world is imploding. How could I be anything but miserable?

"Yes, I understand this moment could be scary. But take in *all* the time and all the experiences since you started your experiment. Really think about it," Marty says. "Are you happier?"

I struggle with this. I know he's about to make a point. I'm not sure I want to follow. I'm not sure I'm ready to admit to anything or to learn a lesson.

But my brain is a horrible traitor. Without my permission, it has launched itself down a path I did not want to travel.

I'm knocking over fruit in the indoor market. I'm eating doughnuts with Delilah on the street outside the bakery. I'm sweating through yoga classes with Darby, trying not to fall over. I'm eating sandwiches with Marty. Getting slobbered on by a golden-colored dog. Meeting Cal's family. Flying kites carried on a warm wind. Driving with the top down. Stealing kisses in the stacks at the library like college kids.

Falling in love.

The words rush at me, unwarranted and unwanted, and I push them away.

"What's wrong?" Marty asks.

I shake my head. I can't put words to any of this. I can't admit out loud that I've fallen for all of them. I've fallen in love with this new life that I accidentally carved out for myself simply by stepping outside my comfort zone. By opening myself up to whatever came my way. I've spent so many years intentionally closing myself off—it reminds me of that line in *Anne of Green Gables* when Anne tells Marilla how much she's missed.

I don't want to be Marilla. I want to be Anne.

I love these people, and it terrifies me.

"Whatever you're feeling, Isadora," Marty says, "let yourself feel it."

My eyes well with fresh tears and I reach for his hand. "I'm feeling scared."

He smiles. "Good. That means you've found something that matters to you—something worth keeping." He shifts his position in his bed and levels his gaze with mine. "It's not the steps that made you happier, Isadora. It's the people you did them with. You found the ones worth spending time with. Don't push them away now without giving them a chance to stick."

My gaze falls to my small hand wrapped up in his larger, more fragile one. "But what if I get hurt?"

He squeezes my hand gently. "You might."

"What if I let people down?"

"You might."

I take in a big breath, in hopes of preparing myself to be strong enough to say the next words.

"What if I fall in love?"

He gently smiles. "You might."

I'm moved to tears at his kindness and grace. I try to gather myself. "Aren't you mad at me?"

"For what?"

"Not being here," I say.

"I'm too old to hold grudges." He pats my hand. "And so are you. You're also too smart to assume you know how something is going to turn out just because of how things have gone in the past."

I frown. "I don't understand."

"Yes, you do," he says. "You saw that ex-boyfriend of yours. It sent you in a tailspin."

"I don't know about any tailspin. I—"

"Don't sugarcoat it. Face it for what it is. Your memory has a way of tricking you into thinking things aren't so bad, or that pain and hurt are okay. They're not. He was a jerk, and you let him have it."

I take a stark look at how I acted. Marty's right.

"And then you decided that because of the way this clown treated you, the professor was going to treat you the same. Which, for some unknown reason, made you think you had to push everyone away. Everyone who cares about you. It was selfish, even for someone with your IQ."

I don't respond. I know he's right.

"And shortsighted."

I lower my head. But then I raise it again. "I told him off."

Marty smiles. "I heard."

"I stood up for myself and let him know how I feel. Exactly how I feel."

"I know," Marty says. "Cal was impressed."

"He was?"

Marty starts to chuckle, straining into a cough. I move to help him somehow, but he waves me off.

"Laughing is good, believe me. It lets me know I'm still alive."

I hand him a small cup of water that is on a nearby rolling tray, and he continues. "You can't see the future any better than a psychic at a carnival. Give people a chance to do the right thing. You're standing in your own way."

I know he's right. I came to this conclusion on my own only a few hours before.

Still, hearing another person say it out loud hits a little differently.

"Do you want to play Scrabble?" he asks.

"Do you want to lose at Scrabble?" I snark back.

"Oh, take advantage of an old man right after he has a heart attack, why don't you?" he says with a returning twinkle in his eye.

And just like that, my relationship with Marty is restored. He beats me once (luck, of course) and I beat him twice before Miriam returns. She thanks me for coming and sends me home so Marty can get some rest.

It's been an emotional day. Self-discovery, realization, being humbled, and frankly, I'm beat. But my brain, ever the traitor, keeps me awake as I imagine returning to work. I wonder how Cal will be around me.

I wonder how I will be around him.

Marty said Cal was impressed . . . so I've got a fighting chance.

As my head sinks into the pillow, I have one final thought.

I've been such *a fool.*

Chapter 41

The next morning, it's me knocking on Darby's door early, and not the other way around. I stand in the hallway nervously bouncing like a newly potty-trained toddler who has to pee.

I've treated my friends badly. I owe apologies all around.

Will she forgive me?

She pulls open the door and frowns at me.

I meet her eyes and then sheepishly say, "Yoga?"

She lifts one eyebrow. "Does this mean you've finally come to your senses?"

I nod. "I'm sorry."

Her demeanor immediately changes. "Let me get my stuff!" She leaves the door open and calls out, "Dante, I'm going to yoga. You've got the kids!"

There's a crash of what sounds like plates, followed by a kid crying.

And just like that, I'm forgiven.

Delilah appears in the living room, a stoic expression on her face.

"Hey," I say.

"Hey."

"I stopped acting like a baby," I tell her.

She watches me for so long I wonder if she heard me. And then she runs toward me and wraps her arms around my waist in a giant hug. She squeezes me so hard I think she might snap me in two.

I hug her back, as best I can in this awkward position, which just means that I wrap my arms around the top of her head. "I'm sorry I flaked on you, Delilah."

She looks up at me, her little porcelain face poking through my sleeves. "It's okay. Everyone gets scared sometimes." She pulls from my grasp. "Wanna watch *Doctor Who* tonight? We left off on the Christmas special. I'll bring you Dad's stuffed shells."

And once again, I'm forgiven. As if it never happened. Slate wiped clean.

The way it feels is unexplainable. First Marty, then Darby, now Delilah. All demonstrating to me the power of forgiveness and grace. I simply don't deserve it.

"Delilah," I say. "How'd you stop being mad at me so easily?"

"That is an excellent question." If she'd been wearing glasses, she would've pushed them from the tip of her nose.

"I wanted to be mad at you forever," she says. "But Mom said that only hurts me. She said if I hold a grudge, I'll get bitter, and bitterness makes our bones brittle. And I don't want my bones breaking inside my skin."

"She said that?"

Darby returns to the living room, dressed and ready for yoga. "Yes, I did. Now scoot, Delilah. Help Dad with the littles."

Delilah points at me. "So is it a date tonight?"

I point back. "Sure thing."

As we turn to leave, I hear her shout from inside the apartment, "Don't flake on me again!"

Darby shrugs. "You heard the girl."

"I won't," I call back. "I promise."

We head outside, into the warm air and we both inhale.

"It's a beautiful day," we say in unison, just as someone passes us, seemingly in a hurry. He looks at us like we're nuts—which we kind of are—and we look at each other and smile. It's as if we have our own secret language, and I can't help but smile at the realization. Darby links her arm through mine, and we start on the familiar trek toward Flow.

I'm quiet on our way. I think through the last few days, I think about Marty, and I imagine what it's going to be like seeing Cal at work later when I finally return. And because of my new friends, I'm thinking about one of the steps I haven't done—step twenty-one: "Let go of grudges."

"Do you think you can teach me how you taught Delilah—the letting go of grudges / brittle bones thing?"

Darby tilts her head, and I can feel her quizzical look without even seeing her face.

"I think maybe I've been holding on to mine."

"You think?"

Sarcasm.

"Isadora, it's not like there's some magic pill you can take to make all the junk in your life disappear. It's a process. And a choice."

"A choice."

"Yes. It's not always easy, but yes. You have a choice to forgive the people who've hurt you. Even Alex. Even your mother."

Darby knew very little about my family, but she's so insightful, she knows that my mother could be a Roald Dahl villain. I don't have kids of my own, but even I know that her version of parenting didn't do me any favors.

"The thing about parenting is, we aren't all naturally good at it," Darby is saying when I tune back in. "We do the best we can, but we literally have no idea what we're doing. And it's possible there are things your mom was working through that spilled over onto you."

In so many ways, I've painted my mother as the enemy. Maybe I've given her too much power.

"Besides," Darby says, "you don't forgive people for their benefit. You do it for yours. Because if you don't, it'll eat you alive. Jealousy, envy, holding a grudge—they rot you from the inside out."

I think about my mother, about Alex, about everyone who's bullied me throughout my life. "How do I simply let it all go?" I stop and look at Darby. "How?"

She stops with me and smiles. "One at a time. And remember, it's not going to be easy."

I think on this, and we continue walking. We've almost reached Flow when Darby stops in her tracks. So I stop. "What's wrong?" I ask.

"What about Cal?"

I look away. "Uh . . . what about Cal?"

"Are you going to call him? See him? Leap into his arms?"

"Darby."

"At least admit that you acted rashly and he didn't deserve to be the target of your emotional constipation."

I grimace at the colorful yet accurate depiction. "This really isn't about Cal."

"No, it's not," she says. "It's about you."

I start toward the door, but Darby stops me.

"You have to talk to him. You owe it to him. Just hear him out, Isadora," she says. "You can't assume you already know how everything is going to go."

"I have a pretty good idea," I say.

She inhales, and I can see frustration on her face. "You're not being fair."

I think about the time I've spent with Cal—how quickly I fell for him, as if someone shoved me out of an airplane without a parachute. Seeing Alex again served as a wake-up call from the universe. Forgetting all that pain wasn't going to do me any good. And I'd forgotten. Because of Cal, I'd forgotten.

And that was foolish.

"Isadora?"

"I know in my head that Cal is a good guy. He's nothing like Alex. I don't think he set out to stab me in the back," I say.

"But . . . ?"

"But I don't want to give someone that power. No one. It doesn't matter if he won't mean to do it; I just can't be put in that position again," I say.

"Oh, Isadora."

Rather than causing me to crumble, her maternal tone enables me to steel myself against the emotions I'm feeling. "Cal and I are better as friends and colleagues, and that's all."

"Except that's not all," Darby says. "You can't stay closed off forever. You can share your heart one piece at a time."

"But I didn't," I say. "I shared it all. And I did it so easily. And that's dangerous for me, Darby. People hurt you. They don't protect you, and they never put you first."

"I'm sorry that's been your truth for so long. But, Isadora"—she puts a hand on my arm—"that's just not true. Not when you find the right people." She squeezes me. "We are the right people. *He* is the right people."

Tears gather in my eyes and I blink them away. "You can't possibly know that."

"Don't throw away something that could be amazing just because you're scared," Darby says. "Nobody ever got anywhere in life by avoiding the things that scared them."

I wince at the hard truth. Then I look up at the entrance

to Flow. "You're right. If that were the case, no one would do yoga."

Darby shakes her head at me and pulls open the door to the yoga studio. "Just remember, Izzy, loneliness isn't good for anyone."

Chapter 42

I'm sitting in my office later that day when I realize I have no one to eat lunch with.

Marty is still in the hospital, and while I have plans to go see him after work, the bench will be horribly empty—a reminder of what I almost lost.

I can't fault him for having a heart attack, but I am looking for someone to blame.

Shellie peeks her head in just before noon and smiles at me. "You're back."

I half smile back at her, careful not to encourage her to come in and sit down. She does both of these things anyway.

"The lab can't stop talking about you," she says as if we're friends now.

I groan.

"No, not in a bad way." She looks out the door, as if to check to see whether anyone is listening. "It's just that you're the first person who's ever really stood up for herself," she practically whispers. "But not the first one who should've."

I look up. And for the first time, truly, I see her. She's striking, hidden behind those glasses.

"Last year," she goes on, "I spent hours working on a paper for Professor Maudlin—do you know him?"

"Mathematician?"

"Yes."

"Ear hair?"

She grimaces. "Yes."

"Please don't tell me you were romantically involved with him," I say.

Her eyes go wide. "No, nothing like that." Then, after a pause, she says, "Wait, were you and Dr. McEnroe . . . ?"

I answer only in silence.

"Oh, I missed that part," she says almost to herself. Then something seems to click. "Oh! Oh, I get it now. Maybe that's why Dr. Baxter punched him in the face."

Now my eyes go wide. "He did *what*?"

She leans in, like she can't wait to spill the tea. "You didn't hear?"

"I haven't talked to Cal," I say, wondering how much I actually missed.

"After you left, Dr. McEnroe walked out of your office, and Dr. Baxter was standing there. They got into it, and Dr. Baxter punched him in the face."

"Cal?" I can't even imagine a scenario in which mild-mannered Cal Baxter would punch anyone.

"Dr. McEnroe fell down, Isadora!" She's practically swooning now. "Dr. Baxter defended your honor!"

"I never asked him to hit anybody!"

"But it's kind of hot, right?"

"Yes," I say, but quickly add, "I mean *no*!" I don't know what to make of it. It doesn't make sense. Cal is the least violent person I know, plus he has a good twenty pounds of muscle on Alex, who is the definition of "scrawny."

"Anyway," Shellie says, clearly not realizing my head is spinning.

"I worked for Dr. Maudlin before moving over here. He gave me hours of research on his project—and let's just say, math is boring."

"That's a fact," I say. "But at least it makes sense." Unlike *feelings* and *emotions*, or *men*, apparently.

"Long story short, when the paper was published, I wasn't even a footnote. Not even a thank-you. Nobody knows how much I contributed to that study."

"You're kidding me." I shake my head in disbelief at the similarity. "And you never said anything?"

"Not a word." She sighs. "I should have."

"Don't blame yourself, Shellie," I say. "We're all learning."

I am learning. I remind myself to be gentle with myself. I might even find a way to be proud of how far I've come. Maybe.

"Anyway, after I heard what you said to Dr. McEnroe, I decided I'm not going to let anyone take advantage of me anymore," Shellie says. "It was inspiring."

I didn't mean for it to be. I simply did what I should've done from the start—occupied my space. How could I ever expect anyone else to value my work if I didn't even value it?

"I'm glad, Shellie," I say. And I mean it.

She smiles. "And to think, this whole time, I didn't even like you. Now you're like my hero."

My forehead pulls at the insult disguised as a compliment, but I choose not to say anything else. How can I, when all I seem to be able to think about is the fact that Cal punched Alex in the face?

Because of *me.*

At lunch, I sit on the bench in honor of Marty and eat my sandwich in silence. The campus is quieter now, with the kids home for summer break. For us, our positions are year-round. We're not ones to get summer breaks, or any breaks for that matter. But we are the minority. There are very few people walking around, which is maybe why I instantly notice Cal the second he steps into the courtyard.

He fixes his gaze on me, and I look down, gathering mental strength. I've played this moment out a million times in my head, but now that it's mere moments away, I need time to prepare myself for the conversation we're about to have.

I've never broken up with someone before.

I've never really been in a position to do that.

He sits next to me but doesn't speak.

I set my sandwich in the wrapper on my lap and press my lips together. My fingers are tingling—this time because I know how his soft beard feels against my skin.

And because a part of me wants to feel it again.

No matter what's best for my heart, I can't deny that I'll miss him.

I already *do* miss him.

"You're back," he says.

"I am."

"You got my texts?"

"Yes."

"You didn't respond."

Neither of us is looking at each other. I feel as though we're both steeling ourselves for what comes next.

"Sorry. I've been trying to sort through some *feelings* stuff."

He hesitates. "Did you get it all sorted?"

I swallow. My throat is dry. "I think I did."

"And?"

I consider. How do I say this? I want us to be friends. Surely he'll understand. "And I think I need some space. Time to myself."

He hesitates before responding again. I can't read him. I'm the worst person in the world.

"Forgive me," he says gently, "but you've had thirty years to yourself." He reminds me that already I've shared too much.

"I'm better off that way," I say. "I'm not good for you, Cal. Not really. We both know it."

He turns to me. "Look at me."

I don't want to. I don't want to see his face. I know it'll unravel every part of me.

"Isadora."

Ridiculously, I face him with my eyes closed, and it's a full five-count before I crack one open. Then, finally, I see him. There's hurt behind his eyes—hurt that I'm causing. The thought of it twists inside me.

He takes a breath, looking as though he's deciding how to proceed. "I'm not like Alex," he says. "This was never about my book for me. I'm not using you."

"I know," I say quietly. And I appreciate he's speaking my language. Forward, clear, to the point.

"Do you?"

"Yes."

"I don't believe you," he says. "I think you're afraid that I'm going to hurt you just like Alex did."

I look into his eyes. "Why didn't you tell me he was the one who told you about me? Why didn't you say you were friends?"

"Because he wasn't the one who told me about you," Cal says simply.

"He wasn't?"

"No, Dr. Miranda Barnett recommended you. She said you were the best."

My mind drifts back to the first day of my experiment. Me, smiling in the bathroom mirror only to discover professional, put-together Dr. Barnett standing there watching me. I assumed she thought I was a possible psychopath after what she witnessed . . . but she thought I was the best?

How many other incorrect assumptions had I made, seeing the world through my jaded lens?

Cal is still watching me. "I think somewhere in that big brain of yours you've somehow missed the most important part of all of this."

"What's that?"

"That I really care about you. That we're good together. That we have a shot at something real—something good."

"I don't deny that there's something special between us, Cal," I say. "I think that's part of the problem. I know better than to let myself get caught up in all of this. I am living proof that there are no happy endings in real life."

He tilts his head ever so slightly. "You haven't seen the end yet, Isadora."

Yes, I have. Whether it's ending up sitting alone at a lunch table at a school, or a desk at work, or a bench in the park, the end is always the same.

He tries again. "I know you wanted to prove Dr. Grace Monroe wrong. I know that's how this began." His eyes search mine. "But that's not how this is going to end."

I look down at my feet.

"Consider it holistically. Are you willing to admit that some of these things actually worked? You fought so hard against being happy, and when you started to be, you sabotaged your own experiment. You corrupted the data. Because the outcome you told yourself you needed wasn't the one you were getting."

"You're wrong," I react. "I'm not sabotaging myself by drawing conclusions."

"This is an *unfounded* conclusion. You haven't even collected all the data. You're quitting before the end—that's scientifically irresponsible."

"Who says I'm quitting? I'm not quitting. I'm going to finish the thirty-one steps."

This stops him. He looks confused.

He should be. So am I.

"Really?"

"Yes. That was always the plan. I'll finish them out, catalog my findings, and move on."

He frowns. "Don't do this, Isadora. Please. Don't put that wall back up. It's taken so long for me to chip away at it, and the second Alex comes back, you're as closed off as you were the day we met."

I look away. I can't see him wrestle with this for another second. I'm terrified of how this is all making me feel. And even more terrified of how it's all making *him* feel. Worse, I know that everything he's saying is true.

I feel desperate. It's that panic of swimming out from shore so you can no longer feel the bottom under your feet.

My desperation defaults me to what I know.

"I can't let this happen to me again," I say, practically to myself. "I can't. I smiled at someone and then Marty smiled back, and then I let him in, and then I almost lost him."

Cal sighs. "Isadora, he's not gone."

"But he almost was!" I blurt. "I almost lost him!" I feel the next words come out of my mouth, and I cannot stop them. "And it will be the same with you!"

His face falters, and he almost looks wounded. "You don't believe that."

He's right. I don't. I'm not even sure why I'm still acting this way or why I've made this choice to push him out of my life. All I know is that I can't let myself get hurt again.

I dig in. It's too late now, anyway. "We were just working on a project together, Cal. That's it. And that's how it needs to be, now that we're finished with it."

"I refuse to believe that." He stands, hurt and angry. "That's not all this is for me, Isadora. Dr. Monroe's steps made me happier—because I got to do them with you." He turns to walk away, then comes back. "And I don't understand why it's so hard for you to believe that I like you. I want to be with you. I'm not going to hurt you."

I don't look up.

I can't.

And after several moments, I hear his shoulders slump and his hands fall to his sides.

And just like that . . . Cal walks away.

Chapter 43

I wake up the following morning to the sound of pounding on my door.

Darby.

I can tell because she's treating the door to my apartment as if it's the door to her kids' bathroom and water is seeping out under it. She is pounding because we have yoga, and also because she knows I'm not out of bed.

This is one of the downsides to having friends.

I pick up my phone and look at the time, aware there is no message from Cal. I suppose I got used to starting my day with a text from him.

I note the disappointment in my chest, brush it aside, and text Darby:

Stop banging on my door, you lunatic.

No signs of life. Had to make sure you weren't trapped under something heavy.

I'm awake.

Great. Let's go.

Can't. Going to skip today. Go without me. Say hi to Meg and Stacy.

Seconds later, I hear the unmistakable sound of my lock being picked. I whip the covers off and vault out of the bed, but Delilah has perfected her craft, and she pushes it open before I get there.

I love that girl.

But not right now.

"Aha!" she says. "I did it!"

"Wonderful, dear," Darby says. "Now go look after the kids."

Delilah looks at me. "You look—"

"Ah!" Darby zips the insult shut before Delilah can get it out. But as soon as her daughter is gone, she finishes it for her. "You look like you got run over by a truck."

"Well then, I suppose I look better than I feel."

Darby only stares.

I recoil a bit. "What? What do you want? I told you I'm not going today."

She keeps staring.

"Darby, you're freaking me out," I say. "*What?*"

"Why are you doing this, Isadora?"

I frown. "I don't know what you're talking about."

I try to go into the kitchen and behind the counter to put some space between us, but she follows me.

"Will you leave me alone?" I plead.

"No," she says. "I'm not going to."

I fold my arms across my chest. "Well, I'm sorry I can't go to yoga."

"Don't change the subject."

"I'm . . . tired," I say, traipsing back to my bedroom. I flop down stomach-first on my bed and pull the covers up over my head.

I lie there for a good ten seconds and pull the covers back only to see that Darby is standing ten inches from my face.

"You know there's nothing wrong with you, right?"

I whip the covers back over my head. "I know, Darby. I'm just tired."

"Isadora. Listen to me." She sits and pulls the blanket off to reveal me actually pouting, arms folded, not looking at her, just as I've seen her children do multiple times.

Great. I've been downgraded from "friend" to "fifth child." Not my proudest moment.

But ever-patient Darby simply waits.

I move my eyes—just my eyes—over to look at her.

"There's nothing wrong with you," she repeats.

"Yes, there is."

"No, Isadora, there's not."

I get suddenly defensive. "Yes, there is! I'm . . ."

"You're what?"

This time, I can't pretend I don't know how I feel. I can't pretend that everything is fine, and in this moment, I shout out exactly how I feel.

"I'm *broken*!" I say, fighting the emotions that are welling up. "Everything about me is screwed up! People smile and feel happy. I smile and I feel naked. People talk and become friends and fall in love, and I talk, and people leave, and I push them away!"

I slam the back of my head onto the pillow in tearful frustration. "There's a huge gap between the things I want and the things I actually do."

"Isadora."

I look at Darby, eyes full of tears, emotionally reaching out of the deep end for a hand.

"What is it that you want? That you *really* want?"

I know exactly what I want, but I look away. I don't have to tell her because I know it's obvious.

I want to belong to someone. I want to be safe. I want to be lifted up. I want to have a spot, I want to share unspoken secrets with a look, and I want the wind to make me soar.

I want Cal.

She places a hand on my shoulder. "You're not a project to be worked on, or an experiment to be conducted. The things you've felt in the past—it is all okay. Honor those feelings. They've brought you here. This is your life, Isadora. And if you love him . . ."

I shoot her a look.

". . . if you *love* him, then let yourself fall. You owe it to yourself to see where it goes."

She stands there for a few seconds, then leaves.

And I roll over and cry myself to sleep.

The next day, I decide to tackle step seventeen: "Create a self-care ritual."

While there are various ways to take care of oneself, I choose to give myself a pampering party. Partly because it's something I've never done, and partly because I want to know if I'm the type of person who enjoys having painted toenails and perfectly manicured fingernails.

Unfortunately, we'll never know, because in order to "perfectly" manicure, you have to have some level of skill.

It takes all of two minutes to conclude I do not possess this skill.

I'm sitting at my kitchen table with a bottle of baby-pink nail polish when it dawns on me that this isn't making me happy. I've globbed it on so thick and uneven, there's no choice but to use the polish remover and begin again.

After three do-overs, I finally give up and decide that taking a hot bath will be my self-care.

I start the bath, add the bubbles, and lower myself in to soak. I've brought a book I can't concentrate on and a crossword puzzle I don't want to do.

Within minutes, I am bored.

And the bubbles have gone away, and the water is getting cold.

Why do people take baths again?

I need a different step. Maybe self-care just isn't my thing.

I quickly jot down: *"Failed at self-care. Need a small team of experts and three months. Found no happiness here. Time to move on."*

I scan the list. There are still a few suggestions I can try, but I'm looking for an easy one. I need to check something off my list, make some progress, move this thing forward.

Nothing jumps out at me.

I know it's because I started this experiment with the intention of doing every step alone.

Even with that plan, I found myself practically adopted by a motley crew of new friends who let me sit at their table. I actually got used to tackling these steps with other people—people who gave no reason to join me except for the fun of it.

It was nice to be a part of something. Even if it was only for a little while.

I force myself to stop dwelling on this and turn my attention to step eighteen: "Plan a trip, even if you don't take it."

I've read in studies and surveys that 97 percent of people say they're happier when they have a trip planned. I wonder if this will have the same effect on me.

As I google vacation spots, Airbnb's, and flight info, my thoughts turn to Cal.

Where would he like to go?

Maybe a beach?

I imagine he'd also like to visit somewhere with some history, like Pennsylvania or Charleston.

This is foolish. I need to stop.

He won't be coming with me on this made-up trip I'm not actually taking.

Still, I click on "Romantic Getaways for Couples."

I create a wish list on Airbnb. I find a bungalow on a beach in St. John. I've never been to the beach, and I'm not a fan of flying, but the bungalow is pristine, calling my name. It's a one-bedroom cottage with stunning views of Coral Bay. The secluded deck is tiled and has a brightly colored outdoor sofa that looks like the perfect place to lounge or read or nap.

The colorful decor is offset with a mix of natural and white wood, stone and tile, making the space relaxing and energizing at the same time.

I want to be there.

But I don't want to be there alone.

I push that traitorous thought away and make a fake list of what I'll bring on this fake vacation, and begin to research things to do in St. John. Most of the activities (obviously) take place on the water, and I wonder if maybe I'd be better off finding a cabin in the mountains where I'm less likely to drown.

Or maybe this trip to St. John would be solely for relaxation. I'd stay in my beautiful bungalow or sit on the beach with a book. That would be all the activity I'd need.

I close my eyes and imagine for a moment.

I can feel the sand between my toes and look up from my imaginary book to consider the secret power of the waves softly crashing on the shore. There's a family struggling to get their umbrella to stand up in the wind that blows in. A few kids are off to my left, having a sandcastle competition—one has made a tower lined with shells he found on the beach. Cal comes back to his chair beside mine, wearing board shorts and an undone button-down shirt. He hands me a bottle of water and asks me if this is what I imagined for our first trip together. I smile, lean over, and . . .

What am I doing?

I'm never going to take this vacation. I'm certainly not going to take it with Cal. I've survived my solitary existence by choosing isolation, locked up in my safe spaces.

Even though this is just an exercise, the fact that I wouldn't have anyone to take with me hits me hard.

I push the laptop away from me, and I'm confronted by my own thoughts.

I have spent so much of my adult life on my own. On purpose. Then I find a friend who is way older than me. Then one who is way younger than me. Then a mom who is way different from me.

Then a guy who is darn near perfect for me.

And yet, somehow, here I am, practically back where I started. Tennyson's saying about it being better to have loved and lost than never to have loved at all is a load of horse manure.

It's not better. It sucks.

This feels so much lonelier than it did before.

Cal's smile. The way his face crinkles at the sides when he laughs . . . the way his eyes don't leave mine when he's listening to me tell a story or share a thought. The way he asks questions and pays attention—it makes me feel like I'm the only one in the room.

For the first time in my whole life, someone actually sees me.

And I sent him away. Of course I did.

I reach over and close my laptop with a sigh. It's like shutting the door on hope.

I can deny it all I want, but these 31 Ways have lost their luster.

I have no one to blame but myself.

Chapter 44

Later that night, I realize I might need a change of scenery—so I go for a walk.

I open my door and almost step on a package sitting on the floor in my hallway. I look around, as if the person who left it here is still lurking in the corridor, but, not surprisingly, no one is there.

I pick up the box and take it back inside, where I set it on my kitchen counter and stare at it, frowning.

I don't like surprises.

I'm 98 percent certain there is no ricin inside this box, but that doesn't keep me from poking it with a wooden spoon.

It's not ticking. A good sign.

I lean over and try smelling it, because in my warped mind I think I can detect trace chemicals. All I succeed in doing is half crawling up onto my counter sniffing a box like a psychopath.

Logically, I know the percentage of unknown academic researchers killed by mail bombs is low—but never zero.

There's no postage, so it didn't arrive in the mail. The simple brown kraft paper isn't giving anything away.

I make my move, bombs and toxins be damned.

I gingerly remove the wrapping and find a thin cardboard box, also unmarked. I pull off the lid and that's when I see a simple white envelope with my name written on it, and because I've been poring over his notes for months now, I know immediately it's Cal's handwriting.

This is his manuscript.

I open the card and read:

Isadora,

I thought you should have the first copy. It's off with my editor now, but I know I couldn't have made it this far without your insight. Thank you for making it better.

Thank you for making me better.

This one's ours.

Cal

Tears prick the corners of my eyes, and I quickly blink them away.

I set the card down and look at the title page.

ANTI-SOCIAL MEDIA

By Dr. Cal Baxter and Isadora Bentley

I stare at this for a long moment. Why is my name on the title page of his manuscript? That wasn't our deal. That wasn't his deal with the publisher. Why then . . . ?

There are multicolored sticky notes throughout the manuscript. I go to the first one and find he's highlighted a paragraph in the introduction:

"I should note: writing a book that requires an excessive amount of research is a huge undertaking, and one I would never want to tackle without the help of Chicago University academic researcher Isadora

Bentley. Truly, she deserves co-credit on this book, which is why you see her name on the cover. Without her insight, talent, and intelligence—not to mention her independent study supporting this project—this book would still be piles of scattered thoughts and half-written chapters."

I skim the words again to make sure I'm not hallucinating.

I'm fully crying, flooded with memories of days with Cal. The collision. The first conversation. The elevator. The park. The ride. The stoop.

All of them made me happy. *Happy.*

And that revelation takes my breath away.

Even working on this book with him brought me joy—a different kind of joy than any other project I've ever tackled.

I flip the pages to the next sticky note: *"Never would've gotten to this conclusion without you."*

The next one, a few pages later: *"This whole section is yours, verbatim."*

A third: *"You really nailed this point and made this sound so much better!"*

He's marked a trail of my fingerprints on a stack of papers that will eventually become a book.

And he's giving me the credit.

I know he doesn't have to. I know he could make my name a footnote or even one of many listed in the acknowledgments. Instead, he's put my name next to his. As if we are a team.

I flip to the next sticky note. There's an arrow to a highlighted paragraph, which reads:

"There is, however, evidence to point to the fact that a lack of technology in a person's life will not guarantee strong interpersonal relationships. In one case study, involving a woman we'll call Doreen, there was clear data that a person must be a willing participant in her relationships in order to reap the many benefits of the human connection."

I frown. What is he saying? Clearly he's drawing some sort of conclusion here—using his psychological expertise to sum up his thoughts on my half-completed experiment. Thoughts he hasn't shared with me yet.

I keep reading.

"Still, as we ultimately conclude based on Doreen's actions in the midst of her experiment, an unwillingness to connect can manifest in many forms, including a retreat into social media—or a retreat into oneself."

I reread the paragraph and then continue, this time out loud. "'Ultimately, what these findings conclude is that *happiness*, like connecting with other humans, is a choice.'"

A choice?

Darby said the same thing. As if it were simple . . . or at least possible. As if I could wake up tomorrow and make a decision to be happy. Forget all the ways I've been hurt over the years, just snap my fingers or click my heels . . . but that's not how this works.

My experiment has proved that.

Right?

Or maybe not. While I considered changing my hypothesis, I never really embraced the belief that I might truly find happiness. I convinced myself that it was always just a little out of my reach, and the second I started to feel something—*anything*—I shut the door.

Why? Why did I do that?

I was afraid of getting hurt. I was afraid of getting my hopes up. I was afraid of believing that Cal saw me and still wanted me.

History has taught me many difficult lessons, and I don't know how to convince myself that any situation I ever find myself in could turn out differently.

Life has been one singular thing for me—disappointing. And that disappointment led to pain and heartache. How am I supposed to forget all that?

How could anyone forget?

I pick up my notebook and leaf through the pages of data I've collected. I've written about the way each step has made me feel. And they all have made me feel something. Not always happiness, but *something.*

Which is more than I can say for the life I was living before.

My gaze lands on the steps I have left to complete, and it's as if some magnetic force pulls my attention to the one that has nagged at me the most.

Step thirty-one: "Confront what is making you unhappy in the first place."

I scoff. I read it again, and I scoff again, louder, right at the words. I toss the notebook down.

What's making me unhappy? How about a whole string of things: The cruelty of other people. Being used. An overbearing mother. A manipulative boyfriend.

"Being overlooked, maybe? What about being forgotten? Take your pick, you stupid list." I talk as if it's going to respond.

Saying those things out loud makes me sound really pathetic. And my inner monologue is strangely silent right now.

"Nothing to add, Sir Attenborough?"

I think back to Cal's words, written out for the world to read. Words about me, about my experiment, about my *unwillingness* to let myself be happy. I get a little belligerent.

"That implies the fault is all my own," I say out loud. "That it has nothing to do with my childhood or all the people who have crushed me over the years."

I pick up Cal's manuscript and talk right to it.

"But that's wrong—*you're wrong*!" I slam it down in frustration, scattering the pages.

If it's not wrong, that means something could've been done about it before now.

And nothing was.

This is just the way it is.

"This is just the way I am, *Cal*," I say to the empty room.

I look at the manuscript, pages now askew, and see all the sticky notes sticking out of the sides. In a flash, I feel guilty and straighten it back together.

I look over at the notebook and pick it up. I run my hand over words that were definitely written in happier times.

In an honest moment, I think that maybe Cal was right. He said that I was sabotaging my own experiment, and that a piece of me never wanted Dr. Grace Monroe to be wrong. That secretly, I started this experiment because a part of me wanted her to be right.

The implication that part of me was trying to sleuth out my own unhappiness so I could course-correct before it was too late nags at me.

My heart rate quickens, and I react without thinking. I angrily crumple the notebook in my hands, shouting into the empty apartment, *"Why am I like this?!"* I pick up the notebook and throw it against the wall, knocking a framed mirror down in the process. It doesn't shatter, but when it lands, I see my own reflection staring back at me.

It's an unwanted answer to an intrusive question I've never dared to ask before.

I don't like it. I stare at myself in the cockeyed mirror and dare it to respond. I don't believe for a single second that this was my choice.

That's a lie.

It's not my choice. Things were done *to* me. I'm *reacting*. This is the *way I am*.

Also lies.

How many times have I justified being alone? How many times have I declared that I work *alone*—I'm better off *alone*?

I know without a doubt that I put myself here on purpose. I

claimed at the beginning of this experiment that this was the life I've designed.

My choice.

I am afraid to feel anything for fear of feeling everything.

But I understand now what Marty has tried to tell me so many times. If I'm not willing to feel the pain of life, how can I ever expect to feel the joy?

The revelation lingers, hanging over me. My instinct is to kick it away like an insect trying to land on my shoe.

But I don't. I sit with the thought. I'm so used to pushing my feelings aside so I can protect myself from any emotional attachment to anything or anyone.

And that has been my choice too.

I pick up my crumpled notebook off the floor and try to flatten it. I find the pages of the original article, paper-clipped to a page near the front. I scan through so many of the steps I've already tackled, and while some of them will never make me happy, I can't deny that some of them did.

And some of them I never quite figured out how to do. Like step twenty-one: "Let go of grudges," which is now glaring at me like a surly toddler.

I hate Dr. Grace Monroe. I don't want to admit that she might've been right with her fluffy article about finding happiness. It was printed in a tabloid magazine, for crying out loud.

Angry, I open the notebook and find a blank page. I rip it out and then tear off small strips of scratch paper. Then I pull out a pen.

"Fine, *Grace.*" I look at her picture at the top of the article. I figure that since I've worked through most of her list, we can be on a first-name basis.

I am going to list off grudges I'm holding on to. Grudges that I've practically sewn in my clothes, falsely protecting me from every shred of harm.

I think back—all the way back—to kindergarten and my mom's red-and-white polka-dotted skirt. It's the first on my list.

Mom—for putting me in that dumb polka-dotted skirt.
Mom—for not sticking up for me when my friends bullied me.
Dad—for never really caring that I existed.
Noah Johnson—for telling his friends he thought I was "a dog."
Mia—for stabbing me in the back.
Alex—

I stare at his name. If my eyes were guns, I would've shot holes through the *A.* I don't want to forgive Alex. He doesn't deserve it. None of them do. *None* of them.

They haven't said they're sorry—why should I forgive them?

"You don't forgive people for their benefit. You do it for yours. Because if you don't, it'll eat you alive."

Darby.

Alex might not be sorry, and he does not deserve my forgiveness. He does, in fact, deserve every evil thing I've wished would happen to him over the years, but it dawns on me that he probably sleeps fine.

He lives rent free in my mind and my heart, and he sleeps fine.

Alex—for using me, betraying me, and breaking my heart.

I stare at the words, and then I cross out "breaking my heart." Because what I know now is that he didn't actually break my heart—not really. Oh, it felt like a broken heart at the time, but what I had with Alex was never real.

Did he use me? Yes. Betray me? Absolutely.

But break my heart? No. That's giving him too much power.

I look over my list of grudges. There's one more I know I need to write down, but I'm afraid to face it.

And then I remember that Marty said I was brave, and I want to prove him right. So I write my own name.

Isadora

My hand trembles as I write honestly.

Isadora—for making me small. For not believing in my worth.
For standing in the way of my own happiness.

I'm not angry with myself for the time I've wasted on these things. After all, you're only responsible for what you know, right? But now that I know it, now that I see it—now, maybe I can change it.

I look over at my never-used fireplace. When Darby was redecorating my apartment, she gave me a lesson on using it.

"*A fire would make such a nice addition to one of your dates with Cal,*" Darby told me at the time. "*Very romantic.*"

She positioned a bundle of logs next to it and stuck a starter log inside, which apparently makes lighting the fire very simple.

I find a lighter in the junk drawer, open the chain mail fireplace grate, and light the paper wrapped around the starter log. A few minutes later, I add two logs to the flaming bundle and it slowly catches and grows.

Then, one by one, I burn my grudges.

I watch as all the hurts I've clung to over the years crinkle and catch at the edges—orange then black—and then curl up and disappear. I make a point not to look away. I make a point to sit with my feelings, to acknowledge them. They have a place here, and they deserve to be felt, to be honored. I've failed to do that in the past.

Once the scraps of paper have all disintegrated, I throw in the last one, and out loud I say, "I forgive myself."

The paper lands on the top log, catches, and is soon eaten up by orange flames.

Gone.

I smell smoke.

It's all of my hurts, the things I've been carrying with me, finally burned away.

No, that's not it. I realize the room has grown hazy. I cough. Smoke is pouring out of my fireplace now, and I have no idea why.

I start to panic. Do I throw a bucket of water on it?

I should know this. I'm a highly intelligent person without a single grudge to my name, and yet my apartment is filling with smoke. I rush out into the hallway and pound on Darby's door, but there's no answer.

Smoke pours out into the hallway, and the fire alarm starts screaming, lights flashing up and down the hall and loud beeps sounding throughout the building.

My neighbors rush out, looking around, seeing the smoke. Confused, they move down the stairs toward the exit as I get on the phone and call 9–1–1.

"Did you start a fire?" my upstairs neighbor calls out.

I shrug as a man shoos me down the stairs. "We should get outside."

I stand on the street, sirens blaring in the distance.

Leave it to me to have an emotional breakthrough that burns down my building.

Chapter 45

I'm standing on the street with many of my neighbors—some I recognize and most I don't—watching smoke pour out of my windows overhead. I'm mildly aware that some of the people around me are grumbling, saying things like, "Who was stupid enough to start a fire in their own apartment? In the summer?" But all of this wafts right over me.

I should feel embarrassed, scared, guilty, but I feel none of these things.

I feel . . . good.

I don't feel good about our having to wait for firefighters to give us the all clear to return to our apartments. I don't feel good about the fact that I'm fairly certain I inhaled more smoke than the CDC recommends.

But I can't deny that a weight has been lifted from my shoulders—a burden I've been carrying, I now realize, for most of my life.

Instead of finding ways to lighten my load, I kept piling onto what was already there, and frankly, it had all gotten too heavy for me.

Now, standing here in the warmth of the summer evening,

listening to my neighbors grumble and watching smoke pour from our building, I feel light. I no longer feel a burden. I feel shockingly relaxed. Like the day I graduated college, and the rigors and responsibilities of studying, learning, working were no longer mine to carry. Up there, on the third floor, mingling with smoke that may or may not ruin every single thing in my apartment, is the pain of my past—finally sent away to its rightful place.

We all watch as the fire truck arrives. Two men hop out, and one of them shouts out, "Do we know where the fire originated?"

I step forward, prepared to own up, but before I do, a man who lives down the hall points an accusatory finger at me. "It was *her* fault!"

He is clearly unhappy to be standing outside in his boxer shorts.

I give the firemen my apartment number and watch as they disappear inside the building.

Darby and her kids appear at my side. "What's going on?"

"She's trying to kill us all!" Boxer Shorts hollers.

"I tried to start a fire," I say.

"What do you mean?" I can see concern on Darby's face.

"In the fireplace, Darby. I'm not an arsonist."

Her frown lines deepen. "Did you open the damper?"

"What's the damper?"

She groans. "Isadora, were you listening to my instructions when I explained how to use the fireplace?"

I feel my face respond for me. "No."

"It's okay. I'm sure they'll figure it out. It's going to smell like smoke for a while, and people might have to get their apartments fumigated, but it's not like the building is going to burn down."

The firefighters emerge from the front door, and they seem to be slightly amused by the whole scene. One of them walks up to me. "Miss, are you familiar with a damper?" he asks. "There's a lever to push that swings it open . . . and it needs to be open if you're going to start a fire."

"I'm really sorry," I tell him. "I think I understand it now."

He turns to the small crowd of my neighbors. "It's safe to go back in! You all might want to open windows for a while!" There are general groans from the group.

I nod at him, still caught up in my own world.

As we walk back inside, Darby turns to me. "What were you doing starting a fire in the middle of June anyway?"

I smile to myself, then at her. "I was letting go of my grudges."

"Next time could you find a way to do that without nearly killing us all?"

When I wake up the next morning, I'm notably lighter. I'm certain if I got on the scale, it would blow confetti into the air and commend me for losing the weight that's been holding me hostage.

Marty is coming home from the hospital, and I want to be there when he does. I want to tell him I put fresh flowers on Shirley's grave and almost set my apartment on fire. I want to share about my epiphany because I know he'll be proud of this emotional breakthrough.

I'm not going to turn into a person whose motto is "Let go and let God!" I'm not looking to completely overhaul my personality here. I just want to let myself enjoy things along the way.

Darby and I pack up a big meal, courtesy of Dante, and bring it over to Marty's house.

It's small and quaint with a neatly manicured yard and perfectly trimmed shrubs. There are pots of flowers on the porch and the red mailbox pops against the white siding. I imagine

Miriam had something to do with the happy little touches and wonder if she's trying to keep the place the way her mother did.

We knock, but Darby doesn't wait for an answer. She pushes the door open, and we walk inside. "Hello?" she calls out.

I've never been to Marty's house, but the second I step through the door, I'm struck by a wealth that could never be quantified or calculated.

Family photos cover the walls of the small hallway, and through the door, I can see a lived-in, well-loved living room, with a sofa and two chairs purposefully arranged for conversation—not for TV viewing.

In fact, I don't even see a television.

The fragrant smell of lilacs fills the air, and I remember the bushes we saw growing on the side of the house. Their aroma must be wafting through open windows, filling the space with their perfume. One last hurrah before they retreat until next year.

"Oh my word, this place is *adorable*," Darby says. Then she calls out, "Marty! Are you here?"

"In the kitchen!" His voice isn't booming or energetic, but if he's up and about, I assume that's a good sign.

We make our way through the living room, in the direction of his voice, and when we reach the kitchen, Darby stops. Marty and Cal are sitting at the table, two empty plates in front of them.

My eyes connect with Cal's, and for a brief moment, I sense the electricity connecting us.

A zinger. Uh-oh. It's still there.

"Marty, you're looking so good." I smile, forcing myself not to be drawn in by Cal's big blue eyes, which are a lighthouse to my ship in a storm.

"Cal brought lunch," Marty says.

"Perfect! Then we brought dinner." Darby holds up the bag. "Don't worry, I didn't cook it—it's all from Dante."

Cal smiles, but I can see the normal light in his eyes is a bit dimmer.

"What's in your bag, Isadora?" Marty nods to the tote I'm carrying, and I'm almost embarrassed to say.

"A self-care ritual?"

"Are you asking me?" Marty asks with a smile.

"No, that's what it is. It's step seventeen: 'Create a self-care ritual.'"

"Ooh. What kind of self-care are we doing? Nail polish? A box of wine?"

Darby laughs and takes Marty's arm. "I'm so glad you're here," she says, squeezing him.

"Me too," he says sweetly.

"There's a mix," I say. "I brought coloring pages and a foot soak and a few other things. I tried this step on my own last night, but it, ah . . . didn't take . . ." My voice trails off, mostly because I feel self-conscious talking about the steps in front of Cal. He was supposed to do this step with me. He had a whole pampering plan, which is, in retrospect, possibly why I botched my solo attempt so horribly.

"We're also tackling step nineteen: 'Spend time with friends.'" Darby flashes a knowing smile at the two men, and for a moment I wonder if she's set me up.

I look at Marty, whose eyes hold an unmistakable twinkle.

Or maybe *they've* set *us* up.

I'm not going to lie, I want Cal here. I want to do these two new steps with him. It hasn't been the same without him, and frankly, I've missed him.

But knowing that in order for us to move forward, I have to have a genuinely honest conversation about *feelings* has me inwardly panicked.

For a flicker of a moment, I consider Darby's advice and

wonder, *What if I let myself fall?* This thought is followed up by, *What if falling is the thing that finally makes me happy?*

That thought is quickly shut down by an onslaught of concerns, coming at me in quick succession like bullets from a machine gun: *Isn't falling scary? What if he hurts me? What if he realizes I'm not what he wants? What if . . . ?*

It's in this moment that I realize changing the way I think isn't going to be a one and done. It's something I'm going to have to intentionally make myself do.

It's a choice. I choose.

"I think you missed a step," Cal says, and I'm grateful to him for pulling me back to reality.

"What? I did? Which one?"

"Eighteen, right? Isn't that 'Plan a trip, even if you don't take it'?" Cal is waiting for a response as I'm silently wrestling with what has turned out to be a less straightforward revelation than I originally thought.

"Oh. Right." I laugh lamely. "I did that one on my own last night. Not worth reliving."

He raises an eyebrow. Great, now his interest is piqued.

"Really. It wasn't that big of a deal."

I pull a variety of supplies from my tote, changing the subject. "So who wants a coloring page?"

Darby pipes in. "Are you not even going to talk about the fire you set in our building?"

The other two pause for a split second, look at each other, then look at me, then overlap their concerned replies: "A fire? What happened?" and "Why start a fire in June?" and "Are you okay?"

I set the colored pencils on the table and look up to see they're all watching me. Even Marty, who is as intrigued as Cal—and Darby, whose expression can only be described as smug.

"Guys. I really don't think it's worth rehashing at this point," I say.

"Oh. It's worth it, believe me." Darby waves her arms as if to indicate the floor is hers. "We took the kids to the restaurant last night, and we're walking home—it's late, the twins *need* to get to bed, and we come around the corner, and there's a fire truck outside our apartment building and a crowd of our neighbors gathered in the street."

Cal snaps his head and looks at me. "What?"

I shrug.

"Danielson was standing outside in his underwear," Darby continues, like a town gossip talking about the mayor's wife's affair. "Probably interrupted his nightly reruns of *Wheel of Fortune.* Everyone was pointing, wondering what the heck was going on."

"I'm fine, by the way," I say, hardly amused.

"Turns out, Isadora tried to start a fire"—Darby pauses and looks at me, setting up the kicker—"but she forgot to open the damper."

I sigh a big sigh, and for a split second, I feel like I'm about to be the butt of a joke. But then she squeezes my hand and says, "I did the same thing the first time I tried to start a fire. If Dante hadn't been there, the fire truck would've been." She smiles kindly at me. "I am now restricted to burning things in the kitchen." She laughs, and I realize something.

She's not laughing at me. She's not making fun of me.

None of them are.

"Those fireplaces can be tricky," Marty says. "But why did you start a fire in the summer?"

I try to deflect. "It . . . just . . . seemed like a good idea at the time."

They all look at me, and I know they're trying to put it all together. I'm not sure how to share this bit. It's embarrassing, revealing, even without the fire fiasco. I was carrying grudges that were nearly three decades old, and after watching them burn to purge them from my system, I came to the hardest grudge of all.

The thing that has been making me unhappy . . . is me.

How in the world do I say all that to other people?

I look at Marty, then Darby, then Cal, and I realize that these aren't just *other people.*

These are *my people.*

And they're safe.

If I want them to be my friends—or more—I have to open up and share about myself, something I've never really been willing to do before.

"I was burning my grudges," I finally say.

"Wait, that was for real?" Darby asks. "I thought you were being dramatic when you said that last night."

"No, the fire truck was dramatic enough." I slide into the fourth seat around the small kitchen table. "I finally confronted what was making me unhappy in the first place."

"Step thirty-one?" Cal asks.

"Step thirty-one."

"So how did that work? Did you write them out?" Cal asks, leaning forward in his chair with renewed interest in my project. With renewed interest in *me.*

"Yes. I wrote down all the people I hadn't forgiven, and specifically what I hadn't forgiven them for, all the way back to kindergarten," I say. "My mom made more than one appearance." I laugh lightly. "Anything I'd been holding on to. Any hurt that still hurt. And then I burned them, one by one."

"And?" Marty asks.

"And . . . what?" I say.

"How did it make you feel?" He says it like he's leading the witness, Your Honor.

I think on it for a moment, so as not to be flippant. "I feel different. Lighter. I never thought a symbolic gesture could make an actual difference. Honestly, it feels like I took off a giant backpack, like the ones legit hikers carry."

"*Not* the ones Eddie Bauer models carry," Cal says, barely smirking.

"Legit hikers." I look at him and smirk back. "I'd picked up a lot of garbage and stuffed it in my pack over the years. It was time to let it go."

Marty reaches across the table and covers my hand with his. "Good for you, Isadora."

I smile at him. "You could've just told me. Don't think I don't know you knew this all along."

"You don't live as long as I have without picking up a few grudges of your own," he says. "But letting them go—there's freedom in that."

"Yeah, I see that now," I say.

"And that's a lesson that needs to be learned through experience," he continues.

"Well," I say quietly, "thank you for sticking around long enough to help me figure it out." My eyes move from Marty, to Darby, and finally rest on Cal.

I wonder if he's going to stick around too.

"So! Self-care?" Darby offers brightly, shifting the mood.

Darby and Marty begin to sort through the coloring pages I printed off that morning, trying to pick the ones that would be the "easiest" and "most relaxing." I watch Cal take one, choose a few colored pencils, and begin on his.

He immediately starts shading, using the pencil to create shadows and depth.

He is an artist as well. Why am I not surprised?

As I choose my own and start remedially trying to stay in the lines, I glance up and find Cal smiling at me.

A smile—I can confidently say because I have grown to know his smiles—of approval.

I smile back, look down at my paper, look up, smile again, and continue working.

And with that small exchange, I know what I have to do.

I'm just scared to do it.

Chapter 46

We spent a few hours at Marty's. I needed it more than I knew—it truly was self-care.

I almost forget that I tried to push them all away.

Regret twists in my belly. I was such a fool.

I can't believe I almost traded them in for a lifetime of loneliness.

I have no idea if Cal will forgive me, but even if he doesn't, I know I still owe it to him to be honest. Really honest.

Maybe that's why I can feel the undercurrent of panic coursing through my veins as the evening winds down. As if my body knows what I can't say out loud.

I'm afraid.

Darby didn't sense this, because she left an hour ago after getting an SOS text from Dante—something about one of the twins biting the other one. "She's a biter, what can I say? I'd better get home before she draws blood."

"I'll come with you," I said.

She waved me off. "Don't be silly. Stay and help with dinner, then Cal can walk you home." A pointed look at Cal. "Right, Doc?"

"Absolutely," he said.

Which is how we got to where we are right now—packing up my things, making sure Marty has what he needs, and heading out the door.

Together.

Marty is resting in his recliner, and I wonder if all the self-care was too much. "You sure you're okay?" I ask. "We didn't overdo it, did we?"

He nods. "Better than okay. I'm happy as a box of birds." He reaches for me and pulls me closer, then whispers one word.

"Bravery."

I pull back, and he winks a secret wink at me. I nod as he squeezes my hand, sending me off with Cal, into a world of uncharted emotions.

Outside, the air is heavy, Chicago now thick in the throes of summer. Or maybe it's just my nerves that are making the air feel smothering.

We start down the sidewalk in the direction of my apartment, both of us quiet with so much still unspoken between us. I know I need to be the one to speak first, but I've had very little practice baring my soul.

"I got your book," I say.

I feel him look at me. "I actually wondered if that was how you started the fire."

I laugh lightly. "It's good."

"Yeah?"

"But you didn't have to put my name on it," I say. "Not on the cover. I didn't cowrite it—not really."

"Yeah, you did," he says. "Really." A pause. "Just like you co-wrote Alex's paper."

"No, I pretty much *wrote* Alex's paper." There is no amusement in my laugh.

He stops. "Why didn't you say anything?"

I look away. The humiliation of my own regret sidles up beside me. "I was stupid."

"No, Isadora," he says. "You were trusting."

"Which is basically the same thing."

He reaches out and takes my hand. "You just trusted the wrong person."

I meet his eyes, and I want to believe him. That ever-present voice calling out at the back of my mind—*He's just like everyone else! He's going to leave too!*—is strangely silent.

"You asked me once what my happiest memory is," I say.

"I remember."

"It's taken me a long time to figure out my answer." I mentally prepare myself to be as vulnerable as I've ever been. I take a deep breath and try to be brave.

"Most of my childhood was about getting through it. Most of my adult life too. I wasn't the girl with shiny, happy memories of good times with friends or family vacations or anything like that. I was a lonely kid, and it seemed like every time I put myself out there, I got burned."

"I'm sorry for that, Isadora," he says. "I want to change that for you."

"That's just it," I say. "What I realized is that *I* have to be the one to change it. Me. I mean, I can't change the past—unfortunately—but I can change the way I think about it. I can change how much attention I give it."

I look him full in the eyes. "Cal. Happiness is a choice."

He smiles. "Huh. I wrote that."

"I know! It was like the words leapt off the page and smacked me right in the face. And every time I thought about my happiest moments, trying to find a time that I genuinely felt joyful . . ." I swallow, and my throat is dry. "I kept coming back to you."

"Me?"

"You," I say. "I've never felt with anyone or any time or place in my life what I've felt when I've been with you."

His face breaks into a slow smile, like the sun peeking through clouds at dawn. "Really." It's more a statement than a question, as if to say, *"I expected this all along,"* but also *"I can't believe it."*

"I'm sorry I pushed you away when Alex came back," I say. "It was a lot to process. Too much. But none of that was about you—it was about me. It was about me realizing that I have the power to change my own life."

"Happiness is a choice."

I nod. "It's a choice."

"That's a big revelation."

"One that almost burned down my apartment."

He laughs, and we start walking again.

"Your book helped me get there," I say. "Your insights about my experiment. About me."

He takes my hand, and I let him. It's familiar. We walk in silence, covered by patterned splashes of light from the streetlamps overhead.

"What other revelations did you have?" he asks.

I draw in a breath. "That I don't want to beat myself up anymore. I did my best, but I'm ready to put it behind me." I pause. "And I also realized I don't want to be alone anymore." As I say the words, something inside me cracks open, and decades of emotion rise to the surface. I try to hide my face, looking away, looking anywhere but at Cal, but he's too intuitive to allow for that. An occupational hazard, I suppose.

He lets go of my hand and moves in front of me, taking my face in his hands. I look into his eyes, and I see the thing I've been afraid to see all along: he truly cares about me.

And maybe it won't work out—maybe we'll end up being

better off as friends. But one thing is certain . . . I don't want to predict that answer without a shred of physical evidence. I don't want to write the end of this story prematurely. Because this story . . . is my life.

And for the first time I can remember, I actually want to go out and live it.

It's as if there's this needling piece of excitement buried underneath my worry, and it seems to be saying, *"I can't wait to see what happens next."*

"You don't have to be alone anymore, Isadora," he says. "Not while I'm around." He brushes my hair away from my face and studies me for a long moment.

I don't try to hide or disguise the angst I'm feeling at allowing him to really see me. Instead, I look back, and I see a man with a deep care and compassion for the people in his life—the way he treated his family said as much. But it was more than that. When nobody else was looking my way, he was, and my prickliness didn't put him off. It was like a protective coating for him to peel away.

And when he uncovered who I am, he didn't run.

I was the one who pushed.

"I'd like to kiss you now," he says, an adorable smile inching across his face. "I say that so I don't startle you. I know you hate surprises."

I smile up at him. "Stop talking about it and just do it then."

He brushes his thumb across my cheek and leans down, and just as his lips are about to move over mine with purpose and warmth, I say, "Oh my gosh, this is going to be the best kiss ever."

Cal stops short. "Are you finished?"

My eyes are still shut. "Yes. Sorry. Please continue."

I stop talking. He draws me close so our bodies are flush against each other, and he brushes a kiss so softly over my lips, my breath catches. I've missed this. I've missed *him*. His kiss grows and I can almost feel his gratitude at having me back in his arms. This realization makes me squeeze my eyes shut even tighter, to keep the tears from escaping.

I focus on Cal. He smells like a pine forest I never want to leave. I inhale every bit of him and chastise myself for ever letting him go in the first place.

And I was right—it *is* the best kiss ever.

In the middle of this pristine moment, a thought hits me and I stop kissing him abruptly. I pull back with wild eyes.

"What is it?" he asks.

"Did you really punch Alex?"

His lips quirk. "I'm not a violent man, I promise."

"But you punched Alex," I say.

Cal shrugs. "I'd do it again too. He didn't deserve to get away with treating you like that."

I wrap my arms tighter around him and lean into his chest, eyes still focused on him. "You're one of the good ones, aren't you, Dr. Cal Baxter?"

"I like to think so." He looks down at me and smiles. "Though I am a little disorganized and I'm a bit of a people pleaser. And I spend way too much time on my fantasy football team."

"Do you?"

"So many things you don't know about me yet," he says with a smile.

He's right. So many things I've yet to discover about him. Maybe it won't all be good, but that's a part of this, isn't it? And I'm glad to be on the journey.

"But you can't make me happy," I say, looking up.

"No. I can't. Only you can do that," he says. "But you'd better believe I'm going to try. And when you're sad or frustrated or setting fires to apartment buildings, I'll be there for those things too."

I try to capture everything about this moment as I stretch up on my tiptoes and kiss him again.

And I can't wait to capture everything about every moment with him from now on.

Chapter 47

It's my thirty-first birthday.

Isadora Bentley stands proud, now a fully grown adult, about to embark on an adventure that she didn't believe she would ever face. The rigors of the wild have prepared her for this journey, and though normally a solitary creature, Isadora has found solace in a new kind of tribe—one that she will be with, foraging and discovering, to the end of her days.

Ah, Sir Attenborough. Haven't heard your voice in a while.

I'm standing backstage in Old Main's lecture hall at Chicago University, wearing what Darby assured me is a "slick black power suit." I can't lie, I do feel a little more powerful than I expected, but perhaps that has more to do with the fact that I'm headlining this event and less to do with what I'm wearing.

Or maybe it's a little bit of both.

After finishing all the steps outlined in Dr. Grace Monroe's article, I turned my findings into a legitimate study on happiness. "A personal account of one woman's quest to change her life," one journalist called it when my report was released. Academic reports typically don't get a great deal of media attention, but for some reason, mine did.

Marty said it was because we're all on a quest to figure out how to live happier lives, and I suppose that's probably true. It turns out, when you start letting people into your life, you uncover far more similarities than differences.

The desire for happiness, it seems, is universal.

And needed now more than ever. I've found in my research that the human race is living in historically unhappy times.

I'm listening as Gary—who should never be allowed to speak into a microphone—introduces me to a crowd of my peers, when I spot Cal in the front row. I'm hiding in the wings, but I can see Darby, Dante, and Delilah are on one side of him, and Marty is on the other. This unusual mix of people I've managed to pick up along the path to happiness has quite literally changed my life.

Now I have an academic paper that has been published, careful credit given to everyone who worked on the project with me, including Shellie, and a promotion Gary claims he's been wanting to give me for months but didn't feel I'd earned until now.

I decided not to challenge him on that.

I knew my work was always good, but now I'm more engaged. More part of a team.

He gave me my own assistant, a young science major named Belle. "You know, after the Disney princess?"

"Admitting that out loud is not your wisest decision," I told her, which humored her more than wounded her.

"They told me you speak your mind, Miss Bentley," she said.

"I view that as a strength," I said.

She smiled. "I do too."

And I decided we'd get along fabulously, me and the Disney princess. Who knew?

I no longer feel I have anything to prove, and I suppose that's what happens with the gift of feeling accepted.

I hear Gary call out my name, and I walk onto the stage, into the lights, aware that the auditorium, while not overwhelmingly large, is full.

All of these students and faculty members hoping to learn the secrets to happiness.

And I have insight now that might help them. For the first time in my life, I have something important to say.

I stand behind the podium and thank Gary, then look out over the people in the seats, eyes falling to my own personal cheering section. Darby lets out a "whoop whoop" and a laugh ripples through the crowd.

"Today is my birthday," I say into the microphone.

Someone in the back calls out, "Happy birthday, Miss Bentley!"

I smile and, almost to myself, say, "Interesting. We wish everyone's birthday to be happy."

I compose myself. "It's important to note the date, because it was on this very day last year that I wasn't happy. It was on this very day that my life began to change. I wasn't aware of it then, of course—I had a lot of introspection to tackle and a lot of baggage to unpack—but changes were being made, to my circumstances, to my comfort zone, and, most importantly, to me."

I glance at Cal and note in my own mind that he has been my biggest cheerleader from the very beginning. Without him, I wouldn't have completed these steps, and I certainly wouldn't have submitted my findings for publication.

He legitimized my work simply by acknowledging my feelings.

"My story starts in Aisle 8," I say into the microphone. "With some Twinkies and a two-liter of Coke."

After my presentation, I go backstage, still a little shaky from the adrenaline of having completed my first public speaking engagement since my speech on Mount Vesuvius in tenth grade. That didn't go particularly well, maybe because I used high-resolution close-ups of burned bodies. I swore I'd never get up in front of an audience again.

Look at me, conquering my fears.

I like the way this makes me feel—a little bit like a rock star.

The crowd is milling around, filtering out into the lobby. I tuck my notes inside my slick, new black computer bag, and when I turn around, there are my people.

"You were so good," Darby says, pulling me into a hug. "You were funny and smart and self-deprecating."

"She's right," Marty agrees. "We're all very impressed."

"Thanks for being here," I say.

I have friends.

The thought nearly chokes me with emotion. I've never felt so supported in all my life. Because of these people, it doesn't even matter that my parents weren't particularly impressed that my paper was published, though I'm betting my mother might be impressed by the makeover Darby gave me before I came here today.

Truly, what I've realized is that the opinion that matters most is my own.

"We'll meet you at the restaurant," Darby says. "We've got to run home and get the kids and relieve the sitter."

I nod, then turn to Cal. "So how'd I do?"

He pulls me into his arms and smiles at me.

"Okay, I get the hint," Marty says, turning around. "I'll wait for you both in the lobby."

"You were stunning," Cal says. "*So* smart. Your brain is the sexiest thing about you."

I laugh and feel myself blush. "Sexy is not what I was going for."

He looks around to make sure we're alone, then kisses me. When he pulls away, he is still smiling. "I'm going to ride your coat-tails all the way to the top, baby."

"I'll happily make room for you."

"Good," he says. Another kiss. "You hungry?"

"Starving."

We walk, hand in hand, toward the lobby, where we find Marty, then head outside. Cal drives us to Dante's restaurant, and when we walk inside, we're met by the hostess and taken to a back room. Hanging on the back wall, behind a big table decorated with balloons, is a banner with the words "Happy Birthday & Congratulations, Isadora" drawn by hand in bold black letters. There's a big, two-layer cake at the center of the table, surrounded by presents.

Darby and Dante and their kids are standing there, along with Gary, Logan, Shellie, and a few others from the office. Meg and Stacy are off to the side, along with Samira, who looks, as usual, like a goddess. Even Cal's family is here, and I secretly hope Sarah has brought me an assortment of her chocolates as a birthday gift. I know I shouldn't be thinking about gifts when their being here is plenty, but what can I say? Chocolate makes me happy.

When I walk in, they all cheer.

Delilah runs up and full-on hugs me, then abruptly pulls back and shoves something in my hand.

It's a leather-bound notebook with a fantastic pen. On the cover is a small bow.

I look down at her, and she's beaming. She excitedly points to the notebook to get me to open it.

When I do, I see that she's written something at the top of the first page.

ISADORA AND DELILAH'S OBSERVATION JOURNAL

Flipping through, I realize she's written something on every page. Inspirational quotes, sayings, prompts, creativity exercises.

I look at her, tears welling up in my eyes.

"It's so we can observe if we're making a difference in people's happiness," she explains.

Without even knowing it, Delilah has found a follow-up to my paper.

And if I ever turn it into a book, I'm going to put her name right on the cover.

Cal's hand is on the small of my back, and when I turn toward him, I see him beaming at the chance to celebrate with me.

To celebrate *me*.

At the center of each table is a basket of my favorite junk food, which I'm sure had to cause Dante physical pain to plate.

They all start singing "Happy Birthday" and surprise tears spring to my eyes.

I've never had a real birthday party before—not one that was truly meant to celebrate me. They reach the end of the song, and I blow out my candles, making a wish that I can hold on to this moment for as long as humanly possible.

I let all of the feelings, the goose bumps, the tingles, wash over me. I'm aware that life will have downs to counteract these ups, but for the first time in my life, I know I'll be able to handle them.

We eat an Italian feast and cake, and I sneak two Ding Dongs when no one is looking. I open presents and mingle with friends, and when it's all winding down, I stand off to the side and take stock of this very different life I now call mine.

Cal is across the room, chatting with Gary, who has finally—*finally*—shaved that horrible mustache, and who seems interested in my yoga friend Stacy, who—for reasons no one will ever be able to explain—doesn't seem put off by the idea of going out with him.

A perfect first entry for Delilah's journal.

I finish off my third Coke when Cal excuses himself from his conversation and makes his way over to where I am.

He stands beside me, and I can feel his look. "What are you thinking about?"

"St. John," I say absently.

"Oh?"

I look at him. "Step eighteen."

"Ah. I was wondering about that."

"I want to go," I say. "Maybe not right away, but someday. I want to do a lot of things."

"Can I do them with you?" he asks.

I smile at him. "I'd hoped you would."

We stand there for a long moment and take it all in. I snap a mental picture, a moment in the middle, so I can pull it back out anytime I feel sad.

"Next time you ask me about a happy moment, I'll have so many to choose from," I tell Cal. "This party for starters. It's amazing."

He faces me then. "You deserve it. You deserve to be celebrated."

I set down my Coke and wrap my arms around him, relishing the bumpy road that has brought me here, to a moment of complete and utter happiness.

He kisses me and whispers "Happy birthday, Isadora" in my ear, and I am certain, for the first time ever, that life really is a grand adventure, and I'm finally ready to discover whatever is around the next corner.

"Thank you," I say. "And thank you for helping me learn what happiness really is."

He kisses me again, in front of the entire room, but nobody seems to notice, or maybe I simply don't care.

I'm too busy being grateful for the highs *and* the lows that brought me here.

And too excited to take the lead in the performance that is my life.

~

As I'm sitting in bed that night, looking through photos on my phone, I open up a new text conversation to my lunchtime crew and message:

Thank you all for throwing me a birthday party. For the gifts and the food and the cake! I feel like the luckiest person in the world. And thank you for helping me complete step 32, the most important step on the journey to happiness.

DARBY: Oh? What's that?

MARTY: 🐎

MARTY: Oops. Wrong picture. Fat fingers. 🎂

CAL: Step 32?

Step 32: "CHOOSE to be happy." Then get out of your own way.

Acknowledgments

Writing is such a solitary journey that one single person could never do alone. I'm so thankful for my tribe. It's small but it's mighty.

Adam. Always. You make me better and your fingerprints are all over this book. I'm so thankful you are my first reader, my biggest cheerleader, and my best friend. Me + You.

Sophia. For growing up to become my friend.

Ethan. For showing me what perseverance looks like.

Sam. For being such a sweet, bright spot in my life.

Becky Wade. I'm so thankful for your balanced, measured, and always kind insight into my life and my writing. You are one of my very best friends, and I'm so thankful God brought you into my life.

Katie Ganshert. I'm so thankful for the years we've been sharing not only writing ups and downs but every little bit of life as well. I admire your passion and creativity, and I'm so glad to call you one of my best friends.

Melissa Tagg. So grateful that you and I can share this working/writing journey. Your encouragement along the way has been invaluable to me, and I'm so thankful for you!

My Parents, Bob & Cindy Fassler. Thank you for setting me on this path and cheering me on along the way. I'm so grateful for you both.

My readers. Your joy in receiving my work. Your excitement for new characters. Your willingness to jump into these crazy story worlds with me . . . all of it blesses me to my toes. I'm so thankful for each and every one of you!

My Studio families. Thanks for being the best of the best. I can't think of anywhere else I'd rather be than hanging out with all of you, making creative dreams come true.

Discussion Questions

1. Isadora is searching for happiness by inadvertently changing some of her habits. What are some habits you might change that could possibly aid in a happier life?
2. One of the key ways that Isadora finds a happier life is by widening her circle to include more people. We aren't designed to live alone, but people are also often the cause of hurt. In what ways have you opened yourself up to or closed yourself off from love and happiness as a result of something that happened in your past? Do you think letting that thing go might help you find more happiness?
3. Everyone has their own definition of happiness. What does it look like for you?
4. Are there any of the 31 Ways that you want to try for yourself? Which one do you think would be the most difficult?
5. Of the new relationships Isadora found along the way, which are the ones that felt the most meaningful?
6. Isadora's past held her back in a number of ways. Do you feel that there are things in your past that hold you back? Do they affect your happiness?

7. One of the most important lessons Isadora learns is that in many cases, happiness is a choice. How can you be intentional about choosing happiness in your own life?
8. Which of Isadora's new friends made the biggest impact on her life? Do you have friends in your own life who challenge your way of thinking?
9. Isadora didn't have a great relationship with her parents, and this affected her own perception of herself. Are there things people have said to you in the past that you still believe today? What would it take for you to move past those things and see yourself in a new light?
10. How does Isadora's transformation affect others, whether people she knows or strangers?

From the Publisher

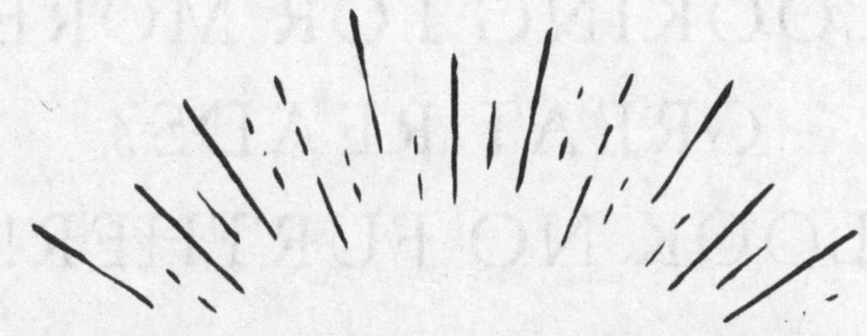

GREAT BOOKS

ARE EVEN BETTER WHEN THEY'RE SHARED!

Help other readers find this one:

- Post a review at your favorite online bookseller
- Post a picture on a social media account and share why you enjoyed it
- Send a note to a friend who would also love it—or better yet, give them a copy

Thanks for reading!

About the Author

Courtney Walsh is a novelist, theatre director, and playwright. She writes small town romance and women's fiction while juggling the performing arts studio and youth theatre she owns with her husband. She is the author of thirteen novels. Her debut, *A Sweethaven Summer*, hit the *New York Times* and *USA TODAY* bestseller lists and was a Carol Award finalist. Her novel *Just Let Go* won the Carol in 2019, and three of her novels have also been Christy-award finalists. A creative at heart, Courtney has also written three craft books and several musicals. She lives in Illinois with her husband and three children.